The
Stone Wall

The Stone Wall

BEVERLY LEWIS

BETHANYHOUSE

a division of Baker Publishing Group
Minneapolis, Minnesota

© 2020 by Beverly M. Lewis, Inc.

Published by Bethany House Publishers
11400 Hampshire Avenue South
Bloomington, Minnesota 55438
www.bethanyhouse.com

Bethany House Publishers is a division of
Baker Publishing Group, Grand Rapids, Michigan

Printed in the United States of America

ISBN 978-0-7642-3308-1
ISBN 978-0-7642-3327-2 (cloth)
ISBN 978-0-7642-3328-9 (large print)

Scripture quotations are from the King James Version of the Bible.

This story is a work of fiction. Names, characters, incidents, and dialogues are products of the author's imagination and are not to be construed as real. Any resemblance to any person, living or dead, is purely coincidental.

Cover design by Dan Thornberg, Design Source Creative Services
Art direction by Paul Higdon

20   21   22   23   24   25   26   7   6   5   4   3   2   1

To
Cousin Lois,
with love and gratitude
for sharing this joyful journey.

As for God, his way is perfect. . . .

—Psalm 18:30

Prologue

"'Tis a waste of time to look back with regret," Mammi Eliza Slaubaugh once told me. "Though we might fret and stew, the past simply can't be changed," she'd added, leaning closer, as if to share a secret. "Besides, if we could change our past, Anna, would we want to?"

Mammi's last question so *ferhoodled* me, I was unable to grasp her meaning. And yet I'd never forgotten her words of wisdom. Truth be told, I was still grappling with that very idea while I picked strawberries with my mother on this exceptionally bright June sixth morning, the one-year anniversary of my breakup with Atley Brenneman, my first beau.

"Do you have any past regrets, *Mamm*?" I asked as I set my bucket on the ground.

Mamm tilted her blond head and smiled quizzically. "Aren't ya a bit young to think about regrets, Anna? You're only twenty."

I sighed, recalling Atley's decision to leave our Beachy Amish community to train to become a pilot. Why hadn't I seen it coming? Atley had done his best to persuade me to leave with him, his arguments sharp as a blade. But with the Lord's help, I stood firm in my upbringing, despite my deep care for him. Even so, our breakup still brought a sense of what-could-have-been.

Mamm flapped her long apron at a bird eyeing a cluster of ripe strawberries. "*Ach*, Anna dear, I can tell where that sigh's coming from. And it's no wonder: Losing your beau to the world was awful hard on you. One of my regrets is how you had to suffer through all of that."

I nodded, remembering how, at the time, I'd taken to writing down my prayers as a way to ease my sadness. At day's end, I would go out to the edge of the woods near our farmhouse and lie in the tall grasses, hoping no one but the critters would notice me there in the fading light. After months of this much-needed solitude, my heart had begun to open to God through His handiwork: the majestic canopy of trees turning red and gold, and the abundance of woodland creatures—red squirrels gathering nuts, deer feeding on underbrush, and birds darting here and there in the rustling branches. And I had known that my heavenly Father was with me, comforting me.

"You feeling all right?" Mamm asked just now, reaching low for more plump red berries.

"*Jah*, but I do wish I'd never gone out with Atley," I admitted, aware of the old pain of disappointment as we finished picking the ripe fruit.

"Your mind's in a whirl today, ain't so?" Mamm gave me a faint smile, her blue eyes discerning. "But you couldn't have known about Atley. Not even his parents suspected anything was amiss." She glanced up at a flock of birds.

Though I hadn't allowed myself to voice it then, the fact was I'd been angry with myself—and him—for allowing us to remain a couple as long as we had. And for the first three months after our breakup, I was downright disgruntled about that, as well as my romantic prospects here in Mifflinburg.

Sadly, Atley hadn't been the only fellow to drift away. On the heels of Atley's exit, the behavior of a handful of other fellows became worrisome, as well, betraying how they were raised. Most shockingly, one of the boys I'd gone to junior high with had decided to join the army, turning his back on the nonresistance our Anabaptist church embraced.

It was around then that I came across God's words in the Bible about looking ahead to the good things He had planned for me. It seemed that the Lord had something better in mind for me than my rehashing the past. I also recognized it wasn't my place to judge Atley, so I'd confessed my resentment and begun to pray for a potential mate who would share my Plain values and way of life, one who had yielded his life to the Savior. Even so, I wasn't sure of the way forward.

Reaching now to take my mother's filled bucket, I carried it and mine as we walked together toward the house. "I wasted nearly a year of my life."

Mamm nodded sagely. "I'm sure it feels that way, but try not to be hard on yourself."

I gave her a smile and realized anew how easy it was to get stuck in the past—all the should-haves and what-ifs.

Mamm and I made our way up the wide back porch steps and into the house.

"It still seems like I should've sensed something was off beam with Atley, though."

"Sometimes it's just not possible, Anna."

"Well, maybe I should prepare for the future, so it never happens again."

Mamm stopped and gave me a look. "How?"

"Honestly, I've been pondering what to do with my life—the next few years, anyhow," I admitted as I followed her into the kitchen with the buckets.

Mamm's eyes widened into soft blue moons as she turned to look at me. "What do you mean?"

Shrugging, I set the brimming buckets on the counter without a word, suddenly unsure of myself. I needed to have a specific plan before I broached the topic, but right now, I didn't have one beyond a desire to do something—*anything*—other than to keep living life as it was in Mifflinburg.

"Well then." Mamm studied me. "Maybe just take some time to think of what that might be."

I nodded and went to wash my hands at the deep double sink, preparing to make a nice hot breakfast of scrambled eggs and bacon for my parents and me. All seven of my older siblings were married and had their own families, so it was quite simple to make meals for just the three of us. I also looked forward to helping Mamm prepare the fresh-picked strawberries for jam making later . . . and a pie, too. The highlights of today's tasks.

Once, Mammi Eliza would have been right here with us, laughing and telling stories of her childhood as we worked side by side. Sharing tales of *"snappin', shellin', picklin', and cannin',"* as she liked to describe women's summertime work. I wished her memory weren't so poor now. How expressive she had always been, prior to her illness. So animated and full of life. It broke my heart to think of her suffering from Alzheimer's at eighty-six, and I wished I could communicate to her how much I appreciated her being such a wonderful role model to me and to all who knew her. *I hope she understands the love and admiration I feel,* I thought, remembering again our long-ago conversations. Just maybe she, too, had once struggled with regrets, and maybe that's why she'd seemed so wise.

For certain I had a few regrets about Mammi Eliza. I missed her smile and missed being able to talk like we used to. And I regretted not being able to share with her my deepest dreams and feelings. *If only I could tell her about my desire to start a brand-new chapter in my life.* A few nights ago, I had even gone so far as to whisper such a prayer before falling asleep.

When I'm Mammi's age, I don't want to regret not heeding this stirring in my heart. . . .

Chapter 1

A nna Beachy, a direct descendant of the founder of the Beachy Amish church, had been up for only three hours the next morning when she completed her indoor chores, including cooking and cleaning up after break-fast, as well as washing the kitchen and mudroom's large vinyl floor with Mamm's string mop.

That afternoon, Anna set out to hoe the annoying weeds from the family vegetable garden, the sound of bird calls all around. And as she worked, she whispered a prayer of gratitude for her family's many blessings.

When the mail truck arrived in the distance, she observed Mamm walk down the driveway toward the road and return with some letters, waving one in the air and calling to Anna, who put down the hoe and went to meet her halfway. Anna immediately noticed the Strasburg, Pennsylvania, return address of Mamm's Old Order Amish cousins, Glen and Sadie Flaud, whom she had visited with her family a number of times through the years. Glancing at Mamm, Anna frowned, then stared again at the envelope clearly addressed to Miss Anna Ruth Beachy. Since she'd never written to the Flauds, she found it very curious that these distant cousins should be writing to *her*.

"Go ahead—see what it says," Mamm urged, standing there with her own look of surprise.

It turned out that Cousin Sadie was writing about a job opening for a tour guide at the Mennonite Information Center in Lancaster County. Anna relayed this to Mamm, then added, puzzled, "I wonder why she thought of me."

"Read on, dear." Mamm clutched the other letters as she and Anna walked barefoot to the back porch.

There, they sat and Anna finished reading Sadie's letter. After refolding it, she looked across the backyard to *Dat's* pony stable, a dark line of birds perched along its peak. Anna pondered this unexpected invitation, clear out of the blue. "Cousin Sadie believes God prompted her to tell me about the tour guide position there." Anna filled her mother in on the particulars.

"Sounds just like Sadie, always thinking of others."

Anna told of the Flauds' offer for her to stay with them in their *Dawdi Haus*. "With my experience at the Mifflinburg Buggy Museum, Sadie thinks the job is something I might be cut out for. She's already talked to the director, Evelyn Leaman, about me."

"You'd really quit your job here?" Mamma asked.

"Well, I've already thought of that, itchin' to try something new." *Somewhere else*, she thought.

Mamm's eyebrows rose slightly. "Wasn't sure you were serious yesterday."

Anna didn't comment that the timing of this offer seemed providential, at least to her. "I'd really like to consider this invitation . . . with your and Dat's blessing, of course. I've always enjoyed the Flauds' company, and Strasburg itself is such a charming village."

Mamm looked thoughtful and said it would be a good idea to talk with her father about this.

"Oh, I certainly will." Anna thought about how she'd recently prayed for something new to happen in her life, though she'd never imagined something as consequential as a move away from Mifflinburg.

"If you *were* to go to Lancaster County, you'd have to make some temporary adjustments—my mother's side of the family originally came from traditional Amish, you know," Mamm said. "A much more conservative environment."

Anna had certainly never considered staying in an Amish farmhouse without electricity. Here in their small Beachy Amish settlement, they enjoyed electricity, phones, and other modern conveniences, even cars if they chose, though a few folk still drove horse and buggy on Sunday to the meetinghouse. In other ways, though, like their simple style of dress, their lives were like those of their Old Order relatives, though many of Anna's ancestors had broken away from that group in 1927.

"It wouldn't be easy," Anna acknowledged.

Mamm breathed out a long sigh and glanced out the window. "Your Mammi Eliza spent a summer there in Strasburg when she was a teenager, working for her Old Order Amish great-aunt Joanna Beiler. It was a difficult time for Eliza and my grandparents, having her so far away."

Anna remembered hearing about that long-ago summer. *Seventy years ago now*, she thought, wondering if Mammi Eliza could possibly have any recollection of that time, considering her severe memory loss. *I'll mention it when I visit her*, Anna decided, suddenly curious.

She was also eager to give Cousin Sadie a call to ask her a few questions and to thank her for the surprising invitation. *Could this be my answer to finding a fresh start?*

The next day, after Friday morning chores, Anna drove her car the two miles to her older sister's home, where Mammi Eliza had been residing comfortably since *Dawdi* John passed away.

The two-story white clapboard house had nine large rooms and an enormous pantry at the far end of the spacious kitchen, which was a good thing, considering that Anna's twenty-eight-year-old sister, Wanita, and husband, Conrad Yoder, currently had nine children under their roof—five biological, including a boy and girl who were twins, and four foster children.

Anna didn't pause to knock at the back door. Like everyone else in her Plain community, she simply announced herself by calling as she opened it and stepped inside.

Instantly, three of the youngest girls came running toward her, all of them wrapping their pudgy arms around her long mint green dress. "*Aendi* Anna's here," five-year-old Bonnie said, grinning up at Anna. Her four-year-old sister, Bethie, beamed happily as she let out a little squeal.

Leaning down, Anna patted each of the girls' cheeks before picking up the smallest of Wanita's foster children—golden-blond Rogene. "Looks like you're wearing breakfast on your face," Anna said as she carried the eighteen-month-old over to the sink to wash the pancake syrup off her chubby face just as Wanita exited the walk-in pantry.

"I didn't hear you arrive," Wanita said, coming to greet Anna after setting two quart jars of tomato sauce on the counter. A blue bandanna covered her dark blond hair bun. "I see you have your arms full of sweetness." Wanita reached out to stroke

Rogene's dimpled arm. "Who's got ya, huh?" she murmured, her deep blue eyes twinkling at the tot.

"Aendi Anna!" the two older girls said in unison from where they still stood nearby.

Anna smiled back at the girls, aware of their fondness for her. She adored children and loved spending time with all of her nieces and nephews. Sometimes Wanita's girls called her their favorite Aendi, which Anna tried to play down—they had plenty of other aunts in Conrad's family to dote on them, too.

Wanita went to the toy chest at the far end of the kitchen and took out some plastic blocks and several little dolls and clothes, then placed them on the floor near the screen door. "Yous can play quietly for a while," she said, telling Anna that the rest of the children were at VBS for the morning. "The oldest ones are helping out."

Anna put Rogene down, and she toddled over to Bonnie and Bethie, who were now talking softly and rocking their dolls.

"Mammi's in the next room," Wanita added in a whisper. "Not having the best of mornings."

Anna frowned, hoping her presence might make a difference. Sometimes it did; other times not. "I'll try to cheer her up."

Wanita nodded, her solemn expression indicating that might be a challenge, then headed back to the kitchen counter.

Having previously experienced a number of Mammi Eliza's not-so-good mornings, Anna had no expectations for this visit. She just wanted to be with her, let her know she was dearly loved and always would be.

Entering the sitting room, Anna saw that Mammi's reading glasses had slid down toward the point of her nose, and a magnifying glass lay on the small table next to her. She didn't look up from her black leather *Biewel* when Anna gently touched her right hand, nor did she respond when Anna took a seat in the nearby chair. Without speaking, Anna observed Mammi's wrinkled hands slowly turning the thin pages of her well-worn *Biewel*. Some pages were marked with homemade bookmarks from her children, grands, and greats, and a whole passage was underlined where the verses must have spoken to Mammi Eliza in a precious way.

Anna's thoughts drifted back to the years when her grandmother was verbally expressive and even at times considered the life of the party, laughing and trading recipes, or engaging the great-grandchildren with her finger puppets made from scraps of leftover fabric. Always, Mammi Eliza had been the family encourager, as cheerful and bright as morning birdsong, and quick to share a Scripture verse that had touched her heart. Never had Anna dreamed that she and her family would lose their beloved matriarch to this dreaded disease.

Sometimes it could be difficult to see how much Mammi had changed, but every so often, Anna saw glimpses of that same lively person in the frail woman before her. "I'm happy to see you again, Mammi," she said softly now. "The sun's shining brightly . . . it's another beautiful day."

Mammi's white hair was pulled back in a bun beneath her white organdy *Kapp*, and she whispered to herself but kept turning the pages, some of their gilded edges worn away from decades of repeated reading. A few pages were even coming loose from the binding.

"I'm thinking of making a trip to Lancaster County," Anna said, aware of the familiar lilac scent of the homemade soap her grandmother had made for years before Wanita took over the task. "Mamm reminded me that you spent a summer in Strasburg, too, many, many years ago."

Mammi's head lifted just then. "Strasburg?"

"*Jah.*" Anna paused, holding her breath. "Do you remember?"

18

Mammi's glassy gray eyes seemed to clear, but her gaze looked beyond Anna. "I'll wait for ya there," she said breathily, as if talking to someone unseen, a faint smile on her face. "By the light of the moon." Then Mammi slowly lowered her head to look at her tattered German Bible and began to turn the pages once again, murmuring to herself as her usual confusion seemed to descend.

The strange momentary response startled Anna. It was almost as if Mammi had actually remembered something from that time decades ago. *What came to her mind?*

Anna went on to talk about her plans to apply for a job there as though she and Mammi Eliza were having a real conversation.

After a while, when it appeared that Mammi was starting to drop off, Anna encouraged her to lean back in the recliner for some rest. It was only a matter of moments before she was fast asleep, her hands resting lightly on the old Bible.

Touched by the endearing sight, Anna leaned down to kiss her damp forehead as if she were a child. *Like Mammi tucked me in when I spent the night with her and Dawdi John,* Anna thought fondly. And glancing again at the ragged Bible, she realized it was the same one Mammi had read aloud to her during those very visits. Sometimes, Dawdi would also come in with her to say good-night and place his soothing hand on Anna's forehead. Both of them had showed such tenderness toward her.

Reluctant to leave Mammi's side, Anna stood there gazing at the sweet wrinkled face, wanting to share more about her hopes and prayers. Eventually, she tiptoed into the kitchen to find Wanita chopping garlic to make a batch of spaghetti sauce.

Wanita looked up. "How's she now?"

"Dozing." Anna didn't mention that Mammi had possibly

remembered her months in Strasburg. *And something about wait-ing in the moonlight . . .*

"She lives for your visits, you know."

"I love seeing her, too," Anna said, retying Wanita's work apron for her where it had loosened in the back. "And *you*, sister." She told Wanita about Cousin Sadie Flaud's letter and the possible opportunity awaiting her in Lancaster County. "If it's the Lord's will for me to live and work there, I trust it'll be obvious and that I'll know without a doubt."

Wanita's eyes grew serious. "I would hate to see ya go, *Schweschder.*" She sighed. "What if you meet someone there— fall in love? How often would we see you then?"

"Well, I'm looking forward to what the Lord has planned for me. To be completely honest, I'm actually hoping to settle down somewhere other than Mifflinburg."

Wanita smiled, but her eyes looked pained, so the effect was more sad than happy. "You're a sensible young woman, Anna. And it may be time to expand your horizons and see where this prospect leads. Must it be so far from home, though?"

Anna grimaced. "I know it won't be easy. I really just need a change—I've felt this way for a while now."

"You'll keep in touch, I hope." Wanita's expression was for-lorn.

"No need to get ahead of yourself," Anna said, glancing toward the doorway that led into the next room. "It's not like I've got the job yet. And if I do end up moving there, I'll defi-nitely stay in touch with all of you . . . Mammi, too."

"You'd come home weekends?"

"I'd miss you too much not to."

Wanita gave the pot in front of her a good stir as she poured in the last of the chopped tomatoes. "We don't know how long Mammi might have."

"But she's in fairly *gut* health other than her memory, ain't so?" Even as Anna said the words, she realized she couldn't bear the thought of losing her.

"Seems to be, *jah*. And I'm thankful for every minute of clarity she has." Wanita washed and dried her hands. "Like those times when she can quote long passages of Scripture or sing hymns without being prompted. Moments like those are blessings." She walked with Anna to the rear screen door, where Bonnie and Bethie looked up from their play and blew little kisses.

"*Kumme* again soon," Bonnie said, eyes pleading.

Anna promised she would and blew a kiss back. Then, heading down the steps to the car, she prayed, *Dear Lord, please watch over Mammi Eliza with Thy tender loving care.*

During the short drive home, Anna passed the deacon's familiar chair shop and a small country store run by one of their two preachers, as well as an Amish quilt shop she and Mamm frequented, owned by Dat's cousins. Rounding the bend, Anna also spotted Atley Brenneman's parents' farmhouse and felt a renewed sense of relief, knowing that if she moved to Lancaster County, the steady stream of updates about his life wouldn't reach her ears via the grapevine.

If Dat and Mamm agree to let me go, she thought, eager to see new places and new people.

Chapter 2

⟪separator ornament⟫

At supper that evening, Anna told her parents that she'd contacted the director at the Mennonite Information Center to request an application. The table was laid with the green-and-white-checkered oilcloth and Mamm's off-white everyday dishes. A lazy Susan holding salt and pepper, sugar, and garlic salt graced its center.

"Based on Cousin Sadie's recommendation, the director wants to have a face-to-face interview with me as soon as I can get to Lancaster County. She said I can hand-deliver my work application," Anna said, cutting into her slice of baked ham with a maple honey glaze.

"So you'd miss a day or so of work here, then." Mamm's voice sounded pinched.

"Actually, I've thought of just giving my two weeks' notice," Anna said.

"You're quitting?" At the head of the table, Dat grimaced and ran a hand through his dark bangs. Anna noticed gray circles under his brown eyes. "Simply because of an invitation from your Mamm's Strasburg cousin?" he asked, looking over at her.

"Not just because of that," Anna replied, going on to explain that she had been contemplating doing something new for some time. "I didn't say anything right away, but I'm sure now that I want to take Cousin Sadie up on her offer to at least visit. I believe the Lord is leading me in all of this."

"Well, the Flauds are God-fearin' folk, but doesn't it give you pause that they're Old Order Amish?" Dat asked, a frown appearing.

Anna wondered why the topic at hand seemed to trouble her father so. She wouldn't have thought that going to the Flauds' would be so problematic.

"A visit's fine, but does it matter that your Mamm and I would prefer you remain here, amongst our own People?" Dat said as he reached for his tumbler of ice water.

"I was hoping for your blessing, Dat."

A slight shake of his head indicated any number of thoughts were going through his mind, but when her father spoke again, there was a softening to his tone. "I realize you're old enough to choose Glen and Sadie Flaud's offer, but if you were to settle down there and rub shoulders with the Old Order youth, that would concern us. I think ya know why."

Anna sighed. *He and Mamm must be worried I'll marry outside the Beachy Amish church.*

"I'll attend a Beachy church," she said respectfully.

"I would assume so," Dat replied, then paused to draw a breath. "But it would be hard on your Mamma if you married and settled down so far away, as well."

Mamm nodded her head. "Both of us would miss ya, dear."

They continued eating the tasty meal, including a vinegary

23

macaroni salad with chopped carrots, celery, and onions, Anna's favorite.

Mamm asked if she had called Cousin Sadie yet.

"I left a message at their phone shanty—hoping to hear back soon." Anna also hoped this conversation might end happily and not the way it seemed to be headed.

"We won't stand in your way, daughter." Dat spooned up some more macaroni salad. "Just be careful not to fix your eyes on Lancaster County. Might be best to think of it as just a short visit."

"But if I get the job I'm hoping for—"

"Well, you haven't even had the interview," he said, stopping her.

She understood, but she could also see he was struggling with letting her go.

"Regardless, I'll pray God will be with you," Dat added, his voice softer now.

"*Denki,*" she whispered loud enough for both parents to hear.

Mid Saturday morning, Anna heard back from both Cousin Sadie and Evelyn Leaman by phone and made plans to arrive in Strasburg that coming Monday morning. She'd have the interview with Evelyn the next day.

Anna was pleased that things seemed to be falling into place so quickly, and she packed a few clothes for the short visit, hoping and praying she would find favor with the director.

But her father's cautious reaction to her plans lingered in her mind.

Monday's breakfast of scrapple, fried potatoes, and sticky buns was especially delicious, thanks to Mamm, who'd gone out of her way. Afterward, Anna loaded her bag into the car and drove through miles of lush green alfalfa and small but unfamiliar towns on her way to Lancaster County. As she passed through busy Harrisburg and beyond, she was glad for Google Maps on her phone to guide her.

When Anna at last reached rural Strasburg, she took Lime Valley Road up to the righthand turn into the Flauds' own long lane, lined with tall oaks that created a lofty, archlike passageway. Cousins Glen and Sadie's stone *Dawdi Haus* was situated off to the east side of the larger main house, where Glen's youngest son and family lived and ran the turkey farm. Both houses were set back quite a distance from the narrow rural road and featured distinctive roof lines and dormers. A rectangular gray buggy was parked near the carriage shed, its black shafts resting against the ground.

Parking her car, Anna had a fleeting feeling of embarrassment at its being the only one on the premises. While no power lines were in sight, a tall windmill stood not far from the white clapboard turkey house and the large woodshed on the opposite side. Colorful flowers were in full bloom, and the light fragrance of lavender permeated the air.

The hem of Anna's dress swished against her calves as she moved up the cobblestone walkway to the *Dawdi Haus* where her mother's cousins had resided for some years now. A large white birdbath surrounded by blooming pink and white ground cover stood off to the side of the walkway, and two red hummingbird feeders hung from the porch.

"'Tis *wunnerbaar-gut* to see ya, Anna!" Cousin Sadie said, her round cheeks rosy as she stepped out onto the back porch. She stood there smiling broadly in her long green dress and black cape apron, her iron gray hair parted down the middle and pulled back into a tight, low bun beneath her white heart-shaped *Kapp*. She was barefoot and held a white dishcloth in one hand.

Anna hurried to greet her. "*Wie geht's?*"

"We're fine . . . chust fine. Been lookin' forward to your arrival." Sadie patted Anna's arm and invited her inside. "Glen's over in the hayfield with the men, but he'll be back come dinnertime." She led Anna into the sunlit kitchen, where the windows were open and a tall glass pitcher of iced tea sat on the counter.

"Mamm sends her love," Anna remembered to say. "And I'm grateful for your kind invitation."

"Well, that's quite all right. We're family, and far as I'm concerned, your folks are salt of the earth." Sadie carried a plate of warm chocolate chip cookies and set it down on the square oak table. "Make yourself at home." Sadie placed her right hand on her ample hip. "Thought ya might need a sweet treat 'bout now."

The sight of the cookies made Anna smile, and she reached for one. Sunbeams spilled through the two curtainless windows near the table, making the kitchen quite cheery, and she noted that the room had been updated with white painted cupboards and woodwork since she and her family had visited here several Christmases ago. *For the annual play at the Amish schoolhouse . . .*

Cousin Sadie offered her iced tea, too, and when Anna politely accepted, Sadie brought over two empty tumblers and set them on the table before joining Anna. Not wasting any time, she asked about Anna's phone conversation with Evelyn Leaman.

"It went well. In fact, I have an interview scheduled for nine o'clock tomorrow morning." Anna could hardly say it without feeling like she might burst with anticipation.

"I'm sure it'll go fine." Sadie nodded as she pushed her white *Kapp* strings over her shoulders.

"*Denki* for saying so." Anna took a bite of the soft, warm cookie, thankful for this chance to catch her breath. The trip here had been a bit unnerving, as she'd never driven such a distance by herself.

Sadie poured some iced meadow tea into each tumbler and offered one to Anna. "Something to wet your whistle."

"I know I'm repeating myself, but it was really kind of you to think of me for this job possibility. And I couldn't help noticing what you said in your letter about believing that God prompted you to write to me."

"*Jah*, it was quite unexpected." Sadie explained that she'd heard about the job opening at Preaching service and immediately thought of Anna. "You kept comin' to mind after that, so it seemed like the Lord had put you on my heart."

"Well, you should know that the moment I read your letter, I felt like it was the chance I've been praying for."

Sadie smiled and went on to ask about Anna's parents and siblings.

Quickly, Anna filled her in on her family back home, including Mammi Eliza's steady decline.

Sadie's eyes were full of understanding. "*Ach*, poor Eliza. And I s'pose it was hard for your parents, sayin' good-bye an' all, considering you're the baby of the family."

"It's only a visit for now. And Strasburg's not too awful far from Mifflinburg. Just under two hours by car," Anna said. She thought of the parting with her parents, especially Mamm, whose tears had welled up despite her reassuring smile. "I'll return home for more clothes if I get the job, so either way, I'll see them again soon no matter what comes of my interview tomorrow. I also want to stay in close touch with Mammi Eliza.

Did you know she spent a summer in Strasburg many years ago? Stayed with her widowed great-aunt."

Cousin Sadie reached for another cookie. "She was just a youth, if I have it right." She paused to chew. "I got this second-hand, though—it happened before I was born."

"It wonders me why she would've left Mifflinburg for the whole summer," Anna said, thinking that surely Cousin Sadie knew that, like much of Mamm's family, Mammi Eliza had been raised Beachy Amish, while Sadie's own family had always been Old Order. *Mammi's great-aunt wouldn't have considered her Amish at all, just as the Old Order around us don't accept my family as Amish, either,* she thought, knowing this from having grown up close to the more traditional Amish.

"She might've come here to help her aunt with produce and canning and whatnot. Or maybe she needed a change of scenery, like we all do from time to time." Sadie eyed Anna.

"Could be." Anna wondered once more why Mammi Eliza had seemed to become more alert at the mention of Strasburg. *She must have strong memories of her days here. . . .*

"It was a long time ago," Sadie said. "And it wasn't talked about."

Anna perked up at this but didn't respond, even though she was very curious.

Sadie's blue-gray eyes twinkled. "Just know that Glen and I are delighted to have *you* with us for whatever time we have together this summer. And, the Good Lord willin', things might just work out for that job."

"Whatever happens will be the right thing."

"I daresay you're wise beyond your years." Sadie folded her hands over her pudgy middle and looked across the table with a sweet expression. "'Tis refreshing."

Anna felt at ease with Sadie, just as Mamm had assured her

she would. In fact, if anything, Sadie was more cheerful and easygoing than Anna had remembered, though one wouldn't think it to look at her—the simple subdued attire seemed to indicate otherwise.

Chapter 3

———— ❧ ————

The next morning, Anna rose before dawn, reached for a light switch out of habit, and smiled to herself as she went to the oak dresser across the room to turn on the battery-powered lamp. A hand mirror lay beside it, and she used it to look at herself, hoping against hope that this day would be filled with good news. Then, going to kneel at the double bed covered with a handmade summer-weight quilt, she prayed as she always did before beginning her day.

Later, after Anna had also read a chapter from the New Testament, she washed up and dressed for the upcoming interview, then checked her text messages. She was glad to see one from Mamm, who was thankful she had arrived safely. Then, going downstairs, she offered to help Cousin Sadie make breakfast. Anna also greeted Cousin Glen, who had returned from helping his son Luke with the morning chore of feeding and watering seventy-five turkeys. Glen was seated at the table in his black suspenders and a dark blue shirt, his graying beard long and thin. A large leather Bible lay inches from his placemat.

"It's another beautiful day, ain't?" Glen said as she brought over a bowl of peach yogurt and a loaf of homemade sweet bread on a small tray. "We pray it's a *gut* day for you, Anna."

"*Denki.*" She was encouraged by his thoughtfulness.

"The Lord is ever faithful," Sadie said, carrying a large plateful of scrambled eggs to the table. Then she and Anna sat down to join Glen for the silent blessing.

While they ate, Glen talked about their large family, with its many grandchildren, especially the greats starting to come on over the past few years. At one point, Glen asked about Anna's grandmother Eliza, which made her think back to the days when Mammi and Dawdi Slaubaugh were young enough to come for an afternoon visit and to see the new ponies Anna's father bred and sold. Dawdi would put Anna high on his strong shoulders and run around the backyard with her squealing, "Faster, faster!" He was the tallest man Anna had ever seen, nearly a giant in her childish eyes, and the world looked so different from high on his shoulders.

Meanwhile, Mammi Eliza would sit with Mamm on the long back porch as Wanita brought out a big pitcher of homemade lemonade and poured it in paper cups for everyone. And sometimes, Mammi Eliza brought along little hard candies in her pockets for Anna and her siblings. After she left, the boys would trade candies among themselves to get their favorite flavors.

Such happy times, Anna thought, enjoying the pleasant company of the Flauds. When the meal was done, they bowed their heads for a second silent prayer, and Anna prayed her own prayer for guidance.

When Anna pulled into the parking lot at the Mennonite Information Center, she recalled Glen's thoughtful words and Sadie's encouraging remarks at breakfast. "They're cheering me on," she murmured, getting out of the car and making her way to the entrance, taking note of the lovely shrubs and blooming flowers. All the while, she did her best to calm the nervousness she felt.

Inside, at the counter, a young blond receptionist wore a cup-shaped prayer cap and a silver name pin with *Helen Weber* engraved on it. She greeted Anna, then took her to the director's office and introduced her as Anna breathed a prayer.

The middle-aged director, Evelyn Leamen, was a pleasant and professional brunette, who gave a thorough overview of the work of a center tour guide. She also mentioned that two others were being interviewed for the same position. "We're looking for the ideal person to represent us to tourists," Evelyn said, tempering her words with a smile from where she sat behind her small desk.

Anna tried to put her best foot forward during the interview and to be articulate and friendly. At its end, she offered her contact information, which included her cell phone number, as well as the address where she was staying.

"Glen and Sadie Flaud are longtime friends of mine," Evelyn said as she showed Anna around the center's bookshop. "They speak highly of you and your family. I understand from them that you've been working as a tour guide in your hometown."

A few minutes later, Evelyn introduced Anna to one of the current tour guides, Martin Nolt, a tall young man with chestnut brown hair and hazel eyes. Evelyn asked him to take Anna downstairs to see the short movie on Mennonite history and life, as well as the other self-guided tour—a replica of the Tabernacle, built as described in the Old Testament.

"What do you think of the place, Anna?" Martin asked as they headed down the hallway to the elevator.

"It's fascinating," Anna replied.

"And a little overwhelming, probably. It was to me at first." He grinned.

"Yes, a little."

"By the way, please call me Mart, okay?" he said. "Nearly everyone does."

Anna nodded. "We shorten names a lot in my family, too." She mentioned her nieces Bonnie and Bethie, nicknames for Beulah and Bethany. "But I'm just plain Anna." She smiled.

"Plain Anna . . . I like that." Pressing the button for the elevator, he chuckled.

"No possibility of shortening that," she replied, enjoying their light banter.

The elevator door opened. "You must have married siblings if you have nieces and nephews," Mart said.

"Seven older siblings, *jah*. How about you?" Anna asked, stepping inside.

"Six," he said. "I'm fourth in the birth order."

"And I'm the last child," she said, avoiding calling herself the baby. She didn't like thinking of herself that way now that she was grown.

As the door closed and the elevator descended, Mart pushed his hands into his tan trouser pockets and asked, "Are you from out of town?"

"*Jah*, Mifflinburg. Ever been there?"

"Once, but I was just a kid, so I don't remember much."

"It's a small town. But it does have a buggy museum, where I've been a tour guide for a couple of years since returning from Illinois, where I helped my aunt and uncle for a time."

Mart's eyes widened. "Well then . . . you definitely have the right experience."

"I do enjoy meeting and talking with tourists. They always seem so curious, and they're generally all-round nice folk."

Mart nodded agreeably. "And appreciative," he added. "Thankful to learn about Plain culture, but even more thankful to still be English when the tour is over."

They shared a laugh as the elevator door opened to the lower level, and Mart motioned for her to exit first. "To be honest, I'd guessed you weren't from around here since you hadn't visited this place before."

"Well, I've heard about it, that's for sure."

Mart walked with her to the large room where the free film about the origins of the Mennonites was shown on the hour. Afterward, as they toured the replica of the Old Testament Tabernacle together, Anna talked with Mart about his work there.

"Ask me anything you'd like," Mart invited. "I've been doing this for five years now, and I'm here to help."

Anna was glad to have this chance and pleased by his friendly attitude. *He must have started in high school,* she thought. "*Denki* . . . er, thanks. I appreciate it." Her happiness at spending time with easygoing Martin Nolt surprised her, and she secretly hoped they would have the opportunity to talk again.

Anna returned to the Flauds' country home, her head awhirl with the interesting things she had learned. *I think I'm a good fit for this job,* she thought while parking her car close to the *Dawdi Haus.* She looked over at the lovely daylilies in Cousin Sadie's flower garden, so brilliantly orange. Getting out of the car, she walked toward them, taking her time there in the sunlight, soaking in the calm beauty around her.

Hopefully I'll hear something from Mrs. Leaman later today, Anna thought, thankful again for the interview.

Sadie Flaud had spent a good part of the morning rolling out dough for homemade noodles, making an extra batch to take to her ailing older sister, Eva Ebersol, whose memory had started slipping since a recent hip surgery. The surgeon had explained to Eva's distressed family that anesthesia administered to older patients had the potential to permanently impair mental function, including memory. That this appeared to have happened to her beloved sister continued to worry and sadden Sadie.

Thinking now of Anna and her interview, Sadie thought, *I hope she liked what she saw.* She lifted the lid on the kettle filled with chunks of tender chicken breast simmering in a rich broth. *Anna deserves a little celebration while she waits for news. . . .*

She recalled Anna's mother, Cousin Rachel, writing some months back about her daughter's heartache over a once-serious beau. *Young love can be painful,* Sadie mused, remembering a few of her own children's romantic struggles.

Setting the table with extra care for this particular meal, she glanced out the window and noticed Anna strolling near the flower beds. Sadie went to fill tumblers with lemonade and remembered how drawn she had always been to Cousin Rachel's youngest. Even as a little girl, Anna had been talkative and engaging, particularly when it came to the ponies her father raised for a living.

Sadie moved back to the window and tried to guess what was on Anna's mind as the young woman tilted her face toward the sun, a gentle breeze ruffling her pastel blue dress, so different in style and fabric than Sadie's own. *She's ponderin' something. . . .*

Eager to build a relationship with her, Sadie hoped it was something Anna might share. *It would be a treat to get to know her better.*

Truth be known, Sadie's own two daughters were mighty busy with their large families these days, and there was little time for the long talks of years gone by. How she missed those one-on-one hours—her girls were young grandmothers themselves now. But she also loved being with her grandchildren and little great-grandchildren, too, each one just as respectful and God-fearing as any Amish Mammi could hope for. So far, every one of the grands who was old enough had either followed the Lord in holy baptism or was taking instruction to do so—heartening to any grandparent.

Seeing Anna heading this way now, Sadie smiled, wanting to hear about the interview, if Anna chose to tell her about it. She had even tucked in a little prayer earlier around the time she guessed Anna might be sitting down with Evelyn.

The familiar screech of the back door meant that her guest had come inside, and Sadie quickly went to meet her.

Chapter 4

W hile admiring Sadie's flower garden, Anna had noticed a sloping expanse of land between the *Dawdi Haus* and the wooded area to the northeast. Several paths overlapped one another like shoestrings before disappearing into the distance. As she entered the back door and was ushered into the kitchen, she washed her hands at the sink. While she reached for the hand towel, Sadie urged her to take a seat, saying she was not to lift a finger for this particular dinner.

Does she think I was offered the position? Anna wondered, thinking she should set the record straight right away.

After Cousin Glen prayed silently over the meal, Anna spoke up. "Evelyn is going to let me know one way or the other about the job. She's interviewing a couple of others, too, but I'm still hopeful."

"Oh, there's no question in my mind you'll get it," Sadie said while dishing up a large portion of chicken and noodles on

Anna's plate. She then passed the bowl of buttered lima beans she'd frozen last summer, and next the dish of chow chow.

Glen chuckled, then quickly cleared his throat. "Let's not count on it, dear," he advised his wife. "Anna should know for sure soon enough."

"*Jah* . . . true. But still." And here Sadie beamed at Anna, seated across the table from her.

Anna could sense they were both waiting to hear more, so she described much of what Evelyn had told her. Then she added, "And there was a nice young man, too, who showed me around the place. Maybe you know of him—Martin Nolt? He's worked there for a while. A Mennonite fella."

Glen salted his noodles, then set the saltshaker down and glanced at Anna. "Well now, there are any number of Martin Nolts round here."

Smiling, Anna nodded as she enjoyed the yummy meal. The same names did have a tendency to keep popping up among even Mennonite Plain communities. She didn't mention how surprisingly easy it had been to talk with Mart about nearly everything—they'd even joked a bit. "I'll need to charge my phone in the car in case I get a call from the director later today," she told them, forking up some noodles. "Such a delicious dinner, Cousin Sadie."

"Aw, chust call me Sadie." She raised her eyebrows. "Okay?"

"Sure, if that's all right," Anna said.

Glen suggested that Anna get reacquainted with Luke and Marianna next door when she was ready. "It's been some time since you visited, so ya haven't seen their two youngest—Sally is all of two, and Baby Jimmy, three months."

"That'd be nice." Anna thought of her own nieces and nephews back in Mifflinburg. If the job panned out, she would miss seeing them so often.

"The older young'uns have the run of the place, as you might've guessed," Glen said as he reached for his lemonade. "More than eighty acres."

"Which reminds me . . ." Anna thought of the paths that crisscrossed the land between the woods and the *Dawdi Haus.* "I noticed some paths on this side of the house. Are they walking trails of some kind?"

"Oh, those." Glen grinned. "I helped Luke's school-age *Kinner* make those: Easy, medium, and hard they like to call them, though in Pennsylvania Dutch, of course. Often they stop by here to get snacks from Sadie to take out to their big tree house."

"Sometimes the boys even sleep out there on a warm night," Sadie added, eyes twinkling.

"You'll have to have yourself a look-see," Glen said, offering to show Anna. "It's really somethin'."

"So, all of the paths lead to the same place?" She found this surprising.

"*Jah.*" Sadie turned her fork in circles to pick up the noodles on her plate.

"How far away is the tree house?"

"Oh, several hundred yards into the woods." Glen motioned in the general direction.

Sadie added, "The children always take along their big watchdog, Brownie, even durin' the daytime."

Anna frowned. "Why?"

"Oh, in case there's a bear or . . ." Glen couldn't keep a straight face.

"*Ach* now, Glen!" Sadie laughed.

Smiling with relief, Anna enjoyed their friendly teasing. It reminded her a little of her pleasant time with Mart that morning.

Later, during a dessert of cookies and homemade vanilla ice

cream, she wondered why she couldn't seem to get Mart out of her mind. After all, she had no idea if she'd even see him again, and she had convinced herself she would be more cautious before letting herself fall for another fellow. *Anyway, it's quite possible he's seeing someone.*

At that moment, her phone rang. "Please excuse me." She rose from the table to answer it, her pulse speeding up as she retrieved the phone from her purse.

Is this Evelyn?

Quickly, Anna opened her purse and removed her phone, seeing on the ID that it was her mother. "Hullo, Mamm."

"Your Dat and I are just sitting here, wondering how your interview went."

"And holding your breath?" Anna asked.

"Jah, s'pose we are," Mamm said, sounding serious.

"To be honest, I am, too." She filled her mother in, then promised, "I'll let you know as soon as I hear something, okay?"

They talked a bit longer, and then Mamm said, "Wanita called to say Mammi Eliza's been asking about you and your trip to Strasburg. Can you imagine?"

Anna was indeed amazed. "Well, when I mentioned to Mammi that I was coming here, she seemed more lucid than she has for years. I'm shocked she remembered that conversation, though."

"Did she say anything else when you mentioned Strasburg?" Mamm asked. "Anything 'bout her time there with her Old Order great-aunt?"

"She didn't say much, really, but she seemed like her old self for a moment. She also said something about waiting for someone . . . 'by the light of the moon.'"

"That's odd." Her mother fell quiet for a moment.

"Maybe she was just mixed up," Anna suggested.

"Well, call me when you hear about the job, okay? Love you!"
"You too." Anna said good-bye and clicked off.

She returned to offer help with the dishes, but Sadie shooed her out the door with Glen, insisting that she could help at suppertime. "Go an' explore the woods . . . see that big tree house," Sadie urged her.

"Okay, but first I must charge my phone," Anna said.

"That's right. Don't miss your important call."

Anna went to her car and started it, then plugged in her phone. While it charged, she went over to join Glen in the side yard where the footpaths started. Nearby was the birdbath, where abundant flowers made a brilliant perfumed tapestry, and several wisteria vines climbed up the side of the house. From down toward the road came the *clip-clop* of a horse pulling a carriage.

"Which path would ya like to take: *leicht, middelmaessich,* or *hatt?*" Glen said, his straw hat on his head and his black work boots on his feet. He had grabbed a sturdy walking stick, as well, one that looked like it had been rubbed smooth.

"Easy, medium, and hard," Anna repeated in English. "Well, they all lead to the same place, right?"

"True, but the hard one is longer and takes unexpected turns along the way," Glen told her. "Just like life does sometimes."

Anna laughed at his analogy. "Then let's take the most challenging path."

Glen slapped his leg. "I like your *Schpank,* Anna."

Spunk, she thought with a smile.

While they stood there, waiting for her phone to be ready, he shared about his life in Strasburg, and she discovered that he was as determined as even her now-deceased Dawdi John had been. Hardworking, too, although Glen had quit working in the hayfield or raising crops and running the small turkey

41

operation on his own several years ago when Luke and his family moved in. "I don't admit to being retired yet," he joked. The way he talked about working alongside Luke so glowingly, it seemed to Anna that work was something he relished. *It might be his antidote for aging,* she thought, remembering how Dawdi John had returned to working in the barn now and then when Mammi Eliza had first become so confused. It was only later that they'd received the shocking diagnosis.

"What about you?" Glen asked. "You come from hardworkin' folk."

"That was one of the most important things Dat and Mamm taught us early on," Anna said. "Next to the importance of following God's ways and respecting our elders, the rewards of hard work were drilled into us."

This seemed to go over well with Glen, who nodded his head approvingly.

After a time, Anna glanced at her wristwatch and went to retrieve her phone, ready for their walk to the tree house.

What if I don't get the job? she thought but quickly dismissed it. There was no sense in borrowing trouble.

Anna followed Glen, and within a minute they were out of the hot sun and heading deep into the woodland, a black crow cawing at them as they went. Despite the heavy shade from the many trees, at first the scent of the nearby farmland hung in the air. Soon, though, they walked past underbrush and thick ferns, and the dank, earthy smells of the woods blocked out everything else. She wondered if sunlight ever touched the low-growing underbrush. If not, how could it grow so profusely?

"It's so beautiful here," she said as birds flitted from branch to branch, their songs part of the inviting sounds of the forest.

"Wait'll ya see the tree house," Glen said, motioning ahead.

An excitement stirred in her as they traversed several

obstacles, including a large downed maple tree, its trunk and wide branches sprawled across the path. A little ways ahead, there was another challenge—a heap of rocks, which Glen and his sons had apparently deposited there years ago after removing them from the fields. The path even skirted a murky pond with noisy frogs making their presence known, and Anna had to take care not to slip in the soft mud near its edge.

When they finally came upon it, the tree house loomed high over them, and Anna marveled at the beauty of the natural wood and the spiral staircase that wrapped around the massive trunk, leading to two levels and then to an even higher lookout far above.

"Did your son build this?" Anna asked, in awe of the amazing structure—so much more than she'd expected.

"Luke contracted a friend of his to construct it a couple of years ago." Glen paused. "An Amish company. I believe its slogan is *Going out on a limb*."

Anna laughed. "That's creative."

"The perfect slogan for a tree house–makin' company, *jah?*"

"I like it!"

Glen motioned for Anna to climb the wooden staircase, following behind. And at the top of the second level, she stopped to look at the lush greenery in all directions—trees of every kind, leafy and lofty. "You could bring a book out here and spend the whole day reading."

"*Jah*, if there was nothin' else to do." Glen pointed out a nest with four pale blue eggs. "Well, lookee here—a brand-new nest," he said as Anna stepped closer to have a peek.

"I'll remind the children not to disturb it," he said offhandedly, as though talking to himself.

Surely they won't, Anna thought as they headed back down the curved staircase to the ground.

43

"Did ya ever have such a fine place to play when you were little?" Glen asked.

"Oh, not really to play, but to dream . . . if ya know what I mean." She paused briefly and wondered if she should share about the attic room where she and Wanita sometimes read aloud from the *Little House* books, as they called them. It might sound a bit slothful to Glen. "Mamm let us sweep out and redd up a little space in the attic. Actually, at first it was for Wanita, but around the time I was reading on my own, she invited me to go up there sometimes, too." Anna didn't describe all they had done to make it cozy and the perfect place for some relief from their six brothers. It had been the spot where the two of them often talked about keeping house and cooking for their husbands some future day, wondering what it would be like to have their own families. "We sometimes watched spiders weave their webs and hoped no one would destroy them."

"Most folk would sweep 'em down without thinkin' a thing of it, I 'spect," Glen said.

"Well, we've always been mindful of nature and honestly rather tenderhearted toward animals. Once, we took care of a wounded tomcat—its paw had a nasty cut. Another time, we cared for an injured bird." Anna thought it was funny to tell Glen these things, but she went ahead and mentioned helping her Dat feed the ponies, as well. "He let me ride them, too, whenever I wanted. Well, once my chores were finished, ya know."

They both laughed at that.

"Well, I s'pose we should head back," Glen said, removing his straw hat to fan his perspiring face. "Which path should we take this time?"

"How 'bout the easy one?" She was thinking of Glen and how winded he seemed, and, too, it was the hottest time of the day.

"*Denki* for showing me this beautiful place," she said, following him over the well-worn path just as he pointed out a raccoon napping high in a nearby tree.

She stared up at the furry critter and removed her phone from her dress pocket to take several pictures. In that instant, her phone rang, and she saw that it was the call she had been waiting for. She purposely lagged behind Glen. "Hullo, Anna Beachy speaking."

Evelyn said she was calling with some unfortunate news. "It was delightful to meet you, Anna, but we've decided to offer the job to one of the other applicants. I'm sorry it didn't work out for you."

Anna felt the air fly out of her. She scarcely knew what to say—she'd been so sure of getting this job. And what about the divine nudge Sadie had felt? Had she only imagined it?

"It was a difficult decision."

"Thanks for letting me know," Anna said politely.

Evelyn mentioned again how lovely it had been to get acquainted with her, then said good-bye and hung up.

Now what? Anna thought, glad she and Glen had taken the easiest path back to the house, because suddenly she felt spent. And that was putting it mildly.

"You all right?" Just ahead on the trail, Glen had turned to look back at her.

"Evelyn called," Anna said, telling him the disappointing news.

Glen pushed his straw hat down more firmly on his head, looking a bit surprised. "Mighty sorry to hear it."

Anna nodded, unable to say more.

Chapter 5

THURSDAY, MAY 13, 1948

Just days before her sixteenth birthday, Eliza Hertzler stepped down from the enclosed gray carriage and looked around at what seemed to be an emerald sea of alfalfa in every direction but one: her great-aunt Joanna Beiler's redbrick farmhouse.

Tired from the trip from Mifflinburg, Eliza stretched her legs a bit, thankful for the charter bus that had brought her to downtown Lancaster. From there, she had taken a taxi to the cobblestoned Strasburg Village Square, where Great-aunt Joanna's neighbor Jacob Zook met her. Eliza's Mamma had informed her that, while Jacob was the bishop for the Beachy Amish church district there in Strasburg, Eliza would be surrounded by predominantly Old Order Amish families.

Eliza straightened her long black apron and headed around to the back of the buggy to retrieve her brown suitcase, anxious to get more comfortable and remove her black stockings and tight black high-topped shoes and go barefoot. She longed to brush out her dishwater-blond hair and tidy it up. She reached to take her suitcase, but Bishop Jacob shook his head, saying he would carry it.

Falling into step behind him, Eliza walked toward the grand back porch, where a large black Labrador stood at the top of the stairs, wagging its tail and panting. She wondered if much had changed about the place since her last visit with Mamma, but since she'd been such a young child at the time, it was impossible to tell.

The realization that it was only the middle of May and Mamma expected her to be there through the end of September hit her hard. *Four and a half months away from home,* she thought, stooping momentarily to pet the dog. *With all of my older sisters, why was I the one sent to help?*

She thought with a measure of frustration about the fun she would be missing back home in Mifflinburg—all the youth-related activities, specifically the many opportunities for pairing up once she was official courting age. But she couldn't let herself think too much about Ephraim Maust, the curly-haired boy she'd admired since fifth grade. Not after seeing him out riding with another girl in his shiny new open buggy last Sunday evening while she sat on the front porch. Now that she was so far away, she mustn't let her mind work on that too much. Being gone all summer surely meant she would lose any hope of catching Ephraim's eye.

Ain't fair, she thought, wishing Mamma had listened when she told her how important it was to spend the first courting-year summer at home.

"That's a mighty light suitcase," Jacob Zook said, reaching up to rap on the back screen door, his straw hat perched on his graying head.

"Well, I'll be sewin' a few more dresses while I'm here," Eliza explained as she tried to muster up a cheerful expression for the kind bishop who'd gone out of his way for her. Still, she could easily imagine how lonely she would feel being away from Mamma and her sisters—Dat, too. But Mamma had said that her coming here might lighten the load for her newly widowed aunt, bringing the poor woman some happiness again.

If only I could be happy here, too. . . .

Chapter 6

Once she'd taken a seat at the kitchen table, Anna told Sadie about the call from the director, and the woman looked crestfallen.

"Well, I'll be," Sadie said, shaking her head.

For the longest time, they both sat there without speaking.

Then Sadie suggested inviting Luke and Marianna and their two littlest ones over for ice cream after supper later, as though that might help to cheer Anna.

But Anna said she didn't feel up for it. "Besides, I'll be leaving this evening. First, though, I should call home."

Sadie nodded. "We understand."

Anna excused herself and rose from the table to make the call.

Keep your chin up, she told herself.

"Someone else was offered the job," Anna told Mamm while sitting in her car. She attempted to sound strong and confident.

"With the way this interview came about, I really didn't think I'd be giving you *this* news."

"I feel for ya, dear," Mamm said, her voice gentle and soothing. "What do ya want to do now?"

"I'll drive home tonight . . . need to be available for tours at the buggy museum tomorrow. And I'll still give my two weeks' notice, too, then figure out something else. Maybe, if the Flauds are okay with it, I'll return here to Strasburg and put my name in at some of the Amish shops."

In the momentary quiet that followed, Anna sensed her mother's reservations. "Don't worry, Mamm," she added, "the Lord is with me."

"Your Dat and I believe that, too," Mamm replied. "Please remember that you're always welcome at home, Anna, if ya change your mind."

"*Denki.*" Anna told her mother when she planned to arrive home, then they said good-bye and hung up.

Anna remained there, looking over at the flower garden and beyond to the paths leading out to the towering tree house. She felt bad now about declining Sadie's offer to invite Luke and Marianna and their children over for dessert this evening.

Getting out of her car, Anna was drawn to the woods again. And taking the narrowest path—the easiest of the three—she hurried off.

"The poor girl's discouraged," Sadie told Glen while they sat in the front room waiting for Anna to return and pack up. "And no wonder."

"Well, there was never any guarantee, so we can't fault Evelyn." Glen looked over his bifocals as he lowered the *Family Life* magazine he'd been reading.

"Even so, Anna had her hopes up. And goodness, I feel

responsible." Sadie sighed, getting up and walking back toward the kitchen window to see what Anna might be up to. The car was still parked where it had been, but there was no sign of her. *Must've taken another walk,* she thought, getting some sugar cookies from the cookie jar and putting them in a napkin for Glen. *Dear man's concerned, too, but won't let on,* she thought before returning to the front room, where a good breeze flowed through the open windows. "Would ya like a treat?" she asked him, unfolding the napkin to reveal the plump sugar cookies.

Just as she guessed, Glen took them, and she went to sit across from him on the rocking chair, where she often sat to think and pray. Pleasant evening though it was, she rocked and wondered how long Anna would stay outside.

Sadie sighed, ever so curious about who had been offered the job in Anna's stead. *Maybe someone with more experience.* But Anna herself had been a tour guide for two years already!

"I feel like goin' out to the phone shack and makin' a call to Evelyn," she said softly, almost hoping Glen wouldn't hear. "See why she didn't favor Anna."

"Why would ya do that?" Glen closed his magazine and placed it on the settee, where a few cookie crumbs had fallen. "She has her reasons, and it wouldn't be right to meddle." He removed his reading glasses and held them in his right hand. "Anyway, she might think Anna put ya up to it."

Sadie groaned. "*Ach,* true." Hard of hearing as Glenn sometimes seemed to be, she hadn't expected him to overhear her. *More like selective hearing,* she thought.

"Ain't the end of the world." Glen rose from his seat. "Somethin' else will turn up for Anna." He headed out through the kitchen and opened the noisy screen door.

Sadie assumed he, too, felt restless, and she again thought

of Anna and where she might have taken herself off to. *That dear girl!*

Just as Anna was climbing the stairs to the second level of the tree house, the mother robin flew off the nest. "So sorry," she whispered, going to lean on the bannister and look out to see where the startled bird had landed.

She spotted her on a nearby branch. "You're out on a limb," she murmured, recalling the slogan of the Amish company that had built this creative and sturdy structure, carefully nestling it around the wide tree trunk. *Is that what I've done by coming to the Flauds' before knowing if I'd get the job?*

She heaved a deep sigh, then turned to sit in one of the wooden alcoves, curious how long it might be before the robin would return to its nest. "Someone else must have needed the work more than I do." Leaning forward, she began to pray, her elbows on her knees. "I will trust Thee for whatever is ahead and offer thanks for the answer when it comes. In the name of Jesus, I pray. Amen."

Straightening on the boxlike seat, Anna saw the robin fly back to the nest and settle in, warming the pretty blue eggs. *I, too, must wait till the time is right,* she thought, gazing at the mother robin. *Till God opens the right door.*

When Anna returned to the house, Glen and Sadie invited her to join them for supper and stay for Bible reading and prayer before her return trip. Sadie had such an encouraging smile on her round face that Anna couldn't bear to disappoint her.

In passing, Glen mentioned the 1927 split of the Beachy Amish church from the original Casselman River Old Order

Amish congregation in Somerset County. "If I remember correctly, your Mamm's an Old Order Amish descendant . . . ain't that right?"

Anna nodded. "And I'm told my paternal great-grandfather was one of the deacons before that."

"'Tis interesting how we get to where we are." As he spoke, Glen glanced at Sadie with a smile.

"Chust so our journey leads us to our Savior," Sadie said sweetly. "That's what our bishop says whenever he preaches."

"*Jah*, every time," Glen agreed.

Anna sat with them in the front room while Glen read from chapter five of John's first epistle. "'And this is the confidence that we have in him, that, if we ask any thing according to his will, he heareth us: And if we know that he hears us, whatsoever we ask, we know that we have the petitions that we desired of him.'"

According to his will . . .

The words lingered in Anna's mind even as she thanked the Flauds for their hospitality and said good-bye, promising to stay in touch. She was especially grateful for Sadie's kind invitation to return and stay with them if she should decide to look for a different type of job here.

Anna drove toward Route 30 on her way back to Mifflinburg, appreciating how light it still was at the end of this long day. "Dear Lord, bless Glen and Sadie for opening their home to me," she prayed softly. "Bless them abundantly."

Once again, she placed her future in God's hands, eager to share with her parents and sister all that she had experienced in Strasburg during this short visit. And she yearned to see Mammi Eliza again, too.

I'll tell her how much I've always loved her. . . .

Chapter 7

A nna's first day back at the buggy museum turned out far better than she had anticipated. When she gave her notice, her boss released her from having to stick around the full two weeks, saying one of the other part-time guides had recently approached him about going full-time. "This will give her that opportunity," he said.

Grateful and relieved, Anna let her parents know that she was free to pursue another job, and that she would be calling Sadie to accept their invitation to stay with them while she searched.

Anna called the Flauds' shanty phone to say she could come back as soon as tomorrow, and Sadie answered right away—she had been out there checking her and Glen's messages. *Goodness, she sounds excited!* thought Anna after hanging up. Sadie had also mentioned wanting to introduce Anna to several Amish shopkeepers when she returned.

That evening, Anna drove over to Wanita's. Conrad and

their older children were out doing barn chores, so Anna visited on the back porch with her sister and the youngest children, and Mammi Eliza, too, enjoying the warm and gentle breezes. Anna filled Wanita in on her plans to look for a job at one of the Amish shops around Strasburg, mentioning Sadie's offer that Anna could stay with them for as long as she wished.

"Real nice of Sadie." Wanita put fussy little Rogene on her lap and jostled her a bit while rocking in one of the several willow rockers there on the porch. "If you get a job in Lancaster County, would you be happy, Anna?" asked Wanita.

"I think so." Anna glanced at Mammi, who seemed to be studying her every time Anna looked her way. "Guess what, Mammi . . . I just got back from a visit to Strasburg," she said for her grandmother's benefit.

Mammi nodded her head like she understood. "A perty place," she said quietly, her stare distant now.

"All the hayfields were so green . . . ready for the second cutting."

"Alfalfa," Mammi said, still gazing out at something none of them could see.

"That's right. Lots and lots of alfalfa." Anna mentioned Luke Flaud's turkey business and how he raised turkeys and sold them fully dressed. "Luke Flaud and his family live next door to Glen and Sadie. They live in the *Dawdi Haus* where Glen's father once lived. That's where I'll be staying, too."

"Oh," Mammi said, returning her gaze to Anna. "You're leavin' again?"

Anna's heart dropped. Did Mammi not want her to go?

Wanita gave a knowing nod to Anna and steered Bonnie, Bethie, and Rogene into the house to get ready for bed, leaving Anna alone with her grandmother.

"I'm going to live in Strasburg, Mammi," Anna said. "I'd like a fresh start, and so much about it just feels welcoming to me. Lord willing, I'll find a job there."

"Lord willin'," Mammi repeated with a blank stare.

"I'll visit you as often as I can, okay?" She reached for Mammi's gnarled hand, marked with brown age spots. "I love you very much," she said, a lump in her throat. "I always have. You've taught me such important things through the years, you and Dawdi John both." Gently she squeezed Mammi's hand, and she felt Mammi weakly return the squeeze, doing so three times in a row.

"You're saying 'I love you,' aren't you?" she whispered, surprised.

Mammi's face was expressionless, but her eyes glinted with tears.

"I'll come see you again." Anna held her Mammi's hand, savoring this moment, as the sun sank lower in the sky.

Sadie sat in bed talking quietly with Glen, a lightweight quilt folded neatly near the footboard, the sheet covering them in their nightclothes. The green shades had been pulled down to the windowsills, but the lamp on Glen's bedside table dimly lit the room they had made their own, setting it up with the furniture brought over from the large farmhouse—same oak bed, bureau, and blanket chest they'd always had. They even still owned the dark brown loveseat they'd sat on during their courting days at Sadie's parents' house more than forty-five years ago.

Downsizing the rest of their accumulations over the years had taken some getting used to, but at least this *Dawdi Haus* had been built to accommodate overnight guests. *Like Anna*, thought Sadie while Glen reached for the cup of cold water on his nearby little table.

"I can't tell ya how happy I am Anna's returning," Sadie said softly, turning slightly to watch Glen.

"*Jah*, and it's *gut* to see you ain't fretting now," he said. "Anna's a capable young woman. I doubt she'll have a speck of trouble finding employment round here."

"I hope you're right." She hated the thought of Anna being disappointed again.

Glen placed the cup back on the table. "We'll trust *Gott*, *jah*?" He patted her hand. "I think ya need some rest, Sadie."

"Maybe so."

"Honestly, we both do." He reached to outen the battery-operated lamp, then scooted down in bed and folded his hands over his middle. Within a few minutes, his gentle snoring commenced.

Sadie sat there pondering the day for a while longer, eventually praying for each member of their large family, from oldest to youngest, asking God to keep them on His path until the perfect day. Tonight she added Anna to the prayer, as well. *Ease her mind and grant her peace, O Lord. And give her hope for the future.*

Sadie hadn't forgotten the way Anna's brown eyes had lit up when she mentioned the Mennonite fellow who'd shown her around the information center yesterday. *Will anything come of that now?* she wondered.

Sadie closed her eyes again, though not in prayer, and rehearsed the various Amish shops and the country store she knew like the back of her hand.

Surely one of them is looking to hire a fine young woman like Anna, she thought, aware, though, that most shopkeepers had already handpicked their summer employees. *After all, it's tourist season.*

57

Halfway between Mifflinburg and Lancaster Thursday morning, Anna stopped for a soda at a convenience store. Just as she was leaving the store, her phone rang. Quickly, she answered, "Anna Beachy speaking."

"Anna, hello. This is Evelyn Leaman calling. Do you have a minute?"

"Yes, of course."

"Well, something quite unexpected has come up," Evelyn said. "The opening for a tour guide hasn't been filled, after all, so if you're still interested, the job is yours."

Anna's heart skipped a beat. "Oh yes, I'm very interested."

"I'm pleased to hear it. Would you be able to come in for training this coming Monday?"

"I'll be there." Anna silently thanked God for this surprising turn of events.

"I've asked Martin Nolt to show you around the places on our list for tourist stops. He's very knowledgeable about the local Amish attractions and such. Is that all right with you?"

All right? Anna was practically grinning now. "*Jah* . . . er, yes."

"And while I have you on the phone . . . just a couple of things," Evelyn said. "Because some of our clients are families with children, you'll be required to be fingerprinted with the FBI, as well as to have a background check."

Anna let Evelyn know she'd been through this process before for her job at the museum. "That's no problem."

"All right, then, we'll see you at nine o'clock Monday. Goodbye, Anna."

Happy and relieved, Anna ended the call and quickly called Mamm to share the good news with her. Afterward, she climbed back into her car and continued on her way. When she arrived at the Flauds' farm roughly an hour later, she saw Sadie outside sweeping the walkway rather vigorously.

She greeted her and said, "You'll never guess who called me."

"Well now, I can only hope." Sadie was smiling even before Anna could share the news.

Anna nodded. "God answered prayer!"

To herself, she thought, *And Martin Nolt will be training me!*

Chapter 8

I t wasn't in Anna's nature to inquire about the first person selected for the job, but sitting in Mart Nolt's car in the parking lot Monday morning, she learned that the woman had balked at the requirement of being fingerprinted. Anna remembered feeling a bit nervous about that herself when she was offered a job as a guide at the Mifflinburg Buggy Museum.

Sitting there behind the wheel, Mart looked sharp in his creased black pants and a white short-sleeved shirt with subtle gray stripes, open at the neck. Anna had dressed well, too, wanting to make yet another good impression on Evelyn and the other staff. *Not just Mart,* thought Anna, smiling to herself a bit.

She listened carefully as he went over the highlighted county map and discussed the most popular stops and places to see around Lancaster County—an Amish broom- and rug-maker shop, a goat farm that sold cheese, a homemade root-beer stand, an Amish hat shop, the Gordonville Book Store, and an Amish bakery. He handed her a copy of the list for her own use.

"First we'll head to the Bird-in-Hand Bake Shop on Gibbons Road," he said. "They even have a petting zoo for children."

Anna made a note of the small zoo in her spiral notebook, and Mart complimented her on her attention to detail.

"If I talk too fast, just stop me, okay?" he said.

She nodded, appreciating his demeanor—efficient, yet in a personable way.

"You'll be conducting car tours for the first weeks and months, perhaps even a year, but at some point, you'll be trained to do coach tours, too."

"I'll do my best," she assured him, nervous at the idea of entertaining a bus full of tourists. *In time*, she thought.

"I have no doubt." His tone sounded almost too positive. "Tomorrow, you'll go on an actual car tour with me," he said as he made the righthand turn onto Route 30 to head east. "I'm booked with a family from New York City."

"*Des gut.* I mean . . ."

He glanced over at her and smiled. "It's okay to let your Pennsylvania Dutch slip now and then, especially with tourists. They'll love it."

It was almost as if he thought it was cute or something, but Anna didn't mind.

At the Bird-in-Hand Bake Shop—voted for many years as having the best shoofly pie in all of Lancaster County—Mart pointed out the sugar-free and gluten-free baked goods. "A lot of your clients will be happy to know they have options," he told Anna. "As you can see, the shop also carries craft items and homemade specialty soaps. Oh, and the cheddar cheese bread is out of this world. I've never had a client buy it and not rave about it."

"Great to know." Anna jotted this down and followed Mart outside, where they passed a food truck with Amish-made soft pretzels on their way to the petting zoo, which featured a few goats and some fancy, fluffy chickens.

Since they were close to a farm that had once served as part of the Underground Railroad, they headed there next. Anna quickly learned from Mart that, in the early 1800s, a devout Quaker named Daniel Gibbons and his wife, Hannah, had built a brick farmhouse along Mill Creek, where for more than fifty years, they had secretly assisted as many as a thousand fugitives by offering them refuge and even new identities on their journey to freedom.

Mart parked the car on the shoulder and pointed out the historic house. "As you probably know, the Underground Railroad helped many people escape all the way to Canada. The network consisted of safe houses and concealed rooms in cellars, attics, and even huts all over the free states," he said. "In fact, this very house was the first station in Pennsylvania."

"Wow," she whispered, "it's like we're on the edge of history." She made a note of this location, one of several stops in Lancaster County on the route to Canada. "You sound just like a tour guide, by the way!"

Mart laughed, and Anna realized she was too close to flirting, though that had never been her style.

The Log Cabin Quilt Shop and Fabrics on the west edge of Bird-in-Hand was their next stop. There, Anna enjoyed talking with the Amish manager, who pointed out a display of how to make the various crafts the store featured. She also took Anna over to one of the large bed frames, where many different quilts were neatly laid out. "Is there a particular pattern you might be interested in?" the lovely woman asked.

Anna explained that she was training to be an area tour guide and would be bringing clients there soon. "But if I were choosing an Amish quilt for myself, it would be hard to decide. They're all so gorgeous." Anna mentioned that she and her mother and sister had made several quilts together, though they were not uniquely Amish patterns.

"We can also custom make anything you'd like," the cheerful owner said. "Any color, any pattern . . . anything at all. Be sure to let your clients know, *jah?*" And she chuckled.

Anna thanked her and, after looking around a bit more, she and Mart left to head up the street the short distance to the large building housing the Bird-in-Hand Farmers Market. Before they went inside, Mart told her to make note of the summer hours, and again, Anna jotted the information down in her notebook.

"Do you like whoopie pies?" he asked as he held the door for her.

"Who doesn't? My favorite flavor is peanut butter."

"The ideal midmorning snack," he agreed.

Mart led the way to Grandma Smucker's, where Anna purchased herself a peanut butter whoopie pie. "It's probably a good idea to sample one before I bring anyone here, don't you think?" she asked with a smile.

"Definitely," Mart said, purchasing the same flavor she'd chosen.

"Wow, these are extra big," she observed.

"More goodness in every bite," Mart replied with a twinkle, sounding like a walking advertisement.

After that stop, they returned to the car and drove past the country housewares store and several other shops featuring Amish goods before they stopped with their sack lunches at Kitchen Kettle Village. They found a picnic table near Lapp

Valley Farms Ice Cream at the far end of the cobblestone walkway.

"Usually the center's new tour guides are more familiar with
Lancaster County, having grown up here," Mart said as they
ate in the welcome shade. "In your free time, you should take
the *Discover Lancaster* getaway guide and spend time driving
around to the recommended locations. You'll especially want
to become familiar with the cemeteries and one-room Amish
schoolhouses, and our historic covered bridges, all of which we
won't have time for today."

"I've heard about a few local highlights, like the Amish Farm
and House, and the Amish Village," Anna said. "And Miller's
Smorgasbord, of course. Are those on the information center's
list of possible tour stops, too?"

"No, and neither is the market we just visited." He grinned
and took a sip of his bottle of sweetened iced tea. "Typically
we don't take tourists to the big attractions that are easy for
them to locate. We go to the out-of-the-way places, ones they
wouldn't necessarily be aware of or be able to find on their own."
He paused and studied her, as if he had something else on his
mind. "Have you ever eaten at Miller's?"

She shook her head and reached for an apple slice from the
plastic bag she'd packed at Flauds'. "Would you care for some?"

"Thanks." He took one, then held out his bag of celery sticks.
"Take as many as you like."

Amused, she reached for one, thinking that she and Mart
hadn't known each other very long, and here they were already
trading food. "*Denki*," she let slip, and his eyes twinkled at her.

"The ins-and-outs of where to go and what to highlight will
become second nature to you over time. Clients really appreciate the chance to see Amish country up close like this—
particularly how the Old Order Amish live and farm." He took

another sip of his tea. "Back-country roads typically offer the best chances to do that—where else can people see eight-mule teams in the fields plowing and cultivating, baling hay, or harvesting field corn, for example?"

Anna stopped eating to jot down these suggestions in her notebook before finishing her turkey and cheese sandwich and the rest of the apple slices.

That afternoon, they stopped to peruse the Gordonville Book Store on Old Leacock Road, which sold books for children, Amish novels, and religious books, along with Amish cookbooks, German Bibles, and homeschool curricula, games, and toys. The inspirational greeting cards caught Anna's attention, as did the scrapbook supplies.

At the Li'l Country Store and Miniature Horse Farm in Ronks, Anna loved seeing the foals in the barn. Children were also outdoors petting and feeding the full-grown miniature horses pellets from a dispenser. Visitors could take rides in carts pulled by the miniature horses, as well as see goats and alpacas. And in the Li'l Country Store gift shop, there were a variety of toy trains. "My favorite part," Mart confessed.

On the drive back to the Mennonite Information Center, Mart asked if Anna had chosen a church to attend. "Since you're new in town."

"I have," she said, and told him where.

"Well, if you'd like to come to my Mennonite church, you're always welcome." Anna thanked him and wrote down the name and address, thinking that it might be useful information for clients.

They made arrangements to finish the remainder of the route Mart had planned, but this time with actual paying customers.

"Trying to squeeze in everything we need to cover is too ambitious for one day," he said as he pulled the car into the lot of the information center and took the key from the ignition. "The places you'll see tomorrow are of particular interest to this family—when I get enough advance notice, I try to customize tours to what clients want to see."

After Anna went inside to meet with Evelyn to fill out the necessary employment paperwork, she drove back to the Flauds', glad Mart had *not* been able to fit their tour into a single day.

Chapter 9

A nna bounded out of bed early the next morning in anticipation of another day with Martin Nolt and eager to summarize yesterday's interesting events in a letter to Wanita.

After a delicious breakfast of scrambled eggs with cheese, toast with strawberry jam, and hot coffee, she listened to Glen read from the eighteenth psalm, "'As for God, his way is perfect: the word of the LORD is tried: he is a buckler to all those that trust in him.'"

Sitting with Glen and Sadie at their table, Anna knew that her parents would be pleased by the Flauds' dedication to reading Scripture every morning and evening. *Like Dat and Mamm do during our own daily family worship,* thought Anna, quickly finding some shared religious practices between the Old Order Amish and her own Beachy upbringing.

Aside from their church forbidding electricity and cars, Glen and Sadie's faith doesn't seem a whole lot different from mine, she thought now. *Maybe it's like Mammi always used to say, "At its heart, faith isn't a matter of rule keeping—it's about having a relationship with God."*

The Brown family of four included their fashionably dressed nine-year-old daughter and Mrs. Brown's gray-haired mother, all of whom arrived at the information center thirty minutes after Anna. Anna was impressed by how Mart warmly greeted each family member. After introducing her to the New Yorkers, he explained, "Anna is training to be a tour guide and will be spending the morning with us." He sent a smile her way.

Mart laid out the itinerary on the nearby counter for Mr. Brown and his wife. "Do you mind confirming these stops for our tour?" he asked the couple.

Anna could hear them talking and chuckling, getting along amiably. *Not surprising,* she thought, *considering how charming Mart can be.*

The Browns' petite dark-eyed daughter, Riley, appeared to take an immediate interest in Anna, coming over with her grandma to stand beside her. "Did you know a place called Down on the Farm Creamery is on today's schedule?" Anna asked her.

"A creamery?" Riley asked, expression puzzled.

"Where ice cream is made," Anna said.

"My favorite food!" exclaimed Riley.

Anna laughed. "That's two of us."

Riley's grandmother raised her white eyebrows and gave her granddaughter a playful poke. "We should go there *first,*" the woman said, trading a smile with her.

Apparently Mart overheard them, as he interjected, "Just wait till you taste their new flavors!"

Riley's cute face broke into a grin, her big eyes dancing.

Once they were settled in the Browns' spacious minivan, Riley's grandmother mentioned that she had her heart set on purchasing a sunbonnet.

Mart promptly added Good's Store in Quarryville to the tour stops, saying he was happy to make their time together everything they hoped for. "Today you're going to see things you've probably never seen before," he told them.

As the day progressed, the grandmother asked Mart numerous questions about Amish customs, and his patient, good-natured responses made Anna appreciate him all the more.

In the back seat beside Anna, Riley asked occasional questions of her own, and Anna was relieved to know the answers. The girl was particularly curious about the dolls she'd seen in an Amish picture book. "Why don't they have faces?" she asked.

"Well, most Amish don't give their dolls faces because they believe it's against one of the Ten Commandments."

Riley pressed her pointer finger into her cheek and frowned. "The second one, right?"

"Yes . . . about not making an image."

Riley seemed to ponder that. "So is that why they don't want their pictures taken, either?"

"That's exactly why." Anna nodded. "Even though I'm not Old Order Amish, I've made those little dolls for myself. But I've never used a book pattern—just created my own. I do that for my clothes, too, just like traditional Amish."

Riley listened, her eyes wide. "Must be hard."

"My Mamm taught me when I was around your age, so I've had plenty of practice. She works her fingers nearly stiff with all the sewing she does for the family, and for other folk, too." Anna explained that her Mamm kept a large wooden box full of fabric scraps. "There was always plenty of material for the small dolls I liked to make when I was younger."

"Did you ever sell them?"

"I liked to give them away, actually, but sometimes in the summer, I'd put a basketful of them out on our roadside vegetable stand, and tourists would offer to pay for them. Whatever they wanted to give was fine with me."

"You're so nice, Anna." Riley smiled up at her.

"And you're very sweet," Anna replied.

Riley asked her then why her head covering was different from those of the other Amish she'd seen today.

"You have a sharp eye."

"Thanks!" The little girl leaned closer to whisper, "I want to be a fashion designer when I grow up."

"Well then, you might be learning to make patterns of your own someday," Anna said. "The reason for our different *Kapp* styles is that each Plain community has a unique head covering. If you pay careful attention when you leave Lancaster County, you'll find you won't see another style of prayer cap exactly like the heart-shaped ones around here."

Riley took this in, looking quite serious. "Oh, that's cool."

Anna smiled and remembered how, at that age, she, too, had often imagined what her life as a grown-up would be like. But because the Beachy Amishwomen she'd known rarely pursued careers, the desire of her heart had been—and still was—to be a loving wife and mother to many children. *Like Mamm . . .*

As they began to head back in the direction of the information center, Anna noticed a large farm ahead, where a stone wall separated a horse paddock from a green meadow. The wall's gray weathered stones looked striking in the noontime sun, and she observed an arched wrought iron sign over the entrance: *Peaceful Meadows Horse Retreat.*

Riley must have noticed it, too, because she announced, "Daddy, look at that ginormous horse farm!" craning her neck to see as they passed the turn into the place.

"Someone sure likes horses." Mart glanced over his shoulder from where he sat up front with Mr. Brown.

Riley nodded her head and grinned. "Can we please stop there, Daddy?"

Mart deferred to Mr. Brown in the driver's seat.

"Maybe later, honey," her father said, explaining that they had lunch reservations coming up soon.

Like Riley, Anna was fascinated by the place and wondered why it was called a retreat. Quickly, she checked her phone for information. *Peaceful Meadows Horse Retreat*, she read silently, *offers horseback riding therapy and is owned by an Amish family whose mission is to offer hope to special needs people from infants to adults.* There were multiple glowing reviews from parents whose children had been helped by the therapeutic program, as well as comments from volunteers.

I should look into this for future clients, she decided.

After work that afternoon, Anna drove back to the horse therapy farm. Entering the long lane from the main road, she came upon what looked at first like a campground retreat, with a high hedge growing on either side and an old stone wall running along the base of the paddock to the south, dividing it from the pastureland. No horses or people were in sight.

She parked and made her way past the cow barn to a large horse stable. Finding that it, too, was empty, she assumed the horses must be grazing in the meadow and meandered around the side of the building. A brawny blond Amishman wearing a short-sleeved gray shirt and black suspenders, his straw hat pushed down hard on his head, was briskly walking her way, his eyes cast to the ground.

"Hello," she said, not even sure he realized she was standing there.

When he lifted his eyes and saw her, he frowned momentarily. "Lookin' for someone?" he asked, as if he thought she were lost.

"Saw the sign out front and was just curious about this farm. I noticed your website says you offer horseback riding therapy."

"*Jah*, that's what we do here." He continued to scrutinize her, running his hand across his closely cropped blond beard. "My uncle owns the place. It's my job to keep things running . . . hopefully smoothly."

"My father breeds ponies, but I've never heard of therapy using horses."

"So, you're a fellow horse person." He paused. "*Ach*, I should introduce myself. My name's Gabe Allgyer." He stepped forward to shake her hand.

"I'm Anna Beachy."

Gabe nodded, a glimmer in his blue eyes. "I've heard the Beachy name before. Plenty of 'em round here, but you're from around Mifflinburg, ain't?"

She was surprised. "How did you know?"

"Your *Kapp*'s like the one the womenfolk up there wear, *jah*? I used to make some deliveries there, back before my wife passed away."

"Oh, I'm sorry," Anna said, thinking how very young he was to be a widower.

"*Denki* . . . it's been two years already," he said solemnly, eyeing her *Kapp* again.

She reached up to touch it.

"What brings ya to Lancaster County?" he asked, his gaze friendlier now.

"Well, I've taken a part-time job working as a tour guide." She looked toward the far meadow, where she could see a palomino, a half dozen chestnut quarter horses, and a black pony grazing. The pony whinnied, bobbing its head up and down. "It's so beautiful here," she breathed, hoping Gabe wouldn't rush her off.

"A tour guide," he said quietly. "Where at?"

She told him and he nodded, saying that he knew several people who worked there. "Helen Weber, for one. She's the receptionist, so I'm sure you've met her."

"*Jah*. What a small world." Anna wished he would tell her more about how riding therapy worked, so she asked.

An expression of curiosity crossed his face. "Do ya know someone who could benefit from our program?"

"No," she said. "I just love horses and find the idea of using them to help people really fascinating."

Gabe seemed eager now to tell her more about the different programs available at the retreat for different needs. "For instance, a child who's never walked can experience the feeling of walking while ridin' a horse." He went on to talk about the confidence this therapy could give to a child or teenager with a disability. "And things like learning to groom or lead a horse can help improve hand-eye coordination."

As he talked more about some of the children they had helped, or how often a typical patient visited, Anna felt herself growing more and more impressed.

"Listen to me, though, goin' on and on," Gabe said, removing his hat and revealing more of his tanned and handsome face.

She smiled. "It's obvious you're excited about what you're doing."

"It's what gets my boots on in the morning," he said with a

chuckle. "Well, if I can answer any other questions, just give me a holler." He removed a business card from his wallet and gave it to her. "Leave a message at the phone shed." He pointed to a narrow wooden structure standing in the middle of the hayfield.

"*Denki* for your time," Anna said, accepting the card and yet another firm handshake from Gabe. Then, making her way back to the car, she smiled at having stumbled onto something so wonderful.

She opened her car door and was about to get in when she heard rapid footsteps. Turning, she saw Gabe waving her down. "Did I forget something?" she asked, leaning on her car door.

"*Nee*, I just wanted to say . . . if you'd like to observe one of the classes we offer, you're certainly welcome to return on a Tuesday, Thursday, or Saturday. Sessions start at nine o'clock, but if you want to come before a session, that would be fine, too. Just come on over to the stable." Gabe gave her a quick grin.

"I might do that," she said, very much liking the idea. "I'm off on Saturdays."

"All right, then, I'll be seein' ya, Anna Beachy."

She nodded, smiling to herself as she got into the car and drove away.

Chapter 10

While at work the next morning, Anna learned from Evelyn that today she would be going on a car tour with a different guide—a young Mennonite woman named Charlotte Meck. "You'll have the opportunity to see how another guide handles tours, as well as where she takes clients and what information she shares about local Amish culture," Evelyn told her.

Anna was grateful for the chance to observe Charlotte, whom she got acquainted with in the break room before setting out. The young woman's face shone when she told Anna that she had just become engaged.

"How wonderful!" Anna said. "Congratulations."

"Austin's just the man for me . . . handpicked by God, I like to say."

Anna smiled at that. "You must feel blessed."

Charlotte nodded. "I couldn't be happier." She asked about

Anna's day yesterday and what stops they'd made on the tour, and Anna recalled most of them from memory.

"Good for you!" Charlotte said. "Well, today you'll get to meet a charming middle-aged couple from England." Her light brown eyes sparkled with obvious anticipation. "I actually took them on a tour last October, and now they're back for more. If you do this long enough, you'll discover that some people will specifically request you, once they get to know you. Since we customize tours, we have a fair number of repeat customers."

"I like that idea." Anna enjoyed talking with Charlotte, who was just as friendly as Martin. And thinking of Mart, Anna realized she had not seen him yet today.

He must already be out on a tour, she assumed.

After Sadie had served the noon meal of fried chicken and mashed potatoes to Glen and thoroughly redded up the kitchen, she walked out to the little wooden phone shed to check for any voice messages. She was surprised but pleased to discover one from Rachel Beachy, Anna's mother.

"Hello, Cousin Sadie," Rachel's voice came over the recording. "I thought I'd call to see how our daughter's getting along there. No hurry, but when you have a few minutes, would you return my call? You have our number."

Sadie clicked off and searched for Alvin and Rachel's number on the paper chart thumbtacked to the bulletin board on the wall near the telephone. The last names were listed in alphabetical order, so it was easy to spot Beachy. "I'll call her now, since I'm here," Sadie murmured, suspecting her cousin was missing her daughter. *I'd miss Anna, too, if she were mine. . . .*

Sadie dialed the number and recalled that her rather modern Mifflinburg cousins had a phone or two inside their house. *Must be convenient come winter,* she thought, though she tried not to covet that for herself.

Her cousin answered, "Rachel Beachy speaking."

"Hullo, Rachel. I heard your message. Everything all right there?"

"Oh *jah* . . . just hoping Anna's doing okay, getting settled in."

"She's fine, from what I can tell." Sadie mentioned that Anna had attended both Sunday morning and evening services at a nearby Beachy Amish church. "And she's talkin' of going tonight to Bible study, too."

"Good to know," Rachel said, then sighed. "Honestly, it's too quiet around here. We're already missing our girl."

"I imagine you are, but I s'pect she'll want to visit yous from time to time."

"And we'll be happy to have her, believe me."

"I remember how tough it can be when a daughter first moves away," Sadie said, hoping to soothe Rachel's qualms. "You've raised a real sweet young woman."

"I hope she can be some help to ya there." Rachel paused a moment. "We pray daily for the Lord's hand on her life."

Sadie caught herself nodding. Cousin Rachel sometimes talked so freely about the Lord God and what she believed He was doing in folks' lives; Sadie rather liked that about her.

"*Denki* again for taking Anna in and looking out for her. Alvin will be sending a check soon."

"*Ach,* ya mustn't."

"*Nee,* it's already been decided."

Recalling Rachel's way of insisting when her mind was set on something, Sadie had to smile.

"Of course, once Anna starts getting a paycheck, she'll be responsible to pay her way," Rachel said, that determined tone still in her voice.

"Maybe Glen and Alvin should discuss this," Sadie suggested, wanting to stay out of it.

"All right, then. I'll have Alvin contact him."

They said good-bye and hung up.

"Rachel Beachy sure knows her own mind," Sadie whispered, opening the wooden door to the phone shack to head home.

Anna was just heading out to her car in the parking lot at the information center when Mart pulled up. He got out and waved to her. "I was hoping to see you, Anna." He came over. "How'd it go with Charlotte?"

"Wonderful. Her style is different than yours, but I really enjoyed the tour. I learned a lot from her, too." Anna went on to say how delightful the British couple had been, sharing some of their customs, including the various times the English took tea during the day. "I didn't let on that I prefer coffee." She laughed.

"Right?" Mart nodded, chuckling.

The wind whipped up, and Anna placed her hand on her *Kapp* to secure it. The sun had disappeared behind a large cloud, and the scent of rain was in the air.

Mart glanced at the darkening sky, then at her. "I was wondering, would you like to have supper with me at Miller's Smorgasbord tomorrow evening?"

She smiled, glad he was welcoming her in this way—a good opportunity to get further insights into local spots of interest to tourists. "That would be nice, sure." She offered to meet him at the restaurant, and he agreed. *Best to drive separately since we're merely co-workers*, she thought, not wanting to give him the impression she was reading too much into his invitation.

"I'll look forward to it," Mart said, then arranged for a time to meet. "It will be great to get to know you better, Anna."

78

She smiled again, still holding on to her *Kapp* in the gusty wind. *"Denki* for inviting me."

After an early supper, Anna left in a heavy rain for Bible study at church. There, while the rain pattered against the church windows, she sat with two sisters, Heidi and Eleanor Denlinger, who said their aunt owned a candle store in Kitchen Kettle Village. They invited her to drop by the shop sometime, indicating they could give tourists a short tour. Anna made a mental note to visit soon, although she knew this particular candle shop was not on the list of suggestions the information center had provided. Even so, she liked Heidi and Eleanor and looked forward to going to a party with them after Sunday night church. Heidi, the more outgoing of the two, hinted that she would introduce Anna to their brother, Lester, at the get-together open to courting-age youth.

Anna's response stuck in her throat—she hadn't anticipated being set up. *When it rains, it pours,* she thought, then chided herself. She *did* want to meet solid Christian young men, so she finally agreed to go along with Heidi's wishes even though Mart had invited her out for supper tomorrow night. Anna would continue to pray earnestly for God to lead her in the right direction.

Momentarily, she thought of Atley Brenneman. *No more unpleasant surprises for me! And no regrets, either!*

Chapter 11

———————————— ❦ ————————————

Outside the redbrick two-story entrance, Miller's Smorgasbord was crowded, with patrons waiting.

Anna spotted Mart standing off to the side, and when she caught his eye, he smiled and walked toward her. "Hi," she said, glad she'd worn one of her best royal blue dresses, because even without a necktie, he looked to be dressed for church, too.

"Nice to see you again, Anna," he greeted her. "I hope the traffic wasn't too congested."

"Oh, just the last few miles on the Lincoln Highway."

"An extra traffic lane would really help. Motorists have complained about that for years." Mart suggested they go inside to the air-conditioned lobby and wait for their number to be announced over the intercom, as he had already put his name in for a table for two.

"I can't believe how busy it is on a Thursday evening," Anna said, surveying the place as he held the door for her. Several families stood just inside the front door, waiting for tables.

"It's like this well into November—tourist season, you know." He led her to a bench, where they sat, speaking just loudly enough to be heard above the din of the room. "We celebrated my dad's birthday here last Tuesday night, and it was this packed then, too."

"I guess word spreads about great food."

"You'll soon find out why," Mart said with a grin. Then he asked, "I'm curious . . . you never really said. What interested you in becoming a tour guide at the buggy museum in your hometown?"

She explained that a friend of her oldest brother had heard they were looking for a history buff for a guide position. "Since I had my nose in history books all the way through high school, it was an ideal fit." She laughed a little. "In fact, I always keep a history book of some kind in my car. You never know when you'll need something to fill your time."

Martin seemed intrigued. "What's your favorite era?"

Anna shrugged. "Oh, Colonial America, I guess. I like reading about the way things were done, especially how the women of the time lived and worked."

Mart nodded. "Nothing like a book to occupy the mind."

"What kind of books do you enjoy?" she asked.

"Lately I've been reading about the Underground Railroad in Pennsylvania," he said.

"So, how did you get involved with conducting tours at the information center?" Anna asked, drawn to his attentive way.

"Well, let's see . . . I started out booking horse-and-buggy rides for a local New Order Amish couple—set up a website for them and helped them attract tourists. I got a kick out of interacting with people who seemed curious about the Plain culture."

"What do most center guides do during the winter months when tourism is down?" she asked.

"Since some are retired, they don't need as much income and just enjoy the time off. A few guides are right out of college, though, so they pick up part-time winter jobs. I work year-round at my uncle's dairy farm, with extra hours during January and February. Things at the center tend to pick up again in March and April," he said.

Their number was called, and she and Mart walked toward the hallway, where a hostess led the way to their assigned table.

Once they were seated beside windows looking out on Amish farmland, Mart brought up that Anna had mentioned attending high school. "I didn't realize your church permitted higher education."

"Well, some Beachy families allow it, and others don't," she explained. "A few families homeschool their children, but our bishop leaves a lot of that up to the individual family to decide. One young man even went on to get his doctorate."

"But is college encouraged?" he asked.

"Not really. Of course, there are also some who leave for so-called greener pastures, just as in any set-apart community." She was thinking now of Atley Brenneman in particular.

"I understand," Mart said, holding her gaze. "The world can certainly be tempting."

The young waitress returned to take their orders, and Anna chose the traditional buffet at Mart's encouragement.

"You'll have plenty of options for meats, vegetables . . . even a variety of soups, salads, and breads," the waitress said.

"And most important, a great selection of desserts," Mart added with a smile.

The waitress agreed and waved in the direction of the separate section for pies, cakes, ice cream, and other sweets. "You'll find the meat station over there," she said, "through that short hallway. Today we have baked ham with a mouthwatering cider sauce, slow-roasted top sirloin, fried chicken to die for, baked cod . . . all of that and more."

Anna thanked her.

"You won't find a better buffet around here," Mart told Anna after the waitress left. Then he folded his hands. "Let's give thanks."

She bowed her head, grateful for Mart's kindness to her and for his prayer, which was reverent yet openhearted—much the way she had been taught to pray.

The rest of the evening was filled with the enjoyment of the many delicious dishes, and Anna tried to pace herself, taking small portions of a variety of things while Mart filled up his plate more than once.

They discussed their mutual hope to share God's love with the clients they met, and Anna confided that it was one of the main motivators behind her pursuing this particular job. "Besides my fondness for local history, that is."

When they were ready to go to the dessert island, Anna smiled when they both reached for the warm chocolate pecan pie. Mart also took a large sugar cookie, one of Anna's favorites, but she was too full to indulge in more than one sweet. And anyway, she could always have something later at Sadie's, since the dear woman seemed to enjoy baking treats of all kinds.

They ate their desserts leisurely in between sips of coffee. When they finished, Anna thanked him for the evening. She and Mart exchanged phone numbers, then walked together to the parking lot.

"Have a nice weekend," he said, waiting by the car until she unlocked it and got settled inside.

"You too." Anna waved to him as he stepped back. She exited

onto the Lincoln Highway and found herself grinning as she drove back to the Flauds'. She'd felt quite at ease with Mart, almost as if they'd grown up in the same circles. For certain, the evening marked a promising start to her new life in Lancaster County.

"I'm thinkin' Anna has found herself a friend," Sadie remarked as she and Glen sat in the front room, where an occasional breeze came in through the west-facing windows, a welcome relief from the warm day.

"A possible beau, maybe?" Glen chuckled.

"Could be one in the makin'."

"I daresay it's real nice for her to have another young person to spend time with around here."

Sadie smiled and agreed. She knew from Rachel that it had been a year since Anna had broken up with her serious beau. "It wonders me if the young man is the Mennonite fella she mentioned before she went home for that short visit."

Glen nodded, but from his vague expression, it looked as if he had something else on his mind. Something completely unrelated.

"Glen?" Sadie said, leaning toward him.

"Oh, I was just thinking of makin' a fresh batch of ice cream for tomorrow night," Glen replied as he got up. He stopped to straighten the embroidered wall hanging Sadie had made years ago. "If Anna's around, it'd be nice if Luke and family came over tomorrow after supper."

"Well, even if she's not. And we can always do with more ice cream." As Sadie rose to go to the kitchen for some cold water, she could hear Glen in the pantry, getting his hand-cranked ice-cream maker. *He really wants Anna to spend some time with*

Luke and Marianna again . . . and to meet their little ones, Sadie thought. *But making new friends her own age is surely her priority.*

Sadie got busy gathering the ingredients for a vanilla sponge cake with chocolate frosting. Summer baking was more tolerable early in the morning or later in the evening, when the sun was low in the sky. *We'll have us a delicious dessert,* she thought, realizing that she, too, hoped Anna might be available tomorrow evening.

Truth be told, the house was ever so quiet with Anna out, Sadie thought as she worked. *Tomorrow morning I'll visit poor Eva. Maybe Anna will come along.* She recalled that, because as a newcomer Anna was considered a part-time employee, she was not on call Fridays and Saturdays. Of course, on Sundays the information center was closed for the Lord's Day, so Anna would be busy with tours only four days a week. *I could show her how to make my little cheer-up cards, if she's interested,* she thought.

Sadie brought the water to a boil for the cake batter, then melted the butter and contemplated Anna's parents' willingness to let her move here to live with Old Order Amish folk, cousins or not. It made Sadie wonder if they knew about Rachel's mother's experiences here decades ago.

Mamm always said Eliza Hertzler was sorely tested that summer, thought Sadie, guessing that Eliza hadn't told her granddaughter much, if anything, about those months.

O Lord, may Anna's time here be pleasant, surrounded by Thy love.

Chapter 12

Eliza Hertzler was busy cutting and bundling what Great-aunt Joanna had happily declared *"a bumper crop of asparagus."* Her aunt was sitting over on the large back porch sipping cold meadow tea this morning as Eliza placed the bundles of asparagus in the faded red wagon that worked fine despite recent years of little use.

After five long days in Strasburg working in the house or garden, Eliza was itching to see more of the area. Today she was responsible for pulling the asparagus-filled wagon up the road to the farmhouse of Joanna's cousin Nellie. *"She'll make good use of it,"* Aunt Joanna had declared at breakfast.

Looking back at the wagonful, Eliza pulled a face at the thought of canning all of that produce. She'd never cared a whit for asparagus, despite its supposedly being a healthy vegetable and *"good for what ails ya,"* according to Mamma. Healthiness certainly didn't stop Eliza from turning up her nose at the green vegetable.

As if somethin' ails me, she thought, picking up her pace on this mild and sunny day. She gazed ahead down the road, glad the pavement wasn't too hot just yet, barefoot as she was. "The only thing ailin' me is that I'm stuck here," she murmured, feeling sorry for herself as she yearned yet again for home and wondered what Ephraim was doing this fine day.

She kept rehashing the fact that Mamma had chosen *her* to come and assist Aunt Joanna. Strasburg had sounded like a foreign country when Mamma had first brought up the idea of sending Eliza here. *Mamma didn't know it, but I felt panicked at the thought of leaving home,* she thought, missing her three older sisters, each one an expert in harvesting and putting up vegetables. Unlike Eliza, they were also skilled in the virtue of patience, knowing when to offer their opinion on a matter and when to hold their peace.

Truth be told, Eliza wished to goodness her great-aunt hadn't contacted Mamma, asking for help. And yet, Eliza did feel sorry for her, pining for her deceased husband as she seemed to be while pacing the creaky floors at night. Eliza had heard her more than twice in the past few days. The poor woman needed comfort, but Eliza wasn't up to the task. Rather, she had simply covered her head with the sheet and quilt, knowing that if she didn't get adequate sleep, she wouldn't be any good for the long list of chores her great-aunt wielded daily.

She keeps mentioning my boundless energy. Eliza lifted her face to look around her as she pulled the wagon to Cousin Nellie's, who wasn't Eliza's cousin at all, at least that she knew of. *So many kinfolk of kinfolk, it's hard to know who's who sometimes.*

One thing she did know, though—the fair-haired Old Order Amish fellow coming this way was mighty hasty over there on the other side of the road. She had just now noticed the young man, and as he approached, she could hear him robustly whistling.

And just like that, the whistling stopped and he crossed the road, coming toward her. "Hullo," he said with a wave toward the wagon. "Mind if I help?"

"I don't need help," she said, struck by how good-looking he was.

"A plucky one, ya are." And without saying more, he leaned over and grabbed the wagon handle from her.

As he began to pull the wagon, leaving her no choice but to fall in step behind him, she was stunned speechless, rare for her. "Where ya headed . . . and where ya from?" He turned back to eye her tan cape dress and white *Kapp*.

It was all she could do not to make up a story, tempted to fool this self-assured young fellow. But she remembered the proverb Aunt Joanna had read earlier about speaking the truth and showing forth righteousness.

"I'm makin' a delivery to Nellie Petersheim," she admitted. "And I'm from Mifflinburg, which may as well be halfway round the world." This last bit she added more softly.

"Ah, so you're the one helpin' Joanna Beiler this summer."

"Goodness—how many people know I'm here?"

"Ain't a single thing hidden from view round here, trust me."

She shook her head. "How on earth can that be?"

"Just is." He glanced at her now, his blue eyes serious—yet she felt sure he was doing his best to hold in a chuckle.

"Okay, then, what's my name?"

"Eliza," he said with a gleeful lilt in his voice.

She wondered why she was still letting this cocky stranger pull the wagon and dominate the conversation. "Listen, if you know so much about me, it's only fair I should know something 'bout you, too, *jah*?"

He couldn't seem to keep a straight face. "Like what?"

"Do ya have a name of your own, just maybe?"

"They call me Eb at suppertime."

"And what do they call ya other times?"

"It's Eb then, too."

"That's not a name, though . . . it's a nickname!" she said, rather enjoying this back and forth now, still looking for Cousin Nellie's house to come into view.

"You're right. It is short for somethin'." He paused and grinned at her. "Ever hear of Ebenezer in the Bible?"

She nodded. "But that wasn't a person."

"Well, no. And how I got it, well . . . it's a complicated story. If ya want, I might tell it to ya sometime, Eliza."

She had to smile. Eb was unlike anyone she'd ever met. He seemed to have more gumption than even her older brother, who liked to nearly tease the life out of her.

"Okay, I don't have to know," she said, though she really wanted to, if only to keep talking with him.

"All right, then."

They walked together without saying more. When she saw Nellie's house, Eliza breathed a sigh tinged with a bit of disappointment, knowing she might never hear Eb's story. "That's the house up there," she said, pointing toward the rise.

Eb chuckled. "I know Nellie Petersheim's place like the back of my hand."

"Oh?"

"I've worked for her husband, Yost, harvesting corn."

So, there was a possibility she'd see Eb again. "Well, how 'bout that?"

He asked if she could find her way back to the widow Beiler's place.

Now she was the one laughing. "I should hope so!" There were only four farms between Nellie's and Joanna's.

Eb pulled the wagon all the way up the rise, to the back door. "There you are." He nodded. "*Gut* to meet ya, Eliza."

She almost said "*You too*," but stood there silently as Eb turned and headed back down the lane, resuming his quick stride and his whistling.

Chapter 13

⸺⸺⸺⸺⸺⸺⸺⸺⸺❧⸺⸺⸺⸺⸺⸺⸺⸺⸺

Anna rose just after dawn Friday morning and slipped out of the house for a walk, replaying in her mind the meal with Mart at Miller's. She felt fairly certain he was interested in her, and goodness, they had learned quite a lot about each other in the space of a single evening.

She strolled along the roadside and relished watching the horses and buggies—the *clip-clop-clip*ping seemed soothing in its own way. "I like it here," she murmured, recalling strolls along this same road with Wanita when their family came to visit off and on through the years. Though the place was as rural and tranquil as her father's in Mifflinburg, it had a specialness about it.

When she returned to the house, Anna partnered with Sadie to cook breakfast—fried eggs over easy and apple oven pancakes. Sadie set bananas in a large bowl for the table, then poured orange juice in small glasses and hot coffee in mugs.

"Would ya like to go with me today to visit my sister Eva?" Sadie asked as they worked together.

"Is this the sister who lives with her *Maidel* daughter?"

"*Jah*, and once a week I spend a good part of the day with Eva to spell off Molly. I often take meals over, too. Eva's sufferin' from dementia, you see."

At that word, a shiver ran through Anna. "Oh," she said softly. "I'm awful sorry."

Sadie bowed her head. "I can't tell ya how hard it is to watch her forget everything she's ever known."

Anna drew in a breath. "I understand . . . I truly do."

"Well, of course you do, with your poor Mammi." Sadie shook her head like she was disappointed in herself. "I've had to learn to be careful what I say around Eva now that she's like this . . . what things to mention and what not to."

Anna listened, nodding. "Mammi Eliza gets really anxious and upset if someone counters what she's saying, even though she may be incorrect. We all simply agree with her, no matter what. One of her doctors shared with us pretty early on in her Alzheimer's that we should come to expect this. It's been so helpful."

"*Gut* to know, Anna. *Denki*."

"It's been painful to witness Mammi's slide from being an outgoing person full of ideas and life to someone so withdrawn and quiet. Such a contrast." She looked away, gathering her thoughts. "It weighs heavy on my heart."

Sadie listened, her eyes bright now with tears. "I understand, dear. And Wanita's sacrifices as a caregiver are a blessing for the whole family, not chust your Mammi Eliza. It takes a lot of extra energy and patience."

Anna agreed, thankful that Sadie seemed to comprehend what she and her family were going through, Mammi Eliza included. "*Denki*, Sadie . . . it really helps to talk about this."

On the ride over to visit Eva and Molly later, Anna gazed out the window at the wild yellow irises blooming along the ditch as the Flauds' horse and buggy moved down the narrow road. It had been some time since she'd traveled this way. Back when her Mamm's parents were both living, they had preferred to travel by buggy, even though they were also Beachy Amish and able to own a car. Sometimes, Mammi Eliza would even take Anna and Wanita to market in their carriage. *Years ago*, Anna thought, savoring the relaxing pace as Sadie commented on each farm they passed, talking about the Old Order Amish families who lived there—all of them devout church members and some ministerial brethren.

"Do you know anything more than what you've already told me about my grandma's time here as a teenager?" Anna asked as they rode along.

Sadie shook her head. "Sorry I'm not more help. Maybe my parents know something."

Tucking a loose strand of hair back into her thick bun, Anna hoped *someone* might know more about that long-ago summer.

She and Sadie rode in silence for a while, the horse trotting faster now, its glossy mane waving up and down.

"Say, Glen and I are thinkin' of having Luke and Marianna and the children over for ice cream this evening. Will ya be home?" Sadie asked.

Anna nodded. "Sure."

"I think you'll enjoy our little toddler girl."

"Sally, right?" Anna loved her name.

"*Jah*, and is she ever a talker."

"I was, too, when I was little, Mamm said. *Bapplich*, ya know."

Sadie smiled at her. "I remember."

"But the older I got, the more shy I became."

Nodding, Sadie said, "I was just the opposite, I'm afraid." She laughed. "I was bashful as a youngster, and now . . . well, listen to me go on and on!"

Anna shared in the laugh, and after a moment, Sadie mentioned little Jimmy, Luke and Marianna's baby. "I can scarcely wait for you to meet both children."

"Are the older boys coming, too?" Anna asked. "The ones who helped Glen make the paths out to the tree house?"

"*Nee*, after supper they usually go and help at the next farm over, but you'll meet them sometime soon."

"Maybe I'll run into them at their tree house." Anna laughed. "I've been there twice already." She paused. "I'm oddly drawn to it. Guess I feel close to God in the woods. Always have."

"Well, it's been quite some time since I managed to get out there." Sadie adjusted the driving lines she held in both hands. "Marcus and Eddy—Luke's school-age boys—wanted me to walk with them on the more difficult path that's blocked by a pile of rocks. I had to say no. Even with their help, I didn't dare risk a fall. Not with my bad knee."

Anna recalled Mammi Eliza's broken ankle a couple years after Dawdi passed away. "You're *schmaert* not to take that path, Sadie."

"*Jah*, the path of least resistance is best for these aging bones."

Anna thought of Sadie's sister Eva and the fall that had broken her hip, leading to the surgery that had left her so confused. "You've very wise," she agreed.

Anna's first impression of Sadie's sister Eva had been that the older woman seemed more wakeful and alert than Mammi Eliza typically was lately. Eva also stared at Anna quite a lot, a puzzled smile on her face, as though trying to place her. And when Sadie introduced Anna as Rachel Slaubaugh Beachy's youngest daughter, Eva had quietly nodded her head as if she understood.

Later, when Anna and Sadie returned from their visit, Anna went to her room and studied the list of sights the information center had given her to work from, as well as the county map. She circled the Amish schools in Strasburg, Paradise, and Leacock, intending to drive to see all of them. She had told Sadie she wouldn't be back for the noon meal, but Sadie had insisted on making a ham, cheese, and lettuce sandwich for her, also packing plastic bags of carrots and celery, and a thermos of cold lemonade.

"I owe you," Anna said, adjourning to the kitchen and thanking Sadie for her thoughtfulness. Then, lunch bag in hand, she headed off to check out the spots she'd marked on the map. This way, she could get some personal experience and better determine how much time to plan for each location.

At the one-room Amish school on Route 741 and Belmont Road, Anna discreetly took pictures of the exterior and the playground from her car, then drove on to do the same at the other Amish schools and even cemeteries in those areas. Tomorrow, she would travel to other nearby townships and burgs populated with Amish folk.

Anna arrived back to the Flauds' well before supper and with time to help Sadie by going out to cut leaf lettuce from the small salad garden. As she headed indoors to wash the lettuce, she could hear Glen and Luke's free-range turkeys gobbling and clucking while meandering through the weeds in the pasture over yonder, foraging for seeds and insects. Once the fresh lettuce was clean, she tore it into bite-size pieces to use for the individual salad plates of lettuce, cottage cheese, and pear halves from one of the many quart jars in Sadie's large pantry.

Meanwhile, Sadie's meatloaf and her scalloped potatoes were baking in the oven, filling the kitchen with wonderful aromas. Sadie turned down the gas under the pot of new snap peas from the garden and went to get some butter for the table.

"Honestly, it feels like I'm s'posed to be here, and maybe not just for the job," Anna told her in the stillness of the kitchen. She didn't let on how, since her breakup with Atley, she had longed to begin anew . . . someplace different from home.

"I s'pose that's one way to say you're hopin' for a beau," Sadie said, glancing at her. "Ain't so?"

Anna only smiled, wanting to let all this newfound happiness settle down—her job, her growing friendship with Mart, and her unexpectedly comfortable relationship with her kind and welcoming host and hostess.

Sadie changed the subject, mentioning that, for their Old Order church district, this Lord's Day was a "between Sunday," which meant no Preaching service. "We'll be goin' round visiting some of Glen's relatives, if you'd like to join us," Sadie invited her.

"Well, I plan to attend the fellowship in Bird-in-Hand," she told Sadie, pleased to discover that the church had been founded by a Beachy Amish bishop.

"It's up to you where ya worship, of course." Sadie wiped her brow with a hankie she'd taken out from beneath her sleeve. "Our house is your house . . . you may come and go as you wish."

Anna appreciated that, looking forward to the next service and even the party later that day. It would give her another chance to make new friends.

After supper, Anna helped clear the table, knowing Sadie and Glen's son and daughter-in-law and children would be arriving soon. Besides Glen's homemade ice cream, there was a cake that Sadie had tucked away on a pretty cake plate with a cover.

While Sadie quickly washed the dishes, Anna swept the floor, moving the chairs and the wooden bench on the side closest to the sink to do a thorough job. "That was a *wunnerbaar-gut* meal," Anna said. "The meatloaf was so moist and tasty."

Sadie smiled. "I put tomato juice in the meat mixture. What about yous?"

"Mamm likes steak sauce or catsup, either one."

"That so?" Sadie said without turning around, still hurrying through her work.

"I'll come and wipe dishes as soon as the floor's swept," Anna promised.

Sadie placed the last plate on the dish rack and drained the sink. She dried her hands on her white work apron, then reached inside the cupboard below to remove two tea towels.

Anna took the second towel, and in just a few minutes, they had everything dried and put away.

Sadie glanced over her shoulder, as if checking to see if her son and his family might be arriving. "We'll have us a real nice time."

"I hope the baby's not shy around me," Anna said. "I can't wait to get my hands on him."

"He's a happy little one. You'll see."

"Aw . . ." Anna felt sure it would be a lovely gathering.

Right away, Anna was reminded of how jovial Luke Flaud was. As he and his wife came into the house, he removed his straw hat, exposing a head full of curly brown hair. Then, reaching to shake Anna's hand, he grinned. "Nice to see ya again, Anna. And *willkumm* to the Flaud turkey farm, small as it is," he said, putting little Sally down on the floor.

"*Denki.* My, your family's grown since I was last here," Anna said, watching Sally head straight for her Dawdi Glen's open arms, jabbering to him about the cloth dolly her Mamma had made, and holding it up close to Glen's face.

Strawberry-blond Marianna smiled as she handed Baby Jimmy to Sadie, then shook Anna's hand, too, her green eyes sparkling. "You're a long ways from home, *jah?*"

"Well, not so far by car," Anna said.

Sadie invited them to sit at the table, where she handed Jimmy to Anna before going across the room to get out the ice cream to dish up. "He's so cuddly . . . just precious," Anna said, taking her spot at the table with the wiggly infant. She gazed down at his little face. "He looks like you, Marianna."

Marianna smiled. "Actually, I see a lot of Luke in him."

"'Tis a *gut* blend of the two of yous," Sadie said, her ears attuned to the table conversation as she removed the cover from the ice cream and began to scoop.

Wide-eyed Sally scooted down from Glen's lap and wandered around the table, stopping at Anna's chair. "Hullo." Sally stroked her baby brother's plump arm while looking up at Anna. "Aendi?" she asked in *Deitsch.*

Sadie tittered, her hand over her mouth, and then Marianna began to explain to Sally that she and Anna were cousins. Wee Sally seemed to take the information in stride, then held up her faceless doll to Anna, its matching blue dress and apron the same as Sally's own.

It wasn't long before Sally tried to climb up on Anna's lap. Anna made room for her by moving the baby over slightly, nestling him in her left arm.

"Well now," Glen said at the head of the table, "I haven't seen Sally warm up to someone new so quickly before."

Marianna nodded. "I daresay Sally likes her cousin Anna."

"I should say so," Luke replied, his eyes brightening as Sadie brought over his big bowl of ice cream.

"You have a special way with children, *jah?*" Marianna said, taking Baby Jimmy from Anna so she could eat.

"I have many nephews and nieces back home, so I've had lots of practice." Anna smiled down at Sally, who'd snuggled with her dolly and leaned her head against Anna.

"Anna will be a right fine Mamma one day," Sadie said as she carried more bowls of ice cream to the table, then went back and brought chocolate syrup, chopped walnuts, and a bowl piled with homemade whipped cream, setting them down, as well. "There are plenty of *wunnerbaar* fellas round here."

"Mamm, for pity's sake," Luke said.

"Pity's sake," little Sally mimicked, bringing a round of laughter at the table.

Oh, to have such darling children, Anna thought. *Lord willing . . . someday.*

Chapter 14

Anna skimmed through the Saturday morning paper after breakfast and then drove over to Peaceful Meadows Horse Retreat. She had been looking forward to this all week. She'd even mentioned it to Sadie last evening, after Luke and Marianna left with their little ones.

Pulling into the long lane, she was impressed again by the natural beauty of the place. She stepped out of the car and walked toward the pristine white horse stable, glad she'd thought to wear her old walking shoes. As Anna tramped through the stable, she saw a number of young Amishwomen, mostly teenagers, each leading a horse out of its stall into a line to be groomed. Standing back near the wall, Anna watched as they prepared for the young clients to help curry the horses they would ride.

At that moment, Gabe Allgyer entered the stable. He walked over to welcome Anna with enthusiasm. "*Wunnerbaar guder Mariye, jah?*"

"*Fehlerfrei.*"

"Some might say that every morning at Peaceful Meadows Horse Retreat is both wonderful *and* perfect," Gabe replied.

"I'd have to agree." Anna looked about her, observing the various volunteers working in an unspoken sort of rhythm.

"Say, we're short one volunteer today." Gabe turned to look at her, a hopeful look on his sun-tanned face. "You've groomed a horse, *jah?*"

"Sure, why not make myself useful?" she said, following Gabe as he directed her toward a small school-age boy wearing black trousers, a blue short-sleeved shirt, and black suspenders. The child's straw hat was the smallest Anna had ever seen.

"His nickname is Freckles," Gabe said, hanging back a bit out of earshot of the boy. "He was born with a rare virus that caused a seizure disorder, but since coming for riding therapy the past two summers, Freckles has gained more confidence and seems more content. He's able to lead his horse around cones slowly with help. And his balance and muscle control are steadily improving when he's *on* the horse, too."

"His parents must be thrilled."

Gabe agreed. "His parents and many others in his family." He asked if she would like to help Freckles curry the chestnut mare. "That's Apple, by the way . . . one of our most docile quarter horses. She knows how to carry her riders smoothly, even at a trot."

"I'd love to help Freckles," Anna said, marveling at the whole program.

Gabe walked with her to meet the lad. "Are ya ready to groom Apple?" he asked him.

Nodding, Freckles leaned against Gabe, who patted his slight shoulders.

"Anna here will give ya a hand."

Freckles looked up at her. With his dark eyes and lashes

and silky brown hair, he was certainly a beautiful child. He nodded. *"Denki."*

"You've done this before, *jah?*" Anna placed her hand over his as he held the curry brush. "How's this?" she asked.

Freckles gave her a big smile, and Anna glanced over at Gabe, who was greeting several Amishwomen carrying small children into the stable. One was a tiny blond girl who closely resembled the beautiful blue-eyed woman accompanying her.

"Emmie always rides Promise," one of the volunteers called to the blond woman, pointing to the black pony at the end of the lineup.

Anna admired the woman and the petite girl—nearly like twins in looks, though years apart. *Like Baby Jimmy and his Mamma,* Anna thought, recalling how good it had felt to cradle a baby in her arms last evening.

Anna returned her attention to Freckles' attempt at making small circles against Apple's sleek coat. "Round and round with the brush, gently . . . gently," she encouraged the boy, who kept looking at her for approval, his tongue poking from the side of his mouth in concentration.

After fifteen minutes or so, Freckles seemed tired, and another young boy was given the opportunity to groom Apple's opposite flank and shoulder with help from one of the Amish teens.

Gabe came over and picked up Freckles, then went to meet a stout Amishman who looked to be the boy's father. The men shook hands and talked briefly before Gabe waved good-bye.

Meanwhile, the assistants helped the riders place and secure their helmets on their little heads. When the tacking up was complete, as well, the riders were either helped up or settled directly onto the saddle. The organization of the volunteers impressed Anna; Gabe did not have to prompt a single one. *Like worker bees. They know exactly what to do,* she thought.

Any disability or hesitation the riders had shown seemed to vanish, and smiles appeared as the horses began to move, each accompanied by a leader and two side walkers, or in some cases, a parent and a side walker.

"Rider and horse build a special bond over time," Gabe told Anna. "Eventually a horse will choose its rider. For some riders, that connection happens almost immediately." He invited her to go along to the sixty-foot round pen, where the horses walked slowly while being led. "The children's parents tell us that they count the days till their next therapy session—the children, I mean. That is, those who can speak." He mentioned that two young riders were nonverbal, one due to autism.

Everything about the program impressed Anna. She was scarcely able to put into words how moved she was by the sheer joy on the faces, the love in their eyes. "What you're doing here is amazing," she told Gabe as they stood near the gate leading into the sandy round pen. "I'm so glad you allowed me to observe."

"*Denki.*" He nodded. "Listen, we're always on the lookout for volunteers who have a gentle way with our youngest children, especially."

She turned to look at him.

"We could use another side walker, if you're interested."

Without considering the time involved, she answered from her heart, "I'm *very* interested and would love to help."

Gabe beamed. He invited her to stay after the session to fill out an application, as well as be available for a screening after a review of the initial paperwork. He also provided a few more instructions about the work, encouraging her to observe how the side walkers firmly held the riders' legs and sometimes arms, as well, to balance them.

"Some riders need to be steadied and made to feel secure

more than others," she said, watching as the groups moved slowly around the pen.

"*Jah*, exactly." Gabe glanced at her. "I couldn't help noticing how you worked with little Freckles . . . helpin' him control the brush and feel its pressure against the horse's flank. You're a natural, Anna."

She blushed—it wasn't only Gabe's remarks that were affirming. His delighted expression was, as well.

"I did something rather impulsive today," Anna told Sadie the minute she arrived back at the house.

"Oh?"

"I applied to be a volunteer at the horse therapy retreat not far from here."

Sadie looked up from the kitchen table, which was covered with a smattering of card stock, fabric, batting, and spools of colored thread. "Did ya, now?" Sadie tilted her head. "Must be Peaceful Meadows."

"So you know the place."

"Well, we know the manager, Gabe Allgyer, who drafted and built the tree house." Sadie smiled.

"Gabe did?"

Sadie nodded and changed the subject. "You're gonna be mighty busy, ain't so?"

"Well, if I'm accepted, it'll just be for two hours on Saturday mornings through September." Anna walked over to the table and looked at the assembly line of sorts that Sadie had going there. "You made these?"

"*Jah*, I call them cheer-up cards." Sadie picked up a completed one that featured a small section of a "quilt"—fabric had been inserted into a cutout in the card stock and plumped out with batting. She opened it to the blank inside. "I've been foolin' with them for years—a way to spread some cheer to folk who need it."

"Never seen anything like them," Anna said, inspecting several others—a daisy, a cat with a fabric bow at its neck, and a cake.

"Would ya like to learn to make them?" Sadie asked. "In your free time, that is." She gave a little laugh.

Anna smiled. "Once I'm caught up with my homework for the tours, I'd love to."

"Okay, then." Sadie grinned and said she used to send them anonymously to people who were sick or shut-in. "But word got out who was behind them, and now it's no secret."

"That's sweet." Anna loved that Sadie was so kindhearted. "Maybe after you teach me how, I'll send one to Mammi Eliza." Anna could think of other relatives she could surprise with such a creative handmade card. "Wanita would be tickled to receive one, too."

"Well, there you have it—a couple folks just a-waitin'." Sadie looked at her as if she wanted to say something more.

"What is it?" Anna asked, going to wash her hands at the sink.

"I'm not sure, really. But you look ever so happy chust now."

Anna nodded. "I can't deny it." And she began to tell Sadie about the therapy session she'd observed and of meeting several delightful Old Order Amish folk, including Freckles.

Chapter 15

Early Sunday morning, Anna rose to open the dark green window shades. She stood there enjoying the beauty of the landscape all around the Flauds' turkey farm. The various corn and wheat fields resembled a patchwork quilt, and farther west, she spotted a tobacco field belonging to an English neighbor.

She slipped into her floral cotton robe and headed for a quick shower in the small washroom just down the hall and through the kitchen. When she'd finished, she brushed through her long, damp hair, thankful to have settled in so easily with the Flauds.

After she was dressed and had gone outside to dry her hair, she received a call on her phone from her sister. "Hello, Wanita," she said, recognizing the number.

"How are you this fine Lord's Day morning?" Wanita asked.

"Getting ready for Sunday school and church. How're you?"

"Oh, just wanted to give you a quick call before church to

hear your voice again," Wanita said. "And I'm curious how you like your new job."

"I like it so far, but I haven't conducted any tours on my own yet. And I'm on call, so I don't necessarily have to go to the information center every day, just be ready to go within an hour's notice." Anna also described how she'd driven around last Friday to take pictures of Amish schoolhouses and cemeteries. "Thursday evening, I had dinner at Miller's Smorgasbord."

"I see . . . and were you with anyone special, like maybe that Mennonite fella you told me about in your letter? The one who trained you?"

Anna laughed. "You remembered?"

"Martin sounds real nice."

"I think you'd like him," Anna said.

Wanita chuckled. "Well, the real question is, do you?"

"We're just getting acquainted," Anna said, not saying how very charming she found him. "So, how's everyone at your house?"

"Oh, fine, including Mammi. She really came alive again when we talked at the table last night about your work as a tour guide there. For a moment, she seemed to be her old attentive self."

"I wish I could have been there to see it. Does that happen often?"

"Not often enough, but every now and then I get a glimpse of how she used to be, much like what you noticed when you first told her you were off to Strasburg. Of course, Mamm and Dat dropped by yesterday, too, so maybe seeing them brightened her up, as well."

Anna couldn't help but wonder if Mammi's keenest memories linked to her earliest years. Others she'd known who suffered with dementia struggled terribly with short-term memory but were quite clear about things that had taken place decades before.

"Excuse me a minute," Wanita said. "Mammi's waving at me. She must want something."

Anna could easily picture dear Mammi Eliza comfortably settled in her favorite chair. Her thoughts raced back to how she'd always felt so at home with her grandmother. She could talk openly with Mammi, who took her seriously and always encouraged her to talk freely and lean on the Lord, giving Anna a solid grounding in the simple ways of faith.

"Anna?" Wanita returned to the line, sounding downright befuddled. "I think Mammi wants to talk to you."

"Are you sure? She hasn't been able to use the phone in the longest time."

"Hold on . . . here she is."

Anna's heart leaped up at the thought of being able to talk to her grandmother again, like they used to before the confusion had descended. Moments like these were so precious. *Don't get your hopes up,* she cautioned herself.

"Hullo, Anna?" came Mammi's quivery voice.

Hearing Mammi like this brought tears to Anna's eyes. "It's so *gut* to hear your voice!"

"Somethin's on my mind," she said. "Bear with me."

"Take your time, Mammi."

"Wanita says you're in Strasburg. Did I ever tell ya I was there?"

"*Jah,* one summer when you were young," Anna said. "I wished I'd paid closer attention that day."

"You and your mother were in my kitchen, the three of us rolling out pie dough." Mammi Eliza began to talk faster, like she was afraid her memory would fail at any moment. "Anyway, not long after I arrived there . . . I, uh . . ." Mammi sighed. "Well, I remember a stone wall."

Anna thought that over. "Do you remember where it was?"

Mammi's breath fluttered into the phone. "Not far from where I was stayin'. I can almost see it—a wall of stacked stone."

"It must be a special memory," Anna said softly.

Mammi went silent then, and Anna wondered if she'd forgotten she was on the phone.

At last, Mammi spoke again. "He wanted to meet me there."

Anna was taken aback. *Who does she mean?*

"And there was a lone tree . . . the tallest ever."

Questions raced through Anna's mind. Where had Mammi's great-aunt lived? But of course, the biggest question was who *he* was. *Did Mammi have a beau before marrying Dawdi?*

"I'm tired," Mammi said softly, and the line went quiet.

Wanita returned to the phone. "Is everything okay? She seems weary all of a sudden."

"I think so," Anna said. "She was trying to tell me more about her months here. Poor Mammi . . . she probably won't even remember this conversation."

"I hope you won't be disappointed if she doesn't," Wanita said.

"It's all right. She can't help it."

Wanita kept talking. "Did I overhear her saying something about meeting someone?"

"She didn't say who. It was decades ago, and as you know, her memory's not reliable."

Wanita agreed. "Well, time to get the family some breakfast. Have a *gut* Sunday, Anna. I'll talk to you again."

"Okay. *Hatyee!* So long!" Anna replied and they hung up.

Returning inside, she continued to puzzle over Mammi's words. *Is knowing that I'm here in Strasburg somehow triggering these memories?* Anna wondered. *Or is her mind playing tricks on her?*

Anna found it hard to stay focused during the sermon later that morning. She recalled the phone conversation with Mammi Eliza, which still seemed so strange—Mammi had been too frightened to talk on the phone for years now. But the way she'd mentioned someone wanting to meet her at a mysterious stone wall had certainly stirred up Anna's curiosity.

The Sunday evening service at Anna's new church was well attended, and afterward she enjoyed eating popcorn and ice cream and meeting more people her age at the monthly youth event. Heidi and Eleanor took it upon themselves to introduce her to their longtime church friends, as well as to their courting-age brother, Lester. When Anna casually asked if he'd ever heard of Peaceful Meadows Horse Retreat, she was surprised that he knew of an Amish family whose son had been going a couple summers. "His nickname is Freckles," Lester said, pointing to his own face. "Like these." He chuckled.

"Freckles? I helped him groom his horse last session!" she said, surprised at this connection.

Heidi's eyes widened. "Didja really? How about that."

Anna told about her experience there and that she hoped to be approved as a regular volunteer. "Oh, you will . . . you will," Heidi said as Eleanor, more shy, nodded her agreement.

"Freckles' mother says they always need volunteers," Lester said.

"And you're so even-tempered," Heidi added.

"*Jah*," agreed Eleanor, smiling now.

"I really want to help if I can," Anna said, embarrassed at Heidi's compliment.

Lester hung around and talked for quite a while, even offering to get more popcorn for Anna, but there were a number of other young adults present who stopped to talk with them, as well, and Anna was grateful not to be singled out too much.

Back at Glen and Sadie's, the house was quiet and the lamps were dark, except for the one directly over the kitchen table. Anna walked quietly to her room, wanting to write another letter to Wanita. She sat at the little corner desk to write, thanking her for calling, then asking how Mammi Eliza had seemed after the surprising phone conversation. Anna also described tonight's after-church party and mentioned that Heidi and Eleanor's brother seemed to be familiar with Peaceful Meadows. *What a coincidence, right?*

She also told about Glen and Sadie and their thoughtfulness toward her, then gave a little more information about Martin Nolt, too—that she liked him, but that she didn't want to jump into a dating relationship too quickly. *If that's where this is heading . . . I'm not even sure at this point,* she wrote.

Anna signed off, then knelt beside the bed and repeated her plea for God to make the way before her plain. "Please make me a blessing to Glen and Sadie," she added, "wherever I'm needed. Look into my heart and know my thoughts."

She got ready for bed, still mulling over Mammi Eliza's words: *"He wanted to meet me there."*

Shadows from the moon played across the far wall as Anna sat on the bed in the darkness. *Was he a beau?* she wondered, lying on top of the sheets, the house still warm from the heat of the day. *And why is this on Mammi's mind all these years later?*

From the bed, Anna could make out the dresser, the small desk, and a tall bookcase on the opposite wall. And as she rested, she pondered many things. How had Mammi Eliza felt those first nights away from home? Had she missed her family as Anna did at this moment? Had she also said her nighttime prayers, not so different from those of her Old Order Amish cousins?

The latter thought prompted a memory. When Anna was younger, her Mammi had kept a daybook of prayer requests and answers. *How long ago did she start doing that?* Anna wondered.

Maybe, if any of those were still around in an old trunk or chest somewhere, they might fill in more of the story. . . .

Down the hall, Sadie was wide-awake next to Glen, who was already asleep. It had been a long but pleasant day visiting her husband's three eldest siblings—two brothers, a sister, and their families. Bubbly Lillian had suggested that Sadie think about making more of her little encouragement cards to sell at market, offering to handle the sales at Lillian's own soy candle booth.

The idea had sparked something in Sadie, and she could scarcely wait to dive in and work to make this happen. She and Glen didn't need the extra income, but the idea of spreading joy and a little whimsy wherever it was needed made her think that this might be a way to cheer up people from all over the country, particularly if tourists found them appealing enough to purchase. *A fun way to shine my little light.* She smiled into the room brightened only by moonglow.

Sadie heard the scrape of a chair in the adjacent room and imagined Anna sitting at the writing desk, sharing her heart with her Mamm or sister, maybe even telling more about her supper out last Thursday evening.

Anna's social life has picked up rather quickly, Sadie thought, smiling all the more.

Chapter 16

*D*er *Weschdaag* was Monday—"or any day that isn't raining or snowing," Sadie remarked to Anna as they worked together the next morning. Fortunately, there was a clear sky and a breeze perfect for drying the washing on the line. Even though Mamm had a dryer, she liked to hang out clothes on a warm day, and Anna soon learned that Sadie was not as persnickety as Mamm about the order in which she hung things. Anna recalled her mother's methodical approach: all the trousers first, then the shirts, dresses, aprons, and so on down the long line. True to her laid-back disposition, Sadie simply pinned to the clothesline whatever was next in the wicker basket.

"I've been thinking about something," Anna said, eager to mention what was on her mind.

"*Jah?*"

"How hard would it be to find out where my Mammi Eliza stayed the summer she was here with her great-aunt?"

Sadie used a clothespin to scratch her head beneath her navy blue bandanna. "Well now, I think someone round here would know."

"I asked my sister to search for Mammi's prayer book—sort of a daily journal she kept of prayers for certain folk and the dates when God answered them. But I don't know whether she did that sort of thing back when she was a teen."

"What an interesting idea." Sadie looked surprised but a bit delighted, too. "I've never heard of anyone doin' that."

"Me either. Mammi Eliza has always been a prayerful person." Sadie nodded emphatically. "'Tis the only way to be."

"Guess I'll just have to wait and see what Wanita says about that," Anna told her.

"Seventy years is a whole lifetime ago, but maybe somethin' will turn up. I'll ask my parents, in case they remember."

Anna pulled another apron from her basket, pinning it to the clothesline, then made sure her phone was in her pocket in case she had a call for a tour. Later, she planned to review everything both Mart and Charlotte had shared with her last week before she drove around again to various shops of interest—a different route than the last time she'd done this and more off the beaten track. She would also keep her word and return to Kitchen Kettle Village to visit the candle shop owned by Heidi and Eleanor's aunt.

When at last Anna finished hanging up her basket of freshly washed clothes, she was more thankful than ever for Sadie's kinship and friendship, as well as her willingness to help bring the past into a clearer picture. *If possible.*

By Tuesday breakfast, the outdoor temperature had turned much warmer. Anna was just putting away the final plate when she received a call from Evelyn saying a college girl from Virginia was interested in having a two-hour tour. "She'd like it to include an Amish bakery, furniture store, and the wooden toy shop."

"I would love that," Anna said, glad the tour would be scheduled for ten o'clock. "Thanks so much, Evelyn."

"Thank *you*, Anna. I'll see you at nine-thirty. Keila Abbott should arrive about ten minutes later."

What a pretty name!

Anna clicked off her phone and spun around, then laughed at herself. "I have my first official tour!"

Anna placed her letter to Wanita in the Flauds' family mailbox, then started out for the information center, wanting to be a bit early. When she arrived, she noticed Mart's car parked beneath one of the large shade trees. *He's early, too,* she thought, happy to see him again.

As she entered the break room, Mart was having coffee with one of the tour guides she hadn't met yet—a pretty young woman wearing a cup-shaped *Kapp* without strings. *All of the guides here must be Anabaptist,* Anna presumed, not interrupting their conversation as she went to the counter to pour herself some coffee.

When it was time to meet with her client, Anna headed to the counter like Mart and the other guides always did after their client had paid for the tour. *I want to do everything just right,* she thought, breathing a prayer for God's love to shine through her this day.

Keila Abbott seemed rather pensive at first, but as she drove and Anna directed her, Keila began to warm up, sharing about her growing interest in Amish culture. "I'd thought of doing a research project on them for one of the summer courses I'm taking, but I decided to just get my feet wet and enjoy a tour."

"Well, you can always pursue that sort of thing later, if you find you're still interested." Anna smiled, glad Keila felt comfortable talking to her.

Keila mentioned that she had always wanted to visit the area. "I've been looking forward to a couple of peaceful days away from my studies."

They stopped at the Bird-in-Hand Bake Shop, and Keila purchased a giant soft pretzel at the large food truck parked to the side of the bakery. All the while, Anna was mindful to be courteous and helpful, hoping she was representing the information center well. As Keila munched on her pretzel, they found themselves discussing Keila's heavy class load and what it meant to be successful, aside from financial gain. "If I may say so, you seem very content," Keila remarked.

Anna nodded. "I have lots to be thankful for, including my work."

"It's nice for a change, meeting someone doing what they love."

Anna shared that she believed God had opened the doors for her to get a job as a tour guide in Strasburg.

Keila smiled. "That's a refreshing way to look at it. A lot of people I know are so caught up in a quest for success that they really don't take time to consider anything to do with faith. That can't be good for a person."

Anna agreed. "What type of major are you pursuing?"

"Gerontology . . . and actually, I'd say it's pursuing me." Keila began to share her lifelong desire to assist elderly people in some meaningful way. "Once I have my master's degree, I want to work as a rehab therapist. I've been drawn to older people since I was a kid."

"Considering how long people live these days compared to decades ago, there must be a real need for people like you."

"Definitely," Keila said, smiling at her.

The remainder of the tour was split between an Amish furniture shop, where Keila had an opportunity to talk with an Amish craftsman, and a shop featuring wooden toys. "I have two young nephews to shop for," she announced to Anna before making some purchases there. "They're such great boys—I can never resist getting them a little something."

As they headed back to the information center, Keila thanked Anna for a terrific time and mentioned possibly returning for a different tour in the future. "I'll have to see when I can come back here again."

"Do you have family or friends in the area?" Anna asked.

"No, but I wish I did." Keila laughed a little. "In some ways, I could really go for the tranquil Plain life."

Anna wondered if all of her clients would be as much fun and as easy to entertain as Keila. She certainly hoped so.

As Anna was about to leave to go to the Flauds' to grab a sandwich, Evelyn asked if she would have time to give an afternoon tour to a middle-aged couple from New Port Richey, Florida. "They're interested in seeing a few covered bridges, as well as the countryside and an Amish school." Anna was delighted to accept and grateful to be able to build her confidence with a second tour.

What a great start! I'll have so much to tell Sadie and Glen, she thought on the short drive back to the farm.

During the afternoon tour with the rather talkative Bruce Hathaway and his demure wife, Kim, Anna directed them to Kurtz's Mill Covered Bridge, mentioning that there were twenty-eight such bridges in Lancaster County. "Some Amish around here call them 'kissing bridges,' since couples can stop in the middle of the dark bridge where no one can see," Anna said.

Bruce chuckled and said he'd never heard that. "I've also noticed some old stone walls in the area, similar to what we've seen all over New England."

"There aren't many walls like that here," Anna told him, wondering why he'd brought this up.

"There's a wonderful book about the history of that kind of wall," Kim said, glancing over her shoulder at Anna in the back seat.

"Is that right?"

Kim nodded her head. "It's really quite riveting—all about who built the many different kinds of stone walls found in New England, and for what purpose."

"Supposedly there are enough miles of stone wall in the northeast to go around the earth ten times," Bruce told her.

"Wow . . . imagine that." Anna thought of the wall Mammi Eliza might have used for a meeting place. Was that particular one still in existence? And if so, where might it be?

Sadie had completed several more cheer-up cards when she heard a carriage clatter up the lane. Leaning out of her chair at the kitchen table, she could see Tessie Flaud, her younger sister-in-law, at the reins. "Well, what do ya know?" Sadie murmured.

It had been months since Tessie had found time in her busy life to drop by for a visit. What with a new set of twins in her daughter's family, Tessie had been occupied with helping her with the older children. *Understandably*, thought Sadie as she rose and went to the back door. "Hullo, Tessie!" she called, stepping out the door and standing there to greet her. "What brings ya?"

"Thought you might be glad to know I'm amongst the living." Tessie chortled as she walked up the steps. "You look right fine, Sadie," she said. Tessie's white *Kapp* was a bit off-kilter, but Sadie decided not to mention it.

"*Kumme* in and rest awhile," Sadie said, leading her into the kitchen. "Would ya like lemonade or meadow tea? Both are nice and cold."

"Tea's fine." Tessie sat on the wooden bench on this side of the table and sighed audibly. She eyed the cards with the fabric inserts. "What are these for?"

"Oh, just some cards I'm making to sell at market."

"I've seen them here and there round the neighborhood," Tessie said. "Looks like you must've been the one who sent them."

Nodding, Sadie smiled. "Chust a little hobby, but Lillian thinks it oughta be something more."

"Ah, Glen's sister's got big ideas."

Sadie moved the finished cards and materials down toward the other end of the table to make way for some refreshments.

"Heard yous have a boarder," Tessie said.

"Well, Anna's family," Sadie said as she took out the pitcher of tea and poured some into tumblers for both of them. She brought the tea over and took a seat across from Tessie, wondering now if she had come just to ask about Anna.

"Any chance she'll go with yous to Preaching next Sunday?" asked Tessie, reaching for her tumbler. She took a quick sip.

Sadie shook her head. "Anna's found a church already. Seems to be quite settled." She took a long drink from her own glass.

"That's *gut* for her sake." Tessie's expression melted into a sorrowful frown. "Not sure how to say this, but I dropped by Molly's with a pie for her and Eva this mornin'. Poor Molly was in tears."

Sadie's throat tightened.

"Seems Eva didn't recognize Molly this morning . . . kept askin' who she was. Dear Molly was beside herself, and who can blame her?"

"*Ach* . . . that's too bad. Far as I know, this is the first time," Sadie said, expecting her niece would have told her otherwise. "I was just there visiting her and Eva last Friday." She gave a long sigh.

"It was bound to happen sooner or later." Tessie shook her head again. "What a dreadful disease."

"For certain," Sadie said. "It breaks Molly's heart every day, seeing her Mamm's decline happening before her eyes." Sadie wished she could comfort Molly somehow. "I'll go over there again this weekend."

"I'm sure she'd appreciate it," Tessie said. "Sorry to bring sad news."

A part of Sadie wished Tessie hadn't told her, but she also wanted to be supportive of Molly and continue to show compassion to Eva, even if her older sister wasn't aware of it. But she didn't think she would invite Anna along to visit again, since it would only remind her of her own dear Mammi Eliza's condition.

As they drank their tea, Tessie moved on from that topic back to Anna, and Sadie just let her talk.

"I'm kinda surprised a Beachy Amish relative would choose to live with ya. A bit unusual, ain't?"

Sadie shrugged, not wanting to comment one way or the other.

"I mean, what do Anna's parents think?" Tessie pressed further. Then she seemed to catch herself. "Guess I'm speakin' out of turn . . . sorry."

Sadie just smiled. "Would ya like some strawberries? I have some extra."

Tessie seemed to get the message and thanked her, saying she had plenty of berries at home.

Once Tessie left, Sadie returned to her card making, a lump in her throat at the thought of Eva not recognizing her own daughter. *These cards may bring cheer to some folk, but not to all,* she thought sadly.

Chapter 17

A nna ran into Mart on Wednesday afternoon and was pleased when he invited her to attend a hymn sing at his church on Friday evening. Anna agreed, looking forward to getting better acquainted with him and meeting his friends. She was also counting the hours till Saturday—that is, assuming she was accepted as a volunteer at Peaceful Meadows Horse Retreat.

In the meantime, Anna hoped to hear back from Wanita regarding the daybooks Mammi had once kept to log her prayers. But knowing how busy she was with her family, Anna chided herself for her impatience.

This could very well be a wild goose chase.

By the end of the Thursday workday, Anna had directed four more tours, each unique in that all the clients were interested in seeing different places. Some wanted more historical sites and information, and she was glad Mart and Charlotte had prepped her for that. Other clients were content to simply see the sights along the rural backroads, hoping to avoid the area's usual tourist traps. One woman even expressed an interest in seeing "the art form" of how Amish hung their clothes out on the line.

After work that day, Anna received her official acceptance letter as a volunteer at the retreat center. *I can't wait to be around horses again—and to see those darling children, too,* she thought later as she pulled over onto the shoulder to take pictures of an old sandstone grist mill. As the sign on the front indicated, Nolt's Mill was no longer a working mill but rather the John Stevens Gallery, which featured the artist's limited-edition watercolors and other exquisite artwork. "To think this place was built in 1770," Anna whispered, in awe of its historic beauty. She took a picture of the cornerstone, as well as the weathervane in the shape of a quill pen atop an attic dormer window. Listening to the powerful rush of the water running through the mill, she thought, My *clients will love this place.*

Anna realized that, had she come upon herself at a Mennonite hymn sing a year ago, she might have wondered what she was doing there. But, new though the experience was, she was enjoying the wonderful music. Two fellows played guitars, and in addition to a piano, there was even a set of drums on the platform. As Mart sat next to her, his deep baritone joining in, Anna felt relieved to be familiar with nearly all of the worshipful, joyful hymns.

Anna pictured her Beachy church back home, where the men and boys always sat on the right side of the congregation, and the women, babies, and young children sat on the left, rather than all together or even paired up as couples, like people were here. Her church taught that being segregated in church helped attendees to keep their focus on the Lord during worship, rather than on their spouse or family.

Paying attention again to the singing, Anna decided she wouldn't let any of this distract her further. After all, the words of the hymns pointed to Christ, and that was what really mattered.

After the hymn sing, Anna strolled out to the lobby with Mart, where he politely introduced her to two other couples, who warmly welcomed her. Anna noticed several young ladies standing near a wall rack of missionary prayer cards and other items, eyeing her and Mart.

Charlotte Meck and her fiancé, Austin Howell, came over to talk, as well. All of them stood around and fellowshipped a bit longer, and soon the group of singles and couples decided to go out for a bite to eat. Mart invited Anna to meet him and the others at a nearby diner, and she agreed, happy for the opportunity to spend more time with all of them.

At the restaurant, Anna ordered a piece of strawberry pie with vanilla ice cream, as did the other two young women. Mart and the other young men ordered burgers and fries while continuing their conversation. Anna especially enjoyed Mart's interaction with Austin, who said that he and Charlotte hoped to be married within the year. "Charlotte and I really want my minister-uncle to marry us, so we've been talking with our pastor about how to go about that," he informed them.

"What if your uncle simply officiated over your marriage vows, and the pastor gave the wedding sermon?" Mart suggested. "It can't be uncommon when someone has a close relative who's a minister."

Austin and Charlotte appeared to like that idea, and Austin said he'd look into it. It struck Anna how engaging and agreeable Mart's circle of friends was—all very supportive of one another.

"How about we all go to the Hershey Story Museum sometime and take the tour? I'd be up for a visit to the Chocolate Lab," Mart suggested with a glance at Anna.

"When?" one of the other fellows asked.

"How about we start by contacting the youth pastor to see if we can borrow the van?" Mart said. "That way we can all travel together, and there'll be plenty of room to include more."

"Great idea. Let us know," Austin said, and the others agreed, as well.

"Definitely. I'll text everyone," Mart said.

"Perfect," Charlotte said, smiling across the table at Austin.

As the gathering was dispersing and they were saying good-bye, Anna looked forward to getting together with all of them again, happy that Mart had invited her.

Sadie was glad her parents had stopped by for a visit that Friday evening. Because it was so warm and humid, Glen had suggested they sit outdoors beneath one of the shade trees in the backyard, where a neat mulch skirt surrounded the base. He carried the porch chairs out there, and Sadie's father helped her frail mother down the walkway to the inviting sheltered spot.

Meanwhile, Sadie went in to dish up generous helpings of vanilla ice cream, then placed all four bowls on a tray to carry outside with a plate of chocolate-chip cookies. With Anna gone, Sadie hoped to broach the topic of Anna's grandmother's stay in Strasburg as a teen. Sadie had no false hopes that she would uncover a trove of information so many decades after the fact, but this way she could at least talk freely to her parents.

Birds flapped their wings and dipped in the birdbath across the yard as Sadie served her parents and Glen. A welcome breeze cooled Sadie's brow as she sat next to her mother, who remarked that the last Preaching service had seemed longer than usual. "Do you think it will be that long again this weekend?"

"Well, there was the members' meeting at the end last time," Sadie reminded her. "A long discussion 'bout dividing the church district, since there are more than forty families now."

"*Ach*, how'd that slip my mind?"

"What's that, Martha?" Sadie's father asked, bending his ear her way, his straw hat firmly set on his gray head.

"She was sayin' the last Preaching service seemed long," Sadie told him, wishing he would get a better hearing aid. Last time they'd dropped by to visit, she had told him as gently as possible that it would make for a more enjoyable conversation. *Maybe that's why they haven't come to see us for a couple of weeks,* she thought.

Glen nodded his head at his father-in-law. "Time to get padded benches for the older folk."

"Well, sometimes they do bring out padded rockers for Preachings," Sadie said.

"And next time we host church, we'll be sure and have them for yous," Glen said, looking at Dat and Mamm. "Don't let me forget, Sadie, *jah*?"

Sadie agreed. All this talk of forgetting and not remembering was weighing on her, what with her sister Eva so heavy on her heart.

A quiet moment or two fell over the four of them while they got more serious about eating their melting ice cream. When her bowl was empty, Sadie asked, "Do either of yous remember

126

where Eliza Hertzler stayed when she came here back in the late '40s?"

"Goodness, where'd *that* come from?" Mamm asked, her thin brown eyebrows knitting together.

"Anna asked me 'bout it . . . says she only knows that she stayed with a great-aunt Joanna. Seems her Mammi mentioned it recently, but with her Alzheimer's, she couldn't supply any details."

"Ah, I see. Well, I was still fairly young then," Sadie's Mamm said. "And it was a long time ago."

Sadie's Dat brightened. "That would've been ol' Widow Joanna Beiler—she passed away not many years after."

"Where was her house located?" Sadie asked with a glance at Glen, who was scraping his bowl clean like he was ready for seconds.

Sadie's father frowned, his face scrunched up in thought. "She lived in an old farmhouse a few miles from here, not far from the smithy's. Of course, that was a very long time ago, so a lot has changed. S'posin' I'd have to think 'bout it."

"That might be helpful," Sadie replied. "I'll let Anna know."

Glen raised his empty bowl and gave her a wink.

Sadie grinned at him. "Dat . . . Mamm, do you want seconds with Glen?"

Her parents shook their heads, but her Dat asked for some cold water.

"I'll second that," Glen said, yawning.

"Mamm?" she asked.

"Nothin' more for me . . . this has been a real *gut* treat, Sadie."

She made her way into the house, thinking ahead to telling Anna what she'd learned, though it wasn't much.

Chapter 18

⁂

The last day of June was a peaceful one at this early hour, and a lone robin's song filled the air. When the robin paused, Anna could hear every other slight sound around her, including the distant creak of the windmill and the turkeys just waking up. Yawning, she moved to the window and raised the shade. The grass was thick with dew, and the sky's golden glow was a sanctuary of anticipation.

At last, it was Saturday! The day Anna had been contemplating since filling out the volunteer application in Gabe Allgyer's rustic office. Had it only been a week?

She glanced at the dresser and saw Gabe's business card, then went to pick it up, recalling how wary he had seemed when they'd first met. However, once she'd mentioned that her father raised ponies, Gabe had quickly warmed up. To think that such a kindhearted man had lost his wife. *He's already suffered such loss. . . .*

Anna recalled how considerate it had been of Sadie to wait

up for her last night just to say she had talked to her parents about Mammi and discovered where she'd stayed. Perhaps she should try to confirm what Sadie's father had remembered . . . once she heard from Wanita.

Eager to see the young riders again, including little Freckles, Anna hurried down the hall to shower and dress.

Anna was greeted at the south entrance of the large horse barn by a slender young Amishwoman who looked to be about Anna's age. She wore a purple dress and matching cape apron, and introduced herself as Dottie Stoltzfus. "Gabe asked if I'd be your instructor today and next Saturday," Dottie said, grinning. "After that, you'll be ready to be a side walker or leader. Maybe even a rider if one of the children needs extra assurance."

Anna was delighted. She had observed both the leaders and the side walkers last weekend, and her experience with her father's ponies meant that she could easily be a rider, too, if necessary. "*Denki*, but how'd you recognize me just now?"

"Oh, Gabe described ya perfectly," Dottie said, eyes twinkling. "Said you're Beachy, so I knew what sort of clothing to look for."

"Do you have Beachy relatives or friends, then?"

Still beaming, Dottie bobbed her head. "Several friends, *jah*."

Anna followed her into the large tack room, where saddles, bridles, horse blankets, bits, and wraps were neatly organized. "I want to learn as much as I possibly can," Anna said as she eyed the well-organized space.

"Gabe says you'll do just fine, so don't ya worry none."

Anna recalled what he had said last Saturday about her being a natural. She certainly didn't want to disappoint him or Dottie.

Once the barn volunteers had tacked up all the horses, an instructor directed the horses and their riders to head over to the round pen, each accompanied by two side walkers, a leader, and sometimes a parent. For this morning, Dottie asked Anna to closely observe the side walkers for a boy named Bennie Glick. She explained that Bennie got around with forearm crutches and was always helped onto the horse by his father, one of the preachers of the local Amish church district.

"Preacher Glick's over here first thing every Saturday with that little boy of his," Dottie added.

While the two side walkers held on to young Bennie's legs, steadying him, one of the volunteers quickly carried the boy's crutches over near the gate, where they were propped up outside the pen.

"Remember that, as a side walker, you'll be responsible for the rider's safety; the leader is responsible for the horse. Unless you're told otherwise, it's your job to always hold on to the rider," Dottie explained. "Of course, we do have some riders who are more capable and can balance themselves in the saddle."

Anna listened carefully even though Dottie had also given her a sheet of instructions to look over at home.

"We create an individual therapy plan for each student," Dottie continued as one of the side walkers got Bennie positioned on the sleek black horse, its body glistening in the sunshine. "Some need to build confidence, and others need soothing for anxiety. We don't focus so much on the particular disability as we do the student's specific needs."

Anna nodded, eager to be ready to do this on her own in two weeks. She and Dottie remained outside the fence while Dottie pointed out what Bennie's side walkers were doing. "A lot of it's common sense, really."

Today Gabe was also inside the pen as a side walker, moving slowly around the circle while holding on to Emmie, the petite blond girl Anna had seen last week—she couldn't be older than five. Anna noticed again how caring and gentle Gabe was. *Especially with the smallest children.*

One of the horses neighed, and then another. But generally, the only sounds were those of the horses' hooves as they moved about.

Toward the end of the first session, Dottie asked if Anna had any questions.

"I do." Anna smiled. "Would I be able to try walking with one of the steadier riders today?"

"You're itchin' to get started, ain't ya?"

"I'd really love to."

Dottie explained that Gabe was firm in thinking that volunteers required a minimum of two sessions of training before they were trusted to do it on their own. "I'm sure you understand."

Anna agreed. "Of course."

Dottie pointed to the stapled sheets of paper. "Be sure to familiarize yourself with everything by next Saturday, okay? Remember that children who are on the autism spectrum are encouraged to say their horse's name and, when they're ready, give it commands. By doing that yourself while side walking, you'll encourage the child to do it, too."

"I'll try to have all of this memorized soon," Anna assured her.

"And I'll ask ya questions, just to make sure you're ready." Dottie turned her attention back to the horse pen. "You'll love lending a hand here. Gabe is so great with all the volunteers . . . you'll see."

"You've been so helpful," Anna told Dottie. "I appreciate it."

"You're welcome. I look forward to seein' you next week." Dottie invited her to stay around for the next session if she had time. "The more you observe the other volunteers in action, the more everything will sink in. It won't be long before you'll feel like you're a part of the group."

Anna thanked her again and headed toward the stable to watch the many volunteers gently assist the children down from the well-behaved horses. Once the riders had dismounted, most rewarded their horses with sugar cubes, the horses lowering their heads to accept the treat.

Anna saw Gabe lift Freckles down from Apple. The boy laughed and gave him a hug before Gabe went over to help a couple other little ones remove their helmets, grinning at them as they smiled back, one jabbering in *Deitsch* about all the fun she'd had. In fact, Anna noticed a lot more noise in the stable at the end of the riding session than at the start of it, and she wondered what effect it had on the horses. *They're surely older and more difficult to spook, or they wouldn't have been selected.* Like her father's more mature ponies, these horses were obviously far more comfortable with commotion and people than the average horse would be.

A large passenger van pulled in close to the edge of the pasture, coming to pick up the children from this first session, and Anna noticed Dottie and some other volunteers either carry or walk with the youngest ones toward the van.

The day was warming up quickly, the sky a pale blue without a cloud to be seen. At that moment, Gabe caught her eye and waved as he came this way. She waited in the shade of the stable, curious to see what was up.

"Did ya enjoy getting acquainted with Dottie?" he asked, running his fingers under his black suspenders, all the way up to his broad shoulders.

Anna tapped on the sheets in her hand. "She was very thorough, but she wants me to study these pages, as well."

"She's a teacher, all right." He paused to wave just then to one of the dads about to climb into the van. "Dottie is my cousin's daughter, by the way. She's been helpin' me here since she was seventeen."

"No wonder she knows her way around." Anna noticed how he brightened at the compliment.

"If there's anything ya need to know, Dottie's the one to ask. Well, besides me." He chuckled. "I hope ya enjoyed yourself, Anna."

"Oh, I did. The staff and horses seem great, and the children are just darling. It must be encouraging for you to know they're being helped by your *wunnerbaar* program."

"Ain't mine, really." Gabe raised his eyes toward the sky. "The Lord God put all this on my heart. It's all His."

Anna was impressed by his humility. "Well, He's entrusting you with it, that's obvious."

Gabe seemed to ponder that, then looked at her, smiled, and nodded. "I never thought of it quite like that."

She studied him. "You could say I like to look for God's fingerprints everywhere."

He glanced away, as if moved by her words. "It was the Lord's work from the very start," he said. "I opened up this therapy program after Emmie, my little girl, became mute . . . she stopped talking when her Mamma died." He paused for a moment as if to gather himself. "She seemed much calmer and less agitated after riding—being around horses is just so good for her. It made me want to help other children with needs and challenges of their own."

Emmie's his daughter! Anna thought, remembering the petite little girl she'd seen among the riders. "*Denki* for sharing this with me," she said. "You must've had lots of help to get all this started."

"People came out of the woodwork, honestly. My uncle has

been especially great, offering his farm like he has. I couldn't have done it singlehandedly."

She nodded, still absorbing all that he'd told her, truly impressed.

"Well," Gabe said, "I'll be seein' ya next Saturday, then."

"If you don't mind, I'd like to stay and observe the next session," she said, remembering what Dottie had suggested.

He agreed, and they parted ways.

Anna headed back to the tack room to offer her help, her heart softened all the more by Gabe's mission here, and the reason behind it.

Gabe's explanation about the beginnings of Peaceful Meadows stayed with Anna as she drove down the narrow lane toward the road. Making the turn, she was aware of the long stone wall running along the edge of the retreat's pastureland, within walking distance from the road. And, as she slowly drove alongside it, she noticed one small portion of the wall had tumbled down. Compelled to remedy it, she signaled and pulled over onto the right shoulder, coming to a stop.

Getting out, she crossed the two-lane road and made her way across the field, toward the wall separating it from the pasture beyond, breathing in the fresh air and enjoying the thick green meadow grass so much that she removed her socks and old sneakers, carrying them as her bare feet pressed deep into the coolness of the grassland.

She stuffed the socks into the shoes before setting them on the ground. Then she picked up the stones that had tumbled down and began to lift them one by one, stacking them in an orderly fashion, the way they seemed to fit best. Stepping back, she brushed her hands together, slapping off the dirt.

The dust of history, she thought, pleased with her efforts.

Anna retrieved her shoes and turned to look down the field at the stony row extending a long way on this side of the road. She recalled Mammi Eliza's remark about meeting someone at such a wall, ever so long ago. Anna even stopped to look around for a tall tree, but there was none.

Shaking her head, she headed back to the car.

Chapter 19

―――――――――――――――――― ⊙⁄⊙ ――――――――――――――――――

SUNDAY, JUNE 20, 1948

It was a warm and humid June evening with a silvery white full moon as Eliza made her way down the narrow road, still wearing her for-good black dress and white organdy cape apron. She'd worn them to the Beachy meetinghouse that Lord's Day morning, then returned to Great-aunt Joanna's to sit with her on the back porch and read aloud from the Good Book. Eliza had also spent quite a bit of that afternoon writing letters home to her older sister and Mamma, so she hadn't even bothered to change her clothes.

Leaving the house after supper hadn't turned out to be as much of a challenge as Eliza had thought. She simply mentioned wanting to go for a walk, and oddly, Aunt Joanna hadn't seemed to mind, nor did she question. *She must be tired and nearly ready to turn in,* Eliza thought.

Now barefoot, Eliza tiptoed through the verdant pastureland, hoping not to be heard or seen. For sure and for certain, it was the first time she'd done anything like this. *Dat and Mamma would disapprove.* . . .

She hadn't forgotten how surprised and pleased Eb Lapp had looked when they'd bumped into each other at market yesterday. Since meeting him, she had seen him a number of times while running errands for her aunt. This time, though, he had suggested they meet privately, over near the towering pin oak tree on this side of a long row of loosely stacked old stones that formed a boundary, defining the property line between two fields. Eliza had objected at first, unsure what it could mean for her or for their budding attraction if they were found out. But Eb insisted it was the best place to talk. *"We won't be noticed there once twilight falls."*

Eliza could see the outgoing young man coming toward her in the near distance. He swung one leg and then the other over the stone wall before ambling across the grass, waving now.

Unusual as Ebenezer Lapp was, Eliza couldn't deny being drawn to him after talking with him several times in the weeks since her arrival—both on the road to buy eggs from Nellie Petersheim and at Saturday market, too. Because he was Old Order Amish and she was from a less traditional Amish sect, they had to be discreet about their conversations. She was, however, quite sure he found her pleasing. Even so, she hoped it wasn't just that she was an out-of-town girl and raised *"part Amish, part Mennonite,"* as Eb had said at least twice lately. She wanted it to be more than curiosity on his part that had caused him to invite her to meet him beneath the bright moon tonight.

Silently, she moved through the meadow grass and past wild black-eyed Susans, until Eb called out, "Eliza . . . you're here." The way he said it sounded as if he'd doubted she'd come.

Her voice was trapped in her throat as she slowed her pace and stopped walking, suddenly worried she was making a dreadful mistake.

Chapter 20

T he first thing Anna noticed upon returning to the Flauds' was Glen and Sadie's blond grandsons, Marcus and Eddy, sitting along the porch railing, legs dangling as they chewed on red licorice sticks. She hurried to get out of the car, looking forward to renewing her acquaintance with them.

"Hullo, Cousin Anna," Marcus, the older one, said, looking her way. "Mammi invited us over to have dinner with ya."

"I was hoping to see you again." Anna went up the porch steps and stood there smiling at the two of them in their white short-sleeved shirts and black trousers. "You look *schee!*"

"Dawdi Flaud said to spruce up for ya," young Eddy explained.

"Well, that was thoughtful." Anna glanced down at her old sneakers. "I best be doin' the same for you."

Marcus gave her a grin. "Were ya out with the horses over at Peaceful Meadows?"

"*Jah.*"

"Was Gabe there?" Eddy asked.

"How do you know him?" she asked, curious.

"He goes to our church," Eddy said, big blue eyes shining.

"And he builds the best tree houses," Marcus announced, unexpectedly turning around and leaping off the railing onto the porch.

"And he calls me Ready-Eddy, like Dat and Mamma," said Eddy.

Anna laughed. "I'll remember that."

Eddy looked over his shoulder at his brother. "Marcus doesn't rhyme with anything, so he's just plain Marcus."

"Nothin' wrong with that." Anna remembered telling Martin Nolt that she was just plain Anna. "Sounds like something a brother might say, and with six older brothers, I should know."

Marcus and Eddy exchanged grins.

Anna walked toward the back door. "Let's see what your Mammi's up to, okay?"

"I'll open the door for ya," Eddy said, running ahead of her and turning the knob on the screen door. "Dat says a *gut* man likes to help out the womenfolk."

"*Denki*," Anna said and walked inside. *This will be fun*, she thought of the upcoming noon meal.

Sadie stirred in the sour cream to complete the dill vegetable dip, knowing how much Marcus and Eddy enjoyed eating their raw veggies that way. She could hear Anna just outside talking to them, glad Anna was back in time for all of them to sit down together.

Hopefully Glen will return from the turkey house soon, Sadie thought as she placed the clear glass bowl of dip on a tray with the carrots, celery, and sliced green peppers fanned around it.

Then, going to the oven, she opened the door and checked on her barbeque chicken chunks. *Looks done!* She reached for her quilted oven mittens and removed the large baking pan, then set it atop the stove. By the time Glen arrived and got washed up, she would have generous sandwiches made and on plates. She liked to use hamburger buns for this recipe, since the juices and filling tended to overflow a bit. Six-year-old Eddy particularly liked the buns because, as he said, he could get his hands around them.

Marcus, nine, was more interested in how spicy certain foods were. So today, she'd added some red pepper flakes into her homemade barbeque sauce, just for him.

Sadie knew for sure that the dessert she'd made would please everyone at the table—strawberry shortcake with heavy whipping cream and fresh strawberries on top.

She turned to see Anna coming in the back door, followed by smiley Eddy, and Marcus behind them. "Chust in time," she called, watching the boys hang up their straw hats on the wooden pegs. She ruffled Eddy's golden locks and motioned him toward the sink. "Wash up quick before Dawdi comes. He'll be hungry the minute he walks in."

"I think we're all hungry," Anna said, removing her sneakers and socks. "Ah, feels so *gut* to go barefoot again."

"How was your training this morning?" Sadie asked, curious.

While she waited her turn to wash her hands, Anna told about some of the things she'd learned. "Those horses are real special . . . calm and gentle with the children."

"S'posin' you're meeting plenty-a new folk, too," Sadie said, making the last barbeque chicken sandwich at the counter.

"*Jah*, I'm getting acquainted with the volunteers. With so many young riders, they need quite a few. My instructor seemed

140

close to my age." Anna glanced at the boys. "Maybe you know Dottie, too?"

Marcus shook his head, and Eddy wrinkled his nose as if trying to remember. "Not unless she came along when Gabe and his crew put together our tree house," Eddy said.

Her potholder in hand, Sadie smiled at the mention of Gabe's name. "A real fine young man, that one," she said for Anna's sake. "All of us had a *wunnerbaar* time talkin' with him when he was here."

"Is the Peaceful Meadows therapy program funded by the community?" Anna asked.

"Oh *jah*, plenty-a folk give of their time and money to keep it goin'," Sadie said. "There's even an occasional pie bake-off where support comes rollin' in. Glen can tell ya more 'bout all that if you ask him." She glanced toward the door, expecting him to walk in at any moment.

"Well, I'm amazed that Gabe can juggle his own work *and* manage the retreat." Anna mentioned that Peaceful Meadows offered a number of sessions three days a week. "The program has really grown since it started. It's impressive."

Just then, the back door screeched open, and there was Glen, removing his work boots and walking stocking-footed into the kitchen. He stood there on Sadie's big rag rug and removed his straw hat as his grandsons flew to his side, smiling up at him. Watching the boys greet their Dawdi with such joy warmed her heart.

"Wanna catch some fish after dinner, Dawdi?" Marcus asked partway through the meal as Anna passed the tray of vegetables and dip around for the third time.

"I'd best be catchin' forty winks first," Glen said, making them all chuckle.

"But you can nap while you're fishin'," young Eddy teased. "Like this. See?" And he dropped his chin against his chest, eyes closed, and pretended to snore.

"Now, how do ya know your Dawdi snores?" Sadie asked with a glance at Glen.

"Don't all men snore?" Eddy frowned as he looked at his brother, who elbowed him.

"*Nee*," Marcus said. "Our Dat doesn't. He slept with us out in the tree house once and never made a peep." Marcus reached for two more carrot sticks and a handful of celery, then spooned up a pile of dip.

"Did ya stay up all night listenin'?" Eddy asked.

Glen was chuckling now. "You two are wound up today. Not sure the fish'll bite if you're this rowdy."

"Oh, we can be still if we want to," Eddy said, scooting forward on the bench, his eyes bright. "Ain't so, Marcus?"

Marcus nodded, still munching on his veggies and dip.

"Well, I s'pose I'll go along, then, since apparently I can snooze and fish at the same time." Glen grinned as he reached for his tumbler of lemonade. "Wonders never cease."

"*Jah*, go an' have yourselves a *gut* time," Sadie said.

"What're yous plannin' here?" Glen asked, looking at Sadie and Anna.

"Well, we could work on some cheer-up cards," Sadie suggested.

Anna was quick to nod. "And afterward, I'll go out and pick more strawberries."

"Speakin' of berries . . ." Sadie rose and went to get the shortcake from the counter.

Glen and the boys turned and watched her carry the dessert over on a clean tray. Then she and Anna spooned up a generous amount of whipping cream to top each helping.

Finally, Sadie nestled the sliced strawberries atop the whipping cream.

"Looks scrumptious," Anna said, offering the first one to Glen.

Eddy and Marcus picked up their forks but waited politely till Sadie sat down again before digging in.

My delightful young cousins, Anna thought, pleased at the chance to get better acquainted with her Amish relatives. *Surely Dat doesn't have qualms about my spending time with these wonderful kinfolk*, she thought. *It's not like I'm falling for an Old Order beau!*

Anna helped Sadie work on her encouragement cards once the kitchen table was wiped clean and the dishes were put away. It gave them a chance to talk while Glen and the boys were down at the fishing hole.

At one point, Anna asked, "This may sound strange, but I keep wondering about something Mammi Eliza said when I was home last."

"If it's on your mind, Anna, I don't think it's strange a'tall."

Anna thought that was sweet. "It's hard to know if Mammi was thinking clearly, but she talked briefly about a stone wall—a spot she went to meet someone. It might have been a young man, 'cause she said *he*."

"Well now." Sadie looked up just then, eyes focused on her.

"I know there aren't many stone walls in Lancaster County. Even one of my tour clients pointed out that New England has many more. He jokingly said that Maine's number one crop is fieldstones. The second, potatoes." She paused to push some batting gently behind the fabric of a robin-shaped design, then held it up for Sadie's smiling approval. "I would love to know where that particular stone wall Mammi mentioned was located."

"Why's that important to you?"

She pondered this. "Maybe it's a way to prove to myself that Mammi Eliza still remembers something from her past," Anna finally said. "You know, still retains part of her former self."

Sadie nodded thoughtfully. "I see what you're sayin'."

"And if it's a genuine memory and I *could* find that stone wall, it would be yet another connection between her and myself," Anna admitted, wanting to hold on to everything possible about her grandmother.

"Do you wonder if it's a fantasy . . . somethin' only in her mind?"

"I just don't know." Anna sighed.

Sadie shared with Anna what little her parents had told her the night before.

"I wish I could help more." Sadie smiled sympathetically. "I really do."

"Oh, and I almost forgot! Mammi also talked about there being a very tall tree nearby. I think she meant it was near the stone wall, but I can't be sure. And I don't know what kind it was. Even if I did, that tree likely wouldn't be around seventy years later."

"Well, there are plenty-a trees growin' near some of the stone walls round here. Mostly black walnut trees."

Anna sighed again. "I don't mean to press you with questions."

"*Ach*, you can ask anything ya like."

Anna smiled. "Mart told me that, too. He's been so helpful preparing me for my touring work."

"This is the Mennonite fella who's sweet on ya?" Sadie asked.

Anna felt herself blush. "Well, I wouldn't say that."

"Oh, I'm sure he knows a special girl when he sees one."

Anna's heart warmed at the compliment. "Mart is every parent's answer to prayer, I'm thinkin'."

"Is that right?" Sadie seemed to study her for a moment, then resumed her work, completing a teddy bear with a fabric bow tie. "Have ya told your parents of this fella's interest?"

"No. Anyway, Mart and I are just getting to know each other. Not dating."

"I see." Sadie gave her a smile. "The more fellas you get acquainted with, the more you'll know what qualities you'd appreciate in a mate."

Anna supposed she was right. "I enjoy talking to you, Sadie," she said. "'Specially with Mamm and Wanita so far away."

"I'm glad ya do, and just know that what you tell me goes nowhere else." Sadie pressed her pointer finger against her thin lips.

"*Denki*," Anna said and picked up some card stock with a cut-out in the shape of a small wicker basket. "I kind of thought so."

They worked in silence for a while; the only sound was of the day clock's measured ticking on the wall above them.

A while later, Sadie said, "My sister-in-law thinks I should have at least fifty finished cards before she'll take them to Saturday market to sell."

"Has she suggested a price?"

"I'll ask her," Sadie said, shaking her head, "since I'm really not sure what to charge."

"Well, you make them much faster than I can. How long does it take?"

"*Gut* point." Sadie scrunched up her face and thought. "Maybe twenty minutes per card, give or take a few minutes."

Anna picked up one of Sadie's finished ones and admired it. "It's not just a card, though. It's more like a keepsake."

"Do ya think so?" Sadie looked surprised as she glanced at the card in Anna's hand.

"I do. Which might raise the price a bit in customers' minds." Sadie laughed softly. "Well, I'll ask Glen's opinion on that."

Anna smiled and wondered if she would think that way, too, once she was married. Would she make her decisions only after talking to her husband?

Mamm doesn't always, Anna realized. *Sometimes she makes up her mind, then tells Dat what she's decided. So, am I more like Mamm or like Sadie?*

Chapter 21

—⟨⟩—

The whole next week, whenever she had free time, Anna helped Sadie make the wonderfully creative cards, one of which she sent to Mammi Eliza. When she wasn't doing that or working around the house, Anna was studying the side-walking instructions Dottie Stoltzfus had given her or reviewing the information she had for tours, making sure she was ready for each new set of clients, of which there were more than a handful, as it turned out. Anna even met a family from Germany who wanted to introduce their two school-age children to some of their Pennsylvania German relatives there in Lancaster. They especially enjoyed hearing Anna tell about the origins of the original Amish settlers.

On Friday afternoon, while Sadie was gone from the house, Anna received a letter from Wanita. Anna was quick to open it and begin reading.

Dear Anna,

Thanks for your letter. I'm hoping you still enjoy your job there in Strasburg.

I talked to Mamm about the prayer book journals you asked about, but she thinks they were discarded when Mammi Eliza moved over here. Mamm doesn't recall the location of the house where Mammi stayed in Strasburg, either—understandable since she's not very familiar with that area. And of course, till here lately, Mammi rarely ever talked about this. Frankly, the bits and pieces we have heard don't make a speck of sense.

The other day, in fact, Mammi was trying to tell me something about cutting asparagus, and how she put the bundles of stalks together in a rusty old wagon. But then she abruptly stopped talking and stared into space, evidently unable to finish the story. It must be frustrating when that happens, although I'm not sure she even realizes her memory is nearly gone.

"Nearly gone?" Anna whispered, wishing she could be with Mammi more often.

She placed the letter on the writing desk where she'd been sitting. Then she wandered out to the kitchen to make chocolate-chip cookies to surprise Sadie, who'd appeared rather glum the past few days since going to visit her sister Eva and Molly—something she'd done at least twice that Anna knew of. *And naturally Glen likes cookies, too, to go along with his nightly ice cream.*

That's when Anna noticed a check lying on the counter near the cookie jar, made out to Glen Flaud from her father. *Dat's kind to do this till I get my first paycheck,* she thought, going around to raise all the windows high, from the kitchen to the front room, creating a nice breeze through the house.

148

Next, she began to gather ingredients, still thinking about Wanita's letter and how Mammi Eliza's memory was further diminishing.

While dropping the cookie dough onto the sheet pans, it crossed Anna's mind to take some for the break room at the information center sometime. And soon, she caught herself daydreaming about Mart's invitation to go to Hershey with him and a group of his friends tomorrow afternoon.

He was grinning when he invited me, she remembered, having enjoyed his company very much.

Saturday morning dawned with a mostly overcast sky, although here and there in the distance sunlight was already sneaking through as Anna rose. She was all set for a walk. She hadn't neglected her morning quiet time while here, and just now she felt impressed to pray for Sadie's elderly sister Eva.

As was her usual way, Anna also tucked in a prayer for Mammi Eliza, who didn't seem to realize all she was losing. Anna also asked God to give Wanita and her husband, Conrad, patience, grace, and understanding as they took care of Mammi.

Dear Lord, it must be so hard for them and for the whole family, she added, thinking she really needed to see Mammi again soon.

While receiving instructions from Dottie at Peaceful Meadows later that morning, Anna happened to see one of the children run over to Gabe. She remembered what Sadie's grandsons had said about Gabe and his crew building the extraordinary tree house in their woods. As Gabe lifted the little fellow high into the air, both of them laughing, she wondered how he had come to have such a wonderful way with youngsters. Were some men just natural with little ones? These young riders were drawn like magnets to Gabe, often vying for his attention. It reminded Anna some of Wanita's husband, Conrad; he seemed content that their house was always filled with many children, whether their own or foster children. Her sister was definitely blessed to have a husband who helped to lovingly bring their youngsters up in the reverence and ways of the Lord.

The flowers near the birdbath looked so pretty as Sadie sprinkled them from her big white watering can. The can had been passed down from her aunt on her father's side, and she had kept it for years in the little potting shed, using it all the time in the spring and summer. Sadie decided that, no matter what anyone said, she would not give up certain items as she and Glen aged. The watering can was one, for certain. True, it had seen better days, but she liked the feel of the smooth handle and the way water flowed evenly from the many holes. *Better for flowers than using a hose*, she thought.

Glen wandered over from the turkey house and stood near. "Been wantin' to talk to ya, dear," he said quietly.

"Oh?"

He glanced at the sky, then back at her. "Now, I hope ya won't misunderstand," he said.

Sadie wondered what could possibly be on his mind. "Go on."

"Well, seems like you've been spending nearly all of your free time with Anna lately."

"*Jah*, since she arrived, in fact." She nodded, agreeing with him wholeheartedly. "Does it bother ya?"

He shrugged and held her gaze. "I just thought you'd wanna pay more attention to your daughter-in-law next door, maybe," he said, offering a smile now. "And your other family members, too."

Sadie hadn't expected this, although Glen's observation rang true. All the same, perhaps he didn't understand her growing motherly connection with Anna or the joy it brought her. "Well, to tell the truth, I'm delighted that Anna seeks me out and shares as openly as she does." *It's just what I need right now,* she thought.

He nodded without saying more and turned to go into the house.

Glen enjoyed spending time with Anna, too, as I recall, Sadie thought. Glen had given Anna a tour of the turkey barn recently, showing her where, in March, the day-old poults were cared for in the large brooder. Those March turkeys would be ready for a summer harvest later this month. Soon, the new crop of tom and hen poults would arrive and go through the same growing process till Thanksgiving season.

Sadie glanced toward the main farmhouse and inhaled deeply. Once it had been the home where she and Glen had lived and welcomed each of their precious babies, taking care to instruct them in the Old Ways of their forefathers and with daily readings from the Good Book.

A house is a tangible thing built with wood or stone or brick, she thought. *But it takes time and memories made to create a home.*

Sadie set down the watering can and walked over there for a quick visit with Marianna, heeding her husband's suggestion.

Chapter 22

⟨⁓⟩

Anna returned to Flauds' from Peaceful Meadows and took time to freshen up and change her clothes, preparing to go with Mart and his friends to Hershey. As she brushed her waist-length hair and redid the thick bun, she recalled the many things she had learned today. Dottie was pleased with her progress, and several of the volunteers had come up to Anna, even more friendly than before, saying how good it would be to have her on board as a side walker starting next Saturday.

It's going to be so much fun! Anna thought, setting the brush down on the dresser and realizing how often her thoughts turned to the therapy program. It occupied her mind almost as much as her work as a tour guide.

"I've never been so invested in two completely different things," she murmured, looking at herself once more in the hand mirror before heading out through the kitchen to the back porch. There, she waited for the church van to arrive, noticing that Sadie was nowhere around. She likely had gone to run an errand or to visit Eva.

I need to keep helping make her cards for market, she thought, eager to see Sadie reach the fifty mark.

Just then, a white van turned into this side of the lane. Seeing Charlotte waving at her from inside, Anna walked down the sidewalk.

The passenger door slid open, and Mart stepped out wearing tan khakis, light brown loafers, and a short-sleeved blue shirt. "Hi, Anna," he said, brightening. "It's great to see you again."

"I'm looking forward to Hershey," she said, aware of the van filled with other young people.

"It'll be interesting," he said as he offered to help her step in.

She spotted a black umbrella tucked under the seat. *Mart thinks of everything!*

Anna was glad to find a spot next to Charlotte, who was sitting directly behind Austin in the driver's seat. Another fellow was up front with him. "I'm glad you're coming with us," Charlotte said, smiling sweetly.

Anna nodded. "I've never been to Hershey."

"The whole town smells like chocolate," one of the girls behind her declared, and everyone laughed, breaking the ice for Anna.

The drive toward the highway took them past farmland— rows and rows of cornstalks and hayfields. And while the others talked quietly, Mart shared with Anna about one of his recent car tours for a family of six. "One child was deaf, so the mom sat beside her, translating everything I said into sign language. It was a first for me."

Anna turned slightly to watch Mart's animated face. "It's wonderful that the child could be so involved," she said softly. "I've recently thought of keeping a notebook of all the different clients I have and their requests."

"And then someday, if you're instructing new tour guides, you'll have all of that at your fingertips," Mart said.

She was a little surprised at his response. It wasn't likely, she hoped, that she'd be conducting tours here for a long time. The Beachy Amishwomen she'd known rarely pursued careers, so she, too, hoped to be married and be home with a family someday. *Like Mamm . . .*

It was obvious when Sadie entered Marianna's kitchen next door that this might not be the kind of visit where they could sit and talk quietly over iced meadow tea or lemonade. Baby Jimmy was wailing in Marianna's arms, and little Sally had cluttered up a large section of the floor with her toys—she'd even dragged a rag rug over to make a small tent of sorts for her dollies.

Sadie went to help Sally pick up her toys, then led her into the front room to read her a story while Marianna nursed Jimmy in the kitchen rocker.

Soon, the baby's crying ceased, and the house was pleasantly still as Sadie and Sally cuddled together on the settee near the open windows. She was happy to spend time with her littlest granddaughter, but Sadie also missed her usual conversation with Anna, who was off on another outing with her Mennonite friends.

Maybe Glen's right and I do need to focus more on our immediate family, but should I deny myself time with Anna? Sadie thought. *If she needs a listening heart, I'll welcome it.*

When Mart held open the Chocolate Lab door for Anna at the Hershey Story Museum, she caught the scent of chocolate, laced with tantalizing hints of vanilla and nuts.

Charlotte and Austin were already discussing whether they preferred dark or milk chocolate, and when Mart asked her, Anna said, "Dark, hands down." Mart agreed, then showed his tickets to the attendant for the unique workshop advertised as "Hershey's sweetest hands-on activity."

The place was already filling up with not only parents and their children but couples of all ages. Anna was eager to learn about the ingredients combined in the making of chocolate, as well as a few Hershey secrets. Following interactive demonstrations by expert chocolate makers, she and the others would get to pour the freshly melted chocolate and have the chance to decorate it.

"Ever seen anything like this?" Mart asked her as they waited for the workshop lab to begin.

"Never! Where'd you hear about it?"

"Folks on the tours have mentioned it, but I've never been myself, so I checked it out online. It looked like fun, so here we are." He winked at her.

Anna's face warmed. "Maybe the information center should put this on their list of things to do and see," she said. "Even though most of the tourists we work with come to see the simpler side of life."

"True, but who doesn't love the taste of chocolate?"

Charlotte glanced their way and nodded her head, apparently having overheard. "This is the sweetest place on earth, right?"

Anna smiled, glad to be a part of such a great group of young people.

Before Anna and the others left the Chocolate Lab to see the interactive museum exhibits, Anna breathed in deeply the amazing chocolate scent one last time. The rest of the place was interesting, as well, especially the rags-to-riches story of Milton Hershey and the chocolate and town that bore his name.

Charlotte and Austin lagged behind, which was fine with Anna, since it felt like she and Mart were more on their own.

After a stop at the chocolate café, where they all enjoyed a late lunch, the group headed through the enormous parking lot to the van. Charlotte and Austin shared a Hershey's chocolate and almond bar as they walked, talking quietly and laughing occasionally, which gave Anna a chance to interact with several others in their group. But it was Mart who kept catching her eye.

Anna found Sadie in the kitchen preparing a beef roast to use for sandwiches tomorrow, since she wouldn't be doing any cooking for the main meal on the Lord's Day. "Sounds like a *wunnerbaar-gut* recipe," Anna said.

"*Jah*, it really is." Sadie rubbed the sides of the meat with a mix of brown sugar and seasonings. "Did ya have fun?" She glanced at Anna.

"Oh yes, there was lots to do." Anna began to describe all she'd experienced. "Have you ever been there?"

"Many years ago, before all the extra attractions were added. Glen took me on a trolley tour of Hershey with several of our older children."

"I think the trolley still runs."

Sadie's eyebrows lifted. "Is that right?"

"We didn't ride it today, but sometime I might." She paused. "Need any help?"

"*Ach*, nothin' to it," Sadie said, picking up the roaster. "Now I chust slip this in the oven for an hour or so. You go an' relax a bit."

"Okay, then." Anna walked through the sitting room to her room, where she closed the door and sat on the bed, recalling the day. Mart had seemed so friendly and attentive, and there'd been that flirtatious wink. Did he want to date her at some point? And if so, how would she feel about it?

Chapter 23

E liza felt frozen in place under the tall pin oak as Eb motioned to her. Except for his white shirt, buttoned at the throat, he was dressed head to toe in black. She'd already come this far from Great-aunt Joanna's farmhouse, but suddenly she was having second thoughts.

"What's a-matter?" he asked, inching toward her.

"Not sure why I'm here," she managed to say, not admitting that she shouldn't be. *But he surely knows I'm breaking the rules. . . .*

Eb chuckled. "Well, since we can't spend time together where we can be seen, this seemed like a *gut* place." He waved for her to follow him. "Besides, I wanted to show you something."

It was getting darker, and without the moon's brilliance, she might have felt even more hesitant. She honestly wished that Eb had stayed on the other side of the stone wall. Then she remembered what her parents had told her about their family's past and how their Beachy church had broken away from the Old Order. *There's more than one boundary between us. . . .*

Looking around her at the shadowy world, she thought of how Eb had shared about his own parents being forbidden to court, since his father was Old Order and Eb's mother had been a Mennonite. Eliza had been very curious about that.

Finally, she agreed. "Well, since I'm here . . ."

Eb flashed a grin. "I wanted to tell ya the rest of my parents' story. Under the covering of night, they spent a lot of time talking right here where we're standin'. Sometimes, when Dat couldn't get a chance to see her, he left her special notes hidden in the stacked stones of this very wall. And in time, she started leavin' some for him, too."

Eliza thought that his parents had taken a big risk sneaking around for their relationship, just as she and Eb were now.

"It took a few months, but Dat managed to convince her to join his church. They married a year later, and when I was born, Dat named me Ebenezer after the stone of help talked about in First Samuel. 'Hitherto hath the LORD helped us,'" Eb quoted. "So ya see, this ol' wall was important to my parents . . . so important I was named after the stones in it."

Leaning down, Eb pointed to the very spot where his father's love notes had been concealed nearly twenty years before.

Even in the dim light, she could see the place where the rocks were a bit looser. "How did your parents manage to find the same spot?"

"Notice that tall oak tree behind us, standin' there all by itself? They claimed it was their special tree. They'd stand next to that, then look straight ahead to this larger dark gray rock. It's kinda hard to see the color in the moonlight, but do you see how it stands out?"

Eliza nodded.

"Mamm said they'd count six rocks over from there, then three up," Eb said. "And that was their secret hiding spot." He chuckled. "If *I* were hidin' a letter in this stone wall, I'd make it real simple to find."

"What do you mean?"

"Well, I'd choose this large dark rock and slip it under there." He shrugged. "But that's just me." He held Eliza's gaze.

Eliza pondered what Eb had said, then asked, "Did the numbers six and three mean something special to your parents, by any chance?"

"*Jah*, those numbers marked the date they first met here . . . June third."

"I like that," she whispered, realizing that her nervousness had vanished, though she didn't know just when. "It's pretty special to think you were named Ebenezer to honor the part this wall played in their courtship."

"*Jah*." Eb was studying her.

She felt her cheeks warm. "*Denki* for sharin' that with me, but I really must get back to my aunt's."

Eb dipped his head. "I've never told anyone that story 'cept you."

Eliza felt the uneasiness return and didn't know what to say.

"Don't worry." He shook his head. "No one will think to look for ya here, Eliza. Your fears are unfounded."

"But still, my aunt would be upset to find me gone."

"Then we'd better not delay. *Kumm*, I'll walk with ya," Eb said, moving toward her, acting like the bold fellow he had been the first time she'd encountered him, with her wagonful of asparagus stalks.

"Oh, I can find my way. Honest." She pointed to the moon.

He nodded but kept walking with her across the meadow, down toward the road . . . then he began to whistle softly.

Eliza did not object again, but the closer they got to her great-aunt's, the more nervous she felt, lest she be seen with an Old Order fellow. *My parents would have my hide,* she thought. Though she couldn't deny there was something charming about nightfall while with such a handsome young man.

When they reached the end of Joanna's pebbled walkway, Eb waited as Eliza headed around to the back door.

She glanced over her shoulder and saw him still there, and a little shiver ran up her spine. *He likes me too much. . . .*

Chapter 24

Anna awoke late into the night. Sighing, she mentally pictured the corner writing desk and the long letter she'd written to Mamm before saying her prayers. In it, she'd mentioned Martin Nolt, in case Wanita had said something to Mamma about Anna's seeing him twice now with his friends.

No official dates yet, but he winked at me today, Anna thought again, smiling at the memory.

She stretched beneath the sheet and yawned. Then, closing her eyes, she realized that Atley Brenneman had not come to her mind even once since she'd started spending time with Mart.

That has to mean something, she thought as she drifted back to sleep.

The next morning, Sadie turned over in bed and reflected on the proverb Glen had read during their Bible reading last evening. *"Pleasant words are as an honeycomb, sweet to the soul, and health to the bones."*

Sadie smiled, thankful now that her husband cared enough to caution her as he had. *Glen was right,* she thought. *Others in the family need my time and attention, too. Not just Anna.*

The cloud cover that hung around all day yesterday had moved out of the area overnight. Presently, the vivid red of the sunrise reminded Anna of the glory she felt at the dawning of each Lord's Day, and she quickly dressed to go walking in the woods. There, alone with God and His creation, she could pray aloud and feel ever so close to her Savior.

When she came to the tree house, she walked up the steps to the first level, then on to the second, gazing out at the beauty in every direction as she breathed in the fresh scent of a new day.

After her walk, she returned to the house and dressed in preparation for worship at her church, renewed from a good night of sleep, the nature walk, and prayer.

As she arrived at the meetinghouse later that morning, she was met by Heidi Denlinger in the church foyer, who again invited her to sit with her and Eleanor. After visiting quietly about the week, Heidi whispered that Lester had inquired if Anna was seeing anyone. "I told him I didn't know," Heidi added with a quick smile.

"Let's talk later, okay?" Anna said as together they walked into the sanctuary and saw where Eleanor was saving two places on a gleaming pew.

The congregational singing was followed by the passing of the offering plate, and then a sermon from Exodus, chapter fifteen. As the minister spoke about the complaints of the children of Israel, it crossed Anna's mind that, despite all the miracles they had witnessed firsthand, they continually doubted Jehovah's promises. Instead, they continued to question or grumble—or worse, disobey. *Even today, we tend to forget God's miracles . . . and His promises.*

After the service, while they waited for the fellowship meal to begin, Anna told Heidi that she had been going out with a mixed group of youth from another church. "Friends of my colleague at work," she said, not mentioning Mart's name.

"So, no one special?" Heidi asked in a whisper.

Anna gave a little shrug. "Time will tell."

Heidi nodded and smiled. "God will guide you."

Anna was counting on that.

The following Saturday, Anna was assigned to be one of the side walkers for little Emmie, one of two young riders who didn't speak. Anna spotted Emmie's shiny black pony, Promise, already waiting in the lineup of horses.

Dottie introduced her to Emmie and explained that Anna would be with her the whole time, as would Katie Blank, another volunteer Emmie was already accustomed to. "You'll like Anna," Dottie assured her in Pennsylvania Dutch, and Emmie glanced briefly at Anna, eyes tentative.

"Promise is all set to ride," Dottie announced, grinning at the little girl. "Can you say his name today? Pro . . . mise."

Fleetingly, a smile appeared, and then Dottie lifted the girl gently onto the pony. Anna helped Emmie get her right foot into the small stirrup while Dottie assisted with the left one, but Emmie still did not make a sound.

The leader turned out to be Gabe, who picked up the line after greeting Anna and Katie, then grinned at Emmie. "All ready, *jah?*"

"*Fix un faerdich,*" Katie repeated in *Deitsch* for Emmie's sake.

"Can ya tell Promise to walk?" Gabe asked Emmie. "Wanna try?"

Emmie remained silent, her little eyes focused on Promise's mane.

Anna held on to Emmie as Dottie had taught her, and they moved slowly through the stable, following the horses and riders in front of them, heading toward the sunshine and the round pen in the near distance. A slight breeze cooled Anna's neck as she kept her eyes on the petite girl in the saddle, as well as their leader, Gabe.

Halfway around the pen, Anna noticed the stone wall across the field, and she couldn't help thinking of Mammi Eliza's remark about meeting someone at such a wall. Had Mammi been clear in her thinking that day, as it seemed?

The second time around, at the halfway point, Anna wondered whether the stone wall within walking distance of her now was the very one Mammi Eliza was talking about. Wasn't it possible?

She firmly held Emmie's arm and leg through her long rose-colored dress, yet never once did Emmie so much as look her way, instead keeping her gaze on the pony's bobbing head and mane. Promise whinnied softly as they went, and Anna wondered if it was a way for the pony to comfort the little girl.

At the end of the session, Gabe helped Emmie down, and Anna went to get a bucket of water for Promise to drink. After Emmie and the other riders headed for the passenger van, Anna and Katie and a few more volunteers began the work of untacking a few of the horses not needed for the second session. Anna and Katie unbridled Promise and put him in crossties, then removed the girth, saddle, and saddle pad, talking softly to him as they worked. Promise bobbed his head, neighing gently in response.

Eager for the next session, Anna offered to help Dottie in whatever way needed.

"I see they're putting you to work," Gabe said when he encountered Anna in the tack room.

"And I'm enjoying it very much."

"*Gut* to know," he said with a smile.

Anna finished hanging up the saddle pad and then stood there, conscious of his continued presence and feeling a bit shy.

"I appreciate your volunteering . . . and I'll look forward to seein' ya next Saturday, too," Gabe finally said, excusing himself to go and meet the incoming riders.

It was more than an hour later that Anna said good-bye to Dottie and headed to the car, grateful to have spent another delightful morning at this very special retreat.

Chapter 25

Monday of the following week, Anna spent time talking with Mart between their individual tours.

"How was your morning at Peaceful Meadows?" Mart asked as he served himself a cup of coffee and walked over to join her at the break room table.

"Oh . . . real nice. I got to be one of the side walkers for a five-year-old girl named Emmie. She doesn't speak."

Mart frowned. "Is she autistic?"

Anna shook her head. "No, Emmie became mute when her mother died," she told him. "She's just darling, and because she's so tiny, she always rides a pony named Promise instead of one of the horses. Come to think of it, Promise reminds me of Misty, one of my favorite ponies that Dat raised."

Mart opened a packet of sugar and stirred some into his mug. "What happened to Misty?"

"We sold her to a family in Peach Bottom," Anna said,

remembering how difficult it had been to part with the sleek beauty. "It was a painful good-bye."

He reached for his coffee mug. "Did you ever visit her?" He took a sip.

"My siblings and I wanted to, but Dat thought it would be too hard on the pony . . . and on all of us, too, so we didn't. Ponies are very intelligent, I'm sure you know. It was important for her to settle in with her new family."

"No wonder you're interested in working at the retreat." He chuckled, then asked more specifics about the kinds of responsibilities she had there.

Anna was happy to fill him in. Then she added, "I can't believe how many new friends I've made since coming here."

"Friends are the whipped cream on the pie of life," he said with a grin.

"Did you just make that up?"

He chuckled. "I actually did."

"Well, whipped cream is the best part of the pie."

"That's what I meant."

They shared a laugh, and then she asked about last Saturday's volleyball tournaments, which Mart had mentioned to her last week.

Mart brightened, clearly pleased as he described a few of the sets. "I wish you could have been there. Some were definite nail-biters."

"Were Austin and Charlotte part of it?" she asked.

"Yes, and they're both quite good. In the end, our church's team squeaked out a win for the championship," he told her, putting his thumbs up. Then he glanced at his watch and said he had to get ready to meet a family coming in from New Jersey.

Anna nodded as he excused himself and headed out to meet

his clients. She decided that this weekend might be a good time to return to Mifflinburg for a visit, since Mart hadn't said anything about going out with the group again.

I'll leave right after my morning at Peaceful Meadows.

The week sped by, and on Friday, Anna helped Sadie clean house. Afterward, they made more of the inlaid fabric cards.

While they worked, Anna shared quietly that Mart hadn't invited her to do anything this weekend. "I guess it shouldn't bother me, since it's not like we're dating. But I'd kind of hoped he would."

Sadie seemed to take her words to heart. "I believe he'll ask ya out again, Anna."

She nodded slowly, thinking how caring it was of Sadie to be so optimistic.

"So, are you still planning to go home for the night tomorrow after working at the retreat?" Sadie asked.

Anna said she was and that she was looking forward to seeing her family again. "I especially want to see Mammi Eliza. I'm worried that if she slips further away mentally, I'll wish I'd visited her more."

"Well, who could blame ya? I feel the same about Eva." Sadie went on to say that, lately, Eva was sleeping a lot more. "She's fatigued even after she wakes up from a nap."

"Does she sleep through the night, do you know?"

"Molly keeps an ear out for her . . . says she's restless. I think they're both sleep deprived, sad to say."

Anna wondered if Mammi was experiencing anything similar, though Wanita hadn't mentioned it.

"Low energy is also a symptom of dementia," Sadie said with a sigh. "Eva's doctor told Molly this recently."

Anna listened for a moment and then put in, "And in the later stages, people suffering with this don't always realize that anything is wrong." She felt truly sorry for Eva . . . and for Molly and Sadie.

"After we make these last two cards, I need to go an' check for messages at the phone shed," Sadie said.

"And while you do that, I'll make supper."

A smile spread across Sadie's wrinkled face. "You've been wanting to do that since ya got here, ain't so?"

Anna nodded. "And how about tonight?"

Sadie just looked at her and tilted her head. "Why don't we cook up somethin' together?"

Anna grinned. "Like you always say."

"It's more fun thataway, *jah?*"

Anna couldn't disagree. "Okay, you win." She laughed. "*Again.*"

Saturday morning at Peaceful Meadows, Anna helped Emmie with the basic grooming, talking softly to Promise, and working closely with the little girl as she moved the curry brush in circular motions. Anna glanced at the sweet girl, whose tiny fingers clutched the small brush as she pressed her lips firmly together.

"Promise is glad to see you, Emmie," she said softly. "Can you say his name today? Can you say Pro . . . mise?"

Looking away, Emmie remained silent and worked with the brush, leaning closer now to the pony.

Gabe soon came around to the left side to lift Emmie up onto the saddle—standard mounting procedure, as Anna knew from all her years working with ponies.

Anna took her own position on the right side, helping to

169

guide Emmie's foot into the small stirrup, just as she had last Saturday, talking softly to the small girl all the while.

Gabe patted Emmie's shoulder gently before he left to assist another young rider. Soon, Dottie came over and stood at Promise's left flank as they waited for the leader. Anna assumed it might be Gabe again, but it turned out to be Katie Blank, who petted Promise's nose and greeted Anna and Dottie before smiling up at Emmie. "Are ya ready to ride?"

Instantly, Emmie reached to hold on to the horn of the saddle, swaying slightly forward and back with her whole body.

Looking up at Emmie, Dottie asked, "Can you tell Promise to go forward?"

Again, Emmie was silent, but she continued to rock gently, as she had done before when sitting in the saddle.

Once Katie was ready to lead, she counted, *"Eener, zwee, drei . . . geh!"*

Playing a small part in this parade-like movement of horses, riders, and volunteers toward the round pen gave Anna goose pimples of happiness. As she had done last week, she kept a firm hold on Emmie's right leg and arm, aware of how very small boned she was. *So tiny for a five-year-old,* Anna thought, recalling her youngest nephews and nieces back in Mifflinburg at this age. Suddenly, she felt even more eager to see her family again.

Will Dat and Mamm have a more accepting view of Old Order Amish, once I tell them about my work here at Peaceful Meadows? she wondered, but she wasn't holding her breath.

During Anna's drive to Mifflinburg, she was glad to be traveling on a Saturday. Considering that summer was officially upon them, there were quite a number of tourists out and about, but as she passed the exit for Hershey and headed toward Harrisburg, the traffic seemed noticeably less than it might be on a weekday.

As was her way, Anna prayed as she drove, offering praise to her heavenly Father for every blessing. She also prayed about Mart, giving their friendship to God, determined not to be discouraged that he hadn't asked her out on a real date yet.

Upon her arrival home, Anna hurried inside and noticed the basement door standing open. "Mamm, I'm home!" she called, then made her way down the steps to see her mother standing in front of the A-L section of the shelves of alphabetized canning jars, counting quarts of chow chow.

"My dear girl!" Mamm said, turning to cup her hands around Anna's face. "You've been gone, what, a month?"

Anna nodded. "Seems longer, I know."

"Well, it's wonderful to see you again!" Mamm beamed. "Are you hungry?"

"I snacked on the way," she reassured her, having assumed that her mother would ask the minute she stepped inside the house. All the womenfolk she knew were like that. *Including Sadie,* Anna thought. *Always wanting to offer food . . .*

They headed upstairs to the kitchen, where they spotted Dat coming up the back walkway. Anna went to meet him, and he went with her to the car to retrieve her bag from the trunk.

"Mighty good to have you home, daughter."

"*Gut* to be back."

They ambled up toward the house. "I understand you've been volunteering at a horse retreat for the disabled," Dat said. It made her smile to see he'd worn his best straw hat with his work overalls.

"Yes, and I can't tell you how much I enjoy it. They're all such wonderful people." She went on to describe how organized the volunteers were, thanks to Gabe's management. "Gabe Allgyer is the nephew of the owner, and he has a knack for making the young riders feel comfortable . . . works well with the volunteers, too."

"And," Dat said, "you're one of those volunteers."

"Yes, and the children are so dear. Many of them don't say much, but they still appear to take joy from their riding experience."

Inside, Mamm had set out fruit for the table—oranges, apples, and bananas—even though Anna had said she wasn't hungry. *Just like Mamm to do that,* Anna thought as she went to sit at the table with her while Dat carried her bag upstairs.

"Surely you have room to nibble on an orange or apple," Mamm said, moving the fruit bowl closer to her.

"It would make you happy, right?" Anna laughed, reached for a banana, and began to remove the peel. "It won't be too much longer, and we'll be sitting down to supper." Anna sniffed the air, glad to be back. "You must be baking my favorite meatloaf."

Mamm nodded, grinning. "I put it in the oven before you came." She glanced at her wristwatch. "Your father wanted to eat earlier than usual, so we'll all be ready again for dessert. We're having peanut-butter dream bars when your eldest brother arrives."

"Wayne's coming over?" It had been a while since Anna had seen him, his wife, Cindy, and their three younger children, all school age now.

"And Cindy's bringing the dessert," Mamm said, eyes shining.

"Oh, this will be so nice!" *A little like Christmas,* Anna thought.

In her old room, Anna unpacked for the night, leaving some

172

things in her small suitcase. Looking around, she was reminded of the contrast between this very familiar room and the one where she was staying at Glen and Sadie's. Her bedroom here was about the same size, but since so many of her personal items had been moved to Strasburg, it felt deserted and lifeless.

She looked out the window and took in the large backyard and the long rope swing on the tree nearest the house. Dat had put it up for Wayne and the other boys long before Wanita and Anna were born. Her gaze traveled to the clearing just before the woods that she loved so, its path nearly grown over with grass and weeds now.

Sighing, she went to sit in her cozy tan chair with its matching hassock and put up her feet, continuing to make comparisons as she looked around the room. *I've managed to make the adjustment to living without electricity in a fairly short time,* she realized with a glance at the pretty electric lamp on the dresser and the reading lamp on the small table near her bed.

To think I expected it to be so hard . . .

Chapter 26

S adie had invited both Molly and Eva for supper, and they'd arrived early, which was quite all right, considering it had been some time since Eva had gotten out of the house. *We'll have more time with her this way,* Sadie thought as Glen helped Eva up the few porch steps and offered his favorite rocking chair, with its padded seat. He began talking with her while Sadie and Molly headed indoors.

Molly sat down at the table with a great sigh, her eyes pink. "What's a-matter?" Sadie asked, going over to sit with her.

Tears welling up, Molly began to pour out her woes, her lower lip quivering as she struggled not to cry. "All the way here, Mamma wanted to know why we were leavin' the house. 'Why are ya taking me away?' she kept saying."

"This is awful hard on you, dear." Sadie reached for her niece's hand and squeezed it gently.

"The worst of it was . . . she wanted to know where I had

taken her daughter. *Me.*" Molly's eyes glistened as she brushed tears away. "It's becomin' so difficult to do this alone, Aendi Sadie. I could use more help—anyone in the family who can spare some extra time."

"We'll talk 'bout that while you're here." Sadie encouraged her to breathe deeply and to enjoy these moments while Glen was occupying Eva's attention just now. "And Anna's gone, so maybe you'd like to go in and stretch out on her bed."

"Are ya sure?" Molly was sniffling.

"I can see you're all in. Help yourself."

Molly was up in a jiffy, thanking her. "I really needed to get out of the house today. *Denki,* Aendi!"

"Have yourself a *gut* long rest." Sadie watched her go, her heart breaking.

She could hear Glen out there reading the newspaper to Eva now. *Poor man, he's probably run out of things to say.*

Anna's sister-in-law Cindy called to Anna as Wayne and their sons—Henry, ten, and Alan, eight—and their youngest child, Gracie, age six, made their way up the porch steps and into the house.

Going to meet them, Anna talked first with Cindy, eyeing her pan of peanut-butter dream bars through the plastic cover. "You've been busy today, *jah?*" she said.

Anna then greeted Wayne, saying it was really nice to see them again.

Wayne grinned and removed his straw hat. "Guess ya had to leave town so you'd miss us."

Laughing, Anna nodded. "You've always been the biggest tease in the family," she said, patting young Alan's shoulder and taking his little straw hat when he handed it to her. She gave it to Henry, who went to hang it, as well as his own and his father's, on the row of wooden pegs.

Cindy smiled. "He certainly is." She carried the pan over to the counter and placed it there, removing the covering. "But in Wayne's defense, it was *his* idea for me to make these bars." She glanced at her husband.

"I take all responsibility for the satisfaction of your taste buds, Anna." Wayne chuckled and smacked his lips.

Anna went over to squeeze little Gracie, who whispered that she was starting school next month. "First grade," she said with a grin, one of her upper front teeth missing.

"Already?" Anna acted surprised.

Gracie nodded her head and glanced at her parents with big eyes.

"She can hardly wait," Cindy said as Anna's mother removed a stack of dessert plates from the cupboard over the sink.

"I'd rather play for longer," Henry said, going over to plop down at the table. "Summer's too short." He leaned his elbows on the tabletop and dramatically rested his blond head in his hands.

"Now, son," Wayne said, "there's plenty of summer left."

Henry turned to look out the window. "Can us kids sit outside to eat Mamma's dessert?"

Wayne gave him a look. "Be polite."

Anna wondered how long before Henry, who was known to push the limits, would ask this again, even though the children were expected to stick around to visit with family.

"It *is* awful hot in here," Dat said. "Why don't we all just go outside and eat?"

Henry hopped up from the bench and began to hurry over to the counter to get his dessert, but Wayne whispered something in his ear. With a sheepish expression, Henry stepped back to let Anna's father and Wayne be first instead.

When they were all outside on the big porch, Anna was reminded of all the many family gatherings here and under the towering backyard trees. She slowly ate Cindy's scrumptious dessert, savoring every bite. Once the boys had devoured their own desserts, she watched Henry and Alan take turns on the rope swing. Little Gracie, meanwhile, was sitting on the porch steps, playing with a doll she'd brought from home, talking to it quietly but glancing up every now and then toward the boys like she hoped to have a turn on the swing, too, eventually.

In time, Henry and Alan headed out to the stable with Wayne and Dat, and Gracie quickly claimed the swing, now sitting with her dolly on her lap as she swayed back and forth.

Anna listened as Cindy talked about their four older children—two close-in-age sons who were in Big Valley for the summer working on Wayne's uncle's farm, and their two older daughters, both of whom were skilled seamstresses.

Soon, the conversation turned to Mammi Eliza, and Cindy mentioned she'd talked with Wanita just this morning. "Evidently something strange happened last night."

Mamm frowned. "Everything all right?"

Cindy assured her that it was nothing to worry about. "I guess Mammi Eliza just said something about needing to get to a stone wall. She seemed real insistent."

Anna perked up her ears. "She said that?"

Cindy nodded. "Wanita said Mammi kept repeatin' it while rockin' in her chair, awful anxious."

Mamm sighed. "She's terribly confused."

"What do you think she meant by it?" Anna asked.

"Wanita couldn't get Mammi to say anything more than

that." Cindy shook her head. "It was downright peculiar. Usually she doesn't fix her mind on things like that."

"True." Anna was intrigued. *It's no coincidence*, she decided.

Glancing at the day clock, Sadie realized that Molly had been sleeping for an hour. Not wanting to disturb her, she stood at the back screen door, where she could see Glen reading now to himself while Eva napped, her double chin resting on her chest, her mouth crumpled closed.

Sadie stepped outside and motioned for her husband. "Do you think we should wait on supper?" she asked, explaining that Molly was sound asleep in Anna's room.

Glen headed inside with her and looked at the clock. "Well, it's already suppertime."

Nodding, Sadie said she could wait another half hour, if he could.

"S'pose so," he said quietly, looking out the door at Eva, still dozing. "She wasn't makin' much sense today. It's hard to see her like this."

Sadie recalled her time on the porch with them earlier, before coming in to put the finishing touches on supper. "We really ought to get more help for Molly than just one day off each week," she suggested. "Molly brought up that she's really strugglin'. Poor thing's tuckered out."

Glen touched her elbow. "Well, you can't keep adding things to *your* day, dear."

He means at my age, she thought.

A smile crept across his bearded face, and he reached for her hand. "We'll get more help for Molly. I'll spread the word to the family."

Sadie looked into his dear face, her heart swelling with love.

Sunday afternoon, Anna took Mamm with her to Wanita's. On the drive over, Anna mentioned that she hoped her most recent visits with Mammi Eliza hadn't caused any anxiety. "You know, because she seems to connect me with Strasburg now."

"I don't think you should be concerned about that," Mamm said, clutching her purse in the front passenger seat. "I really don't."

"Well, she's been talking about a stone wall ever since I first said I was going to Strasburg. And it seems like it might have upset her."

Her mother nodded. "True, but according to the doctor, her failing memory has more to do with the progression of the disease than anything we say to her. At this point, the way she remembers personal experiences might just be faulty."

Anna listened, feeling all the more uncertain as to what they could depend on from Mammi's memories . . . and what they could not.

During most of Anna and her mother's visit with Wanita and the children in the sitting room, Mammi Eliza sat there snoozing. Anna's eyes were drawn to her grandmother's peaceful countenance, and she felt impressed to memorize her dear face. Oh, she loved being with her . . . and with Mamm and Wanita and the children, too. But there was something about Mammi Eliza's restful state that made Anna thankful for this particular visit.

"Who wants a strawberry popsicle?" Wanita asked. "I made a batch yesterday."

Bethie and Bonnie followed her out to the kitchen, and

soon little Rogene wiggled off Mamm's lap and toddled out there, too.

Just then, Mammi Eliza's eyes fluttered open, and seeing Anna there, she sat up a bit, her shoulders rising with a deep breath. "*Ach*, Anna . . . you're here," she whispered.

Nodding, Anna moved her chair closer. "I've sure been missing you, Mammi." She reached for her hand and patted it.

"Well now . . ." Mammi looked pleased.

"I pray for you every day; don't forget."

Mammi's eyelids fell to half-mast now. "Did ya find the stone wall?" She murmured it so softly that Anna wasn't sure she'd heard correctly.

Frowning, Anna turned toward her mother. "What do you make of that?" she whispered. "She's talking about the wall again."

Mamm's smile was faint as she motioned for Anna to go with her to the front room. "You can't trust what she says anymore, Anna," Mamm told her, looking concerned. "She might be hallucinating or coming out of a dream. The doctor says that can happen sometimes."

Anna didn't know what to think. All the same, Mammi's repeated mentions of a stone wall were hard to ignore.

"I tend to believe Mammi," she told her mother quietly. "Honestly, it seems like she's trying to tell me something important."

Her mother paused uneasily, then said, "Just don't let your imagination run away with you, Anna." Her Mamm held her gaze, and Anna let it be.

Before they left, Anna asked her sister if she could run up to the attic and look around.

"If you're thinking about the journals you wrote about, I went through Mammi's blanket chest. There are no journals anywhere to be found, and I searched quite thoroughly," Wanita said.

"Well, would you mind if I look?"

Wanita shrugged. "Not at all," she said. "Guess it's possible I overlooked something."

"I'll search carefully," Anna said, feeling only slightly hopeful.

Chapter 27

SUNDAY, JULY 11, 1948

Eliza waited till she knew Great-aunt Joanna had gone to bed for the night, then crept outside, walking down the dirt lane to sit on the stone steps leading to the springhouse just south of the farmhouse. There, she pondered her situation, going over in her mind the fact that she had not run into Ebenezer Lapp either out on the road or at market for days now. It was odd, really, since for the first few weeks after coming to stay here, she had repeatedly bumped into him. As she stared at the moon, a sliver of a fingernail tonight, she wondered if he might have left the area to help a relative.

She'd brought her flashlight along, in case she decided to give in to her inclination to walk down the road to the stone wall. The desire to visit it was ever so strong, and sighing, she admitted to herself that what she actually wanted was to see Eb. She missed him. Getting up from the steps, she headed down toward the road, the light from her flashlight bobbing along, leading the way.

Locating the lone pin oak tree on this side of the stone wall, Eliza took several steps forward until she stood at the very spot where Eb's parents had supposedly hidden their notes as a courting couple. *Eb seemed so sure about it,* she thought, her curiosity growing as she spotted the dark gray stone Eb had pointed out. Struggling to slip her fingers beneath the heavy stone and the one below it, she remembered what Eb had said about making it simple to find a letter in the wall. She stared at the large gray stone and pushed hard on it, and, managing to find a slight crevice underneath, she fished around, searching for what, she really did not know.

To her surprise, she felt something. And when she directed the light from the flashlight toward it, she saw a folded piece of paper with her name on the front.

"What on earth?" she murmured, pulling it from its hiding place, her pulse racing.

Ever so curious, she opened the note and began to read.

Dear Eliza,

I hope you think to come here looking for a note from me, though I figure the chances are probably low, since we didn't really talk about doing this. But if you're reading this, then know I'm very happy how much we think alike.

As I write this, three weeks have passed since you met me here, and truth be told, I've missed seeing you, Eliza. I like spending time with you. But since we really shouldn't be seen together because of our different backgrounds—if you would even like to see me again, that is—I wondered if you might leave a note here for me, too . . . if you've found this one.

Your friend,
Eb Lapp

"He must be *ferhoodled*," Eliza whispered, refolding the note and forcing it back into the small crevice. She backed away from the stone wall and leaned against the wide trunk of the tall tree, her heart still beating fast as the moon slid behind a cloud.

The boundary between us is stronger than any stone wall, she thought as she turned off her flashlight. Encompassed in darkness, she breathed deeply and tried to calm down, letting her eyes become accustomed to the dark.

She turned to head back to Great-aunt Joanna's. Eb had taken a risk by declaring that he enjoyed spending time with her. But why had he even suspected she might think to look in the wall for a note that she had no idea he'd write?

Glad again for her flashlight, Eliza switched it on to cross the dark road. *Maybe Eb thinks that if notes worked to get his mother to join the Amish and marry his father, they'll work with me.*

Eliza tittered at the notion, then pressed her hand over her mouth as she made her way up toward the big back porch. "That'll never happen," she whispered as she took a seat in her aunt's rocking chair, the black Labrador, Grady, wagging his tail nearby, having come out of his resting place.

Eliza leaned back and stared at the night sky, more conflicted as the moments passed. She remembered the words Eb had written and wondered what had prompted her to look for a note in the very wall where Eb's father had first hidden notes decades before.

She stiffened, upset with herself now for even venturing out to look. And continuing to ponder this, it occurred to her that, if she was so dead set against Eb's note and his apparent fondness for her, then why was she suddenly blinking back tears?

Chapter 28

———— ⟨⟨⟨⟨⟩⟩ ————

Anna wasn't surprised to discover that Wanita's attic was
as neat as the rooms in the rest of the house. Going
over to the long wooden chest in the far corner, she
hoped her sister didn't mind her coming up here. *I need to see
for myself about Mammi's prayer journals,* she thought, lifting
the lid back from the chest, yearning to find them. "Wouldn't
it be wonderful if they still existed?" she murmured, leaning
the open lid against the slanted attic beams.

One at a time, she removed Mammi's old linens, embroidered doilies, and blankets no longer needed to bring cheer
and warmth to a home. Anna even unfolded some of the larger
blankets and quilts, making extra work for herself, but she was
determined not to miss finding something that might confirm
the existence of the Strasburg stone wall that seemingly fascinated her dear Mammi.

She found old books, as well as letters from relatives who
had passed on, and, encased in a plastic bag, a lovely autumn

wreath made with twine and twigs from the woods. Some of
the berries had fallen off, but a few remained, as did a soft gold
velvet ribbon.

Admiring it, Anna wondered if it might be something
Mammi would like to see again. On the other hand, she didn't
want to confuse her unnecessarily. *Not for the world.*

Looking around to make sure she'd refolded and placed everything back as it had been, Anna sighed as she reached for the
hinged lid and gradually brought it down. Discouraged, she sat
on the lid and looked out the attic dormer window toward the
pastureland.

"So that's it," she whispered, leaning her head into her hands
and closing her eyes tightly. "I need to let this go."

After a time, she rose and tiptoed around the opposite side
of the chest.

Then, seeing what looked like a dusty book peeking out from
beneath the old chest, she reached down to pick it up. Thrilled,
she brushed off a small diary with a lock and tiny key dangling
by a thin yellow ribbon.

The key fit the minuscule lock easily, and Anna noticed the
name and date on the first page: *Eliza Hertzler, 1948.* Without
thinking about invading Mammi's privacy, Anna turned to the
month of June and scanned through the pages, looking for any
mention of a stone wall.

Mammi won't mind, she thought, still hoping this might be
just the thing to confirm her grandmother's attempts to reveal
something about her past.

Anna read further. The entries were short and rather
obscure—a few mentions of her great-aunt Joanna and a black
Lab named Grady. Nothing about a beau . . . or a meeting at
a stone wall.

Wanita called up the steps, and Anna let her know that

she'd found something. "Bring it down and we'll have a look-see," Wanita said as Anna made her way to the steep staircase.

Anna carried the still dusty diary downstairs and placed it in Wanita's hands. "I'd love to look through it more thoroughly, if it's all right," Anna said.

Wanita looked quite surprised. "Where did ya find this?"

Anna told her, hoping Mamm wouldn't be upset at this discovery, but secretly, Anna was thrilled.

Early Monday morning, the day after Anna's return from Mifflinburg, she bounded out of bed before her alarm sounded and hurried to the dresser drawer where she'd placed Mammi's diary for safekeeping. Grateful for Mamm's approval to bring the diary back to Strasburg, Anna tenderly turned the pages she'd stayed up last night reading. There were no revelations about any young man, but as Anna read forward now, she noticed a different sort of entry, a page on the righthand side of the diary with a description that caught her attention:

Look for the tall pin oak tree a few yards from the stone wall. Straight ahead, in line with the tree—the only tree around—is the dark gray stone. Search for the crevice under the large stone, and look for the note underneath.

"Wow," Anna whispered. "Mammi wasn't hallucinating after all. There *was* a stone wall."

She couldn't help but wonder about the pin oak tree, though, knowing that if it was that tall seventy years ago, it would have long since reached maturity. "Pin oaks don't live as long as some trees," she murmured, realizing that even if she could find the wall, the marker for the gray stone couldn't possibly be in existence now.

Instead of waiting in the break room between her tours, Anna walked over to the Lancaster Mennonite Historical Society to do some quick research on the historic stone walls of Strasburg. Fortunately, she was able to get the locations of three and was itching to drive to see them after her second tour of the day, this one with a woman and her daughter from Australia who'd requested a three-hour tour. They were interested in seeing an Amish housewares store, the wooden toy shop, and an Amish farm with quilts and crafts and a buggy for photo ops, as well as the Mascot Roller Mills in Ronks.

As soon as that tour was over, Anna asked Helen, the helpful receptionist at the information center, if there were any tours lined up for her tomorrow.

"It looks like you could have three, assuming you can fit them all in," Helen said, showing Anna the log. "One is scheduled for nine o'clock, one for eleven-fifteen—that couple wants to be taken to an authentic Amish restaurant, so I would suggest Dienner's, if you're familiar with it. The third tour would begin at two-thirty, which gives you plenty of time to get back here between the second and third."

"Sure, I'll do all three," Anna said, delighted yet again by how well this job was working out. "Thanks so much."

Walking into the break room, she noticed Mart talking to one of the other fellows and waved at them as she went to get some coffee at the counter.

Evelyn Leaman peeked in at that moment and motioned for Anna. "May I speak with you briefly?"

Anna nodded and, taking her coffee, followed her to the main office down the hallway. She sat across from Evelyn's desk, feeling more at ease with her now.

"You'll be pleased to know that I've received glowing remarks from clients regarding your tours, Anna," Evelyn said, a pen between her fingers.

Anna smiled. "I'm glad to hear they enjoyed them."

"I wanted to pass along the encouragement." Evelyn seemed to study her. "Anna, you must surely miss your family in Mifflinburg."

Nodding, Anna mentioned having just returned from a weekend visit. "My parents understand why I wanted to spread my wings. And I appreciate that."

"Well, we're certainly delighted to have you on board here."

Anna thanked her again, and after the short visit, Anna noticed Mart talking in the hallway with another tour guide, the same young Mennonite woman he often sat with in the break room. Anna kept walking toward the entrance and to her car, feeling a little down, though she wouldn't let on, just as she hadn't let on how nervous she'd been for her interview weeks ago.

Once inside her car, she took out the small notebook from her purse to look up the locations for the stone walls, then opened Google Maps on her phone to enter the first destination. As she backed out of her spot, she saw Mart heading across the parking lot to his car. He raised his hand in a high wave and gave her a big smile.

She waved back.

Before returning to Glen and Sadie's place, Anna drove to the first wall on her list. It was a lovely setting, across the road from pastureland with a pond. She slowed her car, moving along the shoulder and wishing she knew more from Mammi, though that was not possible now. There were many tall black walnut trees—a grove of them—on the north side of this wall. *Just as Sadie mentioned*, thought Anna. *But not a single pin oak.*

Anna drove farther up the road and turned around, then backtracked, creeping along as she scrutinized the wall and the trees again. Next, she drove to a smaller stone wall a few miles away, and later, the last wall, which turned out to be the one running between the wide meadow and Gabe's uncle's property at Peaceful Meadows. She was the most familiar with this one, of course, having admired it whenever she was there to volunteer.

Eventually, Anna returned to the Flauds' farm and hurried to her room to change clothes from work.

That evening, after supper, Anna could tell that Sadie seemed blue. "Let's go for a walk," she suggested.

Sadie shook her head. "*Ach*, I oughta keep workin'."

"It might make you feel better if you come," Anna said while sweeping the kitchen floor.

"Well, ya know, I *have* been wanting to go an' see the tree house again. . . ."

"And I know the easiest path to take there." Anna finished sweeping. "It'd be *gut* for me, too," she admitted.

"All right, then." Sadie dried her hands and untied her white half apron and hung it in the pantry across the room.

Being in the dense woods felt refreshing to Sadie as she walked with Anna on the little path that led through the familiar underbrush, though it had been a while since she'd last walked there. "Feels nice in the shade," Sadie said, making small talk.

"It's the middle of summer, so I guess we can't really complain, *jah?*" Anna said, smiling.

190

Sadie chuckled, glad she'd let Anna convince her to come. After the recent visit with Eva and Molly here at the house, Glen had gone to the phone shanty that very evening to con-tact each of Eva's sisters and sisters-in-law. Based on what Glen had lined up, Sadie made a chart to keep track of who would be helping Molly every other day. Glen had even asked Sadie why they'd waited so long to do this. But thinking about it now, Sadie didn't want to spoil her peaceful walk with Anna. Besides, she felt sure that Anna was noodling on something. "You all right?" she finally asked.

"Oh, it's just that Mammi Eliza brought up that stone wall once again. It's supposedly somewhere round here. So I actually drove past three after work today."

"So you're certain she's remembering a real wall?"

"It might be a partial memory, but she's not able to talk about it fully," Anna said, mentioning the diary entry.

Sadie whistled her fascination, thinking that if Eliza's mem-ory was as poor as Eva's, there wasn't a whole lot that made sense.

Anna stopped walking to wipe her forehead with the back of her hand. "How long do pin oaks live, do you know?"

"Well, a hundred and twenty years or so, compared to white oaks that can live for centuries. Pin oaks put down more shal-low roots," Sadie said.

"I guessed you might know."

"But does it change anything, really?" Sadie asked, the tree house coming into view.

Anna began walking again, not saying anything, as though contemplating this. "I don't like to think I might never find the stone wall . . . not when Mammi's so fixated on it." She sounded a bit sad. "Mammi supposedly exchanged love letters in a stone wall."

Though Sadie was surprised, she felt for her. "I don't usually pray 'bout such things, but if it's on your heart . . ."

Anna nodded. They walked to the tree house, and Anna sat down on the third step, sliding over to make room for Sadie. "One thing's for sure." Anna raised her face to the patches of sky visible through the thick canopy above. "I'm at peace here," she said softly, her hands folded on her lap. "Have you ever felt so calm as when you're spending time in the woods?"

Sadie hadn't really thought about it. "I feel like that when I'm sewing or quilting, or pinning the washing to the clothesline . . . doin' what I'm called to."

Anna glanced at her and leaned back, her face tilted up again. "Just listen."

Sadie closed her eyes, enjoying this moment with Anna. But the only sounds she heard were birds and insects, and after a time, the distant sound of a train whistle, likely the Strasburg Railroad, heading toward its short run to Paradise Township. But she didn't mind sitting there with Anna, who seemed in need of this respite.

"Do you hear it?" Anna asked softly at last.

"The forest sounds?"

"*Jah* . . . the tranquility."

Sadie agreed. "'Tis mighty nice, *jah*."

Anna glanced over her shoulder. "By the way, why did Luke and Glen decide to have this tree house built here?"

"No particular reason." Sadie shrugged. "Maybe Gabe Allgyer thought it made sense for it to be away from the house, yet protected from the harsh sun . . . ideal for Luke's boys, 'specially, who like to be rowdy and a bit noisy," she said. "We really enjoyed havin' Gabe round here while he worked on it. All of us got better acquainted with him."

Anna smiled. "He's so comfortable around children, as you know."

"That he is," Sadie said, wondering what else Anna had discovered about the wonderful young man.

"Would you like to come up with me?" Anna rose and started climbing the steps to the first level of the tree house.

Just then, Sadie heard the rustle of quick footsteps and looked over to see Marcus and Eddy running this way, down the most challenging path, with their large German shepherd, Brownie. Their faces were red and sweaty.

"Mammi!" Eddy called, grinning from ear to ear. "You came!"

Sadie rose slowly from the step, pleased how happy they were to see her there. She followed Eddy and lively Brownie up the wooden steps, Marcus trailing behind.

On the first level, they found Anna peering at a bird's nest, and the boys hurried over, not touching.

"The baby birds all flew away," Marcus told them.

Sadie crept closer to the nest. Sure enough, it was empty. "Remember that sometimes a nest is used a second time for the base of a new one," she said, glancing at Anna, hoping she wasn't being too obvious.

Anna looked Sadie's way and held her gaze.

She understands, thought Sadie happily.

Chapter 29

─────── ❦ ───────

After Anna returned from her morning tour on Wednesday, Mart entered the break room where she sat, making a beeline for the coffee. He greeted her, then poured himself a cup and took his time to look at the tour guide schedule near the coffee pot.

Coming over to where she was sitting, he pulled out a chair at the small table, and it was then that she realized for the first time that Mart took his coffee black. She also realized that the two of them were alone.

Leaning forward, Mart asked, "I was thinking . . . would you like to go on a picnic with me this Saturday?" He paused. "After you're finished volunteering at Peaceful Meadows."

Pleased, Anna agreed.

"I thought we could drive out to Long's Park. Have you been there?"

She shook her head.

"Well then, I'll have the pleasure of introducing you to one of the prettiest places in Lancaster County." He grinned.

"What can I bring?"

"Thanks, but my mom's got that covered."

Anna was touched that he'd already put so much thought into this. "How kind." *His mom knows about me,* she thought, suppressing her smile. And since Mart hadn't brought up Charlotte and Austin or any of the other youth this time, she was fairly sure it would just be the two of them.

They continued to sip their coffee, discussing their morning tours.

Anna asked if he'd ever had a client who wanted to learn Pennsylvania Dutch.

"No, have you?"

"Just this morning, in fact—a Texas college professor and his wife. They were quite curious about it, asking lots of questions about how different it is from standard German. I was able to find a Pennsylvania German to English dictionary for them to purchase at the Gordonville Book Store, where we stopped during the tour. Should be a fun souvenir for them."

"I'm not certain I would have thought of that," he said, his attention wholly on her. "Good thinking, Anna." Then he asked about her trip home. "Did you get to see the grandmother you told me about?"

Anna nodded. "We had a precious time together, and I even happened across an old diary she kept the summer she was here as a teen."

Mart seemed interested.

"I've already read snippets of it," she told him, adding how pleased she was that her mother and sister didn't mind her bringing it back to Strasburg. "It's comforting, in a way . . . makes me feel close to Mammi Eliza."

"My mom likes old things, too, especially memoirs," he said, glancing at his watch. "I really hate to end our conversation, but I need to meet my next clients."

"Of course," she said, smiling back at him and looking forward to their picnic.

The following Saturday, Anna talked with Dottie Stoltzfus and Katie Blank in the tack room at Peaceful Meadows, both young women in pale green dresses and matching cape aprons. Anna again noticed that most of the other volunteers were young women, although there were several teenage boys, too. Likely most married couples were too busy working the fields or at home tending to their families—the only married people here accompanied their child.

Later, when she saw little Emmie arrive in the passenger van, Anna hoped she might be assigned again as her side walker. She wondered once more why the little girl did not speak. Was it that she couldn't, or was something else keeping her from doing so? Gabe had once mentioned she'd stopped talking when her mother died. Emmie moved normally and seemed to understand everything that was spoken to her, with eyes that were bright and focused and even an occasional faint smile.

It turned out that Dottie asked if Anna would like to help Emmie groom Promise again, and Anna jumped at the chance. At one point while she and Emmie moved their brushes over the pony, Emmie leaned her head against his flank.

"Aw, you like him, don't ya," Anna said in *Deitsch*, and Emmie turned to look unwaveringly at her. "He's so gentle and sweet . . . like you."

Then Anna began to talk softly to Promise, as she liked to

196

do, and Emmie resumed brushing, her attention back on the shining black pony.

After the session, Anna helped get Emmie's right foot out of the stirrup and waited for Katie to help her on the left. Then, reaching to lift Emmie out of the saddle, Katie set her down. The girl stood back from the pony, as all the riders had been taught, waiting patiently for whoever was in charge of picking her up and taking her home.

Eventually, Emmie approached the front of the pony and stood practically nose to nose with him, patting him gently. "I think Promise likes that," Anna said softly, only observing and not moving toward Emmie.

The pony dipped his head at Emmie just then, and she broke into a big smile.

"See? And Promise likes you."

After Emmie and the other children left in the passenger van, Gabe came over to help Anna remove the bridle and saddle. "I couldn't help noticing you with Emmie," he said.

"She seems really taken with Promise." Anna ran her hand through the pony's thick, dark mane.

"Well, I think Emmie likes *you*, too," he said more quietly, lifting the saddle off the pony. "She's very fond of you, Anna."

"And I love being her side walker," Anna replied. "I was glad to get the chance again today. She's such a sweet child."

"Would you consider being one of Emmie's permanent side walkers?" he asked, his eyes searching hers, his smile warm. "For the rest of this season, that is?" he added as he walked with her to the tack room.

"Sure," she said, surprised by his lingering gaze. "*Denki.*"

He hung up the saddle. Then, turning to her, he added, "I hope we'll have the opportunity to talk again."

Later, while driving home, Anna realized she hadn't looked even once today at the stone wall. Her mind had been completely preoccupied with Gabe's remark about talking with her again.

And she wondered why she felt so happy about that.

Anna was met by Sadie at the back door as Anna returned from Peaceful Meadows.

"Your church friend Heidi Denlinger dropped by a little bit ago," Sadie told her.

"*Ach*, sorry I missed her." Anna set her purse on the wood bench by the table. "Did she come by just to visit?"

"Well, she was hopin' you'd go swimming with her and some of the other young women from church."

"I wish I'd known they were planning something," Anna said, thinking about the upcoming picnic with Mart. "Maybe next time. Also, don't forget that I won't be here for the noon meal."

"Oh, I remembered," Sadie replied with a knowing smile.

Anna grinned and headed to her room to go over her notebook tallying tours and tips, as Mart had suggested. *I'll see him soon!* she thought, taking time to freshen up.

Long's Park was an eighty-acre haven of beauty on the northwest side of Lancaster. Anna was happy to be there with Mart, wanting to get better acquainted with him, one to one. Besides a large cooler and Thermos from his mother, he had brought along tennis balls and two racquets.

"It's been a couple of years since I've played," Anna admitted when they were settled at a pavilion picnic table.

"I'm out of practice, too," Mart said. "So, we'll play just for fun. No keeping score." He removed the lid on the cooler and set out an array of food—chicken salad sandwiches on homemade hamburger buns, a pea salad with diced cheese and chopped sweet pickles, and potato salad made with mustard and eggs.

Anna eyed the food. "Your mother outdid herself," she said, also noticing the chocolate glaze on the individually wrapped cookies. "Please thank her for me."

"Mom loves to cook." Mart handed a paper plate and plastic utensils across the wooden table to Anna.

"My Mamm does, too." She felt silly saying it, since all the Plain mothers she knew seemed so inclined. "My sister and I used to cook together all the time before she left home to start her new life with her husband, Conrad. I miss those days."

He nodded. "My married sisters like to come over and help Mom make jam and put up vegetables and dried meats. They always have a great time together," he said, folding his hands just then. "Shall I ask the blessing?"

She bowed her head, touched again by the picnic lunch Mart's mother had taken time to make for someone she didn't even know.

I should do something for her in return. . . .

Anna was grateful for the clouds that moved in after lunch, making it less hot for playing tennis. Mart had been modest in saying he was out of practice, but it was obvious he was holding back on the court, hitting the balls directly to her, not making her run back and forth to return his plays.

After an hour of hitting the ball around, they put the racquets away and took a walk over to a bridge and around the banks of the water, where they enjoyed watching the ducks and swans. Mart was a good conversationalist, she realized once again. He politely asked about her family and her interests, showing special concern for her grandmother Eliza.

"You haven't told me much about your married sisters," Anna mentioned.

"Well, Sharilyn and Cordelia are both busy wives and mothers, but they like to have fun in their free time baking specialty cupcakes to sell at their bakery. It's in the historic section of downtown Strasburg," he told her. "You should see their elaborately decorated cupcakes. I almost hate to bite into them."

"Funny . . . I don't think I'd have a problem with it." Anna laughed. "Have they always enjoyed making such creative baked goods?"

He smiled. "Far as I know. Ever since my seventh birthday, when they began helping Mom decorate my brothers' and my birthday cakes. Each year they tried to outdo themselves."

"What a great family tradition."

"Mom has a whole album of photos of all their cakes through the years," Mart said.

Soon, they were talking about his involvement with the youth volleyball teams, and she shared about her church youth group, too, especially her friendship with the Denlinger sisters.

All the while, Anna wondered if this might be the first of more solo dates with Mart, even though she had enjoyed interacting with his church friends, too. *Is this the beginning of something special?*

Later that afternoon, when Anna returned to the Flauds', she helped Sadie peel the apples that Glen had picked while Anna was out with Mart. Sadie was all abuzz about making two large pans of apple crisp for tomorrow.

"I'll take one next door to Marianna, and some over to Molly and Eva, too," Sadie told Anna.

Anna thought it was kind of Glen to pick the apples—in addition to her bad knee, Sadie had been having some balance issues in the past months. As Anna and Sadie worked side by side, Anna asked what she knew about Gabe Allgyer.

Sadie set down the apple she had just finished peeling and reached for another. "Well, I'm sure ya know he's a young widower."

Anna nodded. "His little girl, Emmie, is one of the children I've worked with at Peaceful Meadows." She paused. "It's awful sad that she doesn't speak."

"*Nee*, not since she was three, when her Mamma died," Sadie replied. "Gabe and his bride had the dearest love story," she went on, revealing that his wife, Emily, had fallen gravely ill with a rare form of leukemia while they were courting. "But that didn't keep him from marryin' her and lovin' her right up to the very end." Sadie explained. "She was the only girl he ever courted."

Now Anna had a lump in her throat. She pressed her lips together, shaking her head at this news. "Gabe knew she might not live long?"

"That's what Luke told Glen and me—Luke knows Gabe especially well, though Glen and I've known Gabe and his family since he was an infant."

Anna was struck by the heartbreaking account. *Sacrificial love*, she thought, deeply touched.

"Gabe and Emily had a couple of difficult years with her health, but then suddenly her cancer went into remission, and the doctors were encouraged. When their baby was born, Gabe wanted to name her Emily for his wife."

"Emmie's the perfect nickname," Anna murmured, putting it together.

Sadie placed a large bowl in front of her and began to slice the peeled apples straight into it, an apple in one hand and a paring knife in the other. "Mind you, I wouldn't have shared this, but you asked."

"Isn't it commonly known?"

Sadie said she didn't know how widely known the specifics were. "But Emily was well loved—more than five hundred people attended her funeral, Amish and English alike."

"She must've been very special," Anna said softly.

"I didn't know Emily quite as well, but you might ask Gabe 'bout her sometime, if the time is right."

"Oh, I don't see how it would ever come up." Anna would never think of pressing him on it, but she found it amazing such a robust and energetic man would choose to marry a woman who was so terribly ill.

Chapter 30

The following Monday evening, after another busy day of tours, Anna asked Sadie if she might have some leftover fabric. "I'd like to make a special thank-you card for Mart's mother," Anna said, describing the delicious picnic lunch she and Mart had enjoyed.

Sadie hurried off to her sewing room, and Anna began to sketch a rectangular picnic basket like the one Mammi Eliza had used years ago. "It's a bit old-fashioned looking," she told Sadie when she returned, "but I like it."

"You're right . . . and it's a *gut* idea." Sadie went to the fridge and began to dish up some ice cream for Glen.

Later, when Anna filled the basket shape with batting, she decided to dismiss any further notions she had about locating Mammi Eliza's stone wall.

I've done all I can, she thought, realizing it was taking up too much of her time and attention.

Before leaving the parking lot of the information center the next afternoon, Anna called her father to thank him for helping with the first weeks of room and board at Flauds'. "I'm ready to take that up now," she said.

"Are you sure?"

"Yes, and I'm helping around the house here as much as I can, too." She also described the imaginative cards Sadie made, many of which Anna had helped to design and create. "Her sister-in-law Lillian is selling them at Saturday market, and I wouldn't be surprised if she gets orders for more. Maybe even custom orders. Who knows?"

"Now that you say this, your mother mentioned that Mammi received one from you. She has it out on her bedside table."

"I'm glad she's enjoying it."

"She talks about you often. We all do, Anna."

"I miss you, too, Dat."

"Any idea when you might come visit again?" he asked.

"It won't be for a while yet."

"Well, don't be a stranger, okay?"

She promised she would be in touch, and they said good-bye and hung up.

He sounds a little glum, she thought while driving back to Flauds'.

When she arrived, she headed right into the house to help Sadie with supper, feeling good about being able to pull her weight now with the room and board. It wasn't nearly what an apartment rent would cost, and anyway, living on her own was the last thing she wanted. Being a part of Glen and Sadie's family was ideal, even though Anna still missed air-conditioning, electric fans, and power for her phone.

At least I don't have to bother with hitching up a horse to a buggy! she thought.

"I told Anna 'bout Gabe Allgyer's great heartache," Sadie shared with Glen that evening as they prepared to retire for the night.

"It's 'bout time ya did," Glen replied, smiling.

"Figured you'd think that." She tried not to smile herself lest she egg him on, as fond of Gabe as Glen had always been.

Glen removed his socks and tossed them into the hamper across their bedroom. "Did I tell ya that Gabe brought up Anna to me the other day, over at the smithy's?"

"Well, I'll be." Sadie was pleased. "Gabe and little Emmie certainly need a kind young woman like our Anna in their lives."

"Honestly, I have a feelin' Gabe's got an eye on her."

Glen's admission got Sadie thinking. "I'll have to pray 'bout how we can help this along."

Glen looked at her. "Now, dear. Maybe we shouldn't."

"*Nee*, I think it's a fine idea, to tell the truth." Sadie walked over and gave him a big smooch.

After the first Saturday session at the retreat, Anna was pleasantly surprised to encounter the blond woman who always accompanied little Emmie, either bringing her or picking her up. The pretty woman came into the stable and introduced herself as "Emmie's aunt Barbara Mast."

"*Wunnerbaar* to meet you," Anna said, thinking she looked even more like Emmie up close, her heart-shaped *Kapp* secured with bobby pins on the sides.

"Emmie seemed particularly happy this morning on the way

205

over here. She loves comin' to ride, that's for sure," Barbara said, her rosy cheeks dimpling as she talked. She glanced down at Emmie. "Ain't so, Emmie?"

Emmie did not respond to her aunt but remained focused on Anna.

"I've heard from folks that many of the children seem especially cheerful on their riding day," Anna said.

Barbara gently reached for Emmie's hand. "Well, this one's only cheerful on Saturdays," Barbara said, her deep blue eyes turning sad.

Assuming she was referring to Emmie's grief, Anna caught herself nodding. *Poor little girl!*

"Say, I'm havin' a little get-together next Friday morning," Barbara said. "Some fresh-brewed coffee and goodies, plus *gut* fellowship. Dottie and Katie will be there. Would ya like to join us, Anna?"

Little Emmie blinked as she kept looking up at Anna.

At first, Anna wasn't sure what to say. Why would Barbara invite her when Anna wasn't as traditionally Plain as she was, or as Dottie and Katie, for that matter? But wanting to be polite, she said, "That's real nice. May I bring some sweet bread to share?"

"Just bring yourself. I'll have plenty to nibble on." Barbara's eyes were shining now, and she put out her hand to shake Anna's. "*Denki* for takin' such *gut* care of Emmie when she rides."

This, too, surprised Anna, since all the side walkers were extra careful with the younger riders. "Well, I'm happy to be Emmie's side walker," Anna said, hardly knowing what else to say; it seemed odd to be sought out like this.

Barbara gave her the address, and Anna thanked her, still not sure what to make of the unexpected invitation.

Anna glanced at Emmie just then and saw a smile appear. Heartened, Anna said, "I'll see you again next Saturday, okay, Emmie?" She held her breath, hoping Emmie might nod her head. Anything in response.

But Emmie turned slowly to go with her aunt Barbara, and Anna stood there, watching them walk quietly together toward the passenger van.

Another lovely surprise happened that afternoon, when Heidi stopped by to see Anna at Flauds'. She brought with her an embroidered doily with yellow roses in the center. "I've been working on this since you first came to our church," Heidi said as the two of them sat on the back porch together. "Just overlook the mistakes if you find any." She sounded apologetic.

"I can't believe this, Heidi. It's so kind of you," Anna said, running her fingers gently over the embroidery. "*Denki*."

"Yellow roses stand for friendship . . . as maybe you know."

Anna nodded. "Which makes this perfect." She smiled at her. "You and your sister have gone out of your way to make me feel so welcome."

Heidi blushed at the compliment.

"I really feel like part of the community here with my mother's Old Order cousins, as well."

"Don't you miss electricity?" Heidi asked, moving back and forth in the porch rocker.

"I really thought I would, but I'm getting used to being without it."

Heidi raised her eyebrows. "I'm not sure I could."

"Well, not having a car would be much harder."

"Right," Heidi said. "My siblings and I all share one presently."

207

She pointed to the older model Ford parked at the end of the yard.

"More affordable," Anna commented, enjoying their relaxed conversation.

"It'll probably end up being Lester's, but for now, we take turns." At Lester's name, Heidi looked at Anna and brightened. "We'll be having another after-church party in a couple of weeks. I hope you'll come again."

"I'll look forward to it."

Their conversation slowly moved to other things—Heidi's work as a part-time nanny for an Englisher in their neighborhood, and one particular fellow in the church who had recently asked her out.

Anna wondered if Heidi might hint about double-dating at some point, but she didn't bring it up. Instead, Heidi unexpectedly brought up Peaceful Meadows. "I suppose you're making some friends there, too," she said.

"Yes, quite a few."

"I'm glad for you," Heidi said. "I doubt I could make the transition to another town as gracefully as you have."

"Well, things are coming together quite nicely, which seems to confirm that it was God's will for me to come here." Anna smiled at her. "And to meet *you*, Heidi."

They talked about going swimming next Friday afternoon with Eleanor and some of the other girls in the youth group. Suddenly, Anna remembered that she would be going for coffee at Barbara Mast's house. "I'd really like to if I'm back in time," Anna said. "I've been invited to have coffee with some Amish friends."

"House Amish?"

Anna nodded. "The woman who invited me is Old Order."

Like her former brother-in-law, Gabe, thought Anna. "I'll tell you all about it, okay?"

Heidi smiled. "Okay!"

Then Anna caught herself, not sure how many people she wanted to know about this visit, lest it somehow drift back to her parents.

Chapter 31

—————————— ❧ ——————————

By nine in the morning the following Friday, the temperature had already risen to ninety-two degrees, and according to Sadie's battery-powered digital thermometer, the humidity reading was nearly as high. Thinking ahead to the coffee gathering at Barbara Mast's, Anna felt at once happy and timid, and she brought this up to Sadie as they were redding up the kitchen.

"That sounds like Barbara, chust bein' neighborly to a newcomer," Sadie said, pausing to wipe her face with a hankie she took from beneath her sleeve. "'Tis awful close in here, ain't?"

"Might be a smart thing to work in the basement, where it's cooler," Anna suggested. "If you have some mending or whatnot."

Sadie nodded. "Ain't the most pleasant surroundings down there, but you're right; it'd be much cooler."

Anna wondered if she should mention what was on her mind. She reflected for a moment, then realized she had been talking rather openly to Sadie for all these weeks, so why not?

"How well do you know Barbara?" Anna asked tentatively.

"Well, she's in my church district, so pretty well. Emmie's mother was Barbara's close-in-age sister."

Anna had wondered. "Little Emmie looks so much like her, *jah?*"

"Sometimes children look more like an *Aendi* or *Onkel* than one of their own parents," Sadie said. "It's strange yet true."

Anna thought of her own nieces and nephews. "I think you're right."

"Barbara keeps very busy cookin' and having folks in. And she dotes on Gabe since Emily passed . . . worries 'bout him might be a better way to say it."

"Worries?"

"Well, since he's a widower with a youngster. Though surely the Good Lord will send along a nice wife for him in due time." Sadie smiled a little. "Say, would ya mind droppin' me off at Molly's, since it's on the way?" she asked.

"Sure, and I can pick you up on the way back, too, if you'd like."

"*Denki.* That's real kind."

"And if Molly needs a ride somewhere while you stay with your sister, I can take care of that, too."

"Oh, I think Molly's just goin' to walk up the road to her cousins' place while I'm spelling her off a bit."

"Well, know that I want to help however I can. And just think, you won't have to hitch up today." Anna grinned.

Sadie gave her an endearing smile. "Such a *wunnerbaar* help you already are! You just don't know . . ."

Anna wanted to go over and hug her, Sadie looked so moved. "Are you all right?"

Quickly, Sadie nodded. "I count my blessings every day, Anna. And when I come to you, I count 'em twice."

Anna didn't know what to make of this. "I think my Mamm would be glad to hear it," she observed at last. "She'd say she raised me right."

"Oh, believe me, I've told her that in my letters."

Blushing, Anna had suspected that Sadie and Mamm were exchanging frequent letters. *Maybe Sadie and Glen feel responsible for me since I'm staying with them.*

"Well, we'd better head out pretty soon," she said, aware of a sudden flutter of nerves. Had Barbara invited any other women besides Dottie and Katie?

The coffee get-together looked to be just the four of them, much as Barbara had indicated last weekend. Not far ahead of Anna's car, Dottie and Katie were parking their buggies on the side yard, north of the driveway. Anna held back a smile; once again, she was parking her car amidst Amish carriages.

Just then, Anna saw Gabe and Emmie standing over near the stable, playing with a white cat with black paws. Anna felt her body tighten.

Do they live here? she wondered, still sitting behind the wheel as though in a daze. *Are they coming to coffee, too?*

A tap came at her window, and startled, she turned to see Dottie standing there, grinning. "Ach, sorry," she said and grabbed her purse, embarrassed.

Dottie stepped back so Anna could open the car door. "*Guder Mariye,* Anna."

"Good morning to you, too," Anna replied, falling into step with Dottie. She hoped her expression hadn't let on how surprised she was to see Gabe and his daughter there. "It's one of those hot and humid August days, *jah?*" Anna commented.

Dottie chuckled. "You can say that again. Our watchdog

somehow managed to get himself clear under the back porch. He was peekin' out between the slats when I left, poor thing. Must be cooler there. We're definitely into the dog days of summer now."

"I wonder where that saying comes from." Anna noticed that Dottie had on a brown bandanna instead of her usual prayer *Kapp*.

"Never really thought 'bout it." Dottie glanced at her as they walked toward the back stoop. "I daresay you're a thinker, Anna."

"Sometimes."

Dottie turned to wave Katie over to join them. "My ol' Dawdi used to say that too much thinkin' gets a body in trouble."

And too little thinking gets people in still more trouble! Anna thought, amused, as she followed Dottie up the steps and in the back door. They proceeded through the tidy screened-in porch into the large kitchen without Dottie announcing their arrival. She didn't need to, for there at a trestle table laid with pretty mint green crocheted placemats and small white dessert plates sat Barbara, fanning herself with the hem of her long black apron.

"*Willkumm*," Barbara said, getting up and greeting them, her brow beaded with perspiration.

"You look all in," Dottie said, then urged Barbara to sit back down.

"Are ya sickly?" Katie asked, looking concerned as she and Dottie hovered near her.

"*Nee* . . . just didn't sleep much at all last night. Neither did Aden," said Barbara.

Dottie perched herself on the wood bench. "Aw, did little Emmie keep yous up again?"

Barbara glanced at Anna, as if thinking she'd better not reveal what was on her mind. "Let's just say it was a very long night."

"Well, we're here now, so let us pitch in an' help," Katie said, going to the fridge and removing a pitcher of ice water. She took down a tumbler from the cupboard and poured the water, then carried it quickly to Barbara. "Sip on this to keep from wilting more."

Barbara accepted the water and began to drink, still fanning her face, sunshine spilling in through the spotless windows.

"We should ice the coffee," Dottie suggested.

Katie nodded. "What do ya think, Barbara?"

Anna felt sorry for Barbara, sitting there looking so fatigued. She wondered why Emmie had spent the night and what would have caused her not to sleep.

"I'm one step ahead of ya," Barbara said, after downing nearly half the glass of water. "Look on the right side of the fridge, and you'll see a Tupperware pitcher of iced mocha."

"*Appeditlich!*" Dottie said.

Katie directed Barbara to just sit. "Dottie and I will bring everything to the table."

Meanwhile, Barbara was motioning for Anna to join her. "You're the guest of honor, so come sit by me," she said, pointing to the chair.

"Maybe some iced coffee will perk you up," Anna said, hoping she wasn't out of line to say so.

"*Ach*, a little caffeine never hurt anyone."

Anna smiled and glanced about the kitchen, noting a built-in bookcase on one wall, with many books neatly lined up. "Someone's a big reader," she remarked.

"My husband, Aden, likes biographies," Barbara said. "'Specially ones 'bout ordinary folk. *Englischers.*"

Like me, Anna thought, knowing she was viewed as fancy, since she drove a car and grew up with electricity.

By the time Dottie and Katie sat down, Barbara had already

214

folded her hands for the silent blessing. Anna bowed her head, too, and appreciated the silent gratitude displayed, even for just iced coffee and sweets.

After the prayer, there was animated talk about picking Glenglo peaches, and Dottie mentioned how eager she was to hear if Barbara and Aden were planning to have a cookout on Aden's birthday again, like last year.

"We might, since everyone had such a nice time," Barbara said, sitting up straighter now.

Anna enjoyed hearing all the chatter, sometimes in *Deitsch*, when they forgot and simply slipped back into their mother tongue. Hers, as well.

After drinking the rest of her water and some of the iced coffee, Barbara changed the subject, turning to ask Anna, "How do ya like your work as a tour guide?"

How does she know? Anna wondered, rather surprised. "Did Gabe mention that?"

"*Jah*, some time ago," Barbara said, a humorous glint in her eye.

"Ain't much that slips by unnoticed round here," Katie said with a smile. "Everyone knows what folks are sayin' or doin', and sometimes even thinkin'!"

"It's a little like that where I'm from in Mifflinburg, too," Anna said.

"Gabe did some occasional construction work up there in Mifflinburg, but that was a few years ago," Barbara said, her eyebrows lifting a little as she said his name. "I tend to view him as my flesh-and-blood brother, ya know . . . even though he's not."

Dottie nodded her head and reached for another slice of banana zucchini bread. "Have ya tried this yet, Anna?" She passed the plate to her. "It's so moist and yummy."

Barbara perked up a bit. "You have my recipe, ain't?"

215

Dottie said she did. "There are chopped walnuts in it, *jah?*"

"An' plenty-a sugar." Barbara beamed. "Gabe makes quick work of it at breakfast time, and so does Emmie."

Hearing this, Anna felt certain now that they lived with Barbara and her husband. She wondered why Barbara kept mentioning them.

"Well, getting back to your tour work," Barbara said. "What's the most interesting thing you've run into with travelers?"

"I'd probably have to say a recent client, a young woman from Phoenix who wanted to attend an Amish wedding. In fact, she insisted on it until I explained that Amish wedding season typically isn't until November. She seemed offended that they aren't conducted year-round, to be honest."

"*Ach*, how funny," Katie said, laughing. "Wonder why she didn't think she'd need to be invited, seeing as she isn't from around here."

"I did my best to educate her," Anna said, taking another bite of the truly delicious banana zucchini bread.

"Tell us more," Dottie said as she passed the plates of cookies and bars around for the third time.

"Well, here's something that happened last week," Anna said, feeling more included now. "A man and his wife from Illinois wanted to know if all the Plain folk in Lancaster County were Amish."

Dottie pressed her hand to her chest. "And what did ya say?"

"I said there are many types of Plain groups, but the Old Order Amish are the most interesting to tourists."

"I don't doubt that," Barbara said. "And why do you think that is?"

"Could be a fascination with the horse and buggy," Anna said. "At least, that's what my clients seem most curious about. It's so different from what they know."

"Seems so," Barbara replied.

Just then, Anna heard footsteps outside, coming onto the porch and into the house. She wondered if Barbara's husband and children might want some treats, too.

Turning to look with the other women, Anna saw Gabe walking into the kitchen with Emmie, his straw hat on.

"Excuse us," he said quietly as he led Emmie into the next room.

Barbara eyed Dottie, but neither made a comment about Gabe or Emmie. "So, back to your interesting stories," Barbara said at last.

"I've been keeping a notebook of all the folks I meet on these tours," Anna replied. "But now I guess I should be writing down the humorous things, too."

"You do that," Katie said with a mischievous smile. "And we'll meet back here in a few weeks to hear what you write!"

This brought peals of laughter around the table. And even though the rest of their fellowship time was pleasant, the lack of an explanation for why little Emmie had kept Barbara and her husband up last night lingered in Anna's mind long after she had bid farewell.

Chapter 32

⁂

A s planned, Anna stopped by Molly's house to pick up Sadie on her return. Seeing how gloomy Sadie looked as she got into the car, not saying much, Anna was concerned about her visit with Eva. But, wanting to avoid bringing up anything difficult, she made small talk and offered to help make the noon meal once they returned home.

"Oh, you needn't do that," Sadie said, her eyes pink, as though on the verge of tears.

Anna insisted. "I *want* to."

Nodding, Sadie said softly, "We'll have us a light dinner, of course, since you're goin' swimming afterward, *jah?*"

Anna almost wished she were staying home with Sadie, as disheartened as she seemed.

I wonder if Eva didn't recognize her today. . . .

With that heavy possibility in mind, Anna felt as if she had frittered away her morning having iced coffee and treats with virtual strangers while dear Sadie was experiencing heartfelt pain.

Back at the house, Anna worked alongside Sadie in the kitchen, wanting to be there for her, in case Sadie opened up about her time with Eva.

After a while, Sadie asked, "How was your visit with Barbara Mast?"

"Oh, real nice. I got better acquainted with her and the two other women," Anna replied, mentioning some of the funny things that she'd shared about her clients on tours. Then she said, "Not that it matters, but I didn't realize Gabe and his daughter live with Barbara and her husband."

"Well, I don't believe they do," Sadie said, looking surprised as she cut homemade bread for sandwiches. "He and Emmie go to Masts' for meals now and then. Gabe's home is across the road and down a ways."

Anna considered that, wondering why that hadn't occurred to her.

"So, was Gabe there?" Sadie asked, curiosity evidently replacing her former sadness.

"*Jah*, with Emmie, but not at the coffee gathering."

"Well, did ya have a chance to talk—with Gabe, I mean?" Sadie looked a bit sheepish.

"*Nee*," Anna replied, as she set the table after making lemonade. *Why's she asking about Gabe?*

After the meal, Sadie headed next door to visit Marianna and help with Sally and Baby Jimmy. It would be nice to have a little fellowship with them while Anna was swimming with her friends.

219

Jimmy was asleep when Sadie arrived, and Sally and the older boys had gone with Luke to run some errands.

Marianna must need a break . . . like Molly, Sadie thought, not wanting to relive her rather difficult morning with Eva.

Marianna suggested they sit on the back porch, where an occasional breeze might cool them. "Would ya like some cold meadow tea?"

"Love some," Sadie said. "Let me get it."

"*Nee* . . . I've been sitting and rocking a fussy baby for an hour or more," Marianna said, heading inside. "Somethin's gotten into him."

Must be the hot weather, Sadie thought, recalling how cantankerous Eva had been, too—grouchy that Molly was leaving her *"alone with a stranger."* Even so, Sadie had tried not to let the reaction get to her.

Marianna brought out the tea, ice cubes clinking as she handed a tall glass to Sadie. She seemed pleased to have company and talked about wanting to start getting the house ready to host church in six weeks. "The time 'tween then and now will go fast, and with Jimmy's colic here lately, I'll have to pace myself."

"We'll all pitch in an' help; don't worry." Sadie mentioned a number of relatives who would be happy to help, too. "And maybe Anna can babysit Jimmy in her spare time," she suggested. "Remember how he and Sally took to her?"

"They certainly did." Marianna nodded and glanced toward the house. "I noticed she had more friends stoppin' by for her again today."

"Oh *jah.* Anymore, our Anna's becomin' a social butterfly."

Marianna turned to look at her. "You sound real happy 'bout that."

Chuckling, Sadie said, "Anna's making *gut* connections,

which might make it more likely she'll stay round here, ya know." All the same, she felt torn. "I doubt Anna's parents would smile on her spendin' time with the family of an eligible Old Order widower, though."

"You must mean Gabe Allgyer."

Sadie nodded. "I feel responsible for her, considering her upbringing's so different than ours. And her parents, 'specially her mother, are trusting Glen and me to look after her."

"Well, she's of age, so Anna's ultimately the one responsible for what she does, *jah?*"

Sadie couldn't deny that.

"Besides, didn't ya say she's been seein' a Mennonite fella she met at work? And Anna is attending the same type of church as back home in Mifflinburg, too, right? I would guess that fella's church would be more in keepin' with what she's used to."

Sadie took a drink of her iced tea. "Honestly, she seems more enamored with the horse-riding retreat and all the Amish folk over there."

Marianna gave a little shrug. "Gabe and his volunteers are harmless. You don't have to worry 'bout them trying to get her to be Old Order."

Sadie thought on that; she was rather hoping Gabe might seek Anna out. *It would keep her round here, if he succeeds in getting her attention.*

Marianna gave her a knowing smile. "Don't borrow trouble."

"Well, I'm not Anna's Mamm, so I have nothin' to fret about."

They sipped their tea and watched the hummingbirds flit and flirt, performing their U-shaped aerials as they showed off for potential mates.

Several cats from the stable wandered over across the lawn, meowing, and Sadie began to fret again over Eva, wishing something could be done to bring her back to herself.

There was a bit of a lull where Marianna leaned her head back against the chair and closed her eyes. Meanwhile, Sadie stared at the clouds, watching the shapes slowly move and change. How she longed for autumn, when cooler days and nights meant time for apple picking and then applesauce making and cider pressing. Eventually, they would butcher a steer for the winter. Many of the turkeys would be sold in late October and early November, too, and Glen would help Luke with the harvesting process.

Marianna sighed loudly. "I want Jimmy to be my last baby," she said out of the blue, jarring Sadie from her reverie.

Sadie looked at her, trying not to overreact. "Havin' a hard day, dear?"

Marianna nodded her head slowly. "I catch myself comin' and goin', all day long. Feels like it's never ending."

Sadie reached to pat the back of her hand. "Bein' a Mamma is hard work, but let me remind ya: These baby days won't last for long."

Marianna glanced out toward the meadow. "I know you're right."

"Taking one day at a time is best," Sadie added, squeezing her daughter-in-law's hand. "Sometimes one hour . . ."

To try to get Marianna's mind off her stress, Sadie mentioned all the fun the upcoming months would bring, including the Lancaster Hot Air Balloon Festival in Bird-in-Hand.

"Would *you* ever go up in one?" Marianna asked, crossing her legs and straightening her long green dress.

Sadie shrugged.

"Just maybe?" Marianna was grinning at her.

"I s'pose at my age, what's there to lose? If the balloon goes down, I've lived a long and happy life."

"Oh now, Mamm . . . don't be thinkin' thataway." Marianna

shook her head. "Luke's been dropping hints 'bout taking me up this year."

"Really, now? Would ya want to?"

Marianna nodded emphatically. "'Wither thou goest, I will go' . . . remember, from the Good Book?"

Sadie chuckled, ever so glad she'd dropped by. *It's been good to forget myself for a while.*

Chapter 33

A nna could smell the barbequed chicken on the grill not far from the Denlingers' pond at their farm, where she, Heidi, Eleanor, and two of their cousins— nineteen-year-old Shelley and sixteen-year-old Carol—were swimming that Friday afternoon. The cool water felt refreshing in contrast to the sun's heat and the sultry atmosphere, the perfect remedy.

They took turns jumping off the end of a weatherworn dock. Each time Anna made her way back through the water to the grassy bank and up to the dock, she wished there was a pond at Glen and Sadie's. *I'll just come here whenever I'm invited,* she thought, also looking forward to the cookout with the whole Denlinger family, except for Lester, who was haying with his married brother. Thinking of that, she remembered that Mart would be cutting hay tomorrow for his dairy-farmer uncle.

Just then, Shelley swam over to Anna, bobbing out of the water, her dripping-wet braids a dark red. "Heidi says you're volunteering over at Peaceful Meadows on Saturday mornings." She blinked water droplets off her eyelashes. "How do you like it?"

"I love it," Anna told her. "Are you interested in being a volunteer?"

"Maybe next summer." Shelley smiled. "I've heard a little about the horse riding therapy, since Gabe Allgyer's building a tree house at our place. I've been talking to him more about it. He's such a nice guy!"

"And he has a real knack with the young riders," Anna replied.

Shelley mentioned that Gabe had been working late hours to complete the structure. "I guess his sister-in-law has been babysitting for Emmie a lot."

Maybe that's why Emmie was at Barbara's overnight, Anna thought.

"Gabe built a tree house for my relatives' grandkids, too," Anna said. "It's really something."

Shelley nodded. "It's been so much fun to watch it come together."

Now Carol swam over to them. "Are you two whispering about boys?"

"No, silly," Shelley said, treading water. "I was just telling Anna about our wonderful tree house."

By now, Heidi and Eleanor were swimming this way, too. And when all five of them were together, Heidi suggested they see who could hold their breath the longest underwater.

This is what it would be like having a bunch of sisters, Anna thought, wondering if Wanita had ever wished for more.

Saturday was just as hot and muggy as the day before, and Anna was happy to have the opportunity to work in the tack room prior to the passenger van's arrival at the retreat.

Bennie Glick and Freckles waved at her, grinning as they walked to their waiting horses and side walkers. Emmie approached with her Aendi Barbara, hanging back a bit as she often did until she spied Promise. Then came the familiar slight smile on her pixie face.

Anna's heart rose at the sight of her, and she walked over, carrying the grooming brushes. "*Guder Mariye*, Emmie," she said, handing her a curry brush. "Promise is happy to see you, and so am I."

Emmie began to work with Anna, standing closer to the pony and to Anna than ever before. Barbara told Emmie she would return for her at the end of the session, and Emmie scarcely seemed to notice when her aunt left.

During the short ride to the round pen, Emmie looked Anna's way several times. And by the time they'd walked once all the way around, Emmie was noticeably staring at her. Dottie was the other side walker today, and she often talked to Emmie during the ride, but Emmie hadn't so much as glanced at her.

Anna felt touched. She had grown quite fond of Emmie. Not that the other children didn't tug at her heartstrings, but there was something about Emmie that called to her. But she wasn't sure she should encourage it—after all, the little girl had many aunts and two grandmothers who surely made over her.

At the end of the first session, Barbara Mast met them in the stable and thanked Anna for coming to coffee yesterday. "We all really enjoyed hearin' your stories 'bout your tours."

"Well, I had a nice time, too. And oh, was your sweet bread ever delicious!"

Barbara smiled, and Anna leaned down to talk to Emmie, whose eyes were fixed on Promise. "Remember what I told ya last week?" She glanced at the pony. "Promise picked *you*."

Anna rose to tell Barbara what she meant, explaining that the pony had clearly dipped his head toward Emmie when she'd stood near him.

"How dear," Barbara said. "Ain't so, Emmie?"

Silently, Emmie walked over to the pony, moving right up next to him and smiling.

"Just watch the two of them," Anna whispered to Barbara as she stood there with her.

Emmie very slowly raised her dimpled hand and patted the pony's nose timidly once, then a second time.

Anna held her breath, captivated again by this precious child.

Barbara clasped her hands in front of her as if transfixed. "I've never seen her do this with Promise," she said softly.

Anna said not so much as a peep, not wanting to interrupt whatever was going through Emmie's head. The little girl and her trusted pony were a sight to behold.

Sadie had been spending her morning at market with Lillian, and after being there for several hours, she remarked to her, "I'd forgotten how busy Saturday market can be during the summertime."

"Well, it really is today." Lillian walked over to the long table and counted Sadie's remaining homemade cards. "Only seventeen left," she said happily. "I knew they'd go over big with tourists."

Sadie felt pleased and a little surprised.

"You know what this means, don't ya?" Lillian asked.

"Prob'ly that I'd best be makin' more." Sadie could hardly believe how quickly the cards had sold, and at the stiff price Lillian had set, too. *I'll have extra money to buy more fabric, and then some,* she thought, thinking it would be fun to save some

of the proceeds to surprise Glen with something special. *Maybe
a new felt hat for winter . . .*

While saying good-bye to Emmie and her aunt Barbara,
Anna was surprised when Emmie crept over behind her and
furtively clutched her long apron. Anna looked around and
saw Emmie staring up at her, her beautiful blue eyes pleading.

"I'll see ya next week, sweetie," she said to Emmie, longing to
reach down and pick her up, though she held back. She watched
as Barbara led her niece out to the passenger van and stepped
inside, out of sight. *Emmie must be lost without her Mamma,*
Anna mused, sorrowful at the thought.

She rounded the bend, heading back to the tack room, where
Dottie looked surprised to see her.

Dottie frowned. "Were ya cryin'?"

Anna wiped her eyes, surprised to find tears. "Didn't realize it."

"You all right?" Dottie asked, touching Anna's arm.

"Oh, my heart just goes out to the riders." That wasn't entirely
true. She shook her head. "I mean . . . mostly for little Emmie."

Dottie nodded. "It's been two long years since her Mamma
passed." Dottie's voice was soft, even solemn. "We keep thinkin'
she'll come out of it, but it's like Emmie's fallen into a cavern
somewhere in her mind. And no one, not even her father, can
lift her out."

Anna mentioned Emmie's growing attachment to Promise.
"Have you seen her with him lately? There's something special
happening."

"Well, I've noticed Emmie with *you,* Anna. She's really taken
to you."

Anna nodded.

A few minutes later, when Gabe poked his head in, Anna

was in the farthest corner, putting the pony saddle away. "Here, let me help ya," he said, taking it from her.

Dottie and the other two volunteers left the tack room, glancing back at them.

"I was hopin' I might catch ya, Anna. Are ya busy after this session?" He paused and looked about the room again to see if they were indeed alone. "I have to run an errand and hoped you'd come along."

"I'll help if ya need me." She really didn't know what he was asking. Did he want to talk about something personal? Emmie, maybe?

"*Denki*," he said. "Meet me at the carriage shed after this session, then, all right?" His eyes sparkled, yet his countenance remained sober.

She could not read him well enough to guess what was on his mind. But she knew instinctively that she wanted to ride along with him.

Yet I really shouldn't, she thought.

Chapter 34

Eliza was murmuring to herself while she and Great-aunt Joanna ate dinner that noon. "I can resist and reject, but in the end, curiosity might just get the best of me."

Aunt Joanna's brow pinched into a glower. "What're ya sayin', Eliza?"

They were sitting at the small square table, lingering over a dessert of peach cobbler made with fresh peaches Eliza had purchased from a roadside stand just up the road that morning.

Eliza held her breath, realizing she'd unthinkingly blurted her thoughts, and now her poor aunt was as befuddled as Eliza was with herself. "*Ach*, sorry."

"Somethin' must be on your mind," her aunt pressed.

Thinking again about the unexpected note Eb had slipped between the stones up yonder, Eliza couldn't imagine telling her aunt about it. *I daresn't!*

"Didn't your Mamm teach ya it ain't polite to start something and not finish telling it?"

Eliza's face burned with shame. She nodded her head, missing home all the more.

"Well then?"

Eliza wished she could hide from her aunt's piercing eyes. *What a pickle I'm in!*

"Maybe your mind's on that there diary you're always scribblin' in," her aunt said.

She knows about it? Fear struck Eliza's heart. *O dear Lord God and heavenly Father, no!*

"Eliza? I'm waiting."

Whatever her aunt asked, Eliza would never, ever share anything about Eb and their friendship—if she could even call it a friendship. By now, Eb might have assumed that she hadn't found his note, which she'd left sitting right where he'd put it. Even so, she wanted to lay eyes on it a second time to believe that it had really been there . . . and she hadn't misread it. And she wanted to write a note back to him if she could just get out from under Aunt Joanna's stern gaze. "I have a bad habit of muttering, Mamma says," Eliza told her aunt at last. "I'm sorry for displeasing you, Aendi."

"Well, mutterin' ain't becoming to a young woman, I'm sure you know." Aunt Joanna sighed so long and deep, Eliza wondered if she might be taking ill. She certainly looked white in the face over there across the table. Since Eliza's arrival, she had seemed to wither, and Eliza wished she could make her aunt's life easier. *The reason I'm here, after all,* she thought guiltily.

"If ya don't mind, I'll get started heating up the dishwater," Eliza said, remembering to excuse herself first. She reached for the dessert plates and forks and carried them over to the sink, still quivering inside.

231

Mamma never said how hard it would be, living here, she thought with a glance over her shoulder at the table. Her great-aunt had slumped down in her chair, undoubtedly exhausted after the confrontation. *Persistent as she is.*

Once Eliza's work in the kitchen was done and her aunt had taken herself off to bed for a long afternoon nap, Eliza hurried to her own room. There, she wrote the note she had been composing in her head repeatedly for the last three days since discovering Eb's own startling note. What had gotten into her to second-guess her feelings for Eb like this? All the same, she'd found herself daydreaming about him. Was she making a mistake upon a mistake?

Lest her aunt get any ideas, Eliza hid her little diary under the bureau, kneeling down to push it far back against the wall and out of sight.

Then, rushing out of the house and up the road to the wall, she looked for the spot where Eb's note had been. *There's the tall pin oak, like a watchman on the lookout. . . .*

She quickly found the crevice in the wall, as well as Eb's note, which was still there. Tugging it out from its well-concealed spot, she opened it with trembling fingers. Her eyes flew at once to the lines that had angered her upon first reading.

> *I've missed seeing you, Eliza. I like spending time with you. But since we really shouldn't be seen together because of our different backgrounds—if you would even like to see me again, that is—I wondered if you might leave a note here for me, too . . . if you've found this one. . . .*

She dropped to the ground and sat there in the sunlight as tears sprang to her eyes. *If you would even like to see me again,* Eb had written.

"*Jah*," she whispered, blinking away these sudden tears. "I *do* want to see you, more than you know."

But I shouldn't, she reminded herself, realizing that Eb had written nearly the same thought.

"What's gotten into me?" she wondered aloud, then remembered what her great-aunt had said about young women and muttering. "*Puh!*" She reached in her pocket for a hankie and promptly dried her eyes. "I best get ahold of myself."

She found her note in the other pocket, the one she'd penned to Eb back at the house, and reread it, her heart beating fast. Then, knowing she could never let him read such friendly-like thoughts, she wondered again what on earth she had been thinking. Was she simply lonely for home and family?

Eliza sat there in the thick green grass and tore up her note, pushing the pieces back into her pocket. *I'd be a* Dummkopp *to give this to him!*

With that, she rose and scurried across the meadow toward the road.

Her eyes were cast down as she hurried on her way, hugging the shoulder as she went. Her thoughts were a combination of self-reproach and bewilderment, and it embarrassed her even more that she had actually thought it was all right to return a note to Eb.

Dat would say I'm playing with fire. Tears threatened again.

The wind was gusting, blowing her skirt as she made the turn in the road, not far from her aunt's house. Just then, she heard a horse's *clip-clop* slow up, and when she looked, there was Eb, bringing his spring wagon to a halt. He waved to her, and her heart sank.

"I was just now thinking of ya, Eliza. Haven't seen ya for a while," he said, looking over her head at the road. "Say, are those bread crumbs, trailin' along behind ya?"

She turned and gasped to see small fragments of her note scattered everywhere. *They must have fallen out because of the wind!* Hurrying, she went to pick them up, one by one, and pushed them deeper into her pocket this time.

"Eliza?" Eb was frowning. Then a knowing look swept across his handsome, ruddy face. "Wait a minute . . . did ya go to the stone wall?"

She wanted to deny it outright and not give him the satisfaction of fessing up to finding his note. Yet at the very same time, she wanted him to ask her to ride with him. It was the strangest feeling.

What's wrong with me?

"Guess the cat's got your tongue," he said, chuckling.

She pressed her lips together, needing to calm down so she didn't say something she didn't mean. Or maybe she *did.* Either way, she would put herself in even worse straits. "I found your note last Sunday night, but I put it back where it was," she admitted.

An endearing smile appeared on his face, but he quickly got control of it. "So did you write one back to me?"

She nodded, her head bowed so he wouldn't see how tenderhearted she felt toward him just now.

"I'm glad you read my note, Eliza." His voice was gentle, with none of the old bluster.

She couldn't speak, her heart was racing so.

"What if we talk this evening at the stone wall—you know the spot. Eight o'clock sharp."

A surge of energy ran through her. "All right," she said, loud enough for him to hear.

"So long for now, Eliza." He signaled the horse to pull away from the shoulder and back onto the road.

She refused to second-guess her decision to see him tonight.

She held her head high as she made her way down the road toward Great-aunt Joanna's old farmhouse, glad she'd gone over to the stone wall and run into Eb on her way back. Ever so glad, yet also ever so frightened that she'd dared to say yes.

Chapter 35

⟨ formatting ornament ⟩

There were a few stragglers at Peaceful Meadows after the second session of Saturday morning riders, primarily volunteers and a few parents. Anna walked from the horse stable over to the carriage shed, just as Gabe had suggested earlier.

Only a moment passed before he appeared with his mare and tied her to the post, then began to pull the gray enclosed carriage out of the shed and into the sunlight. Gabe backed the mare into the shafts, giving Anna a kind of tutorial as he worked. He seemed quite serious about the hitching-up process—as an essential part of his life, it had become second nature to him. But Anna had to wonder why he was giving her a running discourse on what he was doing, step by precise step.

When at last they were on their way, Anna beside him on the front seat, Gabe began to talk about her "excellent involvement" with the other volunteers. "Also, with one rider specifically," he added.

She assumed he meant Emmie but wondered what he might say further.

"My sister-in-law Barbara Mast—I know you've met her—has been sayin' what I believe, what I hope, to be true."

She turned to look at him, there on the driver's side of the carriage, holding the driving lines in a more relaxed manner than Sadie ever had.

"Barbara thinks Emmie might be on the verge of a break-through," he continued.

Anna remembered holding her breath as Emmie nuzzled up to Promise, leaning her head against his flank as though Emmie didn't know Anna was observing her. And then today, she'd reached for Anna's apron.

"What do you think?" Gabe glanced her way.

Anna shared with him what she had observed. Then, for no particular reason, she asked why he thought Emmie had stopped speaking when her mother died.

"Emmie's life was stitched into Emily's," he began. "Emily liked to call her a Mamma's girl, since her every waking minute was spent with my wife. Their bond was precious." Gabe also mentioned that he'd built his first tree house for his wife and Emmie. "They played house in there, took naps in the after-noon, had picnics, and whatnot all." He paused and looked the other way for a moment.

Then, his voice quieter now, he went on. "Emily adored Emmie and had so many plans for her when she grew up. She wanted to teach her to cook and do piecework and quilt and garden and sew, like all the other Amish girls. But Emmie was only three when Emily died of cancer after a short remission."

Anna was aware of how Gabe's face softened whenever he

spoke of his daughter. "Emmie's your gift from heaven," she said, hesitant to say more yet appreciative of how frank Gabe had been about such a painful subject.

"I can't help but think that you and Emmie have a special connection, too," Gabe said, startling her. "She doesn't respond even to her Mammis the way she does to you, Anna."

But I'm basically a stranger, thought Anna.

Gabe turned to look at her, his eyes meeting hers. "Do ya understand what I'm sayin'?"

Anna was rather embarrassed. "I think so."

"Well, I've been considering something, but I don't want to seem presumptuous." Pausing a bit, he returned his gaze to the road. "What would ya think of spendin' more time with Emmie in addition to bein' her side walker?" He added that, since the horse riding therapy would come to an end after September, which really wasn't far away, Emmie would miss Anna and perhaps regress. "Just think about whether it's something you're interested in."

Anna sensed his apparent earnestness. *I'm already so busy,* she thought, wondering if this was a good idea. Yet when she thought of Emmie, how could she refuse?

Gabe continued, "I was thinkin' maybe once a week at the house."

I really ought to consider doing this, she thought, then reminded him that, besides the Lord's Day, she only had Fridays and Saturdays off. "Whatever I can work out, it would have to be during one of those two days."

"Don't ya want to think 'bout it first?" Gabe's eyes were questioning.

"Well, I'd like to help Emmie, if I can."

"This wouldn't be babysitting, mind you. And I don't expect ya to work for nothin'," he quickly added.

Anna shook her head. "Oh *nee* . . . I wouldn't accept pay."

Gabe's shoulders rose and fell as though a weight had been lifted. "*Denki*, Anna. You don't know what this'll mean to her." He directed the horse onto a paved driveway that led back off the road to a large dairy farm. "Here we are," he said, halting the mare. "I need to pick up some butter and cottage cheese." He indicated he would just be a few minutes. "Feel free to wait here if you like."

She presumed he was just being thoughtful, or that he didn't want to introduce her to whoever was selling the butter and cottage cheese. *But why did he need my help today if I'm just sitting here while he loads the back of the buggy?* she wondered, guessing he'd used it as an excuse to talk with her about Emmie.

As she sat there waiting, she realized more fully what she'd agreed to do. What if perhaps *Gabe* was also hoping to have more time with her? If that was the case, what would happen to Emmie if Anna were to step back at some point, away from the two of them? Wouldn't it be hard on the little girl?

The last thing I want to do is to jeopardize her progress, she thought. *Oh goodness, am I doing the right thing?*

Sadie tried not to let on, but she thoroughly enjoyed hearing Anna tell about her carriage ride with Gabe. *Her parents won't be pleased if this leads to something more than friendship,* she thought, yet she couldn't help but be tickled at the thought of a spark between Gabe and Anna.

"Gabe's concerned that Emmie might have a setback after the horse riding therapy season is over," Anna explained.

"So, she's become attached to ya?" Sadie asked.

"Apparently. At least it sounds like Emmie's aunt thinks so."

"Well, I'm not surprised, seein' ya with our little ones next door," Sadie said, chopping celery on the cutting board for a Waldorf salad at noon.

"If I can make a difference for Emmie, I'd like to try." Anna went on to say that Gabe had offered to pay for her time on Friday mornings, the day they'd settled on. "But it's not necessary. It's the right thing to give of oneself for another, just as God expects."

Sadie agreed, but she could just hear it now: If Anna got more entangled in Gabe Allgyer's life and family, what would Rachel and Alvin Beachy say? *They'll wonder why I didn't step in and put a stop to it!* she thought.

The following Friday, Anna drove to the address Gabe had given her, taking note of Aden and Barbara Mast's farm on the right side of the road as she neared Gabe's smaller white clapboard house with its black shutters. She could easily spot the silver numerals on the big black mailbox out front, where a nearby half barrel contained red and white petunias.

Here we are, she thought, thinking that she hadn't seen Gabe since going to get butter and cottage cheese with him last Saturday. She wondered what he'd told Emmie about this visit today.

Walking around to the back yard of the house, she found Gabe throwing a large pink ball to Emmie, his laughter filling the air as she caught the lightweight ball. He looked relaxed and handsome in his gray short-sleeved shirt, its top button undone, and black broadfall trousers with black suspenders. His usual straw hat rested on the back porch steps.

Emmie was completely silent as she threw the ball, then opened her arms, her fingers stretched wide, in an attempt to catch it. She looked adorable in her mint green dress and matching long apron, her hair twisted rather loosely into a tiny chunk of a bun. Several strands had come free, and Anna wondered who had helped with her hair.

Not wanting to startle Emmie or interrupt their play, Anna hung back, waiting for the right time to make her presence known.

In a few minutes, the ball rolled toward her, and Emmie turned to fetch it. When she did, she spotted Anna there at the end of the walkway. Stopping in her tracks, she broke into a genuine smile.

"Hullo, Emmie," Anna said, slowly walking toward her. "Looks like you're having fun." She glanced over at Gabe, who motioned for her to join them, eyes alight.

"Would ya like to play three-corner catch with us?" he asked, waiting for Emmie to return to her spot on the lawn with the ball.

"Okay!" Anna set her purse on the back porch step beside his hat and hurried to join them.

After playing for a while, Emmie went to the back porch to get her faceless dolly from one of the chairs and proceeded to walk across the yard to the modest tree house. Gabe suggested that she wanted Anna to go with her.

"How can you tell?" Anna asked as she stood near the porch with him. "I mean, how does she communicate with you?"

"It wasn't easy at first, but now I can understand her pretty well."

"And she's never spoken?" Anna finally ventured forward with the question she'd had since meeting the girl.

"She was slow to walk *and* talk, but she had been trying to put words together before Emily passed." Gabe paused and sighed. "I think she just quit tryin' after the person closest to her was gone."

"I am so sorry." Anna shook her head.

Gabe nodded. "I know she's still stingin' from the pain of loss, even though I don't see how she remembers Emily well. Not anymore." He drew a breath. "She was so young when Emily died; I doubt she could comprehend what was happening, really."

Listening to Gabe, Anna continued to watch Emmie, who had climbed up the ladder and was now sitting on one of the wooden benches in the tree house with her white cat and her doll, just staring down at them.

"There," Gabe said. "See that look in her eyes?"

Anna nodded. "She telling you something?"

"She wants me to leave so you can join her in the tree house."

"You're getting that from one stare?"

"I've had a little experience." He grinned. "And if I'm right, she'll smile once you're up there with her." Turning, he headed across the yard to his shop.

Anna took along the picture book she'd picked up at the library and walked over to the ladder. "Lookee what I have," she said when she reached the top of the ladder.

Emmie's stare evolved into a smile.

Chapter 36

WEDNESDAY, JULY 14, 1948

It was still light as Eliza made her way to the stone wall that evening. Thankfully, she hadn't needed to say that she was leaving to meet a friend, since Aunt Joanna had fallen asleep in her rocking chair there in the kitchen. If the pattern was the same as usual, her aunt would wake up in about forty minutes and then head off to her room for the night, never aware that Eliza wasn't in her own room reading the Good Book, as was *her* pattern this time of the evening.

When Eb saw her coming, he climbed over from his side of the stone wall and walked toward her, carrying a paper bag. "Hullo, Eliza . . . you're right on time."

"I am," she replied, ever so glad to be with him again, though she never would have thought so a week ago.

He asked if she'd like to sit with him in the grass and have some cookies he'd brought from home, and she agreed. "Did ya have a *gut* day?" he asked once they were seated near the tall oak tree.

"Since ya saw me last, ya mean?" She smiled.

"There's that spunk again." He winked at her. "So, what did ya do this afternoon?" He seemed eager to know as he opened the sack and offered her some sugar cookies, still warm.

"Well, I helped mend and sew, since it's Wednesday, ya know. Does your Mamma mend midweek, too?"

"*Jah.* Does your Mamm back home?"

"Her daily chores are similar to my aunt's, *jah.*" She took a bite of the moist cookie. "Ooh, are these ever delicious. How'd ya get them out of the house without bein' seen?"

"I asked if I could have some extras is all," he told her, a grin on his handsome face.

"Some extras." She stifled a giggle. "Ain't you a case!"

"Well, I figured you'd want some, and I was right."

She looked away; his gaze had become too intense. Clearly, he was attracted to her, and there was no doubt how she felt, either.

Eb mentioned that his family was having a special birthday celebration for him next week. "I'm turnin' eighteen and wish you could be there, but I know it ain't possible because you ain't traditional Amish," he said quietly.

"*Jah,* our church broke away from the Old Order, my Dawdi told me."

"Well, let's not talk 'bout that," he said, looking at her with soft eyes. "I just wanted you to know that my birthday wish would come true, Eliza, if we could celebrate together."

She thought carefully before replying. "Well, I'm sorry I can't be there, and it *would* be nice to get to know your family. But like ya said . . ." Suddenly, as she was speaking, she felt terribly sad that their friendship could never move forward.

244

"Will ya write me a birthday note and put it in the wall for me to find?"

At that, she smiled. "I could do that, *jah*. What day's your birthday?"

"A week from today, Wednesday, July twenty-first."

It was so quickly decided that it seemed easy compared to her repeated deliberation of the past few days about replying to his note.

"Are ya all right with that?" he asked.

"I wouldn't do it otherwise."

Eb chuckled. "Do ya get your *Schpank* from your Dat or your Mamma?"

"Both."

He asked if her siblings were as spunky as she was.

"A couple of them are, but Mamma always said the Good Lord must've thought I needed more pluck than the others."

"I like that." Eb looked up at the sky just then, his head back for a moment. "A real nice evening, ain't?"

She agreed and told him she really shouldn't be out too late.

"Doesn't your aunt retire early, though?" he asked, a seeming urgency now in his words.

"*Jah*, but if she wakes up and needs something, and I'm not home . . ."

"So, we'll have to talk fast," he said, looking at her. "Make as much of our time together as possible."

"As *friends*."

"Friends," he repeated.

She asked what kind of cake he was hoping for on his birthday, and he immediately said German chocolate. "The darker the chocolate, the better," he said, and she made a note of that for no particular reason.

"Will all of your siblings and their families come to celebrate?" She tried to imagine the gathering.

"I'm sure they will. And Mamm will want to have it outside in the evening, after the sun drops in the sky a bit. Prob'ly a picnic supper with fried chicken and all the fixings she's so *gut* at makin'."

"Sounds *wunnerbaar*. I'm real happy for ya." Eliza got up and brushed the grass off her dress, saying she'd best be going.

Eb rose quickly, too. "Seems like we just got here."

"I'm not sure why we're doin' this, Eb," she blurted without thinking. "Meetin' like this . . ."

"Maybe 'cause we're *s'posed* to be friends," Eb said, moving toward her.

She stepped back. "But only friends, remember."

He pushed his hands into his trouser pockets. "*Jah*." Then he insisted on walking her partway back to her aunt's place.

"Well, if you're sure," she said, secretly glad he wanted to see her home for at least a little ways. But she did not want to think too far ahead, when she and Eb might see each other again.

Chapter 37

August plodded into September, and the shorter days turned cooler as the weeks passed. Anna saw Mart occasionally—he seemed to prefer doubling up with another couple or spending time with the church youth group to outings with just the two of them. One of those times, they drove to the Green Dragon in Ephrata to walk around and eat kettle corn. Anna purchased a bag to take home to Glen and Sadie as a treat. She also enjoyed stopping at Newswanger's Sausage for homemade sausage sandwiches, attending the small animal auction, and visiting Beulah's Candyland and Lapp Valley Farms Ice Cream.

On the days and evenings she spent at home with Sadie, Anna continued to help make the cheer-up cards for market; they had become very popular from just word of mouth. Occasionally, Anna had also taken care of Baby Jimmy next door while Marianna and her sisters had prepared the main farmhouse for the Preaching service they'd hosted Sunday.

Friday mornings were kept solely for Anna's time with Emmie. She relished reading to and playing with the little girl from around ten o'clock until Gabe finished up in his woodworking shop at noon and walked Emmie over to Barbara's, where the two of them ate their noon meal while Anna left to have her own dinner with Glen and Sadie.

It had become a favorite ritual for Emmie to sit on the back porch steps waiting for Anna to arrive. Then, together, they would walk over to the tree house, where Bootsie, Emmie's white tomcat, would sometimes amble over to join them. Hoping to encourage Emmie to talk, too, Anna would talk to the handsome feline, whose paws were as black as if it had walked through ink. Anna also recalled how Emmie seemed to relax whenever Anna talked to Promise—maybe the little girl appreciated having attention directed away from her and toward the animal.

"I think Bootsie's happy today," Anna said after arriving this fourth Friday in September. "He's looking at ya, Emmie. Want to pet him?" Anna stroked the cat's tummy when he turned over onto his back. She laughed softly and glanced at Emmie in her little black coat and black outer bonnet. "See, like this," she said, hoping Emmie might join her. "Bootsie likes to be stroked as much as Promise does." She waited and wondered if that might encourage Emmie to mimic her.

Slowly, cautiously, Emmie reached over to pet his tummy with Anna, Bootsie's purring rumbly and strong now. Pleased that Emmie had copied what she was doing, Anna touched the back of Emmie's hand. "Anna likes Emmie, too," she said softly.

Emmie looked at her shyly but turned her attention back to Bootsie.

Later, when the cat got up and padded away, Anna showed Emmie the picture book she'd brought from the library, *An Amish Christmas*, written by Richard Ammon. "This is a story about a boy and his sister celebrating Christmas," Anna told her. "Let's go up and sit in the tree house to read it," she said, leading the way.

Emmie followed and climbed up the short ladder, taking a seat next to her on the wood floor.

The Friday before, Emmie had chosen to sit farther away for their story time, but each week, she moved noticeably closer. Anna's hope was for Emmie to someday sit right beside her while she read, without any prompting. *I believe it will happen*, she thought while reading aloud and showing Emmie the beautiful illustrations. At one point, she noticed Emmie lean forward suddenly to look closely at the page where the children's parents rode with them in the sleigh.

Anna also made a practice of talking with Emmie about their heavenly Father and His loving care for all of God's children, including Emmie and her Dat. And when she did, Anna fixed her gaze on Emmie . . . and Emmie smiled.

As usual, Gabe was just a shout away, busy drafting plans and working in his woodworking shop. Considering that she wasn't traditional Amish, Anna was still surprised at Gabe's trust of her with his daughter.

Today, however, Anna noticed Gabe walk over to the well pump and draw water to wash his hands. Unexpectedly, Emmie's eyes met hers, as if to say she'd seen her father there. "Do you want to go down to him?" Anna asked.

Emmie shook her head no.

Anna tried not to react, but inside, she was thrilled. Emmie had responded! Oh, Anna wanted to clap her hands, but she knew better than to frighten Emmie.

Anna tested the waters again. "Are ya sure you don't want to go down the ladder and see your Dat?"

Again, Emmie shook her head, her eyes focused on Anna.

"Okay, we'll keep reading, then." Anna could hardly wait to tell Gabe.

Bootsie came up to them again, flopped down near Emmie, and rolled over, all four paws in the air.

Anna laughed at the silly cat. "I think Bootsie wants you to pet him again." She watched, wondering if Emmie might reach over and stroke his tummy as before.

Emmie didn't even look at the cat.

"Let's finish the book and maybe Bootsie will listen, too," Anna suggested.

Emmie surprised Anna again by nodding her head.

Hoping to take some of the pressure off the girl, Anna said, "Well, Bootsie, you've missed out on some of this *wunnerbaar-gut* story, but here's what's happened so far." She laughed a little, hoping Emmie wouldn't be confused and think her cat actually understood the story. But she was on to something, because as Anna was reading, Emmie slowly reached over and began to lightly pet Bootsie's back as the tomcat slept now on his side there with them in a pool of sunlight.

Trying to keep her voice from cracking with emotion, Anna could hardly contain herself. *A breakthrough!* she thought, turning to the next page. *What a perfect day!*

When Emmie went into her room for a moment, Anna shared with Gabe in the kitchen how she'd very clearly replied to questions with nods and shakes of her head.

"That's great news!" he exclaimed, his smile spreading wide. He stepped closer. "And I have you to thank, Anna. I mean that."

"Well, whatever's making her feel comfortable enough to respond today, I'm very happy she's doing it." Anna placed the picture book on the counter. "In case you'd like to read it to her again," she said, mentioning it was due back at the library a week from tomorrow, so she would return it then.

"I'll do that," Gabe said, still grinning. "You're a teacher at heart, ain't?"

"Maybe it goes hand in hand with being a tour guide." She felt a bit awkward at the warmth in Gabe's expression as he looked at her. "Emmie's so easy to be with," she added.

He nodded thoughtfully. "But she definitely has a preference for you, Anna."

"And I enjoy her, too," Anna said, gathering up her things and slipping on her coat. "Very much."

"Say, I was wonderin' if ya might join Emmie and me for dinner at Barbara and Aden's next Friday noon. Barbara's been askin' to have ya over again."

Ach no, Anna thought, thinking of how complicated it might make things if he was actually interested in her. *Don't ask me!*

But his endearing smile made her want to take the risk. "It would be nice to see Barbara again, and to meet Aden, too," she said, emphasizing their presence.

Gabe had never before walked with her out to the car, but he did this time.

Chapter 38

⁓⁓⁓⁓⁓⁓⁓⁓⁓⁓⁓⁓⁓⁓⁓⁓⁓⁓⁓⁓⁓⁓⁓

That afternoon, Anna sat down at Sadie's kitchen table and wrote her weekly letter to her Mamm while Baby Jimmy slept in his Pack 'n Play and Sadie was over at her sister Eva's. Anna wanted to write to her mother about little Emmie and her budding connection with her and her father. But she was careful how she worded things, lest Mamm misunderstand. Anna also mentioned the invitation for dinner with the Allgyers this Friday, October fifth, at Emmie's uncle and aunt's up the road. *They're God-fearing, wonderful people,* she wrote in the letter, *and I think you'd like them as much as I do. You and Dat both.*

Anna planned to tell Sadie, as well, so she wouldn't set a place for her at the noon meal that day. Continuing on with her letter, Anna wrote about her activities with Mart and his delightful Mennonite friends, making a point to be clear that she still saw the handsome young man now and then.

The sun cast slanting lines across the wide-plank floor, and the sound of buzzing bees came through the nearby open window as Sadie sat with Eva in the sunny bedroom just off the front room. As she read aloud to her sister several comforting psalms, she realized yet again that the poor dear did not even recognize her.

The thought crossed Sadie's mind that it really didn't matter, because this time together was about being there for her sister and letting her know that she cared.

This ain't about me, Sadie thought, sitting there in the rocking chair while Eva dozed propped up in bed. *It's about giving the kind of love anyone would yearn for from a sibling, whether they know who you are or not.*

A few days later, Anna's Mamm called, sounding anxious.

"I received your letter," she said as Anna, seeking more privacy, settled into a white wicker chair on the front porch. "Sounds like you're spending a lot of time with that Amishman and his daughter."

Anna sighed and braced herself for what could be an unpleasant call. "I'm helping little Emmie," she said politely. "And she's beginning to respond to me, Mamm. I'm truly happy about that."

"It's not the child that concerns me" came her mother's prickly words.

"Well, rest assured that Gabe and I are merely friends. And I'm not there to spend time with him."

"But friendship is where things begin," Mamm replied. There was an awkward pause before she continued. "Honestly, Anna,

253

I didn't think the need to tell you this would ever arise, but it seems like it's time. You see," she said, her voice momentarily faltering, "my mother was a very young woman—just turning sixteen—when she went to Strasburg. And while she was there, she met an Old Order fellow. They were supposedly 'just friendly,' as you might say. But there was more to the story."

"So, Mammi fell for a traditional Amishman?" Anna had rather suspected the beau had been Old Order, but hearing it directly from her mother still took her aback.

"Fortunately, it was short-lived, and no one really knows what happened to bring it to an end." Mamm sighed. "Your Mammi Eliza's mother revealed this to me a long time ago, as a warning."

Solemn as Mamm sounded just now, Anna knew it wasn't a good idea to ask for more information.

"Remember how, before you left home, your father cautioned you about not getting mixed up with someone outside our community like this?" Mamm asked. "Anna, I urge you not to turn your back on the Light you've been blessed with. Knowing we're saved by grace through faith is essential . . . it's not only about good deeds, I'm sure ya know."

Anna knew her parents were trying to protect her, and while she understood their reasons for that, she felt reined in, too.

"Your Mammi Eliza wasn't herself for quite some time after returning from Strasburg. Such relationships can only lead to heartache."

No matter what I've said, she doesn't believe Gabe and I are simply friends, Anna thought, not knowing how to respond, except to repeat what she'd already said.

Mamm suddenly mentioned needing to check on something boiling over on the stove, so she said a quick good-bye.

Anna clicked off her phone and sat there on the porch, looking out at the road, feeling not only blue for the heartbreak

Mammi Eliza must have suffered so long ago, but also feeling like she'd just been reproached herself—and for absolutely no reason.

I am not falling for an Old Order Amishman! she thought.

Wednesday and Thursday of that week were exceptionally busy with numerous requests for car tours through the back roads of Amish farmland. Mart sent a text just to say hi and that he was swamped with tourists—and suspected she was, too.

Anna texted back that he was right. Now that harvest was in full swing, out-of-towners were eager to see mule teams out working in the fields and wanted to visit roadside stands where jams, jellies, and homemade Amish root beer were available. Several families had also requested a stop at Kauffman's Fruit Farm and Market to sample the many varieties of apples, or at Stoltzfus Gourd and Pumpkin Farm, where they could purchase decorative gourds and pumpkins of all sizes. Between her job and volunteering at Peaceful Meadows, Anna had felt like she was living the good life, and she was going to miss the latter now that horse-therapy sessions had ended for the season. Of course, being around little Emmie on Fridays was still one of the high points of the week, as well as seeing Mart now and then.

So, why am I not more content? She tried to dismiss her mother's phone call as she turned in to Aden and Barbara Mast's driveway that Friday with Gabe and Emmie along. This time Anna felt more at ease going to Barbara's home, having talked with her for a number of months now whenever the woman brought Emmie for horse riding therapy.

On their walk up toward the back door, Anna pointed out to Emmie two robins tugging at earthworms in the surrounding grass.

"We've got grasshoppers tryin' to escape from the birds over at our place," Gabe said, chuckling as he walked with them. "Extra protein, *jah?*"

Anna wondered if Emmie was understanding any of this. "*Hungerich*, Emmie?" she asked, not expecting an answer.

Emmie nodded, once more surprising Anna, who was glad Gabe was there to witness it. "I'm hungry, too," Anna told her, glancing at Gabe, who beamed at them both.

At Barbara's table, Gabe placed Emmie atop an old dictionary on a chair between Barbara and Anna. Gabe then took the chair up near the head of the table, to Aden's left. After the silent blessing, Barbara served a generous dish of lazy day lasagna, saying it was a dish her boys especially liked. "One of their favorites, really."

Anna remembered that the Amish one-room schools had started more than a month ago now. She hadn't met Aden and Barbara's two sons, but Emmie brightened at Barbara's comment about the lasagna being her cousins' favorite.

Gabe must have picked up on that, as well, because he asked his daughter, "Did ya hear that? Jesse and Chris like this meal, too."

Emmie turned to look at Anna, still smiling.

"I daresay that's a *jah*," Barbara said, reaching now to pass the buttered pole beans and then the cucumber salad.

Aden and Gabe began to talk about the tree house construction business and how much more time Gabe had for his primary work since the horse-therapy sessions were done for the season.

Anna heard Gabe say that he hoped to recruit more volunteers for next year. *I wonder if he'll talk with Heidi and Eleanor's cousin*, she thought, recalling Shelley's interest when they'd gone swimming.

Barbara asked Anna if she was doing any handiwork at present, and Anna mentioned the unique fabric-inset cards she was making with Sadie. "She's been selling quite a lot at Saturday market."

Barbara glanced at Emmie, then back at Anna. "Do ya sew, Anna?"

"Well, I make all my clothing," Anna replied, wondering why she'd asked.

"Have ya ever made doll clothes?"

"When I was younger, all the time."

Emmie's faint smile grew into a full-blown grin, and Anna made a mental note.

Later, while eating their apple Danish dessert topped with homemade vanilla ice cream, Anna caught Gabe looking her way, and she felt herself blush. *Why did he and Barbara invite me here?* she wondered.

Chapter 39

The after-dessert conversation grew more lively when Gabe brought up the Harvest Days Festival coming up next weekend at the Landis Valley Village and Farm Museum. Barbara quickly said she thought Anna would enjoy it, while Emmie rubbed her eyes and yawned.

Barbara rose from her chair and reached for Emmie's hand, and the two of them left the kitchen for what Anna assumed was a nap. As soon as it was appropriate, Anna would thank Barbara for inviting her, then make her exit.

Gabe will surely just walk the short distance home, she thought, hoping that was the case.

When Barbara returned to the table, she began to pour more coffee and even offered warm cider. To be polite, Anna lingered as the conversation turned to apple harvesting, and Aden voiced his opinion about the kind of apple that was the sweetest. He was a big fan of the Fuji, saying its sugar levels were higher than those of the Gala or Golden Delicious.

"The best apple variety depends on what you're usin' them for," Barbara said with a smile. "A good apple for dumplings isn't the same as a good apple for cider, for instance."

"True," Gabe said, excusing himself to go and rinse out his coffee mug. As he stood by the sink, he said, "It's time to get back to work. Do ya mind givin' me a lift home, Anna?"

Surprised, she nodded, hoping the worry didn't show on her face. "Okay," she said, ready to get going, too.

"Emmie can nap while you're workin'," Barbara offered.

Anna thanked her and Aden for the delicious meal.

"You must come again," Barbara said as she followed her and Gabe out through the screened-in porch.

"*Denki*. It was a real nice time," Anna told Barbara when Gabe opened the door for her, and they stepped out.

In the car, Anna started the ignition and drove down the driveway to the road.

"The meal lasted longer than I anticipated," Gabe remarked as if to apologize. "They're such fine folk . . . have been helpin' me with Emmie from day one since my wife died."

"They're certainly a comfort to your daughter." She didn't say that Emmie surely saw a lot of her mother in her aunt Barbara.

"*Jah*, a comfort for both of us," Gabe agreed, then casually pointed out one of his tree houses they passed on the way back to his house.

"I understand you built the tree house at Glen Flaud's farm, where I'm staying," Anna said, making small talk.

"For Luke's *Kinner, jah*, and what a *gut* family." Gabe looked over at her. "So, how're ya related to Glen and Sadie?"

"Sadie's my Mamm's distant cousin."

Gabe was still, as if thinking about that. Then he said, "So evidently someone in your family jumped the fence—or, as we might say, left the Amish."

"My parents haven't told me a whole lot about that," she said, not wanting to delve into this with him.

"*Ach*, didn't mean to pry."

"*Es allrecht*," she said in *Deitsch* by mistake. "I mean—"

"*Nee*, it's *gut* ya forget and talk Amish sometimes." He was smiling. "*Emschtlich*."

"You say seriously, but I've been speaking Pennsylvania Dutch more lately since moving in with Mamm's cousins."

"You fit in with them, ain't so?" he said more softly.

As she made the turn into his lane, she wondered why he'd mentioned this. "I'm still getting accustomed to their Old Ways."

He nodded. "I s'pose it is quite different from your upbringing."

"In some respects, very much so," she was quick to say.

"Well, I appreciate the ride, Anna." He gave her a big smile. "I'll see ya next Friday mornin'." He got out of the car, made his way toward the house, then turned and waved.

She backed the car out toward the road. During the drive, her thoughts sifted through the past months—first meeting Gabe that June afternoon, his seeming eagerness to have her observe the work at Peaceful Meadows, then her being assigned to his cousin Dottie to learn to become a volunteer and Emmie's side walker. And now, dinner today with Aden and Barbara Mast. *More family.*

Why hadn't she seen the signs? Gabe was almost certainly interested in her; she was ever so sure now.

Suddenly, the memory of Mamm's warning resounded in her mind.

Having supper at Katie's Kitchen with Mart got Anna's mind off her conversation with Gabe, though she told Mart in passing about helping with Emmie on Fridays. "She's making a real connection with me. Her father thought it would be beneficial for me to spend more time with her, and it seems to be paying off."

"I'm sure you're a blessing to the little girl," Mart said with a quick smile.

"That's my hope and prayer."

After the meal, he suggested a drive down to the Susquehanna River for a walk, and she was happy to agree.

There, he talked politics for a while, and some about the book he was reading on how to build a deck. She enjoyed listening for a time, but if the truth were known, she had hoped he might begin to talk about more personal things at some point. *Will he ever?*

Later, on the drive back to Strasburg, she realized the two of them really weren't moving forward at all. *We're still stuck at friendship. . . .*

Saturday afternoon, Anna received a call from Wanita with news that Mammi Eliza had fallen out of bed and shattered her right wrist. "She's suffering terribly . . . please pray."

Anna's heart broke for dearest Mammi. It had been a little over two months since Anna's last visit home, and she knew she couldn't wait any longer. "I'll come as soon as I pack a change of clothes."

"Well, I don't expect you to, Anna, but I know it'll make all the difference to Mammi."

Her eyes misted with emotion. "I'll be there as soon as I can, *Schweschder.*"

After Anna hung up, she told Sadie about Mammi Eliza's fall, then went to her room to pack her overnight case. "I'll return tomorrow evening," she told Sadie, her right wrist aching with sympathy pains.

Sadie's face registered her concern. "Glen and I will keep her in prayer . . . and you, too, for traveling mercies."

Two handmade quilts were spread over Mammi Eliza when Anna tiptoed into her bedroom later that afternoon. *She must be chilled from the shock*, Anna thought, aware also of the light scent of lavender. She wondered if Wanita had dabbed some essential oil on Mammi's temples to make her feel a little better. *Did she tell her I was coming?*

Seeing how very pale Mammi looked, there with her right wrist immobilized by a splint, Anna held her breath as she sat down in the upholstered chair near the bed. *Dear Lord, please help my poor, suffering Mammi,* she prayed silently, her hands folded in her lap. *She needs Thy touch, Father. Draw out the pain and heal her wrist by Thy power. I'm so grateful for Thy loving care over Mammi Eliza all these many years. In the name of Thy son, Jesus Christ, I pray. Amen.*

A few minutes later, Wanita stepped inside, frowning and tilting her head toward Anna as if to ask how Mammi was doing. She looked nice in her violet cape dress and the matching half apron that accentuated her deep blue eyes. Her dark blond hair looked as tidy as always in its bun, and her crisp white *Kapp* was perfectly in place.

"Mammi hasn't moved since I slipped in," Anna said. "I didn't want to bother you coming in, in case you were with the children."

"I was upstairs with Rogene, who's teething again."

"Poor baby girl." Anna couldn't help noticing the dark circles under Wanita's eyes.

"Mamm always used peeled gingerroot and rubbed it on our gums," Wanita said. "But I'm all out of ginger, so I put a washcloth in the freezer, hoping that might help." She paused and sighed. "I didn't want to tell ya this, but Mammi Eliza hasn't known any of us in the past few days."

"Then she won't know me, either," Anna said, stiffening at the truth of this as she looked at her precious grandmother.

"Glad you came, Anna. I'll leave you two alone now." Wanita wiggled her fingers and left the room.

Anna nodded and reached over to touch Mammi's left hand. It was cool to the touch, the veins particularly visible. Anna began to pray again, wanting to be a comfort, just as Mammi had been to her when she was a little girl. Once, she'd fallen headlong off the rope swing, hitting her forehead, where a very sore goose egg emerged. Mammi had known just what to say so that Anna wouldn't be alarmed, young as she was, and she took her hand and led her inside to sit on the wooden bench while she went to the refrigerator. "Jesus loves the little ones like you . . . you . . . you," she had sung as she gently tended to the protruding bump with an ice pack.

Fondly remembering that moment years ago, Anna began to hum the song, and when she finished, Mammi's eyes opened slightly, and a sweet smile swept over her face. "Anna . . . you're here."

"Mammi," she managed to say, overcome with emotion. "I've been sitting here and praying . . . remembering that big bump on my forehead when I stayed with you and Dawdi John one weekend."

Her eyes found Anna's again. "You hit your noggin, *jah*."

"I was *dopplich* . . . fell off the swing."

Mammi nodded her head but didn't speak again. Her gaze held Anna's for a long time before she sighed and dozed off again.

It didn't matter, though, because Anna cherished those few moments of recognition and decided to keep them to herself. There was no need to tell Wanita or Mamm, neither one.

Chapter 40

WEDNESDAY, JULY 21, 1948

Eliza had spent time thinking about and writing Eb's birthday note. At one point, she'd actually come close to admitting her affection for him, but then she came to her senses and discarded that note and started over. By the morning of Eb's birthday, she had come up short, with nothing to show for her efforts.

The only minutes she could take to write a new attempt were in between canning and cleaning and being a companion for finicky Great-aunt Joanna. These days, Eliza had very little time for herself until after nightfall, when her aunt's heavy eyelids drooped tightly shut.

Her aunt must have become suspicious about her behavior, however, because several days ago now, she had asked Eliza right out why she was sneaking out of the house after supper. The way her aunt had phrased this made it sound suspicious, and Eliza had felt uncomfortable. *I'm not good at hiding my guilt,* she thought.

The confrontation had *ferhoodled* her enough that she was having trouble fulfilling Eb's birthday request. And, too, she wondered who had told her aunt about her leaving the house. Could it have been that neighbor cousin, Nellie Petersheim?

While her aunt rested that afternoon, Eliza opted to make a simple birthday card, instead of trying to create the perfect note. As she made the swirls and curlicues, she wished she'd thought of this sooner, because it was much easier than writing her thoughts in a note for him.

Finally, Eliza neatly printed, *May this be the best birthday ever, with our heavenly Father's blessing. Your friend, Eliza Hertzler.*

It was a simple yet honest note. Now the only thing left to do was get it to the stone wall and place it in the appointed spot while Great-aunt Joanna still napped. So, as quietly as she had done before, Eliza hurried outdoors and over to the wall. There, she stood in front of the tall oak and walked straight ahead until she spotted the large discolored rock and pushed on it.

To her surprise, she found another note from Eb already there! Eliza removed it and put her little homemade card in its place, then returned the rock and dashed back to her aunt's farmhouse.

Like Eb's first note, this one was folded up. She wished again that she'd kept that first sweet message where he had stuck his neck out about his feelings, risking rejection.

Back at the house, Eliza went straight to her aunt's room and looked in, her heart pounding from running all the way back. Relieved that Joanna was asleep and seemed not to have missed her one iota, Eliza counted her blessings.

Then she made her way to her own room, closed the door, and began to read Eb's latest note.

My dear friend Eliza,

I'm smiling as I write this, because it's strange to call you "friend" when I catch myself thinking otherwise at times. Now don't go running scared, because I understand the way things must be. And although that's unfortunate, we have at least two more months for our friendship to continue. So let's enjoy the time we have, jah?

I'll anticipate your birthday note on July twenty-first.

Your friend,
Eb Lapp

Eliza leaned back on the bed, falling into the pillows and staring up at the ceiling, wishing she could go over to his house, just up the road, and join in the birthday celebration. Oh, how she longed to see him again! "Yet what I feel for him can never be," she whispered.

SATURDAY, JULY 24, 1948

That Saturday at market, Eliza happened upon Eb by sheer coincidence. Just seeing him made her heart leap up as he caught her eye and smiled. Then, just as quickly, he turned back to unload more produce for the man who was presumably his father or uncle.

She returned her attention to her aunt's shopping list, delighted to have seen Eb again, even from afar. Then, heading to the fudge market stand, she wondered if purchasing some for Great-aunt Joanna might sweeten her up a bit. *Wouldn't that be something?*

266

Eliza chided herself. *Maybe Aunt Joanna can't help being crochety.* Eliza's mother had written something to this effect in her recent letter. *Growing old takes courage,* Mamma had penned, as though encouraging Eliza to continue to show kindness.

It's easy to be kind and caring when a person appreciates it, Eliza thought, choosing a box of fudge and paying for it with part of the monthly allowance her father sent her. *It's the sour attitude that's hard to bear,* she decided.

She was glad for the grocery cart, which was filling up so quickly she knew she'd have to call a taxicab to get back to Great-aunt Joanna's. She made her way outdoors to the pay phone around the side of the building where the farm market was held and placed her emergency coins in the slots.

The phone began to ring just as she heard a knock on the glass door of the phone booth. Turning, she saw Eb silently waving his hands to get her attention.

She hung up the phone and cracked open the folding door. "What're ya doin'?"

"I've got my Dat's buggy if ya need a ride," he said quietly.

"Won't we be seen?"

"Not if ya sit in the back seat and I close both doors."

"It'll be hot in there, won't it?"

He frowned. "Do ya want a lift or not?"

She nodded, suppressing her laugh.

"Go behind this building to the third buggy parked on the right, and get in," he told her. "I'll meet ya there in five minutes."

"*Denki,*" she said, dumbfounded that he was willing to take this risk.

Eliza felt like a fugitive all slumped down in the second bench seat, directly behind Eb in the driver's seat. But that didn't keep the two of them from talking a blue streak. Eb said he'd found her birthday card and thanked her, saying it was the "topping on his cake," and she admitted that she'd wanted it to be special.

"I was thinking of writing another letter to you and putting it in the stone wall, but I didn't know if you'd look there for one from me again," he said. "So, I got this idea . . . what if we just leave letters for each other there every Tuesday? What do ya think of that?"

She loved the idea but tried to be measured in her response. "If you want to."

He let out a chortle. "I think you want to, too, Eliza. If not, speak up now."

There was that sassy side of him again, and she snickered and covered her mouth.

"I can hear ya back there." He sounded comically stern.

She laughed all the harder.

"So, look for a letter next Tuesday, late afternoon," he said.

"While my aunt's napping. It's the only time I can leave the house, 'cept at night."

"What if ya just told her you were goin' out with a friend?" he suggested.

"Then she'd want to meet that friend—and approve of that friend, too. She's awful strict, just like Dat and Mamma would want her to be."

"Hmm, I see what ya mean. Guess we're stuck with just letters, then." Eb sounded sad.

"*Jah*, stuck," she whispered. "In more than one way."

"What's that?"

"Sorry, I was muttering. A bad habit I have, according to Aunt Joanna."

"But who doesn't mutter?" Eb wasn't laughing now.

She could see that they were turning into a lane that led to a beautiful wooded area. "Thought you were takin' me to my aunt's place."

"I wanna show ya this real perty spot first." He directed his gelding to slow as the carriage wheels rumbled over rocky terrain. "Whoa, Buckeye. Whoa."

They came to a halt in what looked to be the middle of nowhere. "Are ya sure we oughta be here?" she asked, a little concerned.

"Let's get out an' walk," he said, opening the door to a rush of fresh air.

She hopped out of the buggy and fell into step with Eb, pleased about the unexpected time with him.

"I had no idea I'd get to see ya today." He reached for her hand, and it felt so good—warm, even comforting. "Must be Providence."

She glanced at him. "Today might be the only time we walk together like this," she said.

He nodded, then stopped and looked at her ever so sweetly. "You're just the kind of . . . well, *friend* I've always wanted, Eliza." His gaze was focused on her. "The best kind, I'm thinkin'."

"Why's that?" she asked as they continued to walk, their fingers interlaced.

"Well, you're a *gut* listener. And I feel so at home with you."

She felt the same way. Oh goodness, she did!

They strolled quietly onward, enjoying the breeze that ruffled the trees and the remarkably beautiful surroundings.

"Maybe we shouldn't go too far into the woods," she said suddenly. "The produce will get warm in the buggy."

"*Jah*, I s'pose I'd best be takin' ya home."

They turned to head back, and lovely thoughts flooded her

mind as they ambled along, his arm brushing against hers now and then. It was apparent that Eb had also turned a corner—that they were no longer acting like friends was obvious. But she couldn't think on that now, wanting to enjoy these tender moments together, in case they might be their last.

Chapter 41

─────────── ⌾∕⌾ ───────────

Anna's return to Strasburg Sunday evening came with lingering sadness over Mammi Eliza's broken wrist. Thankful to have spent some time with her, Anna also felt guilty that she lived so far away, especially now. If she had any regret about moving to Strasburg, it was that she couldn't see Mammi Eliza as often as she would like.

Now that she was back at the Flauds', though, Anna looked forward to returning to work. She felt a bit impatient, as well, waiting for *all* the trees in the nearby wood to turn as vividly bright as the red sumac shrubs and sugar maples near the tree house. The several times she'd gone there to pray recently, she had noticed even more depth of color.

Prior to leaving for Mifflinburg yesterday, Anna had sketched out homemade patterns for small outfits for Emmie's doll—a soft pink dress and white apron for one, and a short black coat, too. Once she got some fabric scraps and sewed them up, Anna was certain Emmie would be surprised and happy to receive them.

271

While sitting out on the back porch, she received a text from Mart asking about her grandmother and inviting her out for supper this Friday evening, which made her smile. *He's always so thoughtful. . . .*

After most of Sadie's chores were done late Monday morning, including hanging out the washing, she went with Glen to stroll around the gardens, making small talk about Anna's coming and the ways it had changed their lives. "All for the better," Glen said, and Sadie agreed.

"I'm sure she'll attract a nice young fella and start her own family," Sadie commented. "I'll miss her if that should happen."

"It's not a question of if, but when."

They moseyed around the yard, and Glen remarked how an early October wind had knocked over the tomato cages and frayed the geraniums and hollyhocks. And Sadie bemoaned the hummingbirds' departure not long ago, recalling how comical it had been to see them fly up close to the windows and flutter there for a time, as if to say good-bye till next spring.

"'Twas a *gut* summer, ain't?" Glen said as they walked up the back porch steps and into the house.

"Ever so *gut*," Sadie said, smiling up at him.

Once in the kitchen, he reached for her hand and kissed the back of it, his expression tender.

"Well, ain't you all starry-eyed," she said, baffled but secretly enjoying her husband's attention.

The next day, after conducting several tours, Anna stopped by the Strasburg Market Place on the way home. Sadie had asked her to pick up some ground turmeric and basil.

Anna was happy to do what she could for dear Sadie, and as she parked and hurried into the store, she made a mental note to pick up a gallon of fresh apple cider as a surprise.

Inside, Anna reached for a shopping basket and was heading toward the baking aisle when she noticed Gabe over near the canned soups, scrutinizing a piece of paper. Her heart fluttered at the sight of him, and after a moment of indecision, she turned to head toward the next aisle instead.

"Anna," he called to her. "What a nice surprise!"

She turned sheepishly. "Hullo, Gabe," she said, eyeing the paper in his hand. "Looks like you've got your grocery list."

"Oh, mostly ready-to-eat foods," he said, flapping the paper. "Things I can warm up quickly, ya know."

Anna recalled that he and Emmie had most of their meals at the Masts'.

"Where's *your* list?" Gabe chuckled.

"Well, Sadie only wants a couple items, but she wants them in bulk containers."

"Bulk items? Come, I'll show ya where those are," Gabe said, directing her to a different aisle and following alongside her even though she could have easily found it on her own.

He asked if she was still enjoying her tour guide work, and she nodded. "Each group is so different, which makes things fun!"

Gabe asked if she had discovered all the back-roads quilt shops and whatnot.

"I spent quite a lot of time tracking them down," she replied. "Of course, the information center had a very helpful list for me, which was a great starting point."

"Speaking of lists." Gabe glanced at his. "Since I'm here, I should get some roasted almonds."

Anna laughed softly. "My brother Wayne eats them by the handful."

"Your brother has *gut* taste," Gabe said, chuckling. "What's your favorite snack?"

"Let's see. I love stove-top popcorn with oodles of butter, salt, and cracked pepper. Oh, and a little sprinkle of Parmesan, too."

"Sounds *wunnerbaar-gut*." He grinned.

"My Mammi Eliza always made it like that, on a hot burner with plenty of oil," Anna said, realizing they were blocking the aisle, where a young mother with a baby and a toddler in the cart wanted to pass. "She didn't use the Parmesan and pepper, though."

Gabe stepped back. "Excuse us," he told the woman, who waved it off as not a problem, her expression a bit scrutinizing.

"Maybe you can make some on Friday when ya come." Gabe's eyes were bright with hope. "Okay?"

She had to smile. "Sure, it can be Emmie's and my morning snack," she teased. "Oh, and yours, too."

He was laughing, and she liked seeing him this happy over something as simple as homemade popcorn. But it gave her pause even while her own heart rose with delight in spite of her reservations.

Come Friday morning, Anna was eager to present the home-made doll clothes to Emmie. "These are for you, honey-girl," she said the minute she arrived.

Without blinking an eye, Emmie left the kitchen and brought back her dolly and sat at the wooden bench next to the table, where she began to undress her. Emmie's little fingers worked methodically, and very quickly, her doll was outfitted in its new dress and apron.

"And what if it's cold outside?" Anna asked. "What will your dolly wear then?"

Emmie reached for the little black coat and held it up to show her.

"That's right!" Anna could have cried, she was so happy. "Is it cold enough today for her to wear the coat?" she asked, delighted by the interaction and hoping for more.

Emmie shook her head.

"Maybe a sweater, then?" Anna asked.

Emmie nodded her head, eyes wide and ever so serious.

Anna couldn't help staring at the darling girl. *Goodness, can this be happening?* "You're talking to me in your own way, Emmie, ain't so!" Anna asked softly.

Emmie nodded again, and Anna could scarcely contain her joy. It was almost as if they were having a conversation. "Is your Dat in his workshop?" she asked rather breathlessly.

Emmie nodded repeatedly, smiling at the dolly now and holding her up to Anna.

Anna was tempted to ask Emmie if she could say "*jah,*" but she didn't want to interfere with this wonderful exchange.

Later, when Gabe came in for some cold meadow tea, Anna told him about Mammi Eliza's fall and broken wrist, saying she'd forgotten to tell him when she'd seen him at the market.

"I'm awful sorry to hear it," he said, his eyes kind.

Anna motioned for him to slip into the sitting room next to the kitchen with her while Emmie was focused on her dolly, showing it off to a much larger brown teddy bear and a petite rag doll.

Smiling, Gabe followed her, and Anna quickly told him what had transpired earlier. "Nearly every time I come here, Emmie seems to open up more. It's so exciting to watch her come alive like this."

Gabe's eyes met hers. "There's a *gut* reason for that," he said quietly. "And if ya don't mind, I'd like to talk to you before you leave today." He glanced toward the kitchen doorway, as though not wanting Emmie to hear. "It'd be just for a minute or so."

She had to respond. "All right," she said, curious to know what was on his mind.

After Gabe returned to his work across the yard, Anna sat on the wooden bench and read aloud to Emmie several children's poems she'd found at the library, trying to ignore that her stomach was in knots. *What does Gabe want to talk about?*

Emmie continued to play on the floor, and Anna hoped the gentle rhymes and the sound of her voice might somehow instill in her a desire to speak. *Just a single word would be wonderful,* she thought.

When Anna paused in her reading, she listened to see if there were any small peeps or sounds coming from Emmie while she engaged with her dolls and teddy bear, but Emmie remained as silent as ever.

Eventually, Emmie got up and carried her newly dressed doll over to the back door, making her doll peek out of the window.

She wants to go outside, thought Anna, so she suggested they go and collect some pretty leaves together. Emmie smiled, and they slipped on sweaters and headed outdoors, where, while collecting orange and red leaves, Anna began to tell Emmie stories about her own childhood with her sister, Wanita. "We made a special place in the attic," she said, describing the cozy spot and remembering finding Mammi's little diary in an attic not so long ago. "Maybe we could make the tree house cozier, too. Would ya like that?"

Emmie frowned and shrugged with her dolly nestled in her little arms.

"Cooler days are here already, and in not too many weeks, winter will come, and it'll be real cold," Anna said, thinking out loud. "But what if we took some old blankets up there for story time next week, if it's not too chilly . . . and a blanket for your dolly, too?" She paused. "I *wish* I knew her name."

Emmie smiled, nodding her head and looking at the tree house, then down at her doll.

"I'll bring the blankets, and you bring your baby, okay?" Anna asked, delighted at all the immediate responses she was getting today. Yet she still yearned to hear little Emmie's voice— she'd even daydreamed about it. What did it sound like?

Does Gabe even remember?

Putting on her coat, Anna hugged Emmie good-bye and noticed the noontime temperature had dropped quite a lot. She stepped onto the porch, where she saw Gabe hurrying this way.

Together, they walked to her car.

"If you'd like to go with me to the Harvest Days Festival tomorrow afternoon, I'll ask Barbara to watch Emmie for a few hours. One of the drivers I use can take us."

This has nothing to do with Emmie, realized Anna with a start. *Gabe's asking me out on a date.*

An alarm bell clanged in her head, and her breath caught in her throat. *We shouldn't,* she thought, and yet . . . she wanted to go. It sounded like fun, and she recalled Barbara mentioning the festival last Friday at the noon meal. Even so, she felt all twisted up, like a pretzel, confused about how she felt toward Gabe. He had been married before, for one thing, and he had a daughter, as well. *They're a package deal.*

Besides, she thought, *falling for someone like that, on top of our very different backgrounds, doesn't make sense at all.*

"Just so ya know, this would be my treat," Gabe said with a chuckle.

His demeanor was so self-effacing that Anna was actually tempted, but, attracted to him as she was, she was terrified where this might lead. "I'll have to think about it," she said at last.

"We could go Dutch, if that'd make ya feel better," he said, sounding just as inviting as before.

"As friends." She pondered this rush of emotion.

"Sure," he added. "Friends."

"Well, all right, then," she agreed, wondering how she would share this turn of events with Sadie, who'd seemed a bit nervous the last time she'd talked with her about Gabe and Emmie.

And so did Mamm, thought Anna.

For most of the afternoon, Anna worked with Sadie redding up the house, since Sadie planned to be at market tomorrow with Lillian again. Anna also made time to write to Wanita and to Mamm, this time not hinting that she would be seeing both Mart and Gabe this weekend. *No need to concern them*, she decided.

She freshened up and changed clothes for her supper with Mart, then received a text from him that said he was on his way. She sat on the back porch waiting for him, waving to Marcus and Eddy, who ran past the yard with Brownie yipping at their heels. The boys headed toward the woods and their wonderful tree house, and she wondered, just then, how it would look tomorrow when a passenger van pulled into the driveway and there was Gabe Allgyer coming to the door to get her.

I didn't think this through. . . .

278

Not long after, Mart arrived. Getting out of his car, he looked so wonderful in his gray dress slacks and tan sports jacket that she felt befuddled as he came up the walkway. Kind though Gabe was, she wished now that she hadn't complicated things by accepting his invitation for tomorrow.

Chapter 42

Anna was having such a nice time with Mart at Yoder's Restaurant and Buffet in New Holland, she found it easy to focus on their supper conversation. Mart shared that his parents had invited the whole family over, including extended family, for Thanksgiving this year.

"A houseful, *jah?*" she said, curious where they'd put everyone.

"Absolutely!" Mart mentioned that his mother was concerned they might not be able to gather everyone in one location next year, considering that a number of his cousins would be graduating from high school and leaving for vocational training, college, or even missions work in Haiti with Christian Aid Ministries. "So I understand why she and Dad want to make this work."

"That's a lot of people for one house," she said.

"That's just the thing—Dad's looking into using our church basement."

She thought unexpectedly of Gabe's family, wondering how many extended relatives he and Emmie had. Where did his parents live? Anna knew of his former sister-in-law, Barbara, but did Gabe have any siblings of his own?

She pushed away such thoughts, wanting to be attentive to Mart, the fellow she *should* be thinking about.

One thing was sure, she wanted to be in Mifflinburg with her own family for Thanksgiving, with at least a third of them sitting around Mamm's extendable table. Wanita, her husband, Conrad, and their nine children would come, as usual, and so would Wayne and Cindy and their family. The other five brothers and families regularly went to their wives' parents' homes for the holiday, trading off with Dat and Mamm for Christmas or Easter instead.

"Anna? You're deep in thought," Mart said, studying her.

She nodded. "Oh . . . sorry."

He leaned forward on the table. "Busy week?"

"Very."

He mentioned key lime pie for dessert. "Are you ready for something sweet?"

"Are you having some?" she asked.

"I wouldn't think of passing up pie of any kind." He motioned for her to go with him to the dessert section.

"What is it about buffets that brings in so many people?" she asked later, carrying her slice of pie back to the table.

Mart set his on the table and went to hold her chair while she was seated. "It's probably that there's so much to choose from—something to make everyone happy."

"Variety's *gut*," she said, staring at the generous piece of key lime before her.

"Some folk here come and sit and eat and talk . . . and then eat again for hours."

"The owners surely lose money on them."

As she looked around the space at the many diners, she

281

spotted a particularly elderly gentleman whose fork shook as he raised it to take a bite, and Anna couldn't help but think of Mammi's broken wrist. Was Wanita or one of the older children still helping to feed her?

After the meal, they returned to Flauds', and Mart got out of the car to go around and open her door. "It was wonderful having supper with you again, Anna," he said, walking with her to the back door.

"Thanks for another special evening."

"I'll see you at the information center Monday," he said, pausing. "Unless, would you like to attend church with me?"

She smiled. "Or you could come to *my* church."

"True, but I thought maybe you'd like to hear our bishop preach, since you didn't get to at the hymn sing." The way Mart said it made her think it was very important to him. "Just know you're always welcome, Anna."

"Thank you, Mart. That's kind of you."

"'Night."

She stepped into the house, feeling rather torn. *Does this mean he's actually getting serious?*

Going through the kitchen and down the hall to her room, she knelt beside her bed and prayed. "O Lord, Mart is such a fine young man—everything I would want in a beau and a husband. Please grant me wisdom."

Later, as she sat in bed in the dark, ready to fall sleep, Anna thought of her bishop's sermon last Sunday back in Mifflinburg, about the Holy Spirit praying for believers through wordless groans.

Right now, Anna felt like *she* was groaning within her spirit. Never having had this dilemma before—two fine young men seeking her attention—she struggled with how she'd gotten to this point.

Then she caught herself. *Gabe isn't an option,* she reminded herself with a sigh. *Much as I like him.*

"God is tenderhearted to our groans," Bishop Wengerd had assured the congregation. *"The Lord can be trusted in our weakness and confusion."* She felt grateful for having heard that sermon, even though she had missed going to her church here in Lancaster County and seeing her friends there.

Was I supposed to hear that sermon last week? She slipped down into bed, knowing that God had a unique way of putting people in the right place at just the right time. And He had given her the ability to make a choice about whom to spend her life with, as well.

When Anna dreamed, it was of Mart, urgently asking her to attend his church. She ended up going reluctantly in the dream, but the pastor didn't speak either English or German, nor Pennsylvania Dutch. For the life of her, she could not understand him. She turned to Mart next to her, in a church where couples could sit together, and she couldn't understand him, either, so she dashed out of the building in a panic.

Feeling all wrung out when she awakened, Anna felt stiff—nearly frozen—taking deep breaths. *What an awful dream!*

She reached for the flashlight in her room and carried it out to the kitchen. Setting it on the counter, she went to the gas-powered refrigerator and removed a gallon jar of cow's milk fresh from the neighboring farm. She poured a small amount in a cup and went to sit at the table in the spot where she always sat next to Sadie at meals.

I have to get my mind off this, she decided, needing to return to sleep. She had a busy day tomorrow, redding up her room, doing some mending, and making the noon meal for Glen, too, while Sadie was gone to market. And then there was the outing with Gabe tomorrow afternoon.

Anna sipped the cold milk and wished she knew what Mart was thinking, because if she had to be a member of his church for them to seriously date, she had better think carefully about his invitation.

If it's God's will, she thought, determined to know for sure.

———

Sadie sat up in bed at the sound of footsteps in the kitchen. *Anna must be restless*, she thought, getting up to pull on her robe.

She wandered out to the kitchen, where she could see a stream of light coming from the table. Spotting the flashlight, she said quietly, "'Tis all right to turn on the lamp, Anna."

"I was trying to be quiet," Anna replied from her place at the table. She looked like she was carrying a weight on her shoulders.

"Well, if neither of us can sleep, we may as well keep each other company." Sadie reached for the switch for the battery-powered lamp overhead. "There now, that's better," she said, squinting over at Anna. "You feelin' all right?"

Anna's slender shoulders rose, then lowered. "*Ach*, I hardly know what to think."

Sadie sat down in Glen's chair at the head of the table, hoping Anna might share what was on her mind. "I've felt like that sometimes, too," she said.

Slowly, Anna began to open up and talk about "her predicament," as she put it, the words coming quickly now, as though she'd been holding this in for too long. Her Mennonite friend Mart had invited her to attend church with him this Sunday, and, of all things, Gabe had asked to take her to the Harvest Days Festival tomorrow afternoon. "Supposedly that's just as friends, but I suspect that's only because I suggested it should be that way." She shook her head. "Even so, Mart's the fella I *should* be interested in," Anna admitted. "I've known him longer, for one thing, and . . . his upbringing is more similar to mine." She traced a finger around the rim of her empty glass. "Honestly, though, I feel something very different when I'm with Gabe, which seems odd to me."

Sadie studied her and wondered if she ought to say what she was thinking. She took her time, though, not jumping into the conversation till Anna stared down at the table, like she was beside herself. "Is it odd, really?" Sadie ventured. "I mean, havin' an attraction to a *wunnerbaar* young man like Gabe?"

"Truth is, I never expected it." Anna sat up straighter now.

"Well, when ya invite God to plant His desires in you, ya must be willing to take one step at a time, as He leads," Sadie said quietly. "Remember, the heart chooses who it loves."

Anna seemed to ponder that. "Surely I'm not supposed to be with an Amish fella, though. A widower . . . with a troubled child who might not be easy to raise." Anna covered her mouth, catching herself. "Oh, it's just so complicated!"

Sadie knew she must be gentle with her reply. "Are you afraid of lovin' again, Anna?"

Frowning at first, Anna nodded slowly. "The way things ended with my first beau, I feel like I need to guard my heart . . . be careful who I let in," she confessed. "I don't ever want to hurt like that again."

"You're wise." Sadie reached to touch her hand. "And I believe you can trust your heavenly Father to make the way clear to you."

They talked awhile longer; then Anna asked if Sadie would remember her in prayer. "More than anything, I want God's choice of a mate." She paused. "And I want my family to be pleased, too. I'd never want to hurt them."

Sadie agreed to pray. "Can ya wait for the Lord to make this known to you?"

"I intend to do that, *jah*." Anna thanked her for taking time to listen and to give good advice, especially in the middle of the night. "You're really a dear," she whispered.

"Well, I care 'bout ya, Anna." Sadie smiled. "We'll talk again."

Chapter 43

⟨⟩

The passenger van arrived around one-thirty, and Gabe walked right up the cobblestone path to the porch, where Anna was sitting. He looked like any Amishman headed for Preaching service, dressed all in black other than his white long-sleeved shirt. His fair beard was neatly trimmed, and he wore a black felt hat since the days were cooler now.

Fortunately, Luke, Marianna, and the children had gone somewhere earlier, and Glen was in the front room reading. At least for now Anna could rest easy about not being seen with Gabe. She smiled when he greeted her, and she happily went with him to the van, where he offered his hand to help her in. Strangely giddy, she sat at the window on the third bench and Gabe slid in next to her.

The van was nearly full with other Amish folk, all of them going to the Harvest Days Festival at Landis Valley Farm, she learned as they rode. Gabe also introduced her to several of them, mostly neighbors or church members, all in a friendly, merry mood.

He must not care what they think . . . that I'm not really one of them.

When there was a lull, Anna asked how Emmie was doing, and Gabe said she was carrying her dolly around everywhere, the doll dressed in Anna's handiwork. He added that she'd also taken the doll with her to Aendi Barbara's before he left to come for Anna. "I didn't tell Emmie that I would be seein' you."

Anna didn't have to wonder why not—he was clearly interested in getting to know *her* better. She tried to smile but felt she'd made a mistake in coming. *What am I doing with Gabe?* she thought, watching as the cornfields seemed to fly by.

Yet she hadn't been able to tear herself away from his company, so she was at once miserable and happy.

What's my heart telling me?

There were countless people at the Harvest Days Festival, tourists and locals alike. Anna was impressed by the colorful autumn decorations everywhere—large wicker baskets of ornamental corn, tiered shocks of cornstalks, pumpkins to decorate for the children—and live music, craft demonstrations, horse-drawn hayrides, and apple butter and cider making, too.

She and Gabe stopped to observe a sheep-shearing exhibit, then watched as previously washed and carded wool was spun into yarn on a spinning wheel, and next, turned into the beginnings of a shawl. Anna told Gabe that her Mammi Eliza had been bequeathed a similar spinning wheel from her grandmother, "my great-great-grandmother," she said.

"Is it still in the family?" Gabe asked, the look on his face showing keen interest.

"It's stored in my sister's attic."

"None of your womenfolk use it?"

"Not that I know of."

"Maybe you could learn . . . since you seem interested." He motioned toward the spinning wheel.

"Maybe I will." She laughed, following him to an indoor exhibit that focused on eighteenth-century life in Lancaster County.

They watched an Amish blacksmith at work, and Anna realized this was really nothing new for Gabe, presuming that he visited the smithy quite often, given he owned at least one road horse.

"I helped our Amish smithy one summer when I was a teen-ager out in Indiana, where I grew up," Gabe told her as they watched. "My parents still live in Elkhart County."

"Do your siblings live there, as well?" She hoped she wasn't being too nosy.

"All six brothers and their families, *jah.*" Gabe glanced at her. "Ya prob'ly wonder how I ended up here in Strasburg even though my Mamm married an Indiana Amishman."

She nodded, hoping he might share that.

Gabe told her that his mother was originally from Strasburg but met his father at an Amish youth convention in Indiana. Then Gabe explained that he had been invited here to help Emily's father on their farm before he'd ever met her. "I answered a request in *The Budget,* actually. And"—he paused for a moment—"after I met Emily, I knew that God had brought me here."

She felt sad for him, realizing the love they must have had together.

"Are ya cryin', Anna?" He stopped to look at her, stepping near, like he wanted to comfort her.

"They're happy tears," she said. "For you and Emily . . . and for Emmie. For the years that you did have together."

Gabe tilted his head, his gaze thoughtful. "Does it bother ya to hear 'bout this?"

"Emily was your bride and Emmie's Mamma, so not at all," Anna said, glad he felt comfortable talking about his wife.

They meandered quietly and companionably for a while, looking at various displays of items for sale, including wooden toys, and then he eventually mentioned how his interest in building tree houses came about. "It struck me that so many Amishmen were building gazebos and toolsheds that the market for those was already swamped, so I carved out my own niche." He smiled at her. "It's been a *gut* livin' . . . the Lord is blessing me beyond what I deserve."

Later, they walked past the children's discovery tent, and Anna thought of Emmie. There was no denying that she cared deeply for her, yet it was *Gabe* who was seeking Anna out. It was also Gabe who made her laugh and forget how complicated her romantic life was right now.

Around five o'clock, they stood in line for bratwursts at one of the food stands and then walked around eating them. Gabe's was loaded up with chili, cheese, and relish—so much so that he ended up needing the extra paper napkins Anna had gotten. "You're about to lose the best part," she teased.

"That's just what Emily would say." He frowned suddenly, looking aghast. "Oh," he groaned. "I'm mighty sorry, I—"

"No, it's all right, really," Anna assured him.

Gabe was silent for a while, and Anna wished she could say something to prove that it really was all right. She was actually surprised he hadn't let his deceased wife's name slip before now.

When Gabe did talk again, he asked, "Have ya been baptized into the Beachy Amish church back home?"

Such a probing question, she thought.

"Well, not just yet," she said, "but it shouldn't be much longer."

He glanced at her. "Is your heart set on it?"

"I've been in prayer about it for quite some time."

Nodding, he said, "Baptism is a holy sacrament, as you know. It's an important step for anyone who's opened their heart to Christ."

Anna agreed, and after they bought root-beer floats and headed over to the hayride, she told him that it was her dear Mammi Eliza who'd led her at the age of nine to accept Jesus as her Savior. "Now it's just a matter of being baptized . . . when the time is right."

Gabe listened intently, and as the sun lowered in the sky and they sat together in the big hay wagon, Anna considered all they had shared in the space of a few hours.

The evening was filled with autumn smells—woodsmoke, caramel popcorn, and newly tilled soil—as the wagon slowly rumbled along over the vacant field. And there they sat, contented with each other, talking about their respective backgrounds.

Toward the end of the long wagon ride, night had fallen and some couples were snuggling a bit, which made Anna very aware of how close she was sitting next to Gabe due to the press of the crowd. So close, she caught the spicy scent of his cologne and could almost feel his heart beating.

On the van ride back to Strasburg, Gabe was silent, and Anna mentally relived their time together today, including the hints he'd dropped, especially having asked if she had joined church back home. *That's very telling for any Plain girl.* She realized she was either on dangerous ground by continuing to help with Emmie and spend time with Gabe, or on the brink of an unforeseen path.

But these stirrings of affection could cloud her thinking, and she didn't want to miss God's will, not when Martin Nolt made better sense. Besides, she had never considered becoming Old Order Amish!

Gabe got out of the van and helped her down, holding her hand a little longer than necessary. "I hope you had a *wunnerbaargut* time, Anna," he said, walking her toward the house.

"I did," she admitted. "Hope you did, too."

"It was one of my best days," he said quietly, "in a very long time."

Since the passenger van was parked and waiting with passengers, she thanked him for suggesting the festival and reached for the screen door.

"Next time it's my treat," he said, grinning before he turned to go.

How can there be a next time? she thought, hurrying into the house.

Sadie couldn't help but notice Anna's unusual quiet as she came inside, and later, too, while they sat in the kitchen together. "Ain't my business, but if you'd like to talk 'bout anything, I'm here," she said.

Anna nodded. "I think I do need some advice." She paused and drew in an audible breath. "I felt something for Gabe today that I haven't felt for Mart," she said. "Actually, both Gabe and I felt it—I'm sure of it."

This confirmed what Sadie had been wondering, although Anna had shared with her before about Gabe's interest.

"It's just that I feel so at home with Gabe," Anna continued. *"Des gut, jah?"*

Anna fell silent for a moment. Then she said softly, "Can you tell me more about your beliefs, and your house-church meetings?"

Sadie smiled. "Well now, I'd be right happy to. . . ."

Chapter 44

F or as long as I can remember, our church youth have courted and married within our Amish district here," Great-aunt Joanna was telling Eliza at breakfast before she was to leave for the meetinghouse down the road.

"Same as my church back home," Eliza replied, spreading apple butter on her toast and glancing across the table at her aunt, wondering what she was getting at.

"Well, I'd be lax if I didn't tell ya that someone saw you talkin' with an Old Order fella at market yesterday."

Eliza's breathing stopped. She and Eb had been seen.

"This was a trusted cousin, so there's no doubt" came the sharp remark.

Should I fess up? Eliza wondered, trying not to fidget as she took a bite of her toast.

"Is the young man sweet on ya?"

"We're just friends."

"Ah, so you were acquainted with him before yesterday." It was a statement, but it sounded like a question.

"I met him when I first came here," Eliza admitted.

"Well, I hope you don't get any notions 'bout him. Your parents have laid down strict orders 'bout no Old Order fellas."

"*Jah*, but we're only friends," Eliza repeated, hoping her aunt would drop it. *Why'd Mamma send me here?* she wondered for the hundredth time. "Would ya like more Postum?" she asked, rising to get some for herself, needing to walk a bit, if only across the kitchen floor.

"I'll have a little more. *Denki*."

Eliza went over with the teakettle and poured more hot water in her aunt's cup, then went to get the jar of Postum.

"I want to believe ya," her aunt said, pursing her lips as she blew gently on her steaming mug.

Well then, please do, Eliza thought. "I'm not lookin' to marry an Old Order boy," she said at last, and meant it.

Three weeks passed, and Eb's letters showed up in the stone wall like clockwork on Tuesday afternoons. Eliza wrote to him, too, each time making excuses to her aunt that she wanted to go for a walk or offering to run an errand, always ending up at the wall.

One of those Tuesdays, Eliza spotted Nellie, her aunt's cousin and neighbor, riding past in her family buggy. This seemed peculiar, considering it was the time of day when most Amishwomen were cooking supper, but Eliza smiled and waved cordially all the same. *She's not seein' anything to report,* Eliza thought, watching as Nellie's buggy headed down the road. *Besides, there's nothing to tattle about!*

Tuesday, August 31, 1948

By the last Tuesday in August, the tone of Eb's letters began to change. He asked her to attend his Preaching service, and while he had written this casually before, there was a marked determination now.

"I can't miss going to the Beachy meetinghouse on the Lord's Day," she muttered to herself on the back porch, knowing she must go in and set the table for supper. *Old Order though she is, Aunt Joanna would be in the phone shanty calling my parents right away if I tried that.* But even worse was realizing that it would likely be the end of Eb's and her friendship.

Sitting there on one of the porch rockers, Eliza scribbled a few lines back to him at the bottom of his note, deciding to take it to the stone wall later tonight, even though she'd already left a note for today. *I cannot give him a speck of hope,* she mused, shaking her head.

Then, hearing her great-aunt calling to her, she slipped the note into her dress pocket and hurried inside.

She left the house right after she redded up the kitchen for her aunt, who was settling down with the Good Book. Eliza had said she was going for a walk and would be right back. Her aunt glanced at her over her eyeglasses, her brows raised, but said not a word.

"I won't be but a few minutes," Eliza said.

"All right, then."

Running toward the stone wall, Eliza hoped Joanna wouldn't contact Dat and Mamma, but she worried all the same.

At the stone wall, she was startled to see Eb standing behind the tall tree, the letter she'd placed there that afternoon in his hand.

"What're ya doin' here?" she asked.

He frowned. "How's that any way to greet your friend?"

"Just mighty surprised to see ya."

"Well, I got tied up workin' with my Dat and just now came lookin' for your note." He held it up. "I should be askin' what you're doing here twice in one day."

Now she smiled. "You're right." She handed him the note where she'd answered at the bottom.

He opened it, and seeing his own handwriting, he asked, "Are ya giving it back?"

"Look after you signed off."

"You wrote me a PS?" He grinned.

"I doubt you'll like it much," she said, moving closer to point out where she'd written her answer to his invitation.

He read it, folded it, and pushed it into his pants pocket. "I'm gonna be frank with ya." He paused. "We've been foolin' ourselves, Eliza. I like you as much more than a friend."

Her muscles tensed. And here she was, coming to end his romantic hopes.

"Truth is, I want to openly court ya," Eb said, "for all the People to see. But to do that, you'd have to join my church."

She should have guessed this. And hearing him talk so made her eyes well up. "I wish I could, but . . ."

He reached for her hand, and she stepped behind the tree with him, hidden from the road. "By now, you must know how I feel 'bout ya."

She nodded as he drew her slowly into his arms.

"I don't want to make trouble for ya," he whispered, holding her near. "Never."

"It's impossible for us to be together," she said, aware of the tenderness of his affection, her face against his chest. How she loved being wrapped in his embrace!

Ever so reluctantly, she stepped back. Eb looked at her with the dearest expression and, to her surprise, leaned forward to kiss her cheek.

Eliza's heart pounded, and in that moment, she remembered having told her aunt that she would be right back. "I'm sorry, but I can't stay," she said, telling him why.

Eb reached for her again.

"I must go." She shook her head. "I'm truly sorry."

"I'll write to you tonight an' leave it here for you tomorrow, okay?" he said.

How she longed to return to Eb's strong arms, to forget how sad she felt when they were apart. It was all she could think about, but she forced herself to walk away, lest her aunt come looking for her and Eliza be found out.

Chapter 45

A nna was hanging out the washing on the clothesline the following Monday when Marianna walked over to invite her to Preaching service this coming Sunday. Momentarily taken aback, Anna couldn't help but remember that it was also Gabe's church.

"A little birdie suggested I invite ya," Marianna said, running her fingers across her lips. "And for the fellowship meal afterward."

Was that bird Sadie? Anna wondered.

Still a bit startled, she said, "Well, I *do* attend my own church in Bird-in-Hand."

Marianna nodded. "I know, but I thought you might be interested in our bishop's approach to sermons. It's not like the majority of Old Order services."

"What are the differences?"

"Well, for one thing, our ministers use the Pennsylvania

Dutch Bible, 'specially the New Testament, for all the Scripture readings and sermons."

Anna was surprised. "How long have they done this?"

"Oh, a few years now." Marianna explained that the change had been prompted by the fact that their youth had not understood the readings from the German *Biewel*.

Anna pondered this, still not giving an answer.

"You can think about it," Marianna said with a smile. "Preachin' will be held at the farmhouse at Peaceful Meadows. I believe ya know the way."

It was obvious Marianna really wanted her to go.

"My car would stick out like a sore thumb," Anna offered as a rather weak excuse.

Marianna smiled again. "*Ach*, no need to worry. If ya don't want to ride with Sadie and Glen, Sadie and I will watch for ya, show ya where to line up with the other visitors and unbaptized youth in the back."

"I shouldn't promise," Anna said, still trying to fathom the possible reason for this unexpected invitation.

"If you're concerned 'bout fitting in with the womenfolk as far as dress and whatnot, I guarantee you will," Marianna said encouragingly. She waved and went back to the main farmhouse, her long dress swishing through the grass.

Intrigued, Anna's mind whirled at the prospect as she warmed up to the idea.

Maybe I should go, just this once. . . .

Anna enjoyed her Friday morning drive to Gabe and Emmie's house. All the autumn colors were competing for superiority; even shrubs that were ordinary-looking all year long were decorated in beautiful hues that dominated the scenery.

Today she had remembered to bring along an old blanket, which Sadie had gladly donated to "cozy up" Emmie's tree house. And because the weather was turning warmer than Anna had expected, she and Emmie only had to wear sweaters again, like last Friday.

Emmie had brought along a book of her own for Anna to read up high in the midst of the orange, leafy canopy. And looking at the front page of *My Bible Friends*, Anna noticed an inscription from Emmie's mother, who'd also written the date. Feeling a twinge of sadness again for Emmie, Anna quickly moved on to the first story and began to read.

When she had finished reading, Anna suggested they climb back down and have some sliced apples and popcorn. Emmie nodded, and they headed to the house.

Recalling the conversation with Gabe about her stovetop popcorn, Anna made enough for the three of them while telling Emmie more Bible stories from memory. The child's eyes brightened when hearing about little baby Moses being discovered in a basket in the bulrushes and adopted by Pharaoh's daughter. And Anna found her heart touched once more by this dear little girl without a mother.

Anna ended up taking her car to Gabe's uncle's farmhouse at Peaceful Meadows, where Preaching service was being held that Lord's Day morning. The round pen was especially quiet as she drove in to park, and fields of stubble where soybeans had been harvested caused her to think of her brother Wayne, who planted a big soybean crop of his own every spring. From thoughts of him, she began to ponder how Dat and Mamm would react to her attending an Old Order Amish Preaching service. *Would they be terribly upset?* She knew they would only want her to be baptized into the fellowship back home if she was ready to promise faithfulness to God and to the Beachy Amish church. *Yet how will I know for sure if I don't visit other churches?* she wondered.

Getting out of the car, she saw many buggies already parked and noticed Marianna and Sadie discreetly waving her over toward the line of women, children, and babies, all of them waiting to go into the temporary house of worship.

Little Emmie smiled broadly when she and her aunt Barbara spotted Anna. Then Marianna, holding Baby Jimmy, led Anna toward the back of the line. "I'll sit with ya during the fellowship meal following the service," she whispered.

Though Anna didn't quite know why, she felt unexpectedly emotional during the congregational singing, even though she wasn't familiar with the melody and didn't recognize all of the German words in the old hymnal, the *Ausbund*. Even so, there was something about the intense fervor with which the People sang the songs of the Anabaptist martyrs that tugged at her heartstrings.

There were two sermons, and the second one was based on Philippians chapter two, with an emphasis on verse eight: "'And being found in fashion as a man, he humbled himself, and became obedient unto death, even the death of the cross.'"

The middle-aged minister spoke of how Christ had demonstrated humility in order to prove his obedience to the Father. "Our Lord wasn't afraid to plead for the cup of suffering to be removed from Him, but when it became clear that His Father's plan required death upon a cross, Jesus was willing to be obedient, surrendering His will," the well-spoken preacher stated. "From this, we can see that meekness and obedience are essential in our own lives. Because without humility, we cannot have obedience, nor the other way around."

Anna thought about her predicament over Mart and Gabe in the context of this idea of surrender. Had she submitted her will fully to God's? She sighed, wanting to humble herself and spend even more time in prayer.

Listening more intently now, Anna was grateful for this inspired message from God's Word. Thankful, too, that she had come on this particular Sunday.

After the deacon's benediction, the womenfolk and children headed outdoors to the backyard—except the women assigned to help set out the light meal on the tables. Anna was happy to walk around following the three-hour-long service, unaccustomed to that, but as she recalled how little Emmie had sat so quietly without fidgeting, it didn't seem right to complain.

Barbara Mast waved and walked over with Emmie to suggest they go out to the calf pens to see the new calves. Three more of Barbara's young nieces came running just then, all of them hugging Emmie and surrounding her before they headed toward the pens. Anna went along, as well, and while they stood and admired one of the newest calves, Emmie slipped her hand into Anna's.

Smiling down at her, Anna wanted to lean over and hug her, but she settled for squeezing Emmie's hand.

"Well, just look at *you*," Barbara said, grinning at Anna, blue eyes sparkling.

Emmie's become very attached to me, thought Anna as she and Emmie ambled to the next calf pen, Emmie not letting go.

When Gabe came looking for Emmie, his eyes widened upon seeing Anna. But he did not comment as Emmie continued to cling to Anna's hand, walking in step with her. It was apparent that Gabe wanted to come over and talk with her, but this wasn't the time or the place.

Hours later, after the fellowship meal, where Sadie and Marianna introduced her to dozens of welcoming womenfolk, Anna returned home, her heart warm but feeling ever more conflicted.

Sadie waited till Anna had slipped over next door to help Marianna with the little ones that afternoon before she went to sit in the front room with Glen. "I've been thinking 'bout this for a while now," she began, mentioning having seen Gabe looking at Anna before the fellowship meal. "And today, we were all out admiring the calvies, but it was as if Gabe wasn't seein' anyone or anything but Anna."

Glen smiled her way. "You'd like the two of them to get together, I'm a-thinkin'."

"Ain't so much that . . . although it would be right nice." She went on to tell Glen that Emmie had been holding Anna's hand.

"Well, the man's not gonna just choose a mother figure for his little girl, remember," Glen said. "Not the Gabe I know."

"*Nee.*"

"He's *schmaert* and wise, too. He'll marry for love, pure and simple."

"*Jah*, true," Sadie said, pondering this. "Anna's parents might need to meet Gabe at some point, if he starts spending more time alone with her."

"Might be just what's needed." Glen reached for his copy of *Die Botschaft* and flipped through the pages to an article he had been reading earlier. "Come to think of it, Alvin Beachy reads this periodical, too. He told me so last time they were here, round Christmas."

"Well, how 'bout that." Sadie perked up.

"We discussed how the scribes from here in Lancaster County and the ones there in Mifflinburg write similar things in their columns. Least it seemed like that to us."

Sadie caught herself nodding in agreement. "There's really only a small difference 'tween their church district an' ours, as I see it."

"Aside from the cars and electric, which is big!" Glen added.

She thought on that, realizing how readily Anna had acclimated herself to living without electric lights and other conveniences here in their home. *Of course, Anna's car might be a big hurdle. . . .*

But Sadie was getting way ahead of herself.

Chapter 46

TUESDAY, AUGUST 31, 1948

E liza's great-aunt was sitting out on the back porch as
Eliza scurried up the steps.

"You were gone longer than you said," her aunt stated.

"I'm sorry . . . forgot the time."

Nodding slowly, her aunt fixed her gaze on Eliza. "I s'pose
you went to meet your so-called *friend*."

Eliza gulped and reached for the handrail.

"The Lord despises deceitfulness."

Eliza wondered how on earth she knew about the chance
meeting with Eb.

"I walked up to where I suspected you were. And for pity's
sake, such goin's on, and right out where anyone could see,"
her aunt said.

Eliza hung her head in shame. Being with Eb like that had

306

thrilled her at first, but terrified her now that she pondered it. "I just want to go home to my family," she pleaded, her voice breaking. "I *need* to go home!"

"*Gut* thing, 'cause I went and phoned your parents." Her aunt mentioned how she'd hobbled out to the little shanty to make the call. "I've just gotten back, in fact."

Eliza couldn't bear to stand there and have her wrongdoings recited, not now. "I best be going to my room," she murmured, excusing herself.

"Your parents will fetch ya in the mornin'" were the last words Eliza heard as she reached for the screen door and stumbled inside.

Falling across the bed, Eliza wept bitterly in this room that had been hers since mid-May. Three and a half months of venturing onto a path of friendship with Eb Lapp had led to this. Such joy . . . and now, such sadness.

Eliza wept for her trickery against Great-aunt Joanna, and her parents, too. And she realized that her poor choices proved she was too young to make a decision about anything so serious as love.

No, she must leave here willingly and set him free to court a girl amongst his own People. That would also spare her parents and her family the heartache she herself was suffering this night.

Thinking of it now, Eliza wished she had told Eb not to waste time writing another letter. All the same, he wouldn't have understood.

Eb has no inkling he'll never see me again. With that thought, she rolled over onto the pillow to muffle her moans.

Eliza sat in the back seat of her father's car as he drove her away from Strasburg the next morning, past Yost and Nellie

Petersheim's farm, where she'd gone to purchase eggs so many times, and past Eb's parents' home farther up the road.

She stared out the window and wondered what the point was of having a friendship, forbidden as it was, with Ebenezer. In the end, what purpose had it served?

She shook her head as big tears rolled down her cheeks.

Chapter 47

Anna was occupied with several tours on Monday, but between clients, she contemplated yesterday's Old Order Preaching service and Gabe and Emmie's obvious affection for her. How was she going to handle that when pulling back now might break little Emmie's heart? And what about Gabe's heart?

Each workday that week, Anna's thoughts revolved around her own growing friendship with Gabe that had started so innocently and now was at the place where he was showing constant interest in her.

Thursday, between tours, Mart mentioned that he would be busy the next two weekends helping with the harvest and filling silo. He really didn't have to tell her this, since they didn't have a standing Friday-night date. But the thought crossed her mind that he must care about her at least a little to make a point of letting her know.

But who do I care for more?

On Friday morning, while Anna helped Sadie make breakfast before she left to see Emmie, she brought up the differences in her church and their own. "I've often wondered why churches differ in the focus of their preaching or what's allowed, when really, our Lord and Savior loves all of His children equally. We're all called into His family and fellowship," she said.

"*Jah*, folk can tend to get hung up on one thing or another."

Anna nodded as she mixed the eggs with a hand beater. "I've begun to realize, just since coming to Strasburg, that there are more similarities between the Anabaptist churches than I ever expected."

"And when all's said and done," Sadie replied, "does it matter how long the Preachin' service lasts, or if the People sit on comfortable pews or hard, backless benches, or even some doctrinal differences? I daresay things like that don't matter to our heavenly Father."

But they matter to my parents, Anna thought.

All the same, she understood what Sadie was saying. "Yet what about the churches that put such an emphasis on works and good deeds, and not as much on grace? All my life, I've heard that Old Order Amish set their church ordinance high, but after visiting your church, I see that not every district is alike." Anna realized that by asking this she might be signaling an interest in their church.

"Well, we're blessed with a devout bishop who reads and studies the Bible, including the book of Romans. He says that works should be a sign of what's inside one's heart. After all, without God's grace, where would we be?" Sadie said, pouring coffee.

Anna listened, shocked that Sadie was stating exactly what she had been raised to believe.

"So, *jah*, I can tell you that we're saved by grace through faith in Jesus Christ," Sadie stated without blinking an eye, "but I don't make a point of boasting 'bout it. I want to continue bein' Amish, as well as a witness of grace amongst the People. There've been a few who've wanted to discuss this with me, and some have received the gift of salvation as a result."

Anna sat quietly, soaking in every word.

Later that morning, Anna made sugar cookies with little Emmie while Gabe worked at installing a tree house for a neighbor. Just as Anna was taking the second batch out of the oven, Barbara and her older sister Leona dropped by, and the four of them sat and ate the soft, warm cookies together.

Anna had the slightly unsettling sense that Barbara had brought Leona along to get acquainted with her and possibly evaluate if she was up to their expectations for their former brother-in-law. Judging from the woman's enjoyment of her cookies and their time together, Leona seemed inclined to like her.

A few minutes before Anna was scheduled to leave, Gabe returned and asked her to walk to his workshop with him while Emmie and her aunts remained in the house. "I'm curious to know what you thought about last Sunday's Preaching," he said.

"Honestly, I was a little surprised how much I enjoyed it, especially the old German hymns and the second sermon."

Gabe smiled as they walked across the backyard toward his large woodworking shop. He opened the door and waited till she stepped inside.

"Oh . . . I've always liked the smell of sawdust," she said, wondering what he wanted to tell her.

"That's another *gut* sign," he said, looking more serious now. *He's looking for a sign?*

311

Pulling up a chair for her, Gabe then sat near his desk, surrounded by sawhorses, a lathe that ran on an air compressor, and other types of woodworking equipment. "This might come as a surprise," he began, "but you've been on my mind all week, Anna. And I felt bad that I couldn't talk with ya before you left Sunday after the common meal, but that's our way—men with men, women with women and children."

She listened attentively, discerning from his expression that he was about to say something significant.

He leaned back in the chair, eyes searching hers. "Anna, spendin' time with you has changed my outlook on many things." He drew a deep breath. "I've been praying, too, about our friendship . . . lookin' forward to learning more about you, your interests . . . your family. Everything."

Anna was touched by his words and his kindness.

"This must seem sudden," he said softly. "And for that I apologize, but I mean all I've said. You see, I'd like to get to know you better, Anna. I've been drawn to ya since the first day we met," he admitted.

She recalled that particular day, surprised that it had also remained significant in her memory. "I experienced a heartbreak once," Anna told him. "I've been putting up walls ever since."

His eyes were soft. "I can promise you that I would never hurt ya that way," he said. "And our Lord and Savior would be at the center of our relationship, wherever it may lead." He paused. "Wherever *He* may lead."

She told him how much she appreciated his kindness and consideration, but still she held back.

He smiled thoughtfully. "I'll wait for your answer and not bring it up again."

She was touched deeply by his considerate way with her. *Gabe wants to court me,* she thought.

"I'll walk ya to your car," he said, going to open the door to his shop.

Across the yard, Emmie was sitting where she always sat on Friday mornings when Anna arrived, on the back steps with her tomcat, Bootsie. Emmie waved, then returned to playing with her cat.

Anna wondered if Emmie could sense something between them. *Likely not, she's so young . . .*

Gabe opened the car door and waited till Anna was inside, then closed it, standing near with a look of expectation on his handsome face.

"So long," she mouthed.

And while driving back to Flauds', tears of happiness—and confusion—welled up.

That evening, after supper with Glen and Sadie, Anna went to her room and spent time reading her Bible, searching the Scriptures and her own heart, too. "Not my will, but Thine be done," she prayed, her heart ever so tender toward God.

Upon pulling in to the information center's parking lot after her last tour Wednesday afternoon, Anna listened to a voice message on her phone from Wanita, left at two o'clock. *Three hours ago,* she thought, sitting in her car in the parking lot.

She called her back, they exchanged greetings, and Wanita jumped right in, saying, "I didn't want to leave a sad message on your phone."

Anna braced herself. "I hope it's not any worse than just sad news."

There was a pause, and her sister said, "I hate to be the one to tell ya, but Mamm said it should be me." Wanita sighed into the phone. "Mammi Eliza passed away during her nap this morning."

"Ooh . . ." Anna hadn't expected this, not yet.

"The funeral will be this Saturday morning."

"I'll leave for home tomorrow evening after work," Anna said, suddenly not feeling up to talking any longer. "Thank you for caring for her so well, Wanita. . . . I love you. See you soon."

"I'm very sorry, Anna," Wanita said. "She loved ya so."

They said a tearful good-bye, and Anna put away her phone.

"Dear Lord Jesus, be ever near my family," Anna whispered before starting the car and leaving the parking lot. It wouldn't be easy to go to work tomorrow, but she would be home again soon. *Saying my last farewells to dearest Mammi.*

Later, while turning in to the Flauds' treed lane, Anna noticed how pretty the leaves looked with the afternoon sun low in the sky, casting a certain special glow.

Like Mammi's own beautiful spirit, she thought.

Anna had a few minutes the next morning to tell Mart that she was heading to Mifflinburg for Mammi Eliza's viewing and funeral this weekend. He was very kind and asked if there was anything he could do. Other co-workers also offered their condolences, as did Evelyn.

Getting in her car, Anna called and left a message for Gabe at the phone shanty, telling him the news and that she'd be unable to spend time with Emmie tomorrow. The drive home gave Anna a time for reflection on her years with Mammi Eliza. *I have so few regrets,* she thought, recalling what her Mammi had often said, that regrets were a waste of time. *And to think how happy and content Mammi was in her marriage all those years to*

Dawdi John, she thought, believing that her grandmother had followed God's plan for her life.

After the funeral, where hundreds of people were in attendance, Anna walked with her mother and Wanita to the burial service, saying how sorry she was for unknowingly choosing to spend Mammi's final months far away, her one real regret. Wanita reassured her that Mammi Eliza hadn't noticed, and Mamm said it was a blessing for Mammi to finally have the burden of Alzheimer's lifted. "She's with the Lord now."

The family dinner had been prepared by the womenfolk of the church and was held in the basement of the meetinghouse. And while it was a sad time, Anna was thankful for this opportunity to have fellowship with her married brothers and their families, and Wanita and Conrad and children, all of them in the same place at the same time. *Funerals are like that,* she thought, *bringing families together to lovingly reminisce . . . and to rejoice in the life of a dear one.*

Anna decided to stay overnight for Sunday worship with Dat and Mamm and her siblings. And even though Mammi Eliza hadn't been able to attend church herself in the past year or so, Anna was still very aware of her absence. Her passing left an enormous hole, yet somehow, heaven seemed all the more near on this day.

Chapter 48

Sunday afternoon, Anna drove back to Strasburg following the fellowship meal, grateful for Mammi Eliza's life and that she had been such a godly influence on all who knew her. After quickly unpacking her few things, Anna told Sadie that she was going out for a while.

"I know you're feelin' awful sad," Sadie said, a look of loving concern on her face.

Anna nodded. "The realization Mammi's gone hasn't hit me fully, but she's very much on my heart."

"Well, of course she is." Sadie went on to say that she was keeping Anna in her prayers.

"There are other things on my mind, too, as you know," Anna admitted. "I'm in a deep quandary." She paused and swallowed hard. "For one thing, Mamm wasn't too pleased with me after I told her more about Gabe while I was home. And she wasn't all that interested in my friendship with Emmie, either. She kept asking about Mart, wondering if we were regularly

dating yet, and given the circumstance of Mammi Eliza's passing, I didn't know how to tell her what I was feeling for Gabe."

Sadie was quick to nod her head, although her expression
was filled with questions.

"Like Mammi, I don't want to have any regrets at the end
of my life," Anna said, thinking again that, from a practical
standpoint, Mart was the only real choice. Yet when she was
honest with herself, she felt only a friendship and an admiration
toward him—a far cry from what she felt for Gabe.

"Regrets can't change the past, and worry can't alter the
future," Sadie said as they walked out to the little porch, where
she stood till Anna pulled out of the driveway.

*I don't want my parents to regret giving their blessing for me to
come here, either,* Anna thought while driving the now-familiar
backroads of Strasburg.

She soaked up the autumn landscape, her prayers less plead-
ings for wisdom and more about gratitude for Mammi's long and
happy life of service to God and others, and for the daily blessings Anna enjoyed from the Lord's hand. Blessings of salvation
and mercy, health and employment, family and friends, too.
And she was thankful for both Mart's and Gabe's kindnesses
toward her . . . and for each man's devotion to Christ.

As she drove, she came upon a wide shoulder on the road
and parked her car. Getting out to walk, she decided to offer
only thankful prayers as she went. Large flocks of birds circled
high above her, then rushed en masse toward the west, where
wispy white clouds moved slowly this way. Anna noticed a hawk
preening atop a tall martin birdhouse in someone's yard, and
a wild turkey dashed across a meadow toward a large pond on
this side of the road. An old stone wall was set apart from the
farmhouses surrounding it, and Anna suddenly realized she
had been walking near a long, dense row of black walnut trees.

Glancing between their furrowed dark trunks, she realized that she had driven past this stone wall quite some time ago.

Moving closer to the trees, she clung to happy thoughts of Mammi Eliza, embracing Mammi's rambling thoughts about Strasburg, stone walls, and a beau. The setting suddenly seemed more meaningful with Mammi having passed on, and in that moment, Anna wondered if she would ever know more about her grandmother's Strasburg love story.

She sank down in the cool grass, enjoying the unusually mild temperature and the occasional breeze as she wrestled with her keen interest in Gabe. It would mean changing her lifestyle if she were to agree to let him court her . . . and if their relationship were to eventually lead to marriage.

She closed her eyes, pondering the kind of life she would live as Gabe's wife. "Very much like the one I'm living with Glen and Sadie," she murmured, wondering if that relationship and her willingness to live in an Old Order home was partly why Gabe had been drawn to her.

"Lord, I've prayed so often about this," she whispered. "Disappointing Mamm and Dat is out of the question." She sighed, remembering her mother's frown when they'd talked earlier that day. "Please make the way clear to me," Anna prayed.

That night, when she dreamed, it was of Gabe, and when she awakened, she brushed the dream aside. *He's always in my thoughts, Lord. What am I to do?*

Monday morning, once the washing was pinned to the line and Anna had left for work, Sadie felt compelled to discuss something with Glen. She'd waited till he came in for his midmorning coffee, and by then she knew exactly what she wanted to say.

"What would ya think if I gave Rachel Beachy a call?" she asked while pouring his coffee.

Glen's eyebrows rose as he sat at the table. "Funny thing, I was thinkin' of suggesting it."

"Really, now?"

He nodded. "Gabe's qualities are second to none, and if he's as interested in Anna as you seem to think, there should be nothin' holding him back from pursuing her."

"Well, Anna's parents might disagree." Sadie sighed. "But I'm hoping Rachel might listen to me. We've been friends as well as cousins all these many years."

"That's a good place to start," Glen said.

"So do I have your blessing?" she asked, bringing his coffee mug over and setting it down before him.

Glen nodded as he reached for his coffee. "It can't hurt . . . and it might help."

"I chust don't want to stick my nose in."

Glen smiled wryly. "Oh, I think ya *do*, dear. And to tell the truth, I'm all for it."

She grinned, and when Glen headed back out to the turkey barn, Sadie made her way to the phone shanty, praying silently for the right words.

The next four days, Anna pondered Gabe's invitation while trying to keep her attention on her work. It was all she could do during her tours not to take note of one Old Order Amish farm after another, one mule team out harvesting, one horse and buggy, and more. In fact, everywhere she turned, there seemed to be Old Order folk working and living their beautiful, simple lives. And even though this was nothing new, it somehow seemed that their way of life was calling to her. *Do I crave a more humble life?* she wondered. *Is that the draw for me?*

Anna realized she was also either thinking about Gabe or praying for him several times a day now. Well, not *for* him, but rather how she could justify continuing her time with little Emmie on Fridays while aware of her strong feelings for Gabe . . . and his for her. Was it right when their relationship seemed like a dead-end street, especially where her parents were concerned?

Thursday after work, Anna stopped at the Strasburg Market Place for Sadie, as she sometimes did, and saw Gabe rushing across the parking lot to assist an elderly man who'd dropped his bag of groceries. Cans were rolling everywhere, and the man had dropped his cane.

Immediately, Gabe took the man's arm, led him to his car, and helped him inside. Then, Gabe ran back to gather up the scattered grocery items and the cane and brought them to the man. Gabe crouched at the car window and talked with the now-smiling man for a few moments, undoubtedly to see that he was all right.

Anna brushed tears from her face, her heart beating for Gabe—a wonderful man, and she realized how terribly sad she would feel to walk away from him. *I'd always regret not accepting his offer to court—to see where things might lead*, she thought, reaching for her purse and grocery list. Unfortunately, however, she still had no idea how to get her parents to understand her romantic interest in an Old Order Amishman.

The very thing they feared . . .

The next afternoon was cold—the wind shrieked down the chimney—and thus an ideal day to stay indoors and sew with Sadie once Anna returned from spending time with Emmie. Anna stood very still on a stool as Sadie marked the hem of her new plum-colored dress, one she'd needed for a while now.

"I'm praying about possibly accepting Gabe's offer to explore a relationship," Anna confided. "But first I should try to resolve my parents' concerns about his church—well, your church."

"Truth be told, I'm glad we're talking 'bout this. You see, I went out on a limb," Sadie said, asking her to turn slowly. "I called your Mamm."

Anna was surprised. "You did?"

Nodding, Sadie admitted, "I talked with her for quite a while about many things, including our church district."

Anna listened, relieved. "I hope it helped."

"I believe it did," Sadie replied. "She said she was surprised at how much grace and mercy there seems to be here."

Anna smiled. "I noticed it right away with you and Glen."

"Turn again," Sadie said, double-checking the hem. "I also happened to put in a few words about what an exceptionally fine man Gabe is." She glanced up at Anna's face and gave her a wink.

"He certainly is," Anna agreed.

"Your Mamm indicated that you have the right to choose who you want to date."

Anna was stunned. *Yet even if Mamm and Dat won't stand in my way, I still have to decide for myself*, Anna thought, stepping down from the stool.

She headed to her room and carefully removed her dress, ready to stitch up the hem, and went to get her pincushion and needle and thread. She felt an invisible yet very real burden lift from her shoulders.

All the same, Anna struggled with the idea of living a traditionally Plain life, if it should come to that. For now, it was enough that thoughtful and caring Sadie had paved the way for her to be courted by Gabe.

Chapter 49

———— ❧ ————

Anna spent the following Saturday thinking about Mammi Eliza and all that she had meant to her and to their family. The afternoon was clear and mild, a good day for walking and praying.

She drove back over to the stone wall where she'd gone after Mammi's funeral last weekend, and after a time, found herself searching, yet again, for a large discolored stone.

Scanning the stones in the wall once more, Anna shook her head, realizing it was a long shot. How could she ever find the spot where Mammi Eliza and her beloved had met?

Even so, she sat in the grass and leaned back, resting her hands on the ground, surprised she'd come here again.

What is compelling me?

Below her palms, she felt a smooth surface, and she turned to see a large smoothed-off tree stump, sunken into the ground so far that it was nearly concealed.

Anna recalled Mammi's writing about a lone, tall pin oak

tree near the stone wall. "Could this be the place?" she whispered with a shiver of excitement. *If this was the tree.*

Surely not. And yet, there was something about it, something she could only describe as a feeling, as if she had been *led* there.

She looked toward the stone wall a few yards away and wondered where Mammi's Amish beau might have hidden his letters to her—if this was, indeed, the spot. She remembered the description in Mammi's diary.

Search for the crevice under the large stone. . . .

Her heart sped up as she rose to walk to the stone wall, where she examined the structure of white and gray rocks. She eyed it for an especially large, dark gray stone, assuming that the years of exposure might have discolored many of the stones there.

She walked toward the north, then turned back to the south, wondering what Mammi would think if she were still alive and knew where Anna was—and what she was doing.

At last, she noticed a very large gray stone, one she'd somehow missed, and she leaned down to scrutinize it. She cupped her face in her hands, dazed, and for the longest time she simply stared at the spot.

Finally, she found the courage to inch forward, trying to walk in Mammi's shoes, so to speak. Placing her fingers into the slight hole, Anna felt around and was astonished when she bumped something thick and folded up. She pulled whatever it was out of the sunken gap and laid eyes on a very weathered gray doubled-up envelope.

Brushing off the dust, she read the words *To Eliza Hertzler.*

"What on earth?" she whispered, stunned to see Mammi's maiden name.

Anna hurried back to the Flauds' and rushed into the house, finding Sadie in the front room reading the newspaper.

Anna placed the letter next to Sadie on the settee. "You're not going to believe this."

Sadie picked up the brittle envelope and looked at Anna with wonderment.

"It's a letter to Mammi Eliza!"

Sadie's mouth dropped open as she examined the old envelope. Their eyes met and held.

"Aren't ya gonna read it?" asked Sadie, her voice soft.

"Looks like it might fall apart," Anna said as Sadie handed her the envelope.

"Do you think your Mammi knew it was there?"

"I don't know." Anna shook her head and exhaled. "Either way . . . it's been there for seventy years." She held the letter gingerly. "Honestly, I wish Mammi had lived long enough to know I found it."

"What's it matter?" Sadie replied, patting the spot on the settee for Anna to sit. "Eliza moved on with her life and met and married your Dawdi John, a fine and godly man."

Anna nodded. "You're absolutely right."

"You oughta read it, dear," Sadie encouraged. "You might have more to tell your family, ya know."

Anna excused herself and headed to the woods, choosing the medium-hard trail and glancing above at the glints of sunlight filtering down through the dense trees still leafed out here and there with brilliance. *Like Joseph's coat of many colors.*

At the tree house, she climbed the custom-made staircase all the way to the highest level and sat there looking out at nature's awning all around her. The old envelope was safely tucked into her pocket, and after a time, Anna carefully opened it and began to read the faded words:

My dearest Eliza,

Even though I haven't known you long, I'm certain that God brought us together as friends for a special reason. Jah, I realize we've talked about our different church backgrounds, and you've never wavered about your Beachy home church in Mifflinburg. I understand that.

But I love you, Eliza, and I don't want to say good-bye. So, what if I left my Old Order community and joined yours so we can be together?

Since I haven't joined church yet, I wouldn't be shunned. Will you please think about this?

With all my love,
Eb Lapp

"Goodness. He must've loved her a lot to suggest such a thing," Anna murmured, staring at the faded words. *And Mammi must've left Strasburg before she found this. . . .*

As she tried to absorb what she'd read, Anna was touched by Eb's willingness to give up his Old Order life to be with Mammi Eliza. And surprisingly, she found a sense of direction in the realization.

She held the letter and reread it, realizing that if her grandmother had received it back so many years ago, these words might have changed the course of her life. "And I never would have been born," she murmured, sobered at the thought.

The letter spoke to her from the past, in a way Eb never could have anticipated. The young man couldn't possibly have known what kind of struggles Eliza's own granddaughter would be facing all these many years later . . . or that his words, though penned for his beloved, would have the power to touch a stranger so deeply!

That evening, Anna wasted no time in writing a letter to her parents. She addressed the issue of how startling it had been to find the old letter from Mammi's long-ago beau. *I believe it's a confirmation of what I've decided to do about Gabe's invitation to court,* she wrote, promising to bring the letter home the next time she visited.

The following evening, after a brilliant Lord's Day morning and afternoon, Anna decided to call Gabe at the number on the business card he'd given her that first day they'd met.

"Hullo?" Gabe answered on the first ring.

"Gabe, it's Anna Beachy."

"Well, how nice to hear from you! Emmie and I are sitting here in the phone shanty while I check my voice messages. What can I do for ya?"

She apologized for giving him such short notice. "If it suits, could I drop by to see you in a little while? I wouldn't stay long."

"That's just fine. Drive carefully, Anna." It was as if he was saying *dear Anna,* he sounded so pleased.

When Anna arrived, little Emmie was wearing her nightclothes and a pale blue bathrobe, sitting in the kitchen with her father.

"I let her stay up to see ya and said maybe you would tuck her in, too." Gabe's eyes shone with affection.

"Did ya visit your Aendi Barbara today?" Anna asked Emmie. She smiled and went to get her doll from upstairs.

Anna wondered if now was a good time to talk to Gabe. "I

honestly don't know how to tell you this," she said. "But I must say that our Lord sometimes works in the strangest ways." Her voice broke, and she could not speak for a moment.

"Anna? What is it?"

She paused and searched his face. "What are you hoping I'll say?"

"That you belong here . . . with my People," he said. "With *me*."

She placed her hand on her chest and breathed several times. "Well then, I'm ready to accept your invitation to court."

Gabe's face broke into a smile, and as she rose from her chair, he got up from his seat and came over to her. "Thank the dear Lord! This is a *wunnerbaar* answer to my prayers," he said, reaching for her hands. The only sound in the kitchen was the *tick-tock-tick* of the wall clock and Bootsie's rumbling purr beneath the table. "I couldn't be happier, Anna," he whispered.

The sound of Emmie's muffled footsteps was on the stairs, and Gabe and Anna stepped apart, still beaming at each other.

Anna turned to sit down, an all-encompassing peace flowing over her. *I've never felt more certain about anything,* she thought.

Emmie made a beeline to Anna and placed her dolly on her lap, standing next to Anna's knee.

Gabe crouched near, on the other side of Anna's chair. "We're going to be seein' Anna more often now, honey," he told Emmie, whose eyes sparkled with delight.

Anna nodded. "That's right." She reached to stroke the top of Emmie's head, her golden hair in long braids. "And I'm looking forward to that."

After some ice cream, Anna tucked Emmie into bed and prayed the Lord's Prayer aloud, wondering what bedtime rituals her mother may have had.

"Sweet dreams, Emmie," she said, standing in the doorway. Emmie grinned up at her, looking adorable with her pretty quilt tucked under her chin, her doll's little head sticking out of the covers next to her.

"*Gut Nacht*, sweetie," Anna whispered, leaving the door open just more than a crack, her heart filled with plentiful joy.

Downstairs, Anna was surprised to see Gabe making coffee. "I really shouldn't be out too late," she said, eyeing the mug he'd placed on the table for her. "And coffee keeps me awake at night if I drink it after noon . . . very sorry."

"Well, I have decaf, too, and tea and hot cocoa," he said, opening a cupboard and showing her the options. "At least you'll have something to sip on while we talk." It did her heart good to see how happy he was as he puttered around the kitchen.

"Decaf coffee's perfect. *Denki*." She sat down at the table as he insisted on serving her, bringing the teakettle over and pouring the hot water into her cup, making instant decaf coffee. "I'm afraid you're spoiling me," she said, scooting her chair closer.

"I've become very familiar with this kitchen these past couple of years," he said. "But I'm not a very *gut* cook, which is why Barbara has us over for meals. I *do* know how to make oatmeal and pour cold milk over cereal, though." He chuckled.

She smiled as he sat down with his own cup at the head of the table.

Gabe began to mention all the places he wanted to take her during their time together, including, should the Lord lead, to meet his parents and siblings in Indiana, too, which opened the door for Anna to say she wanted him to meet her parents at some point, as well.

Gabe also brought up that he'd already talked with his bishop to discuss what would be expected from Anna before they could court properly, within the ordinance of the church.

She listened intently, watching his face, the way his eyes

shone . . . his beautiful blond hair. *What a handsome man God handpicked for me*, she thought.

"Imagine my surprise when Bishop said that, since you have an Anabaptist upbringing, he would give us the go-ahead to court before you join my church."

Pleased, she told him how much she looked forward to all that was ahead, even though she knew it held its own set of challenges. "What about my car?" she asked, fairly certain what he would say.

"Before ya start baptismal classes next spring, you'll want to sell it."

He didn't say need to, she thought with a smile. "It might happen before then," she said, wanting him to know she was fully on board with everything that would be expected of her.

"That can all be worked out in time, along with other things you'll learn." He revealed that one of their preachers let it be known that the hardest thing he ever gave up to join church was his wheels.

They laughed about that, and she asked Gabe if he had ever driven a car.

A mischievous smile skittered across his face. "I really shouldn't have, not havin' any training. But one of my cousins went a little wild durin' his *Rumschpringe* and bought a car, and he let me drive it out on the backroads a couple times."

"Why was that?" she asked, fairly amused.

"Oh, he wanted me to experience what I would miss out on when I was baptized, and I went along with it for a while." Gabe glanced toward the ceiling. "But ya know, it made me realize how settled I was . . . content to be Amish."

"I understand what contentment feels like now," she said, thinking she could sit for hours like this, enjoying Gabe's company.

Then, noticing the time on the wall clock, she thanked him for the ice cream and the decaf coffee, as well as the "best evening ever."

The strong smell of a neighbor's bonfire of leaves filled the air as Gabe walked with Anna outside, where he reached quickly for her hand. His large flashlight lit the way to her car. "Why don't ya join Emmie and me at Barbara's for supper Saturday night—a little celebration," he suggested.

"Okay, if it's not a surprise to Barbara."

"*Puh!* One more person at her table won't matter, but *jah*, I'll let her know."

On the drive to Flauds', Anna caught herself singing one of the hymns from her Beachy Amish church, knowing that soon she would be learning the German hymns at Gabe's. And also to hitch up a horse to a carriage.

Staying with Glen and Sadie has been good preparation for dating a traditional Amishman and possibly becoming his bride, Lord willing.

She thought just then of Heidi and Eleanor and the other youth at her present church, knowing she would miss them, but she remembered Heidi's promise of enduring friendship. *I may need someone to talk to along the journey,* Anna thought, thinking ahead to the process of embracing the Old Ways.

Chapter 50

───────────── ✺ ─────────────

At work on Monday, Anna's first clients were three young women from Philly having a friends' day out. Anna took them to some of her favorite spots, including Riehl's Quilts and Crafts in Leola, where all three purchased quilted potholders, oven mitts, and spiced hot mats. One of them even ordered a queen-sized Mariners Star quilt to be shipped to her home. Anna couldn't help but grin at how much fun they were having.

Between the first and second tours, there was time for her to sit down for coffee with Mart in the break room. He was full of stories about his recent travels and mentioned wanting to talk to her, hinting that he enjoyed their relationship as good friends. Anna felt this was her moment to tell him about her decision about Gabe.

Surprisingly, Mart didn't react at all the way she thought he might. But he did indicate that he had been trusting God for guidance and said he'd guessed for some time now that she was quite taken with Gabe and his daughter.

Thankfully, they seemed to be in mutual agreement, and the conversation wasn't difficult for either of them. Mart suggested they continue to pray for the Lord to lead them each individually, and Anna agreed wholeheartedly.

After Tuesday breakfast, Sadie donned her warmest sweater and walked with Glen out to the tree house, enjoying the unseasonably warm autumn weather. Many squirrels skittered about, gathering acorns for the winter, and a little red fox could be seen near a tree, seemingly oblivious to them.

"The woodland creatures know winter's a-comin'," Glen said, smiling at Sadie.

"And before we know it, next fall will roll around again," she said, sharing a little about Anna's recent conversation with her.

"So ya think there might be a wedding come a year from now?" he asked.

"Well, young folk don't wait long once they know they've found the one. And being Gabe's a widower, I expect they'll marry as soon as she's baptized."

"Then we've got us a year with Anna, if that." Glen coughed a little, and Sadie looked at him, asking if he was all right. "*Jah*, just choked up, I guess."

"Aw . . . that's sweet," she said, leaning her head against him as they stopped to embrace beneath the colorful remnants of God's leafy shelter overhead. "I just hope Anna's parents are truly okay with her choice."

He looked down at Sadie quizzically. "At least I know for certain that I made a *wunnerbaar-gut* choice in you, Sadie, dear."

She smiled and snuggled in for another hug.

During the Saturday supper at Masts', Anna learned even more about Barbara and Aden, as well as their sons, Jesse and Chris. She felt especially relaxed this time and once again appreciated Gabe's good humor and his patience when seven-year-old Chris spilled his milk all over right next to Gabe. Barbara also seemed unfazed by this, despite the fact that Chris's older brother burst out with a snicker.

Although Gabe didn't announce it, Anna sensed that Aden and Barbara were aware of her and Gabe's romantic interest in each other. For one thing, they offered to babysit for Emmie. "Any time ya need us," Barbara said, that gleam in her eye. It was almost as if she had been not-so-secretly wanting this to happen.

Later, Anna returned on foot with Gabe and Emmie back to their house, and Emmie headed upstairs to dress for bed. Once she was tucked in by both Gabe and Anna, Gabe suggested they say the Lord's Prayer together. Emmie closed her eyes and folded her hands as they prayed. It was a tender time with the dear little girl who would most likely become her stepdaughter someday. *Lord willing*, thought Anna.

Downstairs, as they were alone in the front room, Gabe asked Anna what had made up her mind to allow him to court her.

"Honestly, I prayed for a definite sign," she said as they sat together on his couch. She told about her Mammi's confused remarks about a stone wall somewhere in Strasburg. "At first I found it frustrating, because I wasn't sure how much was reality rather than maybe a faulty memory. But then I found an old diary of hers that convinced me it was real, so I spent some of my time searchin' for the wall." She gave him a little smile. "That probably sounds a little silly, but I really wanted to see with my own eyes the place that used to be so important to my Mammi Eliza. And apparently, it was a hiding place for love letters from her Old Order beau."

Gabe's eyes widened, and he frowned as if puzzled. "What're ya sayin'?"

Anna explained that, seven decades ago, her Mammi had come to Strasburg for the summer to assist a great-aunt. "While she was here, she met an Old Order fellow, and they exchanged letters using a hiding spot in a stone wall." She shook her head. "And . . . I know it sounds incredible, but I found the wall . . . and discovered one unopened letter that'd evidently been left behind."

"Do ya know who wrote it?"

"It was signed by someone named Eb Lapp." She paused, wondering what Gabe thought of all this. "Unfortunately Eb's not a name I've heard round here."

There was a weighty pause, and then Gabe said slowly, "I know an Eb Lapp. He's up in years, though, so I'm not sure he'd remember much 'bout this."

Anna's eyes widened. "What do you mean?"

Reaching for her hand, Gabe said, "Eb is my grandfather's nickname. Ebenezer Lapp."

She stared at him. "You can't be serious!"

"Oh, it's mighty true."

"So . . . *your* Dawdi was in love with my Mammi?" Anna felt so shocked, it was hard to get the words out.

Gabe nodded, looking as surprised as she felt. "Through the years I've heard snippets from my older relatives 'bout a long-ago forbidden love, but I never gave it much thought."

Anna shook her head and glanced down at their hands, clasped together.

Gabe was chuckling now. "What a story, ain't!"

"I'll say," Anna said, wishing with all her heart that Mammi Eliza could have been alive to overhear this conversation.

That Lord's Day, Anna attended church one last time in Bird-in-Hand, then drove over to meet Gabe at his house, where he was waiting beside the hitched-up horse and buggy. He smiled and waved when he saw her, clearly eager to take her to meet his Dawdi Eb. On the way, they stopped at Aden and Barbara's and took Emmie inside to spend the afternoon.

As they rode, Anna learned more about the elderly gentleman who had yearned to court her Mammi Eliza so long ago. Gabe also told her that Eb lived in a small *Dawdi Haus* next to his daughter and son-in-law's place. "He has Parkinson's, so his hands shake," Gabe said, a noticeable softness and respect in his voice. "But he's as sharp as ever, thank the Lord. And he'll enjoy meetin' ya, Anna . . . 'specially given the letter you found."

"To think that I'm the granddaughter of his first love," Anna said, having brought the letter with her, wanting to show it to both Gabe and his grandfather whenever it seemed appropriate.

Gabe glanced at Anna as he held the driving lines. "Are ya nervous?"

"A little," she admitted.

He winked at her. "You won't have to say a word to win him over, Anna. Trust me."

"I do," she said, love filling her heart.

The meadow lay fallow in clover on either side of Ebenezer's little house. The meadow's edges were lined with a profusion of sumacs, wild-raspberry canes, and the browned stalks of wild flowers, no longer blooming due to several hard frosts.

Pretty sandstone steppingstones made a pathway around to

the *Dawdi Haus*, where they found white-haired Eb Lapp in his toasty kitchen, sitting peacefully in his rocker close to his black heater stove.

"Hullo, Dawdi, I've brought someone to meet ya," Gabe announced as they let themselves in the back door.

Eb pushed his glasses up onto the bridge of his nose and looked their way. "Well, 'tis 'bout time ya found yourself a perty girl again." He chuckled and pulled on his long white beard. "Don't mind me, dear," he said, his voice frail and husky.

"*Jah*, Dawdi Eb doesn't always think before he speaks." Gabe was grinning now.

"It's nice to meet you," she said, stepping forward to shake his hand. "I'm Anna Beachy."

Eb frowned, tilting his head this way and that. "Say now, ya look like someone I used to know." He kept his eyes on her. "Someone I knew when I was chust a young fella."

Gabe brought two chairs over from the table and offered one to Anna. He scooted closer to Eb and sat down. "Anna's from Mifflinburg," Gabe said, glancing now at her.

"Mifflinburg, ya say?" Eb's brow wrinkled as his face grew more serious.

"*Jah*," Gabe replied.

The grandfather clock in the small sitting room next to the kitchen struck a resounding two.

"You wouldn't be related to the Hertzlers, would ya?" Eb tugged again on his long beard. "*Ach*, ya must think I'm all but *ferhoodled*." He sighed.

"Not at all, Dawdi," Gabe spoke for Anna, nodding to her.

Anna moved her chair a little closer to Eb's. "Do you remember a girl named Eliza Hertzler?"

Eb glanced at the ceiling and stared at it for a moment. "Honest to Pete, never forgot 'bout her . . . not to say I wasn't devoted to my wife, Miriam," Eb added, looking now at Gabe. "There's just something 'bout one's first love. . . ."

Anna thought of Gabe just then; *his* first love had gone to be with the Lord.

Eb kept studying Anna, not concealing his scrutiny in the least. "You must be somehow related to Eliza, then."

Anna nodded, delighted to be talking to this man who had once meant so much to her beloved Mammi. "I'm her grand-daughter." She didn't say that Eliza was no longer living. *One thing at a time . . .*

"Well, what do ya know." Eb shook his head and looked over at Gabe like he was in a daze. "I have to say, I never expected this."

Glancing at Gabe, Anna removed the letter from her purse.

"Anna has somethin' mighty special to show ya, Dawdi," Gabe said, giving Anna courage with a thoughtful smile.

"Go right ahead, young lady." Eb turned in his rocker just a bit, leaning his head to look at her through the upper part of his spectacles.

"I believe I've found what might've been the last letter you wrote to my Mammi," Anna said, handing it to him. "One she probably never read."

Eb looked baffled. "*Ach*, are ya sure?"

For a moment, he studied it and held it out away from him, peering down through his bifocals. Then after a time, he shook his head and handed it back to Anna. "I always thought Eliza read it and was offended by it . . . ran away. According to the grapevine, she left town with her parents."

Anna didn't go into the details of how she had discovered the letter in the stone wall, seeing how Eb was trying to wrap his mind around this.

"Guess Eliza never got it." Eb still looked confused. "And all that time, I thought it was me suggestin' to leave my church for hers that scared her off."

"I really don't know what made her return home. Mammi was always rather tight-lipped about that summer here." Anna added that she could ask her mother about it if he'd like.

"*Ach*, no need," Eb said, waving it off. He sat there rocking now, his eyes closed as though suddenly weary. After a time, he opened them and looked Anna's way again. "How'd ya come to know 'bout the stone wall?"

She had wondered if he might ask and told him that Mammi Eliza had first mentioned it when Anna told her that she was coming to live in Strasburg. "At the time, Mammi's memory wasn't too reliable, but there were moments when it was clear. After that, whenever I spoke of Strasburg, she'd try to talk about a stone wall, even though none of it really seemed to make sense to my family."

"But it did to you?" Eb asked, nodding sagely.

"Since my childhood I've been very close to her, so maybe I just picked up something about her sincerity when she'd bring up the stone wall. That and a tall pin oak tree . . . evidently she waited for you there," Anna said.

With a handkerchief, Eb wiped his moist eyes, then his forehead. "A couple years after that summer, I married a *wunnerbaar* young woman. My disappointment over Eliza's leavin' actually led me to Miriam, my bride of sixty-five happy years."

Anna glanced at Gabe, and he held her gaze, his eyes full of affection.

"You two . . . are yous a couple?" Eb asked, slowing his rocking some.

"Just started dating," Gabe said, winking at Anna.

"But you ain't Amish, are ya, Anna?" Eb asked.

338

Gabe intervened and said she was Beachy Amish. "A close cousin to our way of life, as you know."

"Ah, same as Eliza." Eb smiled. "Makes sense."

"But Anna says she'll be joinin' the People here, doin' much like what *you* offered to do for Eliza," Gabe explained.

"Well, how about that. A fine turnabout," Eb said, shaking his head again. "Praise be!"

"Only the Lord knows the path our lives will take. Feels a little to me like your relationship with Eliza's come full circle, Dawdi . . . and right here before your eyes," Gabe said, looking earnestly at Anna.

She nodded, deeply touched by his words—and this remarkable visit. *To think that Eb and Mammi's heartbreak made it possible for Gabe and me to meet and fall in love,* she thought, marveling at the goodness of God's plans.

"The Lord knew this all along," she whispered, sighing happily.

Epilogue

My parents accomplished the joyful challenge of hosting the Beachy clan for Thanksgiving Day. I enjoyed helping with the large spread of food and seeing all my nephews and nieces, as well as dear Wanita, too.

"We sisters must stick together," Wanita whispered to me, and I knew she was still struggling with the loss of Mammi Eliza and of me, living now in Strasburg for good.

The day following that reunion, I welcomed Gabe and Emmie to Mifflinburg, having invited them to meet my parents. After the initial greeting there in Mamm's warm kitchen, I was heartened to see Dat invite Gabe out to the pony stable while Emmie and I enjoyed our fill of leftover cookies and bars from yesterday's variety of desserts.

I had previously shared with my parents that Emmie did not speak, but that didn't keep my mother from engaging her with a musical top and other toys she kept in a box for the grandchildren.

It was during the noon meal that I became convinced that Gabe was winning my father over. To my surprise, the two began to discuss Scripture verses that had ministered to them through the years. My prayerful hope that, given time, Dat would come to appreciate Gabe was already coming true.

While passing the creamy, buttery mashed potatoes and thick chicken gravy, I noticed that Emmie was eating particularly well today, enjoying Mamm's good cooking. Mamm had also been thoughtful to set Emmie's place right next to mine.

Truly, I had so much to be thankful for. To think that Gabe had been willing to come the distance to spend this special time with my parents and me. *I'm falling more in love with him every day,* I thought, catching his gaze.

Deep autumn's winds and frost swept away the last of the dazzling leaves, and with December's cold and snow, my schedule at the information center slowed to three days a week. On my days off, I stayed indoors with Emmie, teaching her easy tasks like making basting stitches, wiping dishes, making her bed, and helping to sort the laundry. Helping Gabe with Emmie during the daytime made sense, and I kept her busy while he drew up blueprints for more tree houses.

On Christmas afternoon, Gabe surprised Emmie with a beautiful palomino pony named Splash. Thereafter, on the mildest days, Gabe and I assisted her as she rode back and forth down the driveway.

So much has changed since I first met them, I thought, excited to see how well balanced and secure Emmie seemed to be on the pony with only her father's help.

All winter long, my bond with Emmie grew like a flourishing flower. I took her everywhere I could, either in the car or around the neighborhood in the buggy, which Gabe had taught me to drive. Of course, I was still getting used to hitching up, but my goal was to complete that chore with ease before the bumblebees flew in early spring. *When we'll start going bare-foot again*, I thought, wondering if Mammi Eliza might just be smiling down from above, seeing as how I'd fallen for an Old Order Amishman.

In early May, when the lavender redbuds and white and pink dogwoods blossomed, Gabe asked me to take him to the spot in the stone wall where I'd found Eb's love letter. It was a superbly sunny morning, with only a few thin clouds over near the green hills to the north. Emmie had gone to spend the morning with Barbara's sons, so it was just Gabe and me walking along the row of black walnut trees. Before today, I hadn't returned to the spot where I'd found the grass-covered tree stump, so it was a bit of a challenge to locate it.

"Are ya sure it wasn't just a dream?" Gabe joked, searching the ground with me for the stump.

"Guess I should've marked it." Oh, I wished I had!

For several minutes, we walked south, traveling along the stone wall.

"Maybe it's farther up," Gabe said.

I shook my head, wondering what had become of it, and looking all the more carefully.

"Wait . . . what's this?" Gabe said, pointing to where a piece of paper was protruding from the wall. He walked forward and tugged on it, managing to loosen it.

Befuddled, I peered at the folded paper.

"Let's see what this says." He opened the paper and began to read aloud. "To my dearest Anna Beachy. I'm certainly not the letter writer Dawdi Eb was, but I can easily write the words *I love you* and say that I don't want to live a single day of my life without you in it. Will you join your heart with mine and be my wife?"

342

By now, I could scarcely see for the tears, and I pulled out a hankie from my dress pocket. "I will," I said, smiling now. "I wondered when you might ask me, Gabe, but I never dreamed it would be in such a meaningful way."

Gabe glanced both ways quickly, then took me into his arms for the first time. "I'll tell ya a little secret," he whispered.

"*Jah?*" I said, eager for our wedding day, when we could lip-kiss.

"It was Dawdi Eb's idea for me to propose to you like this." Gabe kissed my cheek. "I daresay he's the hopeless romantic in the family."

"Well, you should talk!" I reached around his neck and hugged him again.

"Are ya ready to start baptismal instruction?" he asked as we walked back toward his horse and buggy.

I said I was.

Gabe took my hand in his. "You're sacrificing so much for me. And for Emmie."

"But oh, what I'm getting in return!" I said, looking into his eyes as he gently helped me into the passenger side of his carriage.

That noon, at Sadie and Glen's dinner table, I shared about my engagement. They smiled nearly in unison. "I called my parents to tell them my happy news, too," I said, "but I wanted you to be the next to hear it."

Glen was grinning now and pulling on his suspenders. He looked Sadie's way.

"We couldn't be happier for ya, Anna," Sadie said, eyes glistening. "Ain't so, Glen?"

He bobbed his head, clearly moved to the point of not being able to speak.

"Looks like I'm going to be a permanent part of your community," I said. "Come next September's baptism Sunday, I'll be one of the People."

"The Good Lord brought you and Gabe together, I do believe," Glen said, finally finding his voice.

I smiled. "And little Emmie, too. A family of three."

After I helped Sadie redd up the kitchen, I headed to my room to read more of Mammi Eliza's journal. Toward the back pages, I noticed something at the end of her November entry that year, where she was counting her blessings at Thanksgiving time. *I don't regret coming home from Strasburg when I did. God's hand was on me, I know that for sure. And, too, a certain young man here in Mifflinburg has caught my attention: John Slaubaugh, who asked me out for a date. I'm so happy!*

That evening, when I visited Gabe, he told Emmie that he was going to marry me come November. "She'll be your new Mamma."

Emmie's eyes widened, and she let out a giggle.

I looked at Gabe, wondering if he'd heard it, too.

Emmie reached for her dolly on the wooden bench next to her and held it up. "Anna," she said clearly, pointing to the doll.

"*Ach*, honey-girl," Gabe murmured softly.

Tears sprang to my eyes. "You named your dolly after me?"

Nodding, Emmie's eyes sparkled.

"Oh, sweetie." I reached for her, and Emmie's little arms slipped around me, holding on as if for dear life.

There were only a handful of perfect moments in an entire

344

lifetime, I realized, and here I'd cherished two such moments in the space of a single day.

Thank you, dear Lord, for hearing my prayers, I prayed silently, looking first at Gabe, then dear little Emmie. *Such an unforgettable day of days!*

Author's Note

During an autumn stay at a New Hampshire inn, I came across a coffee table book titled *Sermons in Stone* by Susan Allport, which intrigued me with its many historical facts about the stone walls of the Northeast. To my surprise, the paperback edition of that same book appeared under the Christmas tree that year, wrapped and tied with a pretty bow from my husband, Dave, and I was happily able to finish reading it. As I often do, I filed away my impressions—the tiny first seeds of this novel—and later wrote the manuscript titled *The Stone Wall*.

While in Lancaster County, Pennsylvania, for Amish-related research a year later, I strolled along the back roads near Strasburg's historic stone walls and took pictures to assist my art director for this book cover. All the while, I remembered those initial stirrings of the story of Anna Beachy and her quest for a fresh start, and I thanked God for small beginnings.

From the research to the production of this novel, there are numerous wonderful people to thank—the fine folk at the Mennonite Information Center; Annie Jean Smucker at Harmony Hollow Retreat in Quarryville; Greystone Manor Therapeutic Riding Center on Hartman Station Road in Lancaster County;

Dr. Max Nevarez and Dr. Kimberly Wagner, for their wealth of knowledge on dementia and Alzheimer's; the Esbenshade Turkey Farm in Ronks; Rachel Stoltzfus's Farmhouse Memories; John Stevens's watercolor art gallery in Nolt's Mill; Lovina Eicher's latest cookbook, *Amish Family Recipes*; and the Amish contacts and friends who answered my many questions and read sections of the manuscript. And thanks, as well, to my sister, Barbara, for the unique inspiration behind Sadie Flaud's "Amish Cheer" encouragement cards.

I'm ever thankful to David Horton and his exceptional editorial team, including Rochelle Glöege and Elisa Tally. My friends in marketing also deserve a shout-out— especially Steve Oates, Noelle Chew, and Amy Green, as well as Dan Thornberg and Paul Higdon for my book covers. Bravo to all!

My husband, Dave, also played a large part, especially when I succumbed to flu during the revision process last winter. Dave is not only a great first editor, but he makes wonderful soft-boiled eggs and delicious chicken soup, too!

For the sake of this story's timeframe, the Landis Valley Village and Farm Harvest Days Festival remained open until after sundown. In reality, however, it closes at five o'clock. Also, the actual Mennonite Information Center would not pair up a woman with a male tour guide, no matter how experienced.

Finally, I offer a heart full of gratitude to you, my dear reader-friend . . . and to our heavenly Father, constant Guide and Provider, and our Peace. *Soli Deo Gloria!*

Beverly Lewis, born in the heart of Pennsylvania Dutch country, is the *New York Times* bestselling author of more than one hundred books. Her stories have been published in twelve languages worldwide. A keen interest in her mother's Plain heritage has inspired Beverly to write many Amish-related novels, beginning with *The Shunning*, which has sold more than one million copies and is an Original Hallmark Channel movie. In 2007 *The Brethren* was honored with a Christy Award.

Beverly has been interviewed by both national and international media, including *Time* magazine, the Associated Press, and the BBC. She lives with her husband, David, in Colorado.

Visit her website at www.beverlylewis.com or www.facebook .com/officialbeverlylewis for more information.

*A long-ago accident,
a family secret,
and the one beau
that got away . . .
Susie Mast's life
in Hickory Hollow
has been shaped
by events beyond her control,
but what seems like the end
may really be just*

The Beginning

The Next Novel from Beverly Lewis

AVAILABLE FALL 2021

BETHANYHOUSE

 Stay up to date on your favorite books and authors with our free e-newsletters. Sign up today at bethanyhouse.com.

 facebook.com/bethanyhousepublishers @bethanyhousefiction

 Free exclusive resources for your book group at bethanyhouseopenbook.com

Sign Up for Beverly's Newsletter

Keep up to date with Beverly's news on book releases and events by signing up for her email list at beverlylewis.com.

More from Beverly Lewis

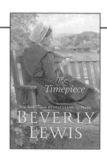

In this continuation of *The Tinderbox*, young Amish woman Sylvia Miller's world is upended by the arrival of Englisher Adeline Pelham—whose existence is a reminder of a painful family secret. Sylvia must learn to come to terms with the past while grappling with issues of her own. Is it possible that God can make something good out of the mistakes of days gone by?

The Timepiece

Also from Beverly Lewis

Visit beverlylewis.com for a full list of her books.

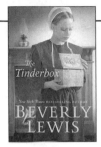

When Sylvia Miller finds her father's old tinderbox left unlocked, her curiosity is piqued. She opens the box and uncovers secrets best left alone. A confrontation with her father leads to a shocking revelation that will forever change not only her own life but also that of her family and her Amish community.

The Tinderbox

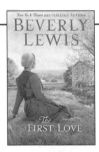

In the summer of 1951, Amish woman Maggie Esh is struggling with a debilitating illness and few future prospects. When tent revival meetings come to the area, Maggie attends out of curiosity. She's been told to accept her lot in life as God's will, but the words of the evangelist begin to stir something deep inside her. Dare she hope for a brighter future?

The First Love

Sent from Michigan to Pennsylvania, Lena Rose Schwartz grieves the deaths of her Amish parents and the separation from her siblings as well as her beau, Hans Bontrager. She longs to return home to those she loves most. However, she soon discovers that Lancaster County holds charms of its own. Is she willing to open her heart to new possibilities?

The Road Home

◊ BETHANYHOUSE

You May Also Like . . .

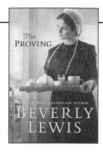

Having left the Amish life for the English world, Amanda Dienner is shocked when she learns that her mother has passed and left her Lancaster County's most popular Amish bed-and-breakfast. The catch is she has to run it herself for one year, acting as hostess. Amanda accepts the terms, but coming home to people she left behind won't be easy.

The Proving

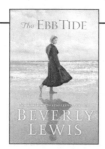

When a young Amish woman takes a summer job as a nanny in beautiful Cape May, she forms an unexpected bond with a handsome Mennonite. Has she been too hasty with her promises, or will she only find what her heart is longing for back home?

The Ebb Tide

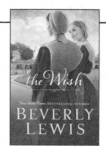

Leona lost her best friend the day Gloria's father was expelled from the Amish church. When she receives an unexpected letter from Gloria, Leona makes up her mind to go after her friend. To the alarm of her fiancé, the deacon's son, she sets out on a mission to persuade Gloria to return to the Amish church. Will Leona's dearest wish lead to her own undoing?

The Wish

BETHANYHOUSE